JOHN SOMER AND JOHN J. DALY

The Anchor Book of New Irish Writing

John Somer grew up on a farm in southern Kansas with a Bohemian father and an Irish mother. Because this wheat country was settled by a variety of European immigrants, it was rich with ethnic cultures. The local Irish were especially vocal and influential. For over thirty years, Somer has read and studied contemporary literature, the agendas of the modern and postmodern literary periods, and Irish literature. He is a professor of English at Emporia State University in Emporia, Kansas, and has long been a student of Yeats and Joyce.

John J. Daly was born and still lives in the family home built by his great-grandfather, which is located a few hundred yards from Joyce's Drumcondra home. Destined to be a Joycean, Daly was educated at Clongowes Wood College (Joyce's alma mater) and later wrote his doctoral dissertation on Joyce. He has taught at school and university level. With his wife, Catherine, he runs Hillsboro Fine Art, a gallery specializing in twentieth-century Irish and British art.

The Anchor Book of
New Irish Writing

THE NEW GAELACH FICSEAN

Edited and with an introduction by
John Somer and John J. Daly

ANCHOR BOOKS
A DIVISION OF RANDOM HOUSE, INC.
NEW YORK

FOR DAVY BYRNES

and

all other moral places

FIC
NEW
IRISH

FIRST ANCHOR BOOKS EDITION, MARCH 2000

Copyright © 2000 by John Somer and John J. Daly

Anchor Books and the Anchor colophon
are registered trademarks of Random House, Inc.

Library of Congress Cataloging-in-Publication Data on file.

Anchor ISBN: 0-385-49889-6

Book design by Oksana Kushnir

www.anchorbooks.com

Printed in the United States of America
10 9 8 7 6 5 4 3 2

CONTENTS

I: Summer Night

II: Nightwind

III: Telling

IV: Persona

V: The Sloe-Black River

VI: The Dream of a Beast

EMILY DICKINSON

From anything that touches her she may recoil
Go no further
But retreat upon it all and reap
Words that are born and unfurl under careful hands
Words that come from her trance
In a silent monotone.

Then the Alice-like fall
Swings from dull thud to thud of her hitting earth.
In her long descent did she howl?
I worry about that sound
And watch how her own nouns
     jostle her now she is down,
Her thoughts are in an empty train, door open,
And no-one getting in.

At times she has nodded drily at the abyss
It is not sunny at this time so there are no shadows
But maybe down there genius lightly spirals,
Words landing squarely, perfect fits;
I edge warily, all blows glancing,
Until my mind connects with a bright shock.
Somewhere, a train pulls off.

—Sara Berkeley

PREFACE

I don't know which we enjoyed more—the exciting new stories we were talking about or the pints of plain we shared the Bloomsday of 1995. We were in Davy Byrne's moral pub in Dublin's Duke Street on a mild, sunny afternoon. Naturally, we started with Joyce, the man of the day, but our conversation kept coming back to the likes of Mary Dorcey, Aidan Mathews, Anne Enright, and Colum McCann. We couldn't describe fast enough how different these writers are from one another and how powerful their imaginations are. As soon as we finished describing a story by Hogan, we were on to Smyth, and Boylan, and O'Connor.

A couple of hours and pints later, we began to lament the fact that most of these amazingly good writers were unknown beyond the shores of Ireland. While a few of these writers, such as Maeve Binchy, Patrick McCabe, John Banville, and Neil Jordan, reach international audiences, most collections of Ireland's new voices are published primarily for Irish readers. We were convinced that the rest of the world's English readers would find these writers as stimulating and entertaining as we did, so we decided to edit a collection of Ireland's recent writers.

Over the next few months, as we considered what stories to include, we read every collection of stories written by Irish writers born in 1940 or later, and we read many stories published only in journals. We found what we thought we would find. These stories share common themes, but they are expressed in as many styles as Joyce's *Ulysses*. The current Irish short story is at times pyrotechnic, yet as nourishing as corned beef; it is playful, yet earnest; Irish, yet universal.

Yes, this fiction is relevant to the rest of the world. Irish writers have long experience with social violence and its human implications, and now that Ireland has experienced its own economic revolution, its writers have mastered the idiom of an accelerated, technological world. With Irish wit, they etch with acid the dilemmas of modern life. They dramatize the clash between lovers, between husbands and wives, between adults and children, and between old values and new freedom—all in the context of a world growing harsher and more violent. With an ear for language, they use style to shape emotional responses to life—responses that lighten the heart rather than burden it.

We begin our collection of recent Irish stories with "Summer Night," a story written when most of our writers were not yet born. Its author, Elizabeth Bowen, is our only representative from Ireland's literary tradition, and we begin with her story because it foreshadows both thematically and technically the current state of the Irish short story. In this story, Bowen searches for "new forms for thinking and feeling," a quest that recent Irish writers continue. The stories gathered here illustrate the common struggle with this issue, and end in Neil Jordan's novella, *The Dream of a Beast*, which manifests just such a form, one that issues from its imagery.

The twenty-six stories we finally selected represent the Irish short story today, and they address the needs of readers everywhere. While these stories dramatize the "new" Ireland's struggle with complex and significant human problems, their authors offer provocative but affirmative solutions to the experience of living. As a result, this collection aspires to give readers what they want: intellectual clarity, artistic affirmation, and new structures for human thoughts and feelings. In both style and theme, then, these stories offer a succinct illustration of the world's contemporary fiction and affirm, once again, the supremacy of the Irish short story.

ACKNOWLEDGMENTS

While reading for this collection, we looked for stories that we enjoyed reading and wanted to talk about. As we made our selections, we used the prevailing schools of criticism and aesthetic taste to inform our search for good stories. We also asked a variety of specialists in Irish literature, ethnic and colonial literatures, and recent literary history to criticize our ideas. Specifically we wish to thank Leslie Lewis, Richard Lloyd, Darrel Lloyd, Laura Marvel, James and Cathy Hoy, Gerry Lynch, Stephen O'Connor, Neal Kirchner, and Christopher Howell. We wish to thank Connie Somer and Catherine Daly for constant support and help. John Somer wishes to acknowledge the continuing influence of his son, John Joseph (1965–1998). He also thanks Emporia State University for a sabbatical to work on the manuscript. Finally, we thank our literary agent, Nat Sobel, for his persistence and clarity of thought, and our editors at Anchor Books, Siobhan Adcock and Mark Maguire, for their perceptions, good taste, and patience. All defects of this book belong to the pints of plain at Davy Byrnes!

Dublin, Ireland
Emporia, Kansas
June 16, 1999

Cathal's "Peculiar Curse": Politics and the Contemporary Writer

Those masterful images because complete
Grew in pure mind, but out of what began?
A mound of refuse or the sweepings of a street,
Old kettles, old bottles, and a broken can,
Old iron, old bones, old rags, that raving slut
Who keeps the till. Now that my ladder's gone,
I must lie down where all the ladders start,
In the foul rag-and-bone shop of the heart.
                                    —W. B. YEATS

When Ireland entered the 1960s, it began to change. Its people abandoned the countryside for city living and doubled their standard of living, even in a time of pressing unemployment. In addition to internal economic changes, Irish society responded to world forces, among them Pope John XXIII's revision of Catholic practices, the American Civil Rights movement, and the women's liberation movement. The Catholic Church, Ireland's unofficial conscience, was losing priests and nuns, and many of those who accepted a vocation were committed to liberation theology, social protest, and intellectual freedoms. Throughout this period of social upheaval, Ireland publicly debated abortion, divorce, and homosexuality. At the same time, a new generation of writers challenged Ireland's values. While Tom Murphy shocked the theater, Edna O'Brien's stories scandalized the nation by portraying the sexual life of Irish women. The most celebrated case, though, involved John McGahern's second novel, *The Dark* (1965). Banned under the Censorship of Publications Act, the book narrates the school days of an unnamed character who is living with his widowed father. The boy prepares for his exams with the help of a drunken teacher and an over-friendly priest. After *The Dark* was published, McGahern was fired from his teaching post without explanation, and, despite much public controversy, the clerical management of the school refused to reinstate him. A bill introduced in 1967 allowed for the unbanning of books after twelve years, and the country began to rely more on public opinion in matters of censorship. *The Dark* and Joyce's *Dubliners* rest now, side-by-side, on a bookshelf.

The Republic of Ireland seemed, then, both economically and politically, to be on its way to equaling the literary achievements of its great writers: William Butler Yeats, James Joyce, George Bernard Shaw, and Samuel Beckett, to mention only a few. Its economy was on the move, its artists were staying at home, its politicians were debating social issues, and its people felt free to think for themselves. But in the mid-1960s, "the Troubles" began in Northern Ireland, marring Ireland's renaissance.

Northern Ireland and its "Troubles" are not simple issues. Declan Kiberd in his monumental 1995 study of Ireland's literary culture, *Inventing Ireland: The Literature of the Modern Nation*, laments that the problem is "obdurate," and "unyielding." He goes on to cite Richard Rose, who declares the problem to be unsolvable. It is this very clash between a progressive Republic and a repressive Northern Ireland that seems to define the contemporary Irish short story. All the old divisions in Irish culture—realism/romanticism, Gaelic/English, Catholic/Protestant, Ireland/England—seem less relevant in the face of this problem. As Dermot Bolger points out in his Introduction to *The Vintage Book of Contemporary Irish Fiction*, these old divisions seem to excite the literary imagination primarily in Northern Ireland. Kiberd also observes that Irish writers have not eulogized the "Troubles" as Yeats might have were he alive today. Rather they seem to have rejected the politics of religion, the politics of state, and the politics of nostalgia in favor of the politics of living. Many Irish writers seem no longer interested in writing the obligatory priest or nun story, sentimentalizing/condemning peasants, or lauding urban guerrillas. It seems that the majority of Ireland's new writers are finding their way back to James Joyce's examination of

Ireland's conscience. Rather than trying to save the world or Ireland, they seem preoccupied with examining the life they have. While this new focus in Irish literature may appeal to an international audience, it seems to have diminished the reputation of Irish writers at home.

In 1996 the magazine *Ireland of the Welcomes* published Eileen Battersby's "Irish Writing Now." In her essay she limits her praise to the poets of Northern Ireland, the playwright Brian Friel, and the older generation of novelists, such as John McGahern and William Trevor, while acknowledging the work of a few new fiction writers, such as Roddy Doyle and Patrick McCabe. She concludes her piece by noting briefly that there are many other Irish writers who have been influenced by American fiction, and she urges critics to study them, but she does not mention any by name. An examination of Kiberd's index to *Inventing Ireland* reveals the same attitude toward Ireland's new writers. Kiberd discusses briefly only three of the twenty-one writers in this collection. As Dermot Bolger argues, if these new writers were studied, their work would reveal a new subject matter in Irish writing. In addition to introducing new themes, however, these stories would also reveal new experiments in forms and techniques.

Irish writers do not have to look far to discover a model for new forms. Joyce's *Ulysses*, published in 1922, is the grand textbook of narrative modes for the twentieth century and likely for the next. Although Joyce is credited with helping to create and define the social and aesthetic movement of modern realism, it is now clear that only episodes 1 through 6 of *Ulysses* focus primarily on this issue. The rest of the novel responds to the pretensions and failures of realism and other rational systems to aptly represent reality and, in the process, defines and demonstrates the potential for at least two ensuing literary movements. The current one, presented in episodes 7 through 14 of Joyce's novel, and now called postmodernism, studies the cultural paradigms and rhetorical systems that humans impose on their experience, however mundane and chaotic, in order to translate it into a significant and bearable reality. The second literary period, which is still in search of a name, shares goals and techniques with both French Surrealism and Robert Bly's notion of deep imagery. This movement, which could well be called "deep realism," is developed in episodes 15 and 18 of *Ulysses* and is a proper reaction to the cynicism of postmodernism. The thrust of this movement is to examine how we use, or misuse, myths and subliminal images and signs in order to infuse meaning and significance into our lives. Declan Kiberd agrees that Joyce equated realism with imperialistic politics and compromised it in *Ulysses* by blending it with myth. In the process, Kiberd notes that Joyce produced a model for South America's recent type of narrative, magical realism. Magical realism is but one of the many guises of "deep realism," and its presence demonstrates how far-reaching is Joyce's influence. Today, writers of many countries continue Joyce's initial experiments in narration, and Joyce's influence is especially strong in Ireland.

Naturally, Ireland's new writers have fashioned their narrative experiments to address their own lives. To read the contemporary Irish short story, then, is to experience life as it anticipates the twenty-first century and to experience the various imaginative responses to the changing human dilemma. Because their stories deal with the fundamental problems of living, new Irish writers have, like Joyce, created a grand mixture of literary styles that hint at the complexities of human experience and represent it honestly. As a result, this anthology of recent Irish short stories includes realistic, postmodern, and "deep realism" narratives.

While reading for this collection, we focused on the new Irish writers, those who were born after 1939 and matured during the 1960s, a period of rapid change in Ireland. Although this collection focuses on new Irish writers, it begins with "Summer Night" by Elizabeth Bowen, our only representative of Ireland's literary tradition. "Summer Night" foreshadows, both thematically and technically, the current state of the Irish short story, by announcing the need for "new forms for thinking and feeling." Bowen explores the potential of this quest by creating her story from a blend of the narrative conventions of realism, postmodernism, and "deep realism." The twenty-four stories illustrating Ireland's recent authors, written by ten women and eleven men from the Republic of Ireland and Northern Ireland, continue this exploration; and the final work, Neil Jordan's novella *The Dream of a Beast*, manifests a narrative order independent of rationalism, one rooted in the subliminal images rising from "the place of understanding."

We have arranged these twenty-four stories in two ways. Within the frame provided by Bowen and Jordan, we grouped the stories in twos by theme, so readers may compare examinations of the same type of social, ethical, or aesthetic issue. Second, we arranged the stories into six larger gatherings. The first group of recent stories, "Nightwind," is a sampling of new realistic writing in Ireland which provides the social background for the next group of eight postmodern stories, "Telling," which challenge realism and its assumptions. The third grouping of six recent stories, "Persona," uses realistic techniques to introduce various features of "deep realism." The last group of stories, "The Sloe-Black River" and "The Dream of the Beast" are "deep realist" stories that gather up and resolve the collection. In "Cathal's Lake," for example, Colum McCann depicts the artist as one cursed to ignore his practical duties in order to respond with beauty to the world's ugliness. Because a young Irishman burned and died in the explosion of his own Molotov cocktail, Cathal, the protagonist of the story, must, once again, surrender to the irrational and dig up a swan from the mud of creation where it waits to be born. To fulfill his aesthetic obligation of liberating beauty, then, the artist must embrace the human condition with all its confusion and corruption, both personal and political. In one sense, Cathal's "peculiar curse" is the job description of all writers, but additionally, it is the destiny of Irish writers.

The interweaving of the realistic, postmodern, and "deep realistic" strands of narration is designed to slowly immerse readers in alternative visions of truth and values. The familiarity of the realistic stories provides a needed insight into the themes of the postmodern and "deep realism" stories. In their turn, the newer narrative modes supply additional imaginative responses to these themes. *The Anchor Book of New Irish Writing: The New Gaelach Ficsean* will introduce you to many interesting writers and to challenging stories set in a familiar context, but finally, it will introduce you to the contemporary Irish short story and to the problems and issues of today's writers.

I

Summer Night

Summer Night

As the sun set its light slowly melted the landscape, till everything was made of fire and glass. Released from the glare of noon, the haycocks now seemed to float on the aftergrass: their freshness penetrated the air. In the not far distance hills with woods up their flanks lay in light like hills in another world—it would be a pleasure of heaven to stand up there, where no foot ever seemed to have trodden, on the spaces between the woods soft as powder dusted over with gold. Against those hills, the burning red rambler roses in cottage gardens along the roadside looked earthy—they were too near the eye.

The road was in Ireland. The light, the air from the distance, the air of evening rushed transversely through the open sides of the car. The rims of the hood flapped, the hood's metal frame rattled as the tourer, in great bounds of speed, held the road's darkening magnetic centre streak. The big shabby family car was empty but for its small driver—its emptiness seemed to levitate it—on its back seat a coat slithered about, and a dressingcase bumped against the seat. The driver did not relax her excited touch on the wheel: now and then while she drove she turned one wrist over, to bring the watch worn on it into view, and she gave the mileage marked on the yellow sign-posts a flying, jealous, half-inadvertent look. She was driving parallel with the sunset: the sun slowly went down on her right hand.

The hills flowed round till they lay ahead. Where the road bent for its upward course through the pass she pulled up and lighted a cigarette. With a snatch she untwisted her turban; she shook her hair free and threw the scarf behind her into the back seat. The draught of the pass combed her hair into coarse strands as the car hummed up in second gear. Behind one brilliantly-outlined crest the sun had now quite gone; on the steeps of bracken, in the electric shadow, each frond stood out and climbing goats turned their heads. The car came up on a lorry, to hang on its tail, impatient, checked by turns of the road. At the first stretch the driver smote her palm on the horn and shot past and shot on ahead again.

The small woman drove with her chin up. Her existence was in her hands on the wheel and in the sole of the foot in which she felt, through the sandal, the throbbing pressure of the accelerator. Her face, enlarged by blown-back hair, was as overbearingly blank as the face of a figure-head; her black eyebrows were ruled level, and her eyes, pupils dilated, did little more than reflect the slow burn of daylight along horizons, the luminous shades of the half-dark.

Clear of the pass, approaching the county town, the road widened and straightened between stone walls and burnished showering beech. The walls broke up into gateways and hoardings and the suburbs began. People in modern building estate gardens let the car in a hurry through their unseeing look. The raised footpaths had margins of grass. White and grey rows of cottages under the pavement level let woodsmoke over their half-doors: women and old men sat outside the doors on boxes, looking down at their knees; here and there a bird sprang in a cage tacked to a wall. Children chasing balls over the roadway shot whooping right and left of the car. The refreshed town, unfolding streets to its centre, at this hour slowly heightened, cooled; streets and stones threw off a grey-pink glare, sultry lasting ghost of the high noon. In this dayless glare the girls in bright dresses, strolling, looked like colour-photography.

Dark behind all the windows: not a light yet. The in-going perspective looked meaning, noble and wide. But everybody was elsewhere—the polished street was empty but cars packed both the kerbs under the trees. What was going on? The big tourer dribbled, slipped with animal nervousness between the static locked cars each side of its way. The driver peered left and right with her face narrow, glanced from her wrist-

watch to the clock in the tower, sucked her lip, manœuvred for somewhere to pull in. The A.A. sign of the hotel hung out from under a bal-
cony, over the steps. She edged in to where it said DO NOT PARK.

At the end of the hotel hall one electric light from the bar shone
through a high-up panel: its yellow sifted on to the dusty dusk and a
moth could be seen on the glass pane. At the door end came in street
daylight, to fall weakly on prints on the oiled walls, on the magenta
announcement-strip of a cinema, on the mahogany bench near the
receptionist's office, on the hatstand with two forgotten hats. The
woman who had come breathlessly up the steps felt in her face a wall of
indifference. The impetuous click of her heeled sandals on the linoleum
brought no one to the receptionist's desk, and the drone of two talkers in
the bar behind the glass panel seemed, like the light, to be blotted up,
word by word. The little woman attacked the desk with her knuckles. "Is
there nobody there—I say? Is there nobody *there*?"

"I am, I am. Wait now," said the hotel woman, who came impassively
through the door from the bar. She reached up a hand and fumbled the
desk light on, and by this with unwondering negligence studied the customer—the childish, blown little woman with winglike eyebrows and
eyes still unfocussed after the long road. The hotel woman, bust on the
desk, looked down slowly at the bare legs, the crumple-hemmed linen
coat. "Can I do anything for you?" she said, when she had done.

"I want the telephone—want to put through a call!"

"You can of course," said the unmoved hotel woman. "Why not?" she
added after consideration, handing across the keys of the telephone cabinet. The little woman made a slide for the cabinet: with her mouth to
the mouthpiece, like a conspirator, she was urgently putting her number
through. She came out then and ordered herself a drink.

"Is it long distance?"

"Mm-mm . . . What's on here? What are all those cars?"

"Oh, this evening's the dog racing."

"Is it?"

"Yes, it's the dog racing. We'd a crowd in here, but they're all gone on
now."

"I wondered who they were," said the little woman, her eyes on the
cabinet, sippeting at her drink.

"Yes, they're at the dog racing. There's a wonderful crowd. But I wouldn't care for it," said the hotel woman, fastidiously puckering up her forehead. "I went the one time, but it didn't fascinate me."

The other forgot to answer. She turned away with her drink, sat down, put the glass beside her on the mahogany bench and began to chafe the calves of her bare legs as though they were stiff or cold. A man clasping sheets of unfurled newspaper pushed his way with his elbow through the door from the bar. "What it says here," he said, shaking the paper with both hands, "is identically what I've been telling you."

"That proves nothing," said the hotel woman. "However, let it out of your hand." She drew the sheets of the paper from him and began to fold them into a wad. Her eyes moved like beetles over a top line. "That's an awful battle. . . ."

"What battle?" exclaimed the little woman, stopping rubbing her legs but not looking up.

"An awful air battle. Destroying each other," the woman added, with a stern and yet voluptuous sigh. "Listen, would you like to wait in the lounge?"

"She'd be better there," put in the man who had brought the paper. "Better accommodation." His eyes watered slightly in the electric light. The little woman, sitting upright abruptly, looked defiantly, as though for the first time, at the two watching her from the desk. "Mr. Donovan has great opinions," said the hotel woman. "Will you move yourself out of here?" she asked Mr. Donovan. "This is very confined—*There's* your call, now!"

But the stranger had packed herself into the telephone box like a conjuror's lady preparing to disappear. "*Hullo?*" she was saying. "Hullo! I want to speak to——"

"——You are," the other voice cut in. "All right? Anything wrong?"

Her face flashed all over. "You sound nearer already! I've got to C——."

The easy, calm voice said: "Then you're coming along well."

"Glad, are you?" she said, in a quiver.

"Don't take it too fast," he said. "It's a treacherous light. Be easy, there's a good girl."

"You're a fine impatient man." His end of the line was silent. She went on: "I might stay here and go to the dog racing."

"Oh, is that tonight?" He went on to say equably (having stopped, as she saw it, and shaken the ash off the tip of his cigarette), "No, I shouldn't do that."

"Darling . . ."

"Emma . . . How is the Major?"

"He's all right," she said, rather defensively.

"I see," he said. "Everything quite O.K.?"

"In an hour, I'll be . . . where you live."

"First gate on the left. Don't kill yourself, there's a good girl. Nothing's worth that. Remember we've got the night. By the way, where are you talking?"

"From the hotel." She nursed the receiver up close to her face and made a sound into it. Cutting that off she said: "Well, I'll hang up. I just . . ."

"Right," he said—and hung up.

Robinson, having hung up the receiver, walked back from the hall to the living-room where his two guests were. He still wore a smile. The deaf woman at the table by the window was pouring herself out another cup of tea. "That will be very cold!" Robinson shouted—but she only replaced the cosy with a mysterious smile. "Let her be," said her brother. "Let her alone!"

The room in this uphill house was still light: through the open window came in a smell of stocks from the flower beds in the lawn. The only darkness lay in a belt of beech trees at the other side of the main road. From the grate, from the coal of an unlit fire came the fume of a cigarette burning itself out. Robinson still could not help smiling: he reclaimed his glass from the mantelpiece and slumped back with it into his leather armchair in one of his loose, heavy, good-natured attitudes. But Justin Cavey, in the armchair opposite, still looked crucified at having the talk torn. "Beastly," he said, "you've a beastly telephone." Though he was in Robinson's house for the first time, his sense of attraction to people was marked, early, by just this intransigeance and this fretfulness.

"It is and it's not," said Robinson. That was that. "Where had we got to?" he amiably asked.

The deaf woman, turning round from the window, gave the two men, or gave the air between them, a penetrating smile. Her brother, with a sort of lurch at his pocket, pulled out a new packet of cigarettes: ignoring

Robinson's held-out cigarette case he frowned and split the cellophane
with his thumbnail. But, as though his sister had put a hand on his
shoulder, his tension could be almost seen to relax. The impersonal,
patient look of the thinker appeared in his eyes, behind the spectacles.
Justin was a city man, a black-coat, down here (where his sister lived) on
holiday. Other summer holidays before this he had travelled in France,
Germany, Italy: he disliked the chaotic "scenery" of his own land. He
was down here with Queenie this summer only because of the war,
which had locked him in: duty seemed to him better than failed pleasure. His father had been a doctor in this place; now his sister lived on in
two rooms in the square—for fear Justin should not be comfortable she
had taken a room for him at the hotel. His holiday with his sister, his
holiday in this underwater, weedy region of memory, his holiday on
which, almost every day, he had to pass the doors of their old home,
threatened Justin with a pleasure he could not bear. He had to share
with Queenie, as he shared the dolls' house meals cooked on the oil
stove behind her sittingroom screen, the solitary and almost fairylike
world created by her deafness. Her deafness broke down his only
defence, talk. He was exposed to the odd immune plumbing looks she
was forever passing over his face. He could not deflect the tilted blue of
her eyes. The things she said out of nowhere, things with no surface context, were never quite off the mark. She was not all solicitude; she loved
to be teasing him.

   In her middle-age, Queenie was very pretty: her pointed face had the
colouring of an imperceptibly fading pink-and-white sweetpea. This hot
summer her artless dresses, with their little lace collars, were mottled
over with flowers, mauve and blue. Up the glaring main street she carried a *poult-de-soie* parasol. Her rather dark first-floor rooms faced north,
over the square with its grass and lime trees: the crests of great mountains showed above the opposite façades. She would slip in and out on
her own errands, as calm as a cat, and Justin, waiting for her at one of her
windows, would see her cross the square in the noon sunshine with
hands laced over her forehead into a sort of porch. The little town,
though strung on a through road, was an outpost under the mountains:
in its quick-talking, bitter society she enjoyed, to a degree that surprised
Justin, her privileged place. She was woman enough to like to take the
man Justin round with her and display him; they went out to afternoon

or to evening tea, and in those drawing-rooms of tinted lace and intently-staring family photographs, among octagonal tables and painted cushions, Queenie, with her cotton gloves in her lap, well knew how to contribute, while Justin talked, her airy, brilliant, secretive smiling and looking on. For his part, he was man enough to respond to being shown off—besides, he was eased by these breaks in their *tête-à-tête*. Above all, he was glad, for these hours or two of chatter, not to have to face the screen of his own mind, on which the distortion of every one of his images, the war-broken towers of Europe, constantly stood. The immolation of what had been his own intensely had been made, he could only feel, without any choice of his. In the heart of the neutral Irishman indirect suffering pulled like a crooked knife. So he acquiesced to, and devoured, society: among the doctors, the solicitors, the auctioneers, the bank people of this little town he renewed old acquaintanceships and developed new. He was content to bloom, for this settled number of weeks—so unlike was this to his monkish life in the city—in a sort of tenebrous popularity. He attempted to check his solitary arrogance. His celibacy and his studentish manner could still, although he was past forty, make him acceptable as a young man. In the mornings he read late in his hotel bed; he got up to take his solitary walks; he returned to flick at his black shoes with Queenie's duster and set off with Queenie on their tea-table rounds. They had been introduced to Robinson, factory manager, in the hall of the house of the secretary of the tennis club.

Robinson did not frequent drawing-rooms. He had come here only three years ago, and had at first been taken to be a bachelor—he was a married man living apart from his wife. The resentment occasioned by this discovery had been aggravated by Robinson's not noticing it: he worked at very high pressure in his factory office, and in his off times his high-powered car was to be seen streaking too gaily out of the town. When he was met, his imperturbable male personality stood out to the women unpleasingly, and stood out most of all in that married society in which women aspire to break the male in a man. Husbands slipped him in for a drink when they were alone, or shut themselves up with him in the dining-room. Justin had already sighted him in the hotel bar. When Robinson showed up, late, at the tennis club, his manner with women was easy and teasing, but abstract and perfectly automatic. From this had probably come the legend that he liked women "only in one way." From the first time Justin encountered Robinson, he had felt a sort of anxious, disturbed attraction to the big, fair, smiling, offhand, cold-minded man. He felt impelled by Robinson's unmoved physical presence into all sorts of aberrations of talk and mind; he committed, like someone waving an anxious flag, all sorts of absurdities, as though this type of creature had been a woman; his talk became exaggeratedly cerebral, and he became prone, like a perverse person in love, to expose all his own piques, crotchets and weaknesses. One night in the hotel bar with Robinson he had talked until he burst into tears. Robinson had on him the touch of some foreign sun. The acquaintanceship—it could not be called more— was no more than an accident of this narrowed summer. For Justin it had taken the place of travel. The two men were so far off each other's beat that in a city they would certainly not have met.

Asked to drop in some evening or any evening, the Caveys had tonight taken Robinson at his word. Tonight, the night of the first visit, Justin's high, rather bleak forehead had flushed from the moment he rang the bell. With Queenie behind his shoulder, in muslin, he had flinched confronting the housekeeper. Queenie, like the rest of the town ladies, had done no more till now than go by Robinson's gate.

For her part, Queenie showed herself happy to penetrate into what she had called "the china house." On its knoll over the main road, just outside the town, Bellevue did look like china up on a mantelpiece—it was a compact stucco house with mouldings, recently painted a light blue. From the lawn set with pampas and crescent-shaped flowerbeds the hum of Robinson's motor mower passed in summer over the sleepy town. And when winter denuded the trees round them the polished windows, glass porch and empty conservatory sent out, on mornings of frosty sunshine, a rather mischievous and uncaring flash. The almost sensuous cleanness of his dwelling was reproduced in the person of Robinson— about his ears, jaw, collar and close-clipped nails. The approach the Caveys had walked up showed the broad, decided tyre-prints of his car.

"Where had we got to?" Robinson said again.

"I was saying we should have to find a new form."

"Of course you were," agreed Robinson. "That was it." He nodded over the top of Justin's head.

"A new form for thinking and feeling . . ."

"But one thinks what one happens to think, or feels what one happens to feel. That is as just so happens—I should have thought. One either does or one doesn't?"

"One doesn't!" cried Justin. "That's what I've been getting at. For some time we have neither thought nor felt. Our faculties have slowed down without our knowing—they had stopped without our knowing! we know now. Now that there's enough death to challenge being alive we're facing it that, anyhow, we don't live. We're confronted by the impossibility *of* living—unless we can break through to something else. There's been a stop in our senses and in our faculties that's made everything round us so much dead matter—and dead matter we couldn't even displace. We can no longer express ourselves: what we say doesn't even approximate to reality; it only approximates to what's been said. I say, this war's an awful illumination; it's destroyed our dark; we have to see where we are. Immobilised, God help us, and each so far apart that we can't even try to signal each other. And our currency's worthless—our 'ideas,' so on, so on. We've got to mint a new one. We've got to break through to the new form—it needs genius. We're precipitated, this moment, between genius and death. I tell you, we must have genius to live at all."

"I am certainly dished, then," said Robinson. He got up and looked for Justin's empty glass and took it to the sideboard where the decanters were.

"We have it!" cried Justin, smiting the arm of his chair. "I salute your genius, Robinson, but I mistrust my own."

"That's very nice of you," said Robinson. "I agree with you that this war makes one think. I was in the last, but I don't remember thinking: I suppose possibly one had no time. Of course, these days in business one comes up against this war the whole way through. And to tell you the truth," said Robinson, turning round, "I do like my off times to *be* my off times, because with this and then that they are precious few. So I don't really think as much as I might—though I see how one might always begin. You don't think thinking gets one a bit rattled?"

"I don't think!" said Justin violently.

"Well, you should know," said Robinson, looking at his thumbnail. "I should have thought you did. From the way you talk."

"I couldn't think if I wanted: I've lost my motivation. I taste the dust in the street and I smell the limes in the square and I beat round inside

this beastly shell of the past among images that all the more torment me
as they lose any sense that they had. As for feeling—"

"You don't think you find it a bit slow here? Mind you, I haven't a
word against this place, but it's not a place I'd choose for an off time—"

"—My dear Robinson," Justin said, in a mincing schoolmasterish
tone, "you seem blind to our exquisite sociabilities."

"Pack of old cats," said Robinson amiably.

"You suggest I should get away for a bit of fun?"

"Well, I did mean that."

"I find my own fun," said Justin, "I'm torn, here, by every single pang
of annihilation. But that's what I look for; that's what I want completed;
that's the whole of what I want to embrace. On the far side of the nothing—my new form. Scrap 'me'; scrap my wretched identity and you'll
bring to the open some bud of life. I *not* 'I'—I'd be the world. . . . You're
right: what you would call thinking does get me rattled. I only what you
call think to excite myself. Take myself away, and I'd *think*. I might see; I
might feel purely; I might even love—"

"Fine," agreed Robinson, not quite easy. He paused and seemed to
regard what Justin had just said—at the same time, he threw a glance of
perceptible calculation at the electric clock on the mantelpiece. Justin
halted and said: "You give me too much to drink."

"You feel this war may improve us?" said Robinson.

"What's love like?" Justin said suddenly.

Robinson paused for just less than a second in the act of lighting a
cigarette. He uttered a shortish, temporising and for him unnaturally
loud laugh.

Queenie felt the vibration and turned round, withdrawing her arm
from the windowsill. She had been looking intently, between the
clumps of pampas, down the lawn to the road: cyclists and walkers on
their way into town kept passing Robinson's open gate. Across the road,
above the demesne wall, the dark beeches let through glitters of sky, and
the colour and scent of the mown lawn and the flowers seemed, by some
increase of evening, lifted up to the senses as though a new current
flowed underneath. Queenie saw with joy in her own mind what she
could not from her place in the window see—the blue china house, with
all its reflecting windows, perched on its knoll in the brilliant, fading air.
They are too rare—visions of where we are.

When the shock of the laugh made her turn round, she still saw day in Robinson's picture-frames and on the chromium fingers of the clock. She looked at Robinson's head, dropped back after the laugh on the leather scroll of his chair: her eyes went from him to Justin. "Did you two not hit it off?"

Robinson laughed again, this time much more naturally: he emitted a sound like that from inside a furnace in which something is being consumed. Letting his head fall sideways towards Queenie he seemed to invite her into his mood. "The way things come out is sometimes funny," he said to Justin, "if you know what I mean."

"No, I don't," Justin said stonily.

"I bet your sister does."

"You didn't know what I meant. Anything I may have said about your genius I do absolutely retract."

"Look here, I'm sorry," Robinson said, "I probably took you up all wrong."

"On the contrary: the mistake was mine."

"You know, it's funny about your sister: I never can realise she can't hear. She seems so much one of the party. Would she be fond of children?"

"You mean, why did she not marry?"

"Good God, no—I only had an idea . . ."

Justin went on: "There was some fellow once, but I never heard more of him. You'd have to be very on-coming, I daresay, to make any way with a deaf girl."

"No, I meant my children," said Robinson. He had got up, and he took from his mantelpiece two of the photographs in silver frames. With these he walked down the room to Queenie, who received them with her usual eagerness and immediately turned with them to the light. Justin saw his sister's profile bent forward in study and saw Robinson standing above her leaning against the window frame. When Robinson met an upward look from Queenie he nodded and touched himself on the chest. "I can see that—aren't they very like you?" she said. He pointed to one picture then held up ten fingers, then to the other and held up eight. "The fair little fellow's more like you, the bold one. The dark one has more the look of a girl—but he will grow up manly, I daresay. . . ." With this she went back to the photographs: she did not seem

anxious to give them up and Robinson made no movement to take them
from her—with Queenie the act of looking was always reflective and
slow. To Justin the two silhouettes against the window looked wedded
and welded by the dark. "They are both against me," Justin thought.
"She does not hear with her ears, he does not hear with his mind. No
wonder they can communicate."

"It's a wonder," she said, "that you have no little girl."

Robinson went back for another photograph—but, standing still
with a doubtful look at Queenie, he passed his hand, as though sadly
expunging something, backwards and forwards across the glass. "She's
quite right; we did have a girl," he said. "But I don't know how to tell her
the kid's dead."

Sixty miles away, the Major was making his last round through the
orchards before shutting up the house. By this time the bronze-green
orchard dusk was intense; the clumped curves of the fruit were hardly to
be distinguished among the leaves. The brilliance of evening, in which
he had watched Emma driving away, was now gone from the sky. Now
and then in the grass his foot knocked a dropped apple—he would sigh,
stoop rather stiffly, pick up the apple, examine it with the pad of his
thumb for bruises and slip it, tenderly as though it had been an egg, into
a baggy pocket of his tweed coat. This was not a good apple year. There
was something standardised, uncomplaining about the Major's movements—you saw a tall, unmilitary-looking man with a stoop and a thin-
nish drooping moustache. He often wore a slight frown, of doubt or
preoccupation. This frown had intensified in the last months.

As he approached the house he heard the wireless talking, and saw
one lamp at the distant end of the drawing-room where his aunt sat. At
once, the picture broke up—she started, switched off the wireless and
ran down the room to the window. You might have thought the room
had burst into flames. "Quick!" she cried. "Oh gracious, quick!—I
believe it's the telephone."

The telephone was at the other side of the house—before he got
there he heard the bell ringing. He put his hands in his pockets to keep
the apples from bumping as he legged it rapidly down the corridor.
When he unhooked on his wife's voice he could not help saying hag-
gardly: "You all right?"

"Of course. I just thought I'd say good night."

"That was nice of you," he said, puzzled. "How is the car running?"

"Like a bird," she said in a singing voice. "How are you all?"

"Well, I was just coming in; Aunt Fran's in the drawing-room listening to something on the wireless, and I made the children turn in half an hour ago."

"You'll go up to them?"

"Yes, I was just going." For a moment they both paused on the line, then he said: "Where have you got to now?"

"I'm at T—— now, at the hotel in the square."

"At T——? Aren't you taking it rather fast?"

"It's a lovely night; it's an empty road."

"Don't be too hard on the car, she—"

"Oh, I know," she said, in the singing voice again. "At C—— I did try to stop, but there was a terrible crowd there: dog racing. So I came on. Darling . . . ?"

"Yes?"

"It's a lovely night, isn't it?"

"Yes, I was really quite sorry to come in. I shall shut up the house now, then go up to the children; then I expect I'll have a word or two with Aunt Fran."

"I see. Well, I'd better be pushing on."

"They'll be sitting up for you, won't they?"

"Surely," said Emma quickly.

"Thank you for ringing up, dear: it was thoughtful of you."

"I was thinking about you."

He did not seem to hear this. "Well, take care of yourself. Have a nice time."

"Good night," she said. But the Major had hung up.

In the drawing-room Aunt Fran had not gone back to the wireless. Beside the evening fire lit for her age she sat rigid, face turned to the door, plucking round and round the rings on her left hand. She wore a foulard dress, net jabot and boned-up collar, of the type ladies wear to dine in private hotels. In the lamplight her waxy features appeared blurred, even effaced. The drawing-room held a crowd of chintz-covered chairs, inlaid tables and wool-worked stools; very little in it was antique, but nothing was strikingly up-to-date. There were cabinets of not rare china, and more blue-and-white plates, in metal clamps, hung in lines up the walls between water-colours. A vase of pink roses arranged by the governess already dropped petals on the piano. In one corner stood a harp with two broken strings—when a door slammed or one made a sudden movement this harp gave out a faint vibration or twang. The silence for miles around this obscure country house seemed to gather inside the folds of the curtains and to dilute the indoor air like a mist. This room Emma liked too little to touch already felt the touch of decay; it threw lifeless reflections into the two mirrors—the walls were green. Aunt Fran's body was stranded here like some object on the bed of a pool that has run dry. The magazine that she had been looking at had slipped from her lap to the black fur rug.

As her nephew appeared in the drawing-room door Aunt Fran fixed him urgently with her eyes. "*Nothing wrong?*"

"No, no—that was Emma."

"What's happened?"

"Nothing. She rang up to say good night."

"But she had said good night," said Aunt Fran in her troubled way. "She said good night to us when she was in the car. You remember, it was nearly night when she left. It seemed late to be starting to go so far. She had the whole afternoon, but she kept putting off, putting off. She seemed to me undecided up to the very last."

The Major turned his back on his aunt and began to unload his pockets, carefully placing the apples, two by two, in a row along the chiffonier. "Still, it's nice for her having this trip," he said.

"There was a time in the afternoon," said Aunt Fran, "when I thought she was going to change her mind. However, she's there now—did you say?"

"Almost," he said, "not quite. Will you be all right if I go and shut up the house? And I said I would look in on the girls."

"Suppose the telephone rings?"

"I don't think it will, again. The exchange will be closing, for one thing."

"This afternoon," said Aunt Fran, "it rang four times."

She heard him going from room to room, unfolding and barring the heavy shutters and barring and chaining the front door. She could begin to feel calmer now that the house was a fortress against the wakeful night. "Hi!" she called, "don't forget the window in here"—looking back over her shoulder into the muslin curtains that seemed to crepitate with dark air. So he came back, with his flat unexpectant step. "I'm not cold," she said, "but I don't like dark coming in."

He shuttered the window. "I'll be down in a minute."

"Then we might sit together?"

"Yes, Aunt Fran: certainly."

The children, who had been talking, dropped their voices when they heard their father's step on the stairs. Their two beds creaked as they straightened themselves and lay silent, in social, expectant attitudes. Their room smelled of toothpaste; the white presses blotted slowly into the white walls. The window was open, the blind up, so in here darkness was incomplete—obscured, the sepia picture of the Good Shepherd hung over the mantelpiece. "It's all right," they said, "we are quite awake." So the Major came round and halted between the two beds. "Sit on mine," said Di nonchalantly. "It's my turn to have a person to-night."

"Why did Mother ring up?" said Vivie, scrambling up on her pillow.

"Now how on earth did *you* know?"

"We knew by your voice—we couldn't hear what you said. We were only at the top of the stairs. Why did she?"

"To tell me to tell you to be good."

"She's said that," said Vivie, impatient. "What did she say truly?"

"Just good night."

"Oh. Is she there?"

"Where?"

"Where she said she was going to."

"Not quite—nearly."

"Goodness!" Di said; "it seems years since she went." The two children lay cryptic and still. Then Di went on: "Do you know what Aunt Fran said because Mother went away without any stockings?"

"No," said the Major, "and never mind."

"Oh, I don't mind," Di said, "I just heard." "And I heard," said Vivie: she could be felt opening her eyes wide, and the Major could just see, on the pillow, an implacable miniature of his wife's face. Di went on: "She's so frightened something will happen."

"Aunt Fran is?"

"She's always frightened of that."

"She is very fond of us all."

"Oh," burst out Vivie, "but Mother likes things to happen. She was whistling all the time she was packing up. Can't *we* have a treat tomorrow?"

"Mother'll be back to-morrow."

"But *can't* we have a treat?"

"We'll see; we'll ask Mother," the Major said.

"Oh yes, but suppose she didn't come back?"

"Look, it's high time you two went to sleep."

"We can't: we've got all sorts of ideas. . . . *You* say something, Daddy. Tell us something. Invent."

"Say what?" said the Major.

"Oh goodness," Vivie said; "*something*. What do you say to Mother?"

He went downstairs to Aunt Fran with their dissatisfied kisses stamped on his cheek. When he had gone Di fanned herself with the top of her sheet. "What makes him so disappointed, do you know?"

"I know, he thinks about the war."

But it was Di who, after the one question, unlocked all over and dropped plumb asleep. It was Vivie who, turning over and over, watched in the sky behind the cross of the window the tingling particles of the white dark, who heard the moth between the two window-sashes, who fancied she heard apples drop in the grass. One arbitrary line only divided this child from the animal: all her senses stood up, wanting to run the night. She swung her legs out of bed and pressed the soles of her feet on the cool floor. She got right up and stepped out of her nightdress and set out to walk the house in her skin. From each room she went into the human order seemed to have lapsed—discovered by sudden light, the chairs and tables seemed set round for a mouse's party on a gigantic scale. She stood for some time outside the drawing-room door and heard the unliving voices of the Major and aunt. She looked through the ajar door to the kitchen and saw a picked bone and a teapot upon the table and a maid lumped mute in a man's arms. She attempted the front door, but did not dare touch the chain: she could not get out of the house. She returned to the schoolroom, drawing her brows together, and straddled the rocking-horse they had not ridden for years. The furious bumping of the rockers woke the canaries under their cover: they set up a wiry springing in their cage. She dismounted, got out the box of chalks and began to tattoo her chest, belly and thighs with stars and snakes, red, yellow and blue. Then, taking the box of chalks with her, she went to her mother's room for a look in the long glass—in front of this she attempted to tattoo her behind. After this she bent right down and squinted, upside down between her legs, at the bedroom—the electric light over the dressing-table poured into the vacantly upturned mirror and on to Emma's left-behind silver things. The anarchy she felt all through the house to-night made her, when she had danced in front of the long glass, climb up to dance on the big bed. The springs bounced her higher and higher; chalk-dust flew from her body on to the fleece of the blankets, on to the two cold pillows that she was trampling out of their place. The bed-castors lunged, under her springing, over the threadbare pink bridal carpet of Emma's room.

Attacked by the castors, the chandelier in the drawing-room tinkled sharply over Aunt Fran's head.

She at once raised her eyes to the ceiling. "Something has got in," she said calmly—and, rising, made for the drawing-room door. By reflex, the Major rose to stop her: he sighed and put his weak whisky down. "Never mind," he said, "Aunt Fran. It's probably nothing. I'll go."

Whereupon, his Aunt Fran wheeled round on him with her elbows up like a bird's wings. Her wax features sprang into stony prominence. "It's never me, never me, never me! Whatever I see, whatever I hear it's 'nothing,' though the house might fall down. You keep everything back from me. No one speaks the truth to me but the man on the wireless. Always things being said on the telephone, always things being moved about, always Emma off at the end of the house singing, always the children hiding away. I am never told, never told, never told. I get the one answer, 'nothing.' I am expected to wait here. No one comes near the drawing-room. I am never allowed to go and see!"

"If that's how you feel," he said, "do certainly go." He thought: it's all right, I locked the house.

So it was Aunt Fran's face, with the forehead lowered, that came by inches round Emma's door. She appeared to present her forehead as a sort of a buffer, obliquely looked from below it, did not speak. Her glance, arriving gradually at its object, took in the child and the whole room. Vivie paused on the bed, transfixed, breathless, her legs apart. Her heart thumped; her ears drummed; her cheeks burned. To break up the canny and comprehensive silence she said loudly: "I am all over snakes."

"So this is what . . ." Aunt Fran said. "So this is what . . ."

"I'll get off this bed, if you don't like."

"The bed you were born in," said Aunt Fran.

Vivie did not know what to do; she jumped off the bed saying: "No one told me not to."

"Do you not know what is wicked?" said Aunt Fran—but with no more than estranged curiosity. She approached and began to try to straighten the bed, her unused hands making useless passes over the surface, brushing chalk-dust deeper into the fleece. All of a sudden, Vivie appeared to feel some majestic effluence from her aunt's person: she lagged round the bed to look at the stooping set face, at the mouth held in a curve like a dead smile, at the veins in the downcast eyelids and the backs of the hands. Aunt Fran did not hurry her ceremonial fumbling; she seemed to exalt the moment that was so fully hers. She picked a pillow up by its frill and placed it high on the bolster.

"That's Mother's pillow," said Vivie.

"Did you say your prayers to-night?"

"Oh yes."

"They didn't defend you. Better say them again. Kneel down and say to Our Lord—"

"In my skin?"

Aunt Fran looked directly at, then away from, Vivie's body, as though for the first time. She drew the eiderdown from the foot of the bed and made a half-blind sweep at Vivie with it, saying: "Wrap up, wrap up."
"Oh, they'll come off—my snakes!" said Vivie, backing away. But Aunt Fran, as though the child were on fire, put into motion an extraordinary strength—she rolled, pressed and pounded Vivie up in the eiderdown until only the prisoner's dark eyes, so like her mother's, were left free to move wildly outside the great sausage, of padded taffeta, pink.

Aunt Fran, embracing the sausage firmly, repeated: "Now say to Our Lord—"

Shutting the door of her own bedroom, Aunt Fran felt her heart beat. The violence of the stranger within her ribs made her sit down on the ottoman—meanwhile, her little clock on the mantelpiece loudly and, it seemed to her, slowly ticked. Her window was shut, but the pressure of night silence made itself felt behind the blind, on the glass.

Round the room, on ledges and brackets, stood the fetiches she travelled through life with. They were mementoes—photos in little warped frames, musty round straw boxes, china kittens, palm crosses, the three Japanese monkeys, *bambini*, a Lincoln Imp, a merrythought pen-wiper, an ivory spinning-wheel from Cologne. From these objects the original virtue had by now almost evaporated. These gifts' givers, known on her lonely journey, were by now faint as their photographs: she no longer knew, now, where anyone was. All the more, her nature clung to these objects that moved with her slowly towards the dark.

Her room, the room of a person tolerated, by now gave off the familiar smell of herself—the smell of the old. A little book wedged the mirror at the angle she liked. When she was into her ripplecloth dressing-gown she brushed and plaited her hair and took out her teeth. She wound her clock and, with hand still trembling a little, lighted her own candle on the commode, then switched off her nephew's electric light. The room contracted round the crocus of flame as she knelt down slowly beside her bed—but while she said the Lord's Prayer she could not help listening, wondering what kept the Major so long downstairs. She never felt free to pray till she had heard the last door shut, till she could relax her watch on the house. She never could pray until they were *all* prostrate—loaned for at least some hours to innocence, sealed by the darkness over their lids.

To-night she could not attempt to lift up her heart. She could, however, abase herself, and she abased herself for them all. The evil of the moment down in the drawing-room, the moment when she had cried "It is never me!" clung like a smell to her, so closely that she had been eager to get her clothes off, and did not like, even now, to put her hands to her face.

Who shall be their judge? Not I.

The blood of the world is poisoned, feels Aunt Fran, with her forehead over the eiderdown. Not a pure drop comes out at any prick—yes, even the heroes shed black blood. The solitary watcher retreats step by step from his post—who shall stem the black tide coming in? There are no more children: the children are born knowing. The shadow rises up the cathedral tower, up the side of the pure hill. There is not even the past: our memories share with us the infected zone; not a memory does not lead up to this. Each moment is everywhere, it holds the war in its crystal; there is no elsewhere, no other place. Not a benediction falls on this apart house of the Major; the enemy is within it, creeping about. Each heart here falls to the enemy.

So this is what goes on. . . .

Emma flying away—and not saying why, or where. And to wrap the burning child up did not put out the fire. You cannot look at the sky without seeing the shadow, the men destroying each other. What is the matter to-night—is there a battle? This is a threatened night.

Aunt Fran sags on her elbows; her knees push desperately in the woolly rug. She cannot even repent; she is capable of no act; she is undone. She gets up and eats a biscuit, and looks at the little painting of Mont Blanc on the little easel beside her clock. She still does not hear the Major come up to bed.

Queenie understood that the third child, the girl, was dead: she gave back the photograph rather quickly, as though unbearable sadness emanated from it. Justin, however, came down the room and looked at the photograph over Robinson's shoulder—at the rather vulgar, frank, blonde little face. He found it hard to believe that a child of Robinson's should have chosen the part of death. He then went back to the table and picked up, with a jerky effrontery, the photographs of the two little boys. "Do they never come here?" he said. "You have plenty of room for them."

"I daresay they will; I mean to fix up something. Just now they're at Greystones," Robinson said—he then looked quite openly at the clock.

"With their mother?" Justin said, in a harsh, impertinent voice.

"Yes, with my wife."

"So you keep up the two establishments?"

Even Robinson glanced at Justin with some surprise. "If you call it that," he said indifferently. "I rather landed myself with this place, really—as a matter of fact, when I moved in it looked as though things might work out differently. First I stopped where you are, at the hotel, but I do like to have a place of my own. One feels freer, for one thing."

"There's a lot in that," said Justin, with an oblique smile. "Our local ladies think you keep a Bluebeard's castle up here."

"What, corpses?" Robinson said, surprised.

"Oh yes, they think you're the devil."

"Who, me?" replied Robinson, busy replacing photographs on the mantelpiece. "That's really very funny: I'd no idea. I suppose they may think I've been pretty slack—but I'm no good at teafights, as a matter of fact. But I can't see what else can be eating them. What ought I to do, then? Throw a party here? I will if your sister'll come and pour out tea— but I don't think I've really got enough chairs. . . . I hope," he added, looking at Queenie, "*she* doesn't think it's not all above board here?"

"You're forgetting again: she misses the talk, poor girl."

"She doesn't look very worried."

"I daresay she's seldom been happier. She's built up quite a romance about this house. She has a world to herself—I could envy her."

Robinson contrived to give the impression that he did not wish to have Queenie discussed—partly because he owned her, he understood her, partly because he wished to discuss nothing: it really was time for his guests to go. Though he was back again in his armchair, regard for time appeared in his attitude. Justin could not fail to connect this with the telephone and the smile that had not completely died. It became clear, staringly clear, that throughout the evening his host had been no more than marking time. This made Justin say "Yes" (in a loud pertinacious voice), "this evening's been quite an event for us. Your house has more than its legend, Robinson; it has really remarkable character. However, all good things—" Stiff with anger, he stood up.

"Must you?" said Robinson, rising. "I'm so sorry."

Lighting-up time, fixed by Nature, had passed. The deaf woman, from her place in the window, had been watching lights of cars bend over the hill. Turning with the main road, that had passed the foot of the mountains, each car now drove a shaft of extreme brilliance through the dark below Robinson's pampas-grass. Slipping, dropping with a rush past the gate, illuminating the dust on the opposite wall, car after car vanished after its light—there was suddenly quite a gust of them, as though the mountain country, before sleeping, had stood up and shaken them from its folds. The release of movement excited Queenie—that and the beat of light's wings on her face. She turned round very reluctantly as Justin approached and began to make signs to her.

"Why, does Mr. Robinson want us to go?" she said.

"That's the last thing I want!" shouted Robinson.

("She can't hear you.")

"Christ . . ." said Robinson, rattled. He turned the lights on—the three, each with a different face of despair, looked at each other across the exposed room, across the teatray on the circular table and the superb leather backs of the chairs. "My brother thinks we've kept you too long," she said—and as a lady she looked a little shaken, for the first time unsure of herself. Robinson would not for worlds have had this happen; he strode over and took and nursed her elbow, which tensed then relaxed gently inside the muslin sleeve. He saw, outdoors, his window cast on the pampas, saw the whole appearance of shattered night. She looked for reassurance into his face, and he saw the delicate lines in hers.

"And look how late it's got, Mr. Robinson!"

"It's not that," he said in his naturally low voice, "but—"

A car pulled up at the gate. Alarmed by the lit window it cut its lights off and could be felt to crouch there, attentive, docile, cautious, waiting to turn in. "Your friend is arriving," Justin said.

On that last lap of her drive, the eighteen miles of flat road along the base of the mountains, the last tingling phase of darkness had settled down. Grassy sharpness passed from the mountains' outline, the patches of firs, the gleam of watery ditch. The west sky had gradually drunk its yellow and the ridged heights that towered over her right hand became immobile cataracts, sensed not seen. Animals rising out of the ditches turned to Emma's headlamps green lamp-eyes. She felt the shudder of night, the contracting bodies of things. The quick air sang in her ears; she drove very fast. At the crossroads above Robinson's town she pulled round in a wide swerve: she saw the lemon lights of the town strung along under the black trees, the pavements and the pale humble houses below her in a faint, mysterious glare as she slipped down the funnel of hill to Robinson's gate. (The first white gate on the left, you cannot miss it, he'd said.) From the road she peered up the lawn and saw, between pampas-tufts, three people upright in his lit room. So she pulled up and switched her lights and her engine off and sat crouching in her crouching car in the dark—night began to creep up her bare legs. Now the glass porch sprang into prominence like a lantern—she saw people stiffly saying goodbye. Down the drive came a man and woman almost in flight; not addressing each other, not looking back—putting the back of a fist to her mouth quickly Emma checked the uprush of an uncertain laugh. She marked a lag in the steps—turning their heads quickly the man and woman looked with involuntary straightness into the car, while her eyes were glued to their silhouettes. The two turned down to the town and she turned in at the gate.

Farouche, with her tentative little swagger and childish, pleading air of delinquency, Emma came to a halt in Robinson's living-room. He had pulled down the blind. She kept recoiling and blinking and drawing her fingers over her eyes, till Robinson turned off the top light. "Is that that?" There was only the reading-lamp.

She rested her shoulder below his and grappled their enlaced fingers closer together as though trying to draw calmness from him. Standing against him, close up under his height, she held her head up and began to look round the room. "You're whistling something," she said, after a moment or two.

"I only mean, take your time."

"Why, am I nervous?" she said.

"Darling, you're like a bat in out of the night. I told you not to come along too fast."

"I see now, I came too early," she said. "Why didn't you tell me you had a party? Who were they? What were they doing here?"

"Oh, they're just people in this place. He's a bit screwy and she's deaf, but I like them, as a matter of fact."

"They're mackintoshy sort of people," she said. "But I always thought you lived all alone. . . . Is there anyone else in the house now?"

"Not a mouse," said Robinson, without change of expression. "My housekeeper's gone off for the night."

"I see," said Emma. "Will you give me a drink?"

She sat down where Justin had just been sitting, and, bending forward with a tremulous frown, began to brush ash from the arm of the chair. You could feel the whole of her hesitate. Robinson, without hesitation, came and sat easily on the arm of the chair from which she had brushed the ash. "It's sometimes funny," he said, "when people drop in like that. 'My god,' I thought when I saw them, 'what an evening to choose.'" He slipped his hand down between the brown velvet cushion

and Emma's spine, then spread the broad of his hand against the small of
her back. Looking kindly down at her closed eyelids he went on: "However, it all went off all right. Oh, and there's one thing I'd like to tell
you—that chap called me a genius."

"How would he know?" said Emma, opening her eyes.

"We never got that clear. I was rather out of my depth. His sister was
deaf. . . ." here Robinson paused bent down and passed his lips absently
over Emma's forehead. "Or did I tell you that?"

"Yes, you told me that. . . . Is it true that this house is blue?"

"You'll see to-morrow."

"There'll hardly be time, darling; I shall hardly see this house in the
daylight. I must go on to—where I'm supposed to be."

"At any rate, I'm glad that was all O.K. They're not on the telephone,
where you're going?"

"No, it's all right; they're not on the telephone. . . . *You'll* have to
think of something that went wrong with my car."

"That will all keep," said Robinson. "Here you are."

"Yes, here I am." She added: "The night was lovely," speaking more
sadly than she knew. Yes, here she was, being settled down to as calmly
as he might settle down to a meal. Her naivety as a lover . . . She could
not have said, for instance, how much the authoritative male room—
the electric clock, the side-board, the unlit grate, the cold of the leather
chairs—put, at every moment when he did not touch her, a gulf between
her and him. She turned her head to the window. "I smell flowers."

"Yes, I've got three flowerbeds."

"Darling, for a minute could we go out?"

She moved from his touch and picked up Queenie's teatray and asked
if she could put it somewhere else. Holding the tray (and given counte-
nance by it) she halted in front of the photographs. "Oh . . ." she said.
"Yes. Why?" "I wish in a way you hadn't got any children." "I don't see
why I shouldn't have: you have."

"Yes, I . . . But Vivie and Di are not so much *like* children—"

"If they're like you," he said, "those two will be having a high old
time, with the cat away—"

"Oh darling, I'm not the cat."

In the kitchen (to put the tray down) she looked round: it shone
with tiling and chromium and there seemed to be switches in every

place. "What a whole lot of gadgets you have," she said. "Look at all those electric . . ." "Yes, I like them." "They must cost a lot of money. My kitchen's all over blacklead and smoke and hooks. My cook would hate a kitchen like this."

"I always forget that you have a cook." He picked up an electric torch and they went out. Going along the side of the house, Robinson played a mouse of light on the wall. "Look, really blue." But she only looked absently. "Yes—But have I been wrong to come?" He led her off the gravel on to the lawn, till they reached the edge of a bed of stocks. Then he firmly said: "That's for you to say, my dear girl."

"I know it's hardly a question—I hardly know you, do I?"

"We'll be getting to know each other," said Robinson.

After a minute she let go of his hand and knelt down abruptly beside the flowers: she made movements like scooping the scent up and laving her face in it—he, meanwhile, lighted a cigarette and stood looking down. "I'm glad you like my garden," he said. "You feel like getting fond of the place?"

"You say you forget that I have a cook."

"Look, sweet, if you can't get that off your mind you'd better get in your car and go straight home. . . . But you will."

"Aunt Fran's so old, too old; it's not nice. And the Major keeps thinking about the war. And the children don't think I am good; I regret that."

"You have got a nerve," he said, "but I love that. You're with me. Aren't you with me?—Come out of that flowerbed."

They walked to the brow of the lawn; the soft feather-plumes of the pampas rose up a little over her head as she stood by him overlooking the road. She shivered. "What are all those trees?" "The demesne—I know they burnt down the castle years ago. The demesne's great for couples." "What's in there?" "Nothing, I don't think; just the ruin, a lake . . ."

"I wish—"

"Now, what?"

"I wish we had more time."

"Yes: we don't want to stay out all night."

So taught, she smothered the last of her little wishes for consolation. Her shyness of further words between them became extreme; she was becoming frightened of Robinson's stern, experienced delicacy on the subject of love. Her adventure became the quiet practice with him. The adventure (even, the pilgrimage) died at its root, in the childish part of her mind. When he had headed her off the cytherean terrain—the leaf-drowned castle ruin, the lake—she thought for a minute he had broken her heart, and she knew now he had broken her fairytale. He seemed content—having lit a new cigarette—to wait about in his garden for a few minutes longer: not poetry but a sort of tactile wisdom came from the firmness, lawn, under their feet. The white gateposts, the boles of beeches above the dust-whitened wall were just seen in reflected light from the town. There was no moon, but dry, tense, translucent darkness: no dew fell.

Justin went with his sister to her door in the square. Quickly, and in their necessary silence, they crossed the grass under the limes. Here a dark window reflected one of the few lamps, there a shadow crossed a lit blind, and voices of people moving under the trees made a reverberation in the box of the square. Queenie let herself in; Justin heard the heavy front door drag shut slowly across the mat. She had not expected him to come in, and he did not know if she shared his feeling of dissonance, or if she recoiled from shock, or if she were shocked at all. Quitting the square at once, he took the direct way to his hotel in the main street. He went in at the side door, past the bar in which he so often encountered Robinson.

In his small, harsh room he looked first at his bed. He looked, as though out of a pit of sickness, at his stack of books on the mantelpiece. He writhed his head round sharply, threw off his coat and began to unknot his tie. Meanwhile he beat round, in the hot light, for some crack of outlet from his constriction. It was at his dressing-table, for he had no other, that he began and ended his letter to Robinson: the mirror screwed to the dressing-table constituted a witness to this task—whenever his look charged up it met his own reared heard, the flush heightening on the bridge of the nose and forehead, the neck from which as though for an execution, the collar had been taken away.

> My dear Robinson,
>   Our departure from your house (Bellevue, I think?) to-night

was so awkwardly late, and at the last so hurried, that I had inadequate time in which to thank you for your hospitality to my sister and to myself. That we exacted this hospitality does not make its merit, on your part, less. Given the inconvenience we so clearly caused you, your forbearance with us was past praise. So much so that (as you may be glad to hear) my sister does not appear to realise how very greatly we were *de trop*. In my own case—which is just—the same cannot be said. I am conscious that, in spite of her disability, she did at least prove a less wearisome guest than I.

My speculations and queries must, to your mind, equally seem absurd. This evening's fiasco has been definitive: I think it better our acquaintance should close. You will find it in line with my usual awkwardness that I should choose to state this decision of mine at all. Your indifference to the matter I cannot doubt. My own lack of indifference must make its last weak exhibition in this letter—in which, if you have fine enough nostrils (which I doubt) every sentence will almost certainly stink. In attempting to know you I have attempted to enter, and to comport myself in, what might be called an area under your jurisdiction. If my inefficacies appeared to you ludicrous, my curiosities (as in one special instance to-night) appeared more—revolting. I could gauge (even before the postscript outside your gate) how profoundly I had offended you. Had we either of us been gentlemen, the incident might have passed off with less harm.

My attempts to know you I have disposed of already. My wish that you should know me has been, from the first, ill found. You showed yourself party to it in no sense, and the trick I played on myself I need not discuss. I acted and spoke (with regard to you) upon assumptions you were not prepared to warrant. You cannot fail to misunderstand what I mean when I say that a year ago this might not have happened to me. But—the assumptions on which I acted, Robinson, are becoming more general in a driven world than you yet (or may ever) know. The extremity to which we are each driven must be the warrant for what we do and say.

My extraordinary divagation towards you might be said to be, I suppose, an accident of this summer. But there are no accidents. I have the fine (yes) fine mind's love of the fine plume, and I meet no fine plumes down my own narrow street. Also, in this place (birthplace) you interposed your solidity between me and what might have been the full effects of an exacerbating return. In fact, you had come to constitute for me a very genuine holiday. As things are, my five remaining days here will have to be seen out. I shall hope not to meet you, but must fear much of the trap-like size of this town. (You need not, as I mean to, avoid the hotel bar.) Should I, however, fail to avoid you, I shall again, I suppose, have to owe much, owe any face I keep, to your never-failing imperviousness. Understand that it will be against my wish that I re-open this one-sided account.

I wish you good night. Delicacy does not deter me from adding that I feel my good wish to be superfluous. I imagine that, incapable of being haunted, you are incapable of being added to. To-morrow (I understand) you will feel fine, but you will not know any more about love. If the being outside your gate came with a question, it is possible that she should have come to me. If I had even seen her she might not go on rending my heart. As it is, as you are, I perhaps denounce you as much on her behalf as my own. Not trying to understand, you at least cannot misunderstand the mood and hour in which I write. As regards my sister, please do not discontinue what has been your even kindness to her: she might be perplexed. She has nothing to fear, I think.

Accept, my dear Robinson (without irony)

My kind regards,
J.C.

Justin, trembling, smote a stamp on this letter. Going down as he was, in the hall he unhooked his mackintosh and put it over his shirt. It was well past midnight; the street, empty, lay in dusty reaches under the few lamps. Between the shutters his step raised an echo; the cold of the mountains had come down; two cats in his path unclinched and shot off into the dark. On his way to the letterbox he was walking towards Bellevue; on his way back he still heard the drunken woman sobbing against the telegraph pole. The box would not be cleared till to-morrow noon.

Queenie forgot Justin till next day. The house in which her rooms were was so familiar that she went upstairs without a pause in the dark. Crossing her sitting-room she smelled oil from the cooker behind the screen: she went through an arch to the cubicle where she slept. She was happy. Inside her sphere of silence that not a word clouded, the spectacle of the evening at Bellevue reigned. Contemplative, wishless, almost without an "I," she unhooked her muslin dress at the wrists and waist, stepped from the dress and began to take down her hair. Still in the dark, with a dreaming sureness of habit, she dropped hairpins into the heart-shaped tray.

This was the night she knew she would find again. It had stayed living under a film of time. On just such a summer night, once only, she had walked with a lover in the demesne. His hand, like Robinson's, had been on her elbow, but she had guided him, not he her, because she had better eyes in the dark. They had gone down walks already deadened with moss, under the weight of July trees; they had felt the then fresh aghast ruin totter above them; there was a moonless sky. Beside the lake they sat down, and while her hand brushed the ferns in the cracks of the stone seat emanations of kindness passed from him to her. The subtle deaf girl had made the transposition of this nothing or everything into an everything—the delicate deaf girl that the man could not speak to and was afraid to touch. She who, then so deeply contented, kept in her senses each frond and breath of that night, never saw him again and had soon forgotten his face. That had been twenty years ago, till to-night when it was now. To-night it was Robinson who, guided by Queenie down leaf tunnels, took the place on the stone seat by the lake.

The rusted gates of the castle were at the end of the square. Queenie, in her bed facing the window, lay with her face turned sideways, smiling, one hand lightly against her cheek.

II

Nightwind

Nightwind

He shuffled down the corridor, trying the handles of the blind white doors. From one room there came sounds, a cry, a soft phrase of laughter, and in the silence they seemed a glimpse of the closed, secret worlds he would never enter. He leaned against the wall and held his face in his hands. There were revels below, savage music and the clatter of glasses, and outside in the night a wild wind was blowing.

Two figures came up from the stairs and started toward him. One went unsteadily on long, elegantly tailored legs, giggling helplessly. The other leaned on his supporting elbow, a pale tapering arm, one hand pressed to her bare collar-bone.

—Why Morris. What is it.

They stood and gazed at him foolishly, ripples of laughter still twitching their mouths. He pushed himself away from the wall, and hitched up his trousers. He said

—S'nothin. Too much drink. That you David.

The woman took a tiny step away from them and began to pick at her disintegrating hairstyle. David licked the point of his upper lip and said

—Listen Mor are you all right. Mor.

—Looking for my wife, said Mor.

Suddenly the woman gave a squeal of laughter, and the two men turned to look at her.

—I thought of something funny, she said simply, and covered her mouth. Mor stared at her, his eyebrows moving. He grinned and said

—I thought you were Liza.

The woman snickered, and David whispered in his ear.

—That's not Liza. That's . . . what is your name anyway.

—Jean, she said, and glared at him. He giggled, and took her by the arm.

—Jean I want you to meet Mor. You should know your host after all. The woman said

—I wouldn't be a Liza if you paid me.

—Mother of God, said Mor, a bubble bursting on his lips.

David frowned at her for shame and said

—You must be nice to Mor. He's famous.

—Never heard of him.

—You see Mor. She never heard of you. Your own guest and she never heard of you. What do you think of that.

—Balls, said Mor.

—O now. Why are you angry. Is it because of what they are all saying. Nobody listens to that kind of talk. You know that. We're all friends here aren't we Liza—

—Jean.

—And this is a grand party you're throwing here Mor but no one listens to talk. We know Mor that your success is nothing to do with— matrimonial graft.

On the last words the corner of David's mouth moved as a tight nerve uncoiled. Mor looked at him with weary eyes, then walked away from them and turned down the stairs. David called after him

—Where are you going man.

But Mor was gone.

—Well, said the woman. Poor Mor is turning into quite a wreck. These days he even has to pretend he's drunk.

David said nothing, but stared at the spot where Mor had disappeared. The woman laughed, and taking his arm she pressed it against her side and said

—Let's go somewhere quiet.

—Shut your mouth, David told her.

Downstairs Mor wandered through the rooms. The party was ending, and most of the guests had left. In the hall a tiny fat man leaned against the wall, his mouth open and his eyes closed. A tall girl with large teeth, his daughter, was punching his shoulder and yelling something in his ear. She turned to Mor for help, and he patted her arm absently and went on into the drawing room. There in the soft light a couple were dancing slowly, while others sat about in silence, looking at their hands. In the corner a woman in a white dress stood alone, a little uncertain, clutching an empty glass. She watched his unsteady progress toward her.

—There you are, he said, and grinning he touched the frail white stuff of her gown. She said nothing, and he sighed.

—All right Liza so I'm drunk. So what.

—So nothing. I said nothing. Your tie is crooked.

His hands went to the limp black bow at his neck, and went away again.

—It's coming apart, he said. The knot is coming apart.

—Yes.

He held her eyes for a moment, and looked away. He said

—You have a sobering effect Liza. How do you live with yourself.

—You always pretend to be drunker than you are and then you blame me. That's all.

—You know I met a woman upstairs and thought it was you. She was laughing and I thought it was you. Imagine.

He put his hands into the pockets of his jacket and looked at the room. The couple had stopped dancing, and were standing motionless now in the middle of the floor, their arms around each other as though they had forgotten to disentangle them. Mor said

—What are they waiting for. Why don't they go home.

—You hate them, Liza said. Don't you.

—Who.

—All of them. All these people—our friends.

He looked at her, his eyebrows lifted.

—No. I'm sorry for them—for us. Look at it. The new Ireland. Sitting around at the end of a party wondering why we're not happy. Trying to find what it is we've lost.

—O Mor don't start all that.

He smiled at her, and murmured

—No.

David put his head around the door, and when he saw them he smiled and shot at them with a finger and thumb. He crossed the room with

exaggerated stealth, looking over his shoulder at imaginary pursuers. He
stopped near them and asked from the corner of his mouth

—They get him yet.

—Who, said Liza, smiling at his performance.

Mor frowned at him, and shook his head, but David pretended not to
notice.

—Why your murderer of course.

Liza's mouth fell open, the glass shook in her hand, and then was still.
David went on

—You mean you didn't know about it. O come on now Liza. I
thought you and Mor had arranged it. You know—we've got everything
at our party including a murderer loose in the grounds with the cops
chasing him. You didn't know Liza.

She turned to Mor, silently questioning. He clicked his teeth angrily
and looked at the floor.

—Shut up David.

—O excuse me, said David, grinning, and coughed behind his hand.
Liza turned to him.

—David what is this joke all about. Seriously now.

—Well Liz it's no joke. Some tinker stabbed his girl friend six times
in the heart tonight. The guards had him cornered here when the rain
came on. The way I heard it they left some green recruit to watch for
him while they all trooped back to Celbridge for their raincoats. Anyway they say he's somewhere in the grounds but knowing the boys he's
probably in England by now. Come over to the window and you can see
the lights. It's all very exciting.

Liza took a drink and laid down her glass. She said quietly, without
raising her head

—Why didn't you tell me Mor.

—I forgot.

—You forgot.

—Yes. I forgot.

David looked from one of them to the other, grinning sardonically.
He said

—Perhaps Liza he didn't want to frighten you.

Mor turned and looked at David, his lips a thin pale line.

—You have a loud mouth David.

He moved away from them, then paused and said

—And uncurl your lip when you talk to me. Or I might be tempted to wipe that sneer off your face.

The smile faded, and David said coldly

—No offence meant Mor.

—And none taken.

—Then why are you so angry.

Mor laughed, a short, cold sound.

—I haven't been angry in years.

He stalked away, and in silence they watched him go. Then Liza laughed nervously and said

—Take no notice of him David. He's a bit drunk. You know.

David shrugged his shoulders and smiled at her.

—I must go home.

In the hall Liza helped him into his coat. He said lightly

—Why don't you come over to the house and visit me some day. The old bachelor life gets very dreary.

She glanced at him with a small sly smile.

—For what, she asked.

He pursed his lips and turned to the door. With his hand on the lock he said stiffly

—I'm . . . I'm very fond of you Liza.

She laughed, and looked down at her dress in confusion.

—Of me. O you're not.

—I am Liza.

—You shouldn't say things like that. Good night David.

But neither moved. They stood and gazed at each other, and Liza's breath quickened. She moved swiftly to the door and pulled it open, and a blast of wind came in to disturb the hall. She stepped out on the porch with him. The oaks were lashing their branches together, and they had voices that cried and groaned. Black rain was falling, and in the light from the open door the lawn was a dark, ugly sea. She opened her mouth to speak, closed it, then turned away from him and said

—Call me.

She stood very still and looked out at the darkness, and the damp wind lifted her hair. David moved to touch her, and dropped his hand. He said

—I'll call you tomorrow.

—No. Not tomorrow.

—When.

—I must go David.

With her head bent she turned and hurried back along the hall.

All the guests had left the drawing room, and Mor sat alone in a high winged chair, a glass in his hand and a bottle beside him on a low table. His tie had at last come undone, and his eyes were faintly glazed. Liza went to the couch and straightened a cushion. From the floor she gathered up a cigarette end and an overturned glass. He watched her, his chin on his breast. He said thickly

—What's wrong with you.

—Nothing. Have they all gone.

—I suppose so.

She went to the tall window beside his chair and drew back the curtains. The wind pounded the side of the house, and between gusts the rain whispered softly on the glass. Down past the black, invisible fields little lights were moving. She said

—I wonder why he killed her.

—They say he wanted to marry her and she wouldn't have him. I think she was maybe a man-eater. A tart. He killed her. Happens every day these days.

There was silence but for the wind and rain beating, and the faint sighing of the trees. Mor said

—I suppose David made his usual pass.

She moved her shoulders, and he grinned up at her, showing his teeth. She said

—He asked if . . . he asked me to go with him. Tonight. He asked would I go with him.

—Did he now. And why didn't you.

She did not answer. He poured himself another drink.

—I know how David's mind works, he said. He thinks I don't deserve you. He's wrong though—God help me.

—You have a nasty mind.

—Yes. Though he must have been encouraged when I took the job. That sent me down a little farther.

He looked at her where she stood in the shadows watching the night. He frowned and asked

—Do you despise me too.

—For taking the job—why should I. Are you ashamed.

—No no. Your father is very good to do so much for me. Yes I'm ashamed.

—Why.

—Don't act Liza.

—It was your decision. If you had kept on writing I would have stood by you. We would have managed. Daddy could have—

She bit her lip, and Mor laughed.

—Go on, he said. Daddy could have kept us. You're right. Kind, generous daddy would have come along with his money-bags to sour our lives. Where's the use in talking. Me a writer—I'd be laughed out of the country. The bar in the Grosvenor Arms would collapse after a week of the laughing. Did you hear how mad Mor knocked up old man Fitz's daughter and moved into the big house and now says he's writing a book. Did you ever hear the likes. No Liza. This place produced me and will destroy me if I try to break free. All this crowd understands is the price of a heifer and the size of the new car and the holiday in Spain and those godblasted dogs howling for blood. No.

She said quietly

—If you hated these people so much why did you marry into them.

—Because Liza me dear I didn't know I was marrying into them.

There was a long silence, then Liza spoke.

—It wasn't my fault he died, she said, sadly defiant.

Mor turned away from her in the chair and threw up his hands.

—Always, he said. Always it comes to your mind. Blaming me.

She did not speak, and he leaned toward her, whispering

—Blaming me.

She joined her hands before her and sighed, holding her eyes fixed on the dark gleam of the glass before her. He said

—Well why don't you just trot along now after old David there. Sure maybe he can give you a better one. One that will live longer and make you happy.

She swung about to face him. Her eyes blazed, and she said

—All right then Mor if you want a fight you'll get one.

For a moment they stared at each other, and her anger went away. She turned back to the window.

—Well, Mor asked, and the word rang in the silence. She lifted her shoulders slowly, allowed them to fall. Mor nodded.

—Yes, he said. We've had it all before.

He stood up unsteadily, pressing his fingers on the arm of the chair for support. He went and stood beside her at the window. She said

—They're still searching. Look at the lights.

Side by side they stood and watched the tiny flashes move here and there in the dark. Suddenly she said

—If he got to the stables he could come in through the side door. If he did I'd hide him.

He stared at her, and feeling his eyes on her she set her mouth firmly and said

—I would I'd hide him. And then in the morning I'd get him out and bring him to Dublin and put him on the boat for England for Liverpool or some place.

She reached out blindly and took his hand. There were tears on her face, they fell, each gathering to itself a little light and flashing in the darkness of the window.

—We could do that if he came couldn't we Mor. It wouldn't be a bad thing to do. It wouldn't be a crime I mean would it. Out there in the dark with the rain and everything and thinking about all the things— thinking and thinking. It wouldn't be wrong to help him. Mor.

He took her in his arms and held her head on his shoulder. She was trembling.

—No, he said softly. It wouldn't be a bad thing.

She began to sob quietly, and he lifted her head and smiled at her.

—Don't cry Liza. There now.

The door-bell rang, and her eyes filled with apprehension. Without a word she moved past him and left the room.

Mor stood and looked about him. Long ago when he first saw this room he had thought it beautiful, and now it was one of the few things left which had not faded. The shaded lamps took from the warm walls of lilac a soft, full light, it touched everything, the chairs, the worn carpet, with gentle fingers. On the table beside him a half-eaten sandwich lay beside his bottle. There was an olive transfixed on a wooden pin. Muted voices came in from the hall, and outside in the fields a shout flared like a flame in the dark and then was blown away. Mor lifted his glass, and when the amber liquid moved, all the soft light of the room seemed to shift with it. He felt something touch him, something of the quality of silence that informs the saddest music. It was as though all the things he had ever lost had now come back to press upon his heart with a vast sadness. He stared at the table, at the little objects, the bread and the bottle, the olive dead on its pin.

Liza came back, her hands joined before her, and the knuckles white. She stopped in the middle of the room and looked blankly about her, as if she were dazed.

—What is it, he asked. Who was at the door.

—A guard.

—What did he want.

—What.

—What did he want. The guard.

—O the guard. He wanted to use the phone.

She looked at him, and blinked rapidly twice.

—They found him, she said. He hanged himself in the long meadow.

She examined the room once again with vague eyes, then she sighed, and went away. He sat down to finish his drink, and after a time went out and climbed the stairs.

Liza was lying in bed, the lamp beside her throwing a cruel light over her drawn face. He sat beside her and watched her. Her eyes were open, staring up into the dimness. In the silence there was the sound of the rain against the window. She said, so softly he barely heard her

—We missed so much.

He leaned down and kissed her forehead. She did not move. He put his hand over her breast, feeling the nipple cold and small through the silk of her night gown.

—Liza.

She turned away from him, and when she spoke her voice was muffled by the sheets.

—Bring me a glass of water Morris. My mouth is dry.

He moved away from her, and switched off the light. He went down the stairs in the darkness, the air cold and stale against his face. On quiet feet he returned to the drawing room and poured another, last drink. Then he went and stood at the dark window, and listened to the wind singing in the trees.

The Bombs

"Once hit by it you are haunted forever." He woke in New York, went to the washroom, threw water over his face. What was it he was dreaming of? Then he remembered. Bombs. Talbot Street 17 May 1974. Running along, a newspaper reporter who that day stalked over blood, gush, bones.

"Jesus."

Outside New York tapered, a sort of winter redolence, lights crushed into the sky. "Like roses," he told himself. Like the beautiful exotic roses his mother used to grow in her Wicklow garden.

He dried himself, looking at the towel as though expecting blood, went back to bed.

This time dreams brought him to Dublin streets, Georgian doors.

Footfalls echo in the memory
Down the passage which we did not take
Towards the door we never opened
Into the rose garden.

He'd been a prize pupil at University College Dublin.

These were the only lines of poetry he could dismember from the general array of quotations. They crossed his mind now, a shadow. The autumn in Dublin had been honest as autumns go, ripe leaves falling and beautiful youngsters performing street theatre in Stephen's Green. He'd left Dublin on a day of lemon and wine leaves to cover the American elections.

Now he was free. He had a month before him. He was leaving next day for the most golden state of all, California.

The plane took off into the sunset and the air-hostess brought him shrimps. He'd always desired this journey. Being young in the early sixties he'd read much of Jack Kerouac and Allen Ginsberg. He made a few hitch-hiking journeys to Belgium and Holland. But then the Irish television station had been set up and they employed him. He watched the sixties burgeon. He was in Berlin in '68 and Paris the same year. His girlfriend for ten years, being five years younger than him, partook in some of these celebrations. But it fascinated him, the sexual candour which people of his generation merely seemed to be imitating. He thought they were so lucky, those young in the late sixties and early seventies.

Yet there was something, a little you might say of which he was augur in Ireland. He'd been quick to read the beats. He remembered them. His apartment in Ballsbridge, Dublin was full of the works of Brother Antoninus and Thomas Merton. He had had Hermann Hesse before anyone else. He even occasionally smoked marijuana with timid and leading personalities of the Irish media.

He stayed in Geary. There he had friends who worked on a liberal San Francisco newspaper. They were out most of the time. He had a lovely room, a window to the street, twenty-five days in San Francisco.

He wrote his impressions in a diary.

"Coming into San Francisco was like—like bordering on the Divine. Hills wearing houses like tiaras. The theme of a generation went through my head. 'If you're going to San Francisco.' It really was, up there, on a Friday evening a golden city."

Finished his diary he wondered whether he should write to Diane.

Their last parting in Grafton Street had been turbulent. She was sleeping with a boy of twenty-five. Their relationship was truly disintegrating. The summer had borne witness to that. Fights in expensive restaurants with wren blue fronts to Dun Laoghaire. She was having an affair with a young actor. There was nothing he could do.

A girl at a party before he left Dublin approached him and said, "So she's sick of you fucking her."

That's what he despised about Dublin. The cynicism that almost seemed to generate from the waste land of the North. He and Diane were lovers because both were vigilant. They journeyed each Sunday to a woodland in Wicklow and walked, or on long weekends visited Celtic ruins hanging beside perilous waters in the West, or maybe even an island hotel, eating mackerel in the slow Atlantic twilights.

She was living apart from him now. She was dressing ravishingly since their break, blues, purples. She looked a bit like the Paris nightline he thought—rather sadly knowing their moments had been counted and that Diane was looking better, finer, newer.

What he really should do was have an affair himself.

All the romanticism possible in a suburban Dublin youth caught up with him in San Francisco. Around the bay there were cafés of such beauty you'd swear time had stopped still and a young poet had posed.

There was no pop music on the juke boxes on North Beach. There were snatches of Puccini or Rossini or, to be cautious, a singular piece of Charlie Parker.

James drank tea, watched by aspiring authoresses.

In one café an Arab lady with a veiled face scribbled what James desired to think was her memoirs.

He was free from journalism yet his journalistic head juggled with phrases or knotted impressions. However that too was slowing down.

He was waking more easily, recalling and picturing his first date, bringing a young lady to the harbour at Dun Laoghaire.

He motored up and down the coast a little.

His first sight of Big Sur: he knew he was destined to change.

Earth postulating under light; the first shots of creation. He knew he'd go back to Ireland a new man. His eyes caught his face in the mirror. He looked at least nine years younger.

Going into a profession, he told himself in San Francisco, you accept its ethics, you become its clichés.

Here clichés fall off. I don't know why.

Maybe it was that Hare Krishna monk with the balloon in Santa Barbara or the old toothless lady giving out diagrams which accurately illustrated Hell on the highway to hitchhikers.

He'd driven south to Santa Barbara, breaching his own commandments to interview an Irish writer, world famous.

He knew this interview to be in the nature of a scoop and well-written and wise. But it wasn't good enough. Eating macro-biotic, honeyed ice-cream in a restaurant on Church Street he decided to call quits, totally for these weeks. He destroyed the interview, burnt it in a blaze coming towards Thanksgiving. The only words left were the Irish writer's in type.

"Ireland is on the brink of moral collapse. Only its young can save it."

That would make you think of Rome. James had been cynical of proclamation. North and South of Ireland he knew to be irredeemably divided. The South peaceful, complacent, much unemployment in evidence in the cities but the country thriving, and men and women enjoying life who had never before allowed enjoyment into their lives. The North was toppling. After eight years reporting on it James could only call it a mess, messy stupid people everywhere, nobody to his knowledge with the courage to transcend clichés, Marxist, IRA, loyalist, middle-class, no one, but no one with gall.

He drove to the sea after this ritual and for the first time since seventeen was amazed, truly astonished by time.

He had already discovered San Francisco to be a garden of restaurants and read Malcolm Lowry's *Under the Volcano* from one to the other. Young gay people abounded, some with east coast accents. There were some with beautiful faces and one spoke to James about the metaphysics of being gay.

He dropped Diane a postcard.

"How's Dublin. I see it's below freezing point. Wish you were here but I know that is not possible. The Indian summer is shaking everything here—with laughter. Love James XX." He picked up the card in a shop in which he found poems in a book of gay poetry by many discreetly known Irish writers. He smiled. The city was full of coincidences.

The first time he saw her was on a bus; he remembered her from somewhere but could not figure where or why his mind boggled him with remembrance. She addressed the conductor in a distinct Irish accent.

He wanted to run after her but realized the thread this time had not been in his favour.

A party? A concert? She had auburn hair turning to gold, fine pointed green eyes.

Her face was what snatched cords of remembrance. A face one would associate with a Botticelli, eager little points in it yet overall a look of abandon, a look of innocence. "Dreaming again," he told himself yet he knew clearly he had seen her before. He started reading Hermann Hesse again. Yes, he was going back, back; to University College Dublin maybe, the green of Iveagh Gardens, discussions on love or morality in the ripe spring of '61. It was as though he had opened a floodgate and innocence was succumbing.

San Francisco had been an inspiration, a goal for him.

Of course he had his friends to contend with. Middle-class Irish. He shared Thanksgiving with them, fire blazing and marshmallows toasted on sweet potatoes. There were American guests; one, an American poet, was fascinating. She was a warm, vibrant person at fifty. She exuded qualities which James could only define as love.

The thought of this auburn haired Irish girl on the bus struck him once or twice until one day in Berkeley he saw her, ran after her. She turned. "Hello." Her name was Sandra. She was from Mayo. "Where could I have met you?" he asked her.

"Don't know."

They ate in a café where each diner was a sunstruck effigy of the Californian dream.

She'd known of him. She read his articles. Her mother often sent her Irish papers.

"You've been here for a while."

"Two and a half years."

"Since."

"Since the Dublin car bombings."

The thought struck him he'd seen her there.

Crazy.

"Where?"

"Talbot Street."

She'd been there.

She'd been a student studying for her final examinations. She'd gone to get a textbook. She was caught in the horror. She'd never forget it. She'd escaped. A friend had been killed. She'd been meant to meet him at Bewley's. They'd been quite close.

"We went to hear Stephane Grappelli that spring. Imagine some months later being dead," she said.

She didn't talk much about him. She whispered about the awfulness of it. She would not forget it. It had been awful, awful. Imagine a whole family being wiped out.

"I was so young then," she said.

"You're still young."

"Yes."

She smiled. "Yes." She'd come to the States on a battered student plane after the bombs. She'd remained in California.

After a while she confessed she was a member of a religious sect.

Could it be he had seen her in those bombs in Talbot Street? Could it be she registered in the mayhem and the bodies and the dirt and the blood. She would have had a very pure face in the middle of all that. Perhaps she'd been dressed in bright colours.

They arranged in Berkeley that noon to meet again.

They met on Saturday in Geary. She was more beautiful than the last time. They had Earl Grey tea. He kept looking at her. She was puzzled by this. He could not help recalling his favourite quotation as a boy.

"There are more things in Heaven and earth Horatio than are dreamt of in our philosophy."

She explained about her group. It lay to the North. They lived by the sea. They studied Saint Matthew and the Ecclesiastes. They were a close knit community. They dealt said Sandra gently in verities.

"Verities—"

"Truths. Sometimes things come as signs. The Dublin car bombings were such for me. A sign. I saw death that day. I turned my face away. But surely death should turn us to something beyond."

"God?"

"Yes. I knew that moment of destruction my life was meaningless. I couldn't cope. I came here. Now I want to sort out. I want to discover. Do people die in vain?"

"Everyday in the North they do."

Her eyes looked away. She wasn't able to cope with strong statements such as this.

"I can see only private tragedies," she said.

He drove with her one day to Monterey and there they had lobster. California was becoming as a jingle of gold. He was very happy. She was from Mayo, a doctor's daughter, had led a wild youth, going to Paris in jeans at seventeen. She studied French at college, she'd been doing her finals during the bombs.

"How did you get into your group?" he asked her.

"A notice in San Francisco."

San Francisco was a city full of notices, signs advertising astrology, religion, sex. There was art and experiment and *Gestalt*. Most of all there were people. Like all cities it had its backbone of morons. What lay between was often beautiful to look at, lovely carefree people, west-coast people.

The girl intrigued him. He wanted to reach her, talk to her, tell her something. One day he watched her handle a copy of *Narziss and Goldmund*, by Hermann Hesse.

"Your generation has had so many more opportunities than ours."

She smiled. "Think of what you missed." That was the first time he felt her being cruel.

He was seeing a lot of her. She was trekking from her community to visit him—perhaps out of loneliness for Ireland and Castlebar and the seeping mountains and the august Wimpy bars. He asked her about her parents, if she missed them, were they anxious about her. She said yes, they were, but inevitabilities had to be pushed through.

How long would she stay here? Maybe a lifetime. Studying. Maybe a short while. Then going on to another life, a different city.

James realized he was in love, that there was nothing but nothing he could do about it, that it too was inevitable, as inevitable as the shooting of birds into Pacific skies.

They ate a lot together, picking their way through cafés where they feasted rather than dined. He observed her losing seriousness. She was laughing considerably. He was losing his pose, grey hairs, odd as they were flying away. His lips were becoming sweet.

She missed her bus back one day and she came with him to spend the night where he was staying. He moved towards her to seduce her. She turned away. He got frightened. Sex was the premium of her contemporaries yet here was one who did not wish to sleep with him. "Go to sleep," she whispered. He woke in the morning to find her arms were about him. They had breakfast out—in a macro-biotic restaurant.

She said "How are you?"

He said fine.

She had to go north for two weeks. She couldn't come down. She would be preparing for Christmas.

"I'll miss you."

"Soon I go home," he added.

"Yes."

She rose. "I'll have to get the bus." He walked towards it with her. She was wearing a fur coat. She kissed him goodbye. He couldn't stand it; he wanted this girl. He desired her. She had to be his. The bus took off. The following week he had an affair with an arts student from Berkeley. It was nice, they drank much Californian wine, but looking at her over a table near Fisherman's Wharf he understood only too clearly his need for Sandra. It was a desire for understanding. Ever since he was a child when his mother moved from Wicklow to Dublin he needed something from life, something journalism could not give him. He'd been a crazily romantic teenager. He'd wanted to create.

He took the Berkeley arts student to *The Nutcracker Suite*. The sight of dancing moved him to ring Sandra. She whispered on the phone, "Yes, I'll see you next week."

He told her then he loved her, he told her then he was obsessed with her. She wept. She said when her friend died and the memory of the bombs surrounded her she felt like the moon, a crazy, alien, friendless planet. There was no meaning left. At his grave she left flowers banded by Vermeer's picture of an artist painting a model in blue. It had been her desire, his, to create. Their youths together had been based on an understanding of creation. He'd been a boy in a multi-coloured jumper. They hoped to create love together, marriage, children. His death finished that. Anyway the bombs would have killed that for her, sight of carnage, sight of a landscape based on the ultimate horror of man maimed and laid motionless by man.

"In Bewley's once Dorian Gray was paged on the megaphone. I looked to see if he would rise, but he didn't and yet I knew that he and I were flirts. We were flirts with fate, flirts with ourselves. The bombs ended all that."

James was staring into a sunrise tequila.

He was drunk.

Like any Irishman he said, "I love you. I love you. Love you."

Her face was very tender.

"Yes. But I must leave you. I must go back now. There are chores I must do."

She'd come for the day to see him.

It was like a dangling farewell for her. She wasn't sure where to search, where to probe.

Women were selling flowers on Union Square.

As James had waited for her a young lady had approached him asking if he'd seen David Bowie.

They were seated in the lounge of the Saint Francis. A boy was playing Mendelssohn on the piano.

Sandra got up to go.

He touched her. "Is this goodbye?" She'd come as she'd said on the phone. She seemed so emotionless.

"When do you leave?"

"Wednesday."

She hesitated.

"There's a car going back. I've got to get it."

"May I visit you?"

She hesitated.

That posed problems. "Ring me." He did, from the apartment. A jet was flying over. "Come on Monday." It was Saturday night.

He replaced the receiver and rang Dublin where he heard it had been snowing and brown, brown leaves were blowing. He'd rung a journalist friend. Many people were inquiring after him. Many were anxious for him. His articles kept appearing.

"I'll be back on Thursday," he told his friend. Just then, the Righteous Brothers were placed on the record player. "You've lost that loving feeling." He considered his days as a teenager as Nelson's Pillar ranged high and the first rock and roll was bursting on rugby hops in Dublin. He recalled the hands of girls, white, and the middle-class vaginal areas he was destined to enter and semen flowing and the nights, the provocative nights of coloured lights and fish and vans with sausages like sore fingers.

"I love you," he said in his sleep. He knew he no longer really understood who or what he was addressing except that he required a love object.

Diane was doing her Christmas shopping now. A number of ex-

mistresses were baking Christmas pudding for former rugby playing husbands.

"I have loved, O Lord, the beauty of thy house and the glory that
dwells therein."

He drove to the sea. The ocean was a Walt Disney blue. He walked
up and down until he considered taking his shoes off.

That wasn't riotous enough. He removed all his clothes and swam in
the cold, cold Pacific.

There was a noise and he wondered if it was a whale going south or a
fog horn. He wrote in his diary that night.

"Seized Jack London's shadow."

The trip north to see Sandra for the last time occurred on a day of
exquisite blue. The sea shimmered. Highway 1 promised an apocalypse.
This he got. She was there to meet him in a pink cardigan and a white
shirt. Around him lay white houses, a white church and flowers,
entwined purple and white, leading to the sea.

A boy, a veteran of Vietnam, blond, short haired in a red check shirt
was reading the Ecclesiastes.

"A time to love, and a time to hate; a time for war and a time for
peace."

A young man who'd been to the Himalayas told him about temples
on mountain-tops and monks in lotus positions at sunrise. A middle-
aged ex-Hollywood director spoke of the Second Coming. A young
Frenchman of rich family, quoted Rilke, recalled for James that life
passes, that we are in danger of losing our little and yet extraordinary significance if we are not always careful.

"'Strait is the gate, and narrow is the way which leadeth unto life,
and few there be that find it,'" said Sandra. "Once I was in a supermarket
when an earthquake came. I closed my eyes and wondered, What next if
this is death? Have I plundered my own areas of holiness, of Godliness?
Or have I lived wisely, catching the right note, remembering the right
score?"

The grass was golden. It seemed to lead to the sea as though to the
birth of Atlantis.

It was as if these children, old and young, were waiting the rise of that
island, a new age and it would not have been surprising to James if the

strange and tremulous light of the sea had at that moment produced a mound of earth. A boy played a guitar. It was Bach's "Jesu, joy of man's desiring." James remembered the night after the bombs in Dublin a boy outside Gaj's restaurant had strummed "Blowing in the Wind." He and Diane had stopped with a meagre crowd. Yet it would take years, years, wouldn't it, before sight of such carnage could be forgotten, integrated, remembered wisely, well and as part of God's symmetry. That day, by the December sea, James felt more than at any time in his life he had touched upon, understood reality.

It was reality as the papers never reported in Dublin, as the telephones never considered, as the bulletins never announced. It was life passing, eternity deciphered, the passage of light transmitted through the ages.

They had strawberry flan and listened to the disquiet of a cello in the church.

Sandra held James's hand.

Her face seemed to grow in intensity. The sound of a jet jarred the music.

"I must go," said James.

"Back to San Francisco."

"Yes."

"Goodbye."

She led him to the door. He looked behind at her and perceived not just the Dublin car bombings but the Vietnam protests of the sixties, the marches with the pigs' heads, the violence, the ugliness, turned to this, solemn questions, spiritual search.

He thought of his generation's sexual envy of hers and knew that sex too poses problems, that its demons had to be controlled that inevitably laughter dies and has to be built again.

Like a kingdom.

It rained next day in San Francisco. Young men in medieval costume sang "Greensleeves" by the docks and he confirmed his ticket to Dublin.

The huge commercialism of Christmas was building to a crescendo. Yet here and there were the street-artists with their paint running in the rain.

He hadn't asked her what exactly she was doing, but understood that what she was doing was the only way she could do it, understand bombs, death and the passing of innocence. The plane arrived in Dublin on a grey, grey morning.

The letters had piled up. The BBC had written again repeating an offer for a post. This time he thought he'd take it. He drove about Dublin that Christmas mesmerized by tinker children. He couldn't help seeing water instead of news of bombings in the North, children instead of colleagues sporting glaring jackets.

One day in the immediate aftermath of Christmas he drove to a certain house near Castlebar to deliver a book of Botticelli prints as a present from Sandra to her parents.

Between Two Shores

It was dark and he sat with his knees tucked up to his chin, knowing there was a long night ahead of him. He had arrived early for the boat and sat alone in a row of seats wishing he had bought a paper or a magazine of some sort. He heard a noise like a pulse from somewhere deep in the boat. Later he changed his position and put his feet on the floor.

For something to do he opened his case and looked again at the presents he had for the children. A painting by numbers set for the eldest boy of the "Laughing Cavalier," for the three girls, dolls, horizontal with their eyes closed, a blonde, a redhead and a brunette to prevent fighting over who owned which. He had also bought a trick pack of cards. He bought these for himself but he didn't like to admit it. He saw himself amazing his incredulous, laughing father after dinner by turning the whole pack into the seven of clubs or whatever else he liked by just tapping them as the man in the shop had done.

The trick cards would be a nice way to start a conversation if anybody sat down beside him, so he put them on top of his clothes in the case. He locked it and slipped it off the seat, leaving it vacant. Other people were beginning to come into the lounge lugging heavy cases. When they saw him sitting in the middle of the row they moved on to find another. He found their Irish accents grating and flat.

He lit a cigarette and as he put the matches back in his pocket his fingers closed around his wife's present. He took it out, a small jeweller's box, black with a domed top. As he clicked back the lid he saw again the gold against the red satin and thought it beautiful. A locket was something permanent, something she could keep for ever. Suddenly his stomach reeled at the thought. He tried to put it out of his mind, snapping the box shut and putting it in his breast pocket. He got up and was about to go to the bar when he saw how the place was filling up. It was Thursday and the Easter rush had started. He would sit his ground until the boat moved out. If he kept his seat and got a few pints inside him he might sleep. It would be a long night.

A middle-aged couple moved into the row—they sounded like they were from Belfast. Later an old couple with a mongol girl sat almost opposite him. The girl was like all mongols. It was difficult to tell her age—anywhere between twenty and thirty. He thought of moving away to another seat to be away from the moist, open mouth and the beak nose but it might have hurt the grey haired parents. It would be too obvious, so he nodded a smile and just sat on.

The note of the throbbing engine changed and the lights on the docks began to move slowly past. He had a free seat in front of him and he tried to put his feet up but it was just out of reach, the parents took their mongol daughter "to see the big ship going out" and he then felt free to move. He found the act of walking strange on the moving ship.

He went to the bar and bought a pint of stout and took it out onto the deck. Every time he travelled he was amazed at the way they edged the huge boat out of the narrow channel—a foot to spare on each side. Then the long wait at the lock gates. Inside, the water flat, roughed only by the wind—out there the waves leaping and chopping, black and slate grey in the light of the moon. Eventually they were away, the boat swinging out to sea and the wind rising, cuffing him on the side of the head. It was cold now and he turned to go in. On a small bench on the open deck he saw a bloke laying out his sleeping bag and sliding down inside it.

He had several more pints in the bar sitting on his own, moving his glass round the four metal indentations. There were men and boys with short hair, obviously British soldiers. He thought how sick they must be having to go back to Ireland at Easter. There was a nice looking girl sitting alone reading with a rucksack at her feet. She looked like a student.

He wondered how he could start to talk to her. His trick cards were in the case and he had nothing with him. She seemed very interested in her book because she didn't even lift her eyes from it as she sipped her beer. She was nice looking, dark hair tied back, large dark eyes following the lines back and forth on the page. He looked at her body, then felt himself recoil as if someone had clanged a handbell in his ear and shouted "unclean." Talk was what he wanted. Talk stopped him thinking. When he was alone he felt frightened and unsure. He blamed his trouble on this.

In the beginning London had been a terrible place. During the day he had worked himself to the point of exhaustion. Back at the digs he would wash and shave and after a meal he would drag himself to the pub with the other Irish boys rather than sit at home. He drank at half the pace the others did and would have full pints on the table in front of him when closing time came. Invariably somebody else would drain them, rather than let them go to waste. Everyone but himself was drunk and they would roar home, some of them being sick on the way against a gable wall or up an entry. Some nights, rather than endure this, he sat in his bedroom even though the landlady had said he could come down and watch TV. But it would have meant having to sit with her English husband and their horrible son. Nights like these many times he thought his watch had stopped and he wished he had gone out.

Then one night he'd been taken by ambulance from the digs after vomiting all day with a pain in his gut. When he wakened they had removed his appendix. The man in the next bed was small, dark-haired, friendly. The rest of the ward had nicknamed him "Mephisto" because of the hours he spent trying to do the crossword in *The Times*. He had never yet completed it. His attention had first been drawn to Nurse Mitchell's legs by this little man who enthused about the shortness of her skirt, the black stockings with the seams, clenching and unclenching his fist. The little man's mind wandered higher and he rolled his small eyes in delight.

In the following days in hospital he fell in love with this Nurse Helen Mitchell. When he asked her about the funny way she talked she said she was from New Zealand. He thought she gave him special treatment. She nursed him back to health, letting him put his arm around when he got out of bed for the first time. He smelt her perfume and felt her firmness. He was astonished at how small she was, having only looked up at her until this. She fitted the crook of his arm like a crutch. Before he left he bought her a present from the hospital shop, of the biggest box of chocolates that they had in stock. Each time she came to his bed it was on the tip of his tongue to ask her out but he didn't have the courage. He had skirted round the question as she made the bed, asking her what she did when she was off duty. She had mentioned the name of a place where she and her friends went for a drink and sometimes a meal.

He had gone home to Donegal for a fortnight at Christmas to recover but on his first night back in London he went to this place and sat drinking alone. On the third night she came in with two other girls. The sight of her out of uniform made him ache to touch her. They sat in the corner not seeing him sitting at the bar. After a couple of whiskeys he went over to them. She looked up, startled almost. He started by saying, "Maybe you don't remember me. . . ."

"Yes, yes I do," she said laying her hand on his arm. Her two friends smiled at him then went on talking to each other. He said that he just happened to be in the district and remembered the name of the place and thought that he would have liked to see her again. She said yes, that he was the man who bought the *huge* box of chocolates. Her two friends laughed behind their hands. He bought them all a drink. And then insisted again. She said, "Look I'm sorry I've forgotten your name," and he told her and she introduced him to the others. When time was called he isolated her from the others and asked her if she would like to go out for a meal some night and she said she'd love to.

On the Tuesday after careful shaving and dressing he took her out and afterwards they went back to the flat she shared with the others. He was randy helping her on with her coat at the restaurant, smelling again her perfume, but he intended to play his cards with care and not rush things. But there was no need, because she refused no move he made and her hand was sliding down past his scar before he knew where he was. He was not in control of either himself or her. She changed as he touched her. She bit his tongue and hurt his body with her nails. Dealing with the pain she caused him saved him from coming too soon and disgracing himself.

Afterwards he told her that he was married and she said that she knew but that it made no difference. They both needed something. He asked her if she had done it with many men.

"Many, many men," she had replied, her New Zealand vowels thin and hard like knives. Tracks of elastic banded her body where her underwear had been. He felt sour and empty and wanted to go back to his digs. She dressed and he liked her better, then she made tea and they were talking again.

Through the next months he saw her many times and they always ended up on the rug before the electric fire and each time his seed left him he thought the loss permanent and irreplaceable.

This girl across the bar reminded him of her, the way she was absorbed in her reading. His nurse, he always called her that, had tried to force him to read books but he had never read a whole book in his life. He had started several for her but he couldn't finish them. He told lies to please her until one day she asked him what he thought of the ending of one she had given him. He felt embarrassed and childish about being found out.

There were some young girls, hardly more than children, drinking at the table across the bar from the soldiers. They were eyeing them and giggling into their vodkas. They had thick Belfast accents. The soldiers wanted nothing to do with them. Soldiers before them had chased it and ended up dead or maimed for life.

An old man had got himself a padded alcove and was in the process of kicking off his shoes and putting his feet up on his case. There was a hole in the toe of his sock and he crossed his other foot over it to hide it. He remembered an old man telling him on his first trip always to take his shoes off when he slept. Your feet swell when you sleep, he had explained.

The first time leaving had been the worst. He felt somehow it was for good, even though he knew he would be home in two or three months. He had been up since dark getting ready. His wife was frying him bacon and eggs, tip-toeing back and forth putting the things on the table, trying not to wake the children too early. He came up behind her and put his arms round her waist, then moved his hands up to her breasts. She leaned her head back against his shoulder and he saw that she was crying, biting her lip to stop. He knew she would do this, cry in private but she would hold back in front of the others when the mini-bus came.

"Don't," she said. "I hear Daddy up."

That first time the children had to be wakened to see their father off. They appeared outside the house tousleheaded and confused. A mini-bus full of people had pulled into their yard and their Granny and Granda were crying. Handshaking and endless hugging watched by his wife, chalk pale, her forearms folded against the early morning cold. He kissed her once. The people in the mini-bus didn't like to watch. His case went on the pyramid of other cases and the mini-bus bumped over the yard away from the figures grouped around the doorway.

The stout had gone through him and he got up to go to the lavatory. The slight swaying of the boat made it difficult to walk but it was not so bad that he had to use the handles above the urinals. Someone had been sick on the floor, Guinness sick. He looked at his slack flesh held between his fingers at the place where the sore had been. It had all but disappeared. Then a week ago his nurse had noticed it. He had thought nothing of it because it was not painful. She asked him who else he had been sleeping with—insulting him. He had sworn he had been with no one. She explained to him how they were like minute corkscrews going through the whole body. Then she admitted that it must have been her who had picked it up from someone else.

"If not me, then who?" he had asked.

"Never you mind," she replied. "My life is my own."

It was the first time he had seen her concerned. She came after him as he ran down the stairs and implored him to go to a clinic, if not with her, then on his own. But the thought of it terrified him. He had listened to stories on the site of rods being inserted, burning needles and worst of all a thing which opened inside like an umbrella and was forcibly dragged out again. On Wednesday the landlady had said someone had called at the digs looking for him and said he would call back. But he made sure he was out that night and this morning he was up and away early buying presents before getting on the train.

He zipped up his fly and stood looking at himself in the mirror. He looked tired—the long train journey, the sandwiches, smoking too many cigarettes to pass the time. A coppery growth was beginning on his chin.

He remembered her biting his tongue, the tearing of her nails, the way she changed. He had not seen her since.

Only once or twice had his wife been like that—changing that way. He knew she would be like that tomorrow night. It was always the same the first night home. But afterwards he knew that it was her, his wife. Even though it was taut with lovemaking her face had something of her care of his children, of the girl and woman, of the kitchen, of dances, of their walks together. He knew who she was as they devoured each other on the creaking bed. In the Bible they knew each other.

Again his mind shied away from the thought. He went out onto the deck to get the smell of sick from about him. Beyond the rail it was black night. He looked down and could see the white bow wave crashing away off into the dark. Spray tipped his face and the wind roared in his ears. He took a deep breath but it did no good. Someone threw a bottle from the deck above. It flashed past him and landed in the water. He saw the white of the splash but heard nothing above the throbbing of the ship. The damp came through to his elbows where he leaned on the rail and he shivered.

He had thought of not going home, of writing to his wife to say that he was sick. But it seemed impossible for him not to do what he had always done. Besides she might have come to see him if he had been too sick to travel. Now he wanted to be at home among the sounds that he knew. Crows, hens clearing their throats and picking in the yard, the distant bleating of sheep on the hill, the rattle of a bucket handle, the slam of the back door. Above all he wanted to see the children. The baby, his favourite, sitting on her mother's knee, her tulle nightdress ripped at the back, happy and chatting at not having to compete with the others. Midnight and she the centre of attention. Her voice, hoarse and precious after wakening, talking as they turned the pages of the catalogue of toys they had sent for, using bigger words than she did during the day.

A man with a woollen cap came out onto the deck and leaned on the rail not far away. A sentence began to form in his mind, something to start a conversation. You couldn't talk about the dark. The cold, he could say how cold it was. He waited for the right moment but when he looked round the man was away, high stepping through the doorway.

He followed him in and went to the bar to get a drink before it closed.

The girl was still there reading. The other girls were falling about and squawking with laughter at the slightest thing. They were telling in loud voices about former nights and about how much they could drink. Exaggerations. Ten vodkas, fifteen gin and tonics. He sat down opposite the girl reading and when she looked up from her book he smiled at her. She acknowledged the smile and looked quickly down at her book again. He could think of nothing important enough to say to interrupt her reading. Eventually when the bar closed she got up and left without looking at him. He watched the indentation in the cushioned moquette return slowly to normal.

He went back to his seat in the lounge. The place was smoke-filled and hot and smelled faintly of feet. The mongol was now asleep. With his eyes closed he became conscious of the heaving motion of the boat as it climbed the swell. She had said they were like tiny corkscrews. He thought of them boring into his wife's womb. He opened his eyes. A young woman's voice was calling incessantly. He looked to see. A toddler was running up and down the aisles playing.

"Ann-Marie, Ann-Marie, Ann-Marie! Come you back here!"

Her voice rose annoyingly, sliding up to the end of the name. He couldn't see where the mother was sitting. Just a voice annoying him. He reached out his feet again to the vacant seat opposite and found he was still too short. To reach he would have to lie on his back. He crossed his legs and cradled his chin in the heart of his hand.

Although they were from opposite ends of the earth he was amazed that her own childhood in New Zealand should have sounded so like his own. The small farm, the greenness, the bleat of sheep, the rain. She had talked to him, seemed interested in him, how he felt, what he did, why he could not do something better. He was intelligent—sometimes. He had liked the praise but was hurt by its following jibe. She had a lot of friends who came to her flat—arty crafty ones, and when he stayed to listen to them he felt left outside. Sometimes in England his Irishness made him feel like a leper. They talked about books, about people he had never heard of and whose names he couldn't pronounce, about God and the Government.

One night at a party with ultra-violet lights someone with rings on his fingers had called him "a noble savage." He didn't know how to take it. His first impulse was to punch him, but up till that he had been so friendly and talkative—besides it was too Irish a thing to do. His nurse had come to his rescue and later in bed she had told him he must *think*. She had playfully struck his forehead with her knuckles at each syllable.

"Your values all belong to somebody else," she had said.

He felt uncomfortable. He was sure he hadn't slept. He changed his position but then went back to cupping his chin. He must sleep.

"Ann-Marie, Ann-Marie." She was loose again. By now they had turned the lights down in the lounge. The place was full of slumped bodies. The rows were back to back and some hitch-hikers had crawled onto the flat floor beneath the apex. He took his raincoat for a pillow and crawled into the free space behind his row. Horizontal he might sleep. It was like a tent and he felt nicely cut off. In the next row some girls sat, not yet asleep. One was just at the level of his head and when she leaned forward to whisper her sweater rode up and bared a pale crescent of her lower back. Pale downy hairs moving into a seam at her backbone. He closed his eyes but the box containing the locket bit into his side. He turned and tried to sleep on his other side.

One night when neither of them could sleep his wife had said to him, "Do you miss me when you're away?"

He said yes.

"What do you do?"

"Miss you."

"I don't mean that. Do you do anything about it? Your missing me."

"No."

"If you ever do, don't tell me about it. I don't want to know."

"I never have."

He looked once or twice to see the girl's back but she was huddled up now sleeping. As he lay the floor increased in hardness. He lay for what seemed all night, his eyes gritty and tense, conscious of his discomfort each time he changed his position. The heat became intolerable. He sweated and felt it thick like blood on his brow. He wiped it dry with a handkerchief and looked at it to see. He was sure it must be morning. When he looked at his watch it said three o'clock. He listened to it to hear if it had stopped. The loud tick seemed to chuckle at him. His nurse had told him this was the time people died. Three o'clock in the morning. The dead hour. Life at its lowest ebb. He believed her. Walking the dimly lit wards she found the dead.

Suddenly he felt claustrophobic. The back of the seats closed over his head like a tomb. He eased himself out. His back ached and his bladder was bursting. As he walked he felt the boat rise and fall perceptibly. In the toilet he had to use the handrail. The smell of sick was still there.

How could his values belong to someone else? He knew what was right and what was wrong. He went out onto the deck again. The wind had changed or else the ship was moving at a different angle. The man who had rolled himself in his sleeping bag earlier in the night had disappeared. The wind and the spray lashed the seat where he had been sleeping. Tiny lights on the coast of Ireland winked on and off. He moved round to the leeward side for a smoke. The girl who had earlier been reading came out on deck. She mustn't have been able to sleep either. All he wanted was someone to sit and talk to for an hour. Her hair was untied now and she let it blow in the wind, shaking her head from side to side to get it way from her face. He sheltered his glowing cigarette in the heart of his hand. Talk would shorten the night. For the first time in his life he felt his age, felt older than he was. He was conscious of the droop in his shoulders, his unshaven chin, his smoker's cough. Who would talk to him—even for an hour? She held her white raincoat tightly round herself, her hands in her pockets. The tail flapped furiously against her legs. She walked towards the prow, her head tilted back. As he followed her, in a sheltered alcove he saw the man in the sleeping bag, snoring, the drawstring of his hood knotted round his chin. The girl turned and came back. They drew level.

"That's a cold one," he said.

"Indeed it is," she said, not stopping. She was English. He had to continue to walk towards the prow and when he looked over his shoulder she was gone. He sat on an empty seat and began to shiver. He did not know how long he sat but it was better than the stifling heat of the lounge. Occasionally he walked up and down to keep the life in his feet. Much later going back in he passed an image of himself in a mirror, shivering and blue lipped, his hair wet and stringy.

In the lounge the heat was like a curtain. The sight reminded him of a graveyard. People were meant to be straight, not tilted and angled like this. He sat down determined to sleep. He heard the tremble of the boat, snoring, hushed voices. Ann-Marie must have gone to sleep—finally. That guy in the sleeping bag had it all worked out—right from the start.

He had a night's sleep over him already. He tilted his watch in the dim light. The agony of the night must soon end. Dawn would come. His mouth felt dry and his stomach tight and empty. He had last eaten on the train. It was now six o'clock.

Once he had arranged to meet his nurse in the Gardens. It was early morning and she was coming off duty. She came to him starched and white, holding out her hands as she would to a child. Someone tapped him on the shoulder but he didn't want to look round. She sat beside him and began to stroke the inside of his thigh. He looked around to see if anyone was watching. There were two old ladies close by but they seemed not to notice. The park bell began to clang and the keepers blew their whistles. They must be closing early. He put his hand inside her starched apron to touch her breasts. He felt warm moistness, revolting to the touch. His hand was in her entrails. The bell clanged incessantly and became a voice over the Tannoy.

"Good morning, ladies and gentlemen. The time is seven o'clock. We dock at Belfast in approximately half an hour's time. Tea and sandwiches will be on sale until that time. We hope you have enjoyed your . . ."

He sat up and rubbed his face. The woman opposite, the mongol's mother, said good morning. Had he screamed out? He got up and bought himself a plastic cup of tea, tepid and weak, and some sandwiches, dog-eared from sitting overnight.

It was still dark outside but now the ship was full of the bustle of people refreshed by sleep, coming from the bathrooms with toilet bags and towels, whistling, slamming doors. He saw one man take a tin of polish from his case and begin to shine his shoes. He sat watching him, stale crusts in his hand. He went out to throw them to the gulls and watch the dawn come up.

He hadn't long to go now. His hour had come. It was funny the way time worked. If time stopped he would never reach home and yet he loathed the ticking, second by second slowness of the night. The sun would soon be up, the sky was bleaching at the horizon. What could he do? Jesus what could he do? If he could turn into spray and scatter him-self on the sea he would never be found. Suddenly it occurred to him that he *could* throw himself over the side. That would end it. He watched the water sluicing past the dark hull forty feet below. "The spirit is willing but the flesh is weak." If only someone would take the whole thing away how happy he would be. For a moment his spirits jumped at the possibility of the whole thing disappearing—then it was back in his stomach heavier than ever. He put his face in his hands. Somehow it had all got to be hammered out. He wondered if books would solve it. Read books and maybe the problems won't seem the same. His nurse had no problems.

The dark was becoming grey light. They must have entered the Lough because he could see land now on both sides, like arms or legs. He lit a cigarette. The first of the day—more like the sixty-first of yesterday. He coughed deeply, held it a moment then spat towards Ireland but the wind turned it back in the direction of England. He smiled. His face felt unusual.

He felt an old man broken and tired and unshaven at the end of his days. If only he could close his eyes and sleep and forget. His life was over. Objects on the shore began to become distinct through the mist. Gasometers, chimney-stacks, railway trucks. They looked washed out, a putty grey against the pale lumps of the hills. Cars were moving and then he made out people hurrying to work. He closed his eyes and put his head down on his arms. Indistinctly at first, but with growing clarity, he heard the sound of an ambulance.

Near the Bone

I only come back once a year if I can help it. Cootehill, County Cavan, where even the faded postcards, if you can get any, can't make it look special. It is not a "must see" town, hasn't acquired enough heritage to build a centre. There's a wide main street with several pubs, two pharmacies, a post office and a two-star AA hotel—the White Horse Inn. I used to dream that I could come back and be able to stay in that place for as long as I liked. Buy it even. Instead I went to Germany to work in a printing works one summer and that was that. The hotel went rapidly downmarket and now is kept running on functions, not guests.

I walk down Bridge Street past clumps of teenage boys hanging out on the corners. Apart from the video shop my mother mentioned, there's just as little to do as when I was young, itching to leave, scornful of anyone who stayed stuck. The smell of singed kebabs leaks out of Giovanni's takeaway, masking the sweetness of turfsmoke. Shankey's supermarket has a spanking new front, and a couple of farmhands perch on the high, pink stools in Paddy's Diner, waiting for Demi Moore to waltz in and make their day.

I find myself in the West End Bar which hasn't changed at all. My eyes take a moment to grow accustomed to the dimness. The faint tangerine glow from the tinted windows always made me think of the rusty water that seeps out and collects in narrow ditches in the bog. The bar still smells the same, like any other—spilt beer, fag-ends, sweaty leatherette, the motionless air laced with the acrid whiff of industrial toilet cleaner, which must eat through enamel. I don't know why I go in there, especially in the afternoon. Most of the people I knew have moved on, to Dublin, London or America. Or else they're married with three kids, a half-finished bungalow, with a swing and a cement mixer in the garden and two eagles mounted on the gateposts. Those guys only come out for stag nights and the World Cup.

I always take my earring out and shave off my moustache before I come home. Nonetheless, I still sense they know I'm different as I walk stiffly to the counter. I don't really drink any more, it's just for appearances and some kind of nostalgia. Though why I'm nostalgic for this place I'll never know. Much of my time in here I spend bluffing. Pretending to fancy Micky's sister, Gerry's cousin, so and so's bloody unmarried aunt. Flirting heartlessly.

"Hey, Desi, how's about you?" calls Malachi, the barman. He's greyer on top. They're friendly alright. My shoulders ease a little. I work out in a gym in Frankfurt. I don't even wear a tight T-shirt that would show it off. Truckdrivers round here would have muscles like mine, but if they thought I went to the gym, they might twig.

"The family well?" Malachi dries his hands on his jeans.

"The best," I supply, the ritual coming back to me with every gesture, every glance. I order a pint and look around, nod at an old school friend I never liked. There's a poster of a red Ferrari on the wall. No one in Cootehill will ever touch inside one, I think sourly. The Triaxles are playing tonight. Then Susan O'Kane tomorrow. I can't believe she's still around. Didn't she sign a record deal?

The pub is quiet, the pool tables waiting and the jukebox silent. It's early yet. Kevin Mulligan's elbows are pinned to the other end of the bar, his face red and pocked, his eyes blue as morning glories. Someone should tell him not to wear a red jacket. He looks as though he is about to smoulder and combust, nose first. Suddenly I imagine him head-to-toe in leather, a Muir cap jammed on his head, and the rush of cruising teems through me like amyl nitrate. I want HiNRG streaming through my muscles, making space between the bones, till they loosen, follow the beat, pull me away from the dark walls into cones of coloured light on the dance floor. Ultra-violet would bathe me till my T-shirt would be radiant, my skin bronzed. The pleasure of being watched would pump me up till I'd be surrounded by an electric band of gazes and the exhilaration of knowing anything could happen. My ears would buzz with the volume, my nostrils embrace the bitter sniff of poppers and sweat. Every pore would focus on desire, taste it in the quick dart of an eye, a glance returned, touch it in the anonymous fondling of men's faces, cupped tits and neat arses. My body would be young, made beautiful, sensuous as a stallion.

I take a gulp of Guinness, lift and adjust my balls, smiling to myself. Here men over twenty-five dance only at weddings.

I study a middle-aged couple sitting in a corner, not talking, staring at the blank TV screen. I recognise them, but have forgotten their name. McConkey, is it? I'll ask Malachi. The man lights one Major after another and each time his wife slides the green and white packet to her side of the table, admonishing him with a roll of her eyes. There are three women on their own. I can tell by their lack of interest in each other, then their sudden, giddy intimacy, that they are family. A mother in purple, the two daughters in peach and cerise. All the same jumper. Dunnes Stores.

My sister never comes back. She's in Newcastle-Upon-Tyne. It would cost her less than me to come. She and our mother fell out over clothes. I tried to keep out of it. Bernie said it was plain fucking crazy, there she was wearing a tie-dye vest which showed her black bra straps and Mum went loopy, calling her a hoor as she went out the door. "Have you no shame? Someone'll grab you," she warned. "It's as if people aren't meant to know I fucking wear one for Chrissakes." Mum never liked her swearing. It got worse in England. I never swear in front of Mum. What's the point in upsetting her?

I spin the cardboard Harp coaster and wait for someone I know to come in. If not, I'll go home, spend the evening reading the paper, watching the box, while Mum and Dad blather on again about who's sick, who's dead, God love them.

The door opens and Flinty McClure comes in. He was several years ahead of me at school, but we both played football for the County. He rushes right over and shakes my hand, asks me what I'm having. He's more friendly than I've ever seen him, his big red mane of hair as wild as ever, his teeth stained yellow. He's lost weight.

"Still writing the poetry then, Flinty?"

I sound more jocular than I feel.

"Aye." He shakes his head. "Not so much lately though." At once the energy of his greeting has evaporated as though he has been exhausted by it.

Unsummoned, Malachi places a large malt in front of Flinty, who reaches into his pocket. Malachi waves his hand to stop him.

"Catch yoursel' on," he scolds kindly.

"And you're getting back into shape, I see." I stand upright and pat my firm stomach.

Flinty sips his whiskey, says nothing. He brings out the old lighter that gave him his name, thumbs the wheel and sucks a cigarette into life. He points the packet towards me. I decline.

"And where's Bob Breen?" I go on as though there's been no break in the conversation. Bob and Flinty always drank together. Bob plays the pipes.

Flinty's face collapses a little. He doesn't look at me.

"Did you not hear, Desi?" He inhales again as if to pump his lungs with courage and turns to me.

"Bobby's dead these three weeks."

"Sure I never heard," I protest lamely. "My mother and father tell me nothing." I am trying not to look into his eyes. I don't know whether to say I'm sorry. I say it anyway.

"What killed him?" I ask gently.

He hesitates.

"Cancer." His voice is hoarse.

I tell him I think it's awful and it's Sellafield and pollution and it must be hard for him drinking alone.

Flinty swirls his drink round in its glass. He has a deep cut on his hand which is not healing. Pale green pus lines its edges. A Paul Brady track breaks out of the jukebox. It takes me back. I am relieved when Flinty changes the subject.

"So you're doing well in Germany, is it?" He clears his throat.

"Well enough. It's not Ireland though."

"You'll be getting married out there soon." He sounds matter-of-fact.

"Soon enough." I look away and catch Malachi's eye, tilting up my almost-empty glass. I fidget with the little finger of my left hand, where I normally wear a ring. I twist the bare skin.

Flinty's sadness is upon him like a big, sulky animal. It sucks in all the air between us until I feel as though I will suffocate unless I move away. I don't encourage him to stay for another when he knocks back his short and says cheerio with pretended brightness. He coughs a loose phlegmy cough, peers round the bar, taps his pockets as if he's lost something, waves to Malachi and walks away. His clothes look too big for him. Crumpled.

Malachi comes up to serve me. "Same again?" I slide my glass towards him.

"Terrible sad," he mutters, gazing at the door.

"No one said at the funeral and we don't let on we all know."

He lowers his voice, leans towards me.

"Bob had AIDS." There is sorrow but no fear in his words.

I gasp through my teeth involuntarily and bend my head into my hands.

"Jesus, I—" My voice dissolves. I didn't know, couldn't have known. Why didn't I comfort the man? I didn't even see him. Christ. Into shape. What in God's name made me say that? I think of my father suddenly. I remember a rare time I went for a walk with him. Up to Annamaghkerrig. It was cloudy but the rain of earlier had eased off. The air was still. He didn't talk much but there was less distance between us then. I lived at home and was uncertain of my desire, not yet guilty of having acted upon it. When we climbed the little hill above the lake he stopped.

"Look," he said.

I gave a bored mumble. The lake was a round grey stone, the trees sloping up the hillside opposite were green. The water was flat. The arc of trees was mirrored on its surface in sharp, jagged dark and light lines. It was not until later as we walked into the woods and I looked back on the lake that I realised how perfect the reflection had been. A flag of small ripples had scattered the crisp glassiness, blotting and fragmenting the image. I hadn't seen what Dad had meant until it was too late to share it.

Malachi asks me if I'm alright. I nod. He goes on wiping the counter, waiting for my Guinness to darken and settle. His body knows patience.

"Flinty never left his side, they say." His voice is soft with admiration. He slices the creamy top off the pint. "Never left his side."

I feel like I am sinking back into the blackness of the bog, vanishing without mercy into the land that made me believe that I was the only one.

My stomach bubbles and churns. I want to chase after Flinty, explain that I understand, take his big hand in mine, look into the light in his eyes. Tell him about Eamonn, Rudolph, about Timothy and the others.

Malachi pushes the pint towards me and waits for the money.

The Little Madonna

Look at this. I found it in *The Sun*. It's about a sixteen-year-old called Dolores and her three-month-old daughter, Marigold. "The Little Madonna," they called her. She has a perfect heart-shaped face and rosebud lips that curve up into a sweet smile. The baby's face was a miniature heart with the same rosebud. Dolores had no job and no one to support her. She was given a council flat. People brought her money and food. Everybody looked forward to seeing her out with the baby, her hair neatly tied in a bunch on top of her head, the baby's scraps of fluff tied up in imitation. Dolores wore a long Indian caftan and the baby had a little Indian smock over her pram suit. People agreed it made you think the world wasn't so bad when you saw them out together. A Mr Cecil Dodd, who owned the shop across the road, said it changed your mind about the female sex.

One day the Little Madonna put the baby out in the playground in her pram because she wanted to take a rest. It was Mr Dodd, rubbing a clear patch on his shop window, wondering if the papers would be delivered on such a day, who saw a ghostly hump beyond the railings of the flats. The pram was completely covered in snow and although his heart hit off his rib cage when he sprinted out to see, he told himself it was only foolishness, no one would put a child out on such a day.

"There!" he reassured himself when he reached the pram for there

was only a toy—a little white woolly bear. It looked so cold he had to touch it and his finger traced beneath the rasping surface, a small, cold slab of forehead, a heart-shaped face, milky blue. His first thought was to wonder who had done it and what they had done to Dolores. He banged on her door, but it was open. She was lying on the floor, near a radiator. He knelt beside her and stroked her face. She opened her lovely gentle eyes: "I was having a sleep. It was cold so I lay down by the radiator."

"The baby . . . !" he said.

"It's all right," Dolores smiled. "She didn't suffer. I read that people who freeze to death just get very sleepy and then drift off with no pain. I was very careful about that."

Mr Dodd told this story in court, in support of Dolores's character, even though the inquest had revealed a dappling of long, plum-coloured bruises underneath the little Indian shirt.

The report in *The Sun* is more economical. You have to read between the lines. "Baby Freezes while Mum Snoozes," it says. Had the baby failed to freeze to death, she would have been a Miracle Baby, but that is beside the point.

I have this propped up against the milk jug while I'm eating my breakfast. I'm trying to work it out. Who would leave a sixteen-year-old to look after a baby? I remember Rory, who was a good child and sensible, relatively, cut her wrists very neatly with a razor blade when she was sixteen. Being an intelligent girl she read up some books first to make sure the slits would not go through, but it was a very bad moment for me and she meant it to be.

I am not young. I'm a has-been. I'm on the heap and let me tell you this, it's quite a comfortable place to be. When my womb packed up I went through a sort of widowhood although my husband was not yet dead. I went around sighing, drinking cups of tea to wash down the nerve-stunning pills I brought from a doctor. For a mother to learn that she can have no more children is for a surgeon to have his hands cut off. What can she do? You can't make the children you have last indefinitely. After a long time it came to me that the void was not in my stomach at all. It was in my head. The womb does not have a brain, but that is like saying that the rat is not an intelligent creature. It comes programmed with the cunning of survival. When a young girl presents her-

self and her head full of dreams to her lover it is natural for the womb to say, "Let me do the thinking, dear. You just use your pretty head for painting your pretty face." That's how it is. No, excuse me. That's how it was.

This emptiness I located in my head was not new. It had been there since I was a young woman, Rory's age. My hands were full and my lap. I used my intelligence as a rat does, to plot a path through the maze. Now that the high walls of the maze had crumbled I found myself in open fields. Thoughts rose up into my head. I realized that the period of mourning which succeeds the menopause is not a grieving. It is the weariness that follows upon the removal of a tyranny. Now I was free. I made up my mind never to cook again and became an enthusiastic collector of complete meals in plastic bags with added vitamins. I began, recklessly, to allow entry to thoughts that were not my immediate concern—none of my business at all, to be perfectly frank.

I gave up *The Guardian* which was still telling me how to raise my children and my political consciousness. I started buying *The Sun* which told me about homicides and sex scandals and the secret vices of the royals and reminded me how bountiful women's breasts were. It was the start of my expanded thinking. Every day I find a new marvel on which to ponder.

Why, I ask myself this morning, would anyone leave a sixteen-year-old in charge of a baby? What about all those people who said they brought gifts of food? Why didn't they sneak inside and offer to change the baby's nappy to see if it was being fed all right or if it was being beaten? Who would leave a baby with a sixteen-year-old?

And it comes to me, quite suddenly, sprouting out of the scrap-heap of my middle-aged head—God did. God the Father! He gave His only son to a girl of fifteen. There, with my cup of tea in one hand and my fag in the other, I am filled with alarm as if there is something I should instantly do. I can see the baby with his nappy on backwards as his mother puts henna in her hair. He's crawling around on his hands and knees in his father's carpentry shop, his little mouth full of nails, waiting with growing hopelessness for his mother to come and make him spit them out. Oh, God.

Now there's a thing just caught my eye. ORGY AND BESS is the heading. It's about an heiress, Bess Hichleigh-Harrow, who is alleged to have

offered the sum of £10,000 to any man who could make her experience an orgasm. She looks a nice ordinary woman. Her coat is good.

There is a great preoccupation with orgasms in the modern world, their frequency, their intensity, their duration. Why choose a muscular spasm as an obsession and not something full of mystery, like a bat or a bee? Why not blame the orange for failing to make us happy and fulfilled?

Because it comes to us from our lover, our husband, our mate, our enemy, with whom all things become possible—whose fault everything is.

Of all the things that rose up in my mind after my womb folded up, orgasms wasn't one. I thought of Rory's bottom, when she was a baby—that hot, clothy acquiescence, serene as a Rajah on its throne, pissing indifferently over her legs and my arms while her own arms, entirely dignified and intelligent, patted my face.

She came in the morning. I called her Aurora—a rosy dawn. I was flabbergasted. At long last, after all the false promises, the beloved had come and she came from myself who, being young, I also loved. Men marvel at rockets to the moon and are not astounded by the journey of a sperm to the womb, the transformation of liquid into life. Only women are amazed. "I'm not pregnant, not me, I can't be!" they tell the doctor. "Why me?" they rail at God, and are further dismayed when the emergent infant shows no gratitude to its host, but shits and spits and screams like the devil.

Rory was not like that. She loved me, not just in the way little girls love their mothers, but with the deep earnest love that some men have for their wives, which also contains a small element of contempt. Unlike other children she respected me as the bearer of her life but she thought of me as a simple, shallow person out of touch with reality. I tried to get myself in shape. I read Freud and Kate Millet and Carl Jung and *The Guardian*. It wasn't easy keeping up. Rory grew up in the seventies when everything happened.

I was full of curiosity about the new woman; to be free of priests, to see the penis as a toy, to open one's body to men and lock the door of the womb. "Tell me," I coaxed her. Do you know what she told me?

"You were lovely," she said, "before Daddy died. Why did you have to change?" My generation were the essential women. We were structured to our role and submitted without grievance. That's what she said. We gave birth in our season without ever giving it a thought. That's what she thinks.

She remembered me in a flowered apron and high-heeled shoes, dabbing on my powder—slap, slap, slap—so that it sat on my nose in a comfortable, dusty way, like icing on a bun. A bright, dry, crimson lip was put on, like a felt cut-out and then blotted on to the lower lip and then the glorious gold compact with its wavy edges was snapped shut with a sophisticated clack, and slipped into a little black bag.

"Remember?" she said. There were tears in her eyes.

Rory comes to visit me once a week although she is not comfortable in the hearthless flat I bought after her father died. I hide *The Sun* under a cushion, but she finds it. "What can you be thinking of?" she asks in exasperation.

She is thirty-two. There are lines around the edges of her eyes and her jaw is starting to set, which is an unnerving thing to see on your own child. So I tell her: "I was thinking of the Virgin Mary!" I light a cigarette but I have to hold it away at an angle because she doesn't like the smoke.

I suppose the point of it all was that she was only fifteen. Who else could an angel of the Lord have declared unto? I wonder now, why people make such a fuss about the virgin birth? As if making love had anything to do with having babies. What do you suppose she said to her mother and father afterwards? "I'm going to be the mother of God!"? "I'm pregnant!"?

"I saw an angel." I'll bet that's what she said. Afterwards, when she remembered, she told them what the angel said, that like any old mother everywhere, she had conceived of the Lord.

What on earth did her mother say, her good Jewish mother from the house of David who had gone to such trouble to make a nice match for the child? Don't tell me she took it on the chin. An easy lay and a liar, yet! She was too old to have her daughter's faith, but if she had, she would have asked: "What was its wing span?"

"Look at this!" Now that Rory has pulled my *Sun* out from under its cushion the gloves are off. "'Bag Baby Found in Bin'!"

This is my favourite story today. It's about Norman who was found in a bag which was then stuffed down into a bin. It is a large denim shoulder bag, well enough worn to be prudently discarded. Baby Norman seemed to accept this as his world, or hiding place, and was angry only when disturbed. He has a very red face with rough patches like a butcher's hands. He is not winsome. The item is an appeal for his mother to come back and claim him but his mother has ditched dour Norman, she has sacrificed her battered denim shoulder bag which she probably quite liked, and callously pinned the name "Norman" on his little vest. She has put the tin lid on him and she is never coming back.

Now I've made my daughter miserable. She says I am growing morbid. As you grow older you see things differently. Cause, you realize, is only the kite tail of effect and God is a lateral thinker. I heard a Chinese fable once which said that fate bestows a gift for life on every child at birth. Perhaps Baby Norman's gift was to be left in a bag. Someday, when he is an ugly man being reviled by a woman, he will tell her that his mother left him in a bag in a bin, and her heart will break and she will take him on. He would have been ugly with or without his mother's indifference, but who else would have loved him if his mother had? Rory says you can't believe anything you read in *The Sun*. I suppose she's right, yet she believes absolutely and without a wisp of doubt that Mr. Gorbachev is ready to lay down all his arms.

There is only one mystery left in life, or at any rate in the Western world, where people have opened out the brain and the soul, analysed the body's responses and claimed for themselves in everything from work to love to life or death, the right to choose. Only the child remains the unchosen one. Who knows whether twin soul or tyrant comes dimpling from the neck of the cervix? Cells gather inside us in secret like a pack of dogs or a flock of angels. It could be the Messiah. It could be the man in the moon. Only a child would open Pandora's Box.

Only a Marigold or little Norman's mother would have the nerve to shut it again.

Rory is right. I was lovely before. I made lemon drops and shepherd's pies and fairy cakes. Women play house to preserve a moment that once was almost theirs, the same way they paint their faces to hold youth a little longer. My husband used to tell me—or tried to tell me—over and over, about a trip in a canoe with his father when he was seven. That's all I remember except for official reports issued daily over the tea table. For all I knew about him he might have been a fish in a bowl. I told this to Rory but she thought I was criticizing him. "You made your choices," she said. And I have.

I used to think that Rory would be my guide dog when I went over the hill, would lead me into the new generation.

Now I see that she was hanging around waiting for me to give her the vital information she needed to grow up. We have nothing to do with each other except love and guilt. The terms of reference change with the times and experience is wear-dated. She thinks I turned to packet foods and tabloid papers because I lost interest in life. In fact it is my interest in life that impels me to labour-saving food and literature—that and an aversion to eating anything that still looks like an animal, although I am too old now for the full routine of nuts and pulses. I talked to an Indian on the bus one day (you have to pick your company with care if you intend to say anything you mean) and told him how I could no longer bear to pick up a fish or a chicken and take it home and eat it, because I suddenly knew they were my brothers, but now I worried that such thinking might in due course lead to a meatless world in which the pleasant cow would become extinct. "But the vast, intensified brother-hood of cows is ruining the ozone layer with its communal breaking of methane wind," the Indian gentleman enlightened me. I found this exchange deeply satisfactory. How fitting for the Almighty to knock us all off with a massive cow fart.

What appeals to me now is the language of the tabloid. People do not fornicate or have carnal knowledge. They have sex romps. They frolic. They do not exceed the permitted number of alcohol units. They guzzle. HE GUZZLED BUBBLY WHILE HE PEDDLED DEATH, ran the banner headline above the story of a drug dealer.

It is not, after all, a chapter of adult corruption but a nursery story of miracle babies and naughty children looking for pleasure or treasure, excitement or escape, and reigning over all is the breast goddess—the giver of forgiveness, of guzzling and joy.

Have we all been let down by our mothers who failed to frolic while we guzzled? Was little Marigold lucky, in spite of the bruises and her cold sleep, to have, for a little while, a mother young enough to romp? If only we had the right to choose.

I have a secret. When you get to my age, your fingers go numb and they lose their grip and then you can choose anything you fancy.

There is a photograph in my secret box of a man and a woman. They are not my parents because I was not born then, but I have chosen them. They do not smile. They watch the camera as if it was a test. The girl clasps her flowers like a doll. She has a dress with square buttons and a hat which claps its brim over her alarmed eyes. The man has a suit but he does not wear it, he is worn by it. Such pure people. When this is over, will they be allowed to take off their good clothes and play again?

After the wedding my mother told me they ate rashers and eggs in a hotel and drank champagne and then went to Blackpool on the boat.

In my mind's eye that is where I see them, leaning on the rail looking into the water that floated them away from the world of rules and responsibilities. They might have played "I spy" or talked about the enormous meal they would eat when they got to their hotel—chicken and salad and soufflé and wine—for they were thin and were probably always hungry. Now and again the boy might have looked at the square buttons on the pale blue dress and thought: she's underneath there and she's my woman now. It is certain that they did not think about me for I did not exist then, just as they do not exist now, and did not exist after I was born and made them grow up. It is almost certain that they did not think about orgasms although they might have kissed and kissed until they were in an ecstasy of deprivation. They might have thought that ecstasy was just a tiny little moment away—a romp, a frolic, away—like the jam at the bottom of the pudding dish when you had eaten most of your rice.

Most likely they just thought that they had all the time in the world now; that they never, ever had to please anyone for the rest of their lives but themselves and one another, which were one and the same; that for tonight they might just hold each other close on the narrow bunk and rock to slumber on the waves and tomorrow, in private, in another country, start off their lives.

En Famille

Catherine turned from her own image in the window. Stiff, yet shaken, the continual clatter, carriage off carriage, bone within socket, even the breast shook in its shaping cup. Something primitive in the constant trundle. A hand reached up to the luggage-rack, it was duplicated in the window, a suitcase slipped down at an angle, can't be far off, she tensed herself, prepared her ears, knowing the steel bridge five hundred yards before the station. The thundering rattle of steel, every bolt shocked into its part in the shattering crescendo.

Lights, always dim at railway stations, she stepped out into a sprinkle of rain, steam hissing from the heating system, shreds of voices, smell of oil, somewhere at her back the engine idling, yet with a mechanical insistence to jerk ahead, pull its load to the next stop. The air is pierced, a jerk, a door banged shut, another, the dull resounding thud. Light flickers across her face, quicker and quicker, figures walk back against the motion, faces, limbs, luggage coming and gone. Finally the black hole in the air, drawing and repulsing as if the eyes were struck. Things settle themselves, a footbridge, the further platform, railings, lights repeating themselves in damp surfaces. Man in the signal-box pulling and twisting, contorting himself about the huge wheel while below, ever so slowly, the gates creak back, cars move again before the gates clash to, shutting off the tracks, the man in the box straightens himself, adjusts his cap.

"Taxi, miss?"

"No thank you, I . . ."

But the taximan was already taking suitcases from a family party and ushering them towards the exit. One of the smaller children stumbled and cried before falling. The fatigue and bother of travelling, well past its bedtime and all the strange excitement drained out of the day. The father picked it up, it leaned on his shoulder, his long step, up and down, the child's hat bobbing away into the distance. . . .

"Catherine! Over here!" Yes, it is her name, called out sharply out of the murk and drizzle. James, of course; his usual hurry, she imagined him being incited, dragged away from his stereo or a book, she felt her coming a mistake, she had been too dazed to object strongly enough, Barbara was so persuasive at a distance. He was taking her bag, still not accustomed to him as a brother-in-law, at once related and alien.

He held her to his rough dufflecoat. Always that awkward hug, must have discovered somewhere that kissing is unhygienic, or else the propensity had atrophied because Barbara does not approve. Leading the way to the car he interrupted his flow of trite remarks to wish people good evening. There was something too determined about the tone he adopted; they could scarcely be more than acquaintances. He seemed anxious to justify his being seen at the station with an unknown woman. And Catherine was being invited to note that the man with the trilby hat was the town's operatic tenor, his wife, president of the ladies' golf committee. At the car she stood aloof waiting for James to unlock the anti-theft device, the boot, the passenger door. She knew that a comment was expected from her on the new model, but she took a spiteful pleasure in letting him search for it.

"Just got the number-plates on yesterday. Continental, you know, way ahead on suspension. Overhead camshaft, low air resistance, real smooth, can't you notice the difference?"

"But I thought you felt the Japanese model to be way ahead on everything!"

"Well, Barbara felt they were becoming too common, besides it was a bit cramped you know, very little leg-room. No harm in having a bit of luxury."

The wipers swished before them. A long suburban road, houses well back, lights placed in an alternate pattern, parked cars on both sides.

Catherine leaned forward to wipe the condensation from the glass with her gloved hand.

"I'd prefer if you didn't, it leaves a smear, besides the blower will clear it in a minute."

"I see. Forgive me, I'm so unacquainted with the technical advances."

She stared at the panel of green dials, a frozen light, easy on the eyes perhaps, yet could all those clocks and dials be necessary; were they just stating the obvious, or was it the intention to create a cockpit interior? A more complicated and overtly technical toy? A red light stopped flashing as James belatedly released the handbrake.

"Barbara would have come with me but didn't dare leave the Infanta. I have a horror of babysitters too—one's own flesh and blood, such a risk nowadays, and having some youngster poke about the house, know what I mean?"

"Of course, an unavoidable disadvantage."

"Leaving the child?"

"No, having to apologise for not leaving it."

Catherine decided to take a grip on her irony, too sharp, too complex, a symptom merely of her nerve-shaken frustration. She settled back in her seat, comfortable after the jolting train. The journey, the city, above all the college, receded, it was as if some other person was involved. Here it was again, the immediacy of James and Barbara, their life blotted out her own, transformed her somehow. The town seemed asleep, the odd pedestrian, the odd dog, a huddle of cars at the hotel. Something negative, something static, perhaps she could get away from herself in this atmosphere, if only she could sustain the attack of domesticity, and the inundation of fashionable pseudo-theories, so stupidly *simplistes*—

"Paternal instinct is quite a phenomenon."

"Really?"

"Yes. I don't think it's quite understood, I mean I instinctively wake up and jump out of bed before I have thoroughly registered the fact that Niamh is whimpering."

"I should think it's because Barbara has you so well trained."

"But I have this strange feeling, bang on, when she needs a nappy change, very odd."

"Surely it doesn't take an extraordinary instinct to discover that?"

"Have you read Cohen on paternal instinct?"

"Sorry, I'm afraid teacher training at present is learning to avoid the detritus of the pseudo-sciences."

"But this is really interesting, remind me to show it to you."

"The paternal instinct?"

"Seems I have been misled. You don't sound in the least out of sorts."

"Does one have to sound it?"

"All this won't prevent you taking your diploma, I hope? It would be a terrible waste?"

"It won't—though it is difficult to decide what is waste in the context."

"You know what I mean, things have become so competitive, it's important to have something to show. You must finish at the training college. Nothing wrong with teaching, good money, of course I have no experience of the primary section, but I feel that they work out better than we do, less pressure, easier to handle the younger kids."

He continued his monologue until he brought the car to a halt in the driveway. The confined sense, the press of the neighbouring façades, as if he might have parked at someone else's front. She stepped out, felt her foot sink in soft earth, flower border, daffodils, whether the car was too big or the driveway specification too meagre, there was nowhere else to step. She concealed her faux pas as James busily locked the car doors, opened the front door, the garage and the boot. She may find her own way in, Barbara will be in the kitchen.

She finds herself moving cautiously along the hallway, the narrowness, the conventional furnishings, telephone, potted creeper, coatstand, an openwork stairway, probably saves material, and a mirror never intended to reflect anything because of its impossible angle. A barometer in under the stairs, it could hardly be read without a bump on the head. She lingers, alone with herself again. If only Barbara would appear or call, she must have heard the door open. She feels an intruder, pushing against an unwelcome, stealing into the house. Again, that confusion, the indecision, too late to turn back, she might be discovered loitering if Barbara suddenly appeared. In shoe shops, department stores, at railway stations, penetrating to the ladies' room in hotels, confusion, hesitation. She tries to overcome the feeling, taps at the kitchen door. No response. The feeling returns much stronger, yet she turns the handle and enters. Nothing. A smell of cooking. Then Barbara came from the outer kitchen with an armful of clothes.

"Oh you've come. Train late? Just finishing the ironing. Would you stir the soup, I must run upstairs with this load."

Catherine removed her gloves and left her handbag on a chair, stepped on a plastic duck which uttered a complaining squeak. She found the soup and a spoon. Glancing about she noticed the newness of things, pretty curtains, ingredients in jars and bottles clearly marked, little zigzag shelves for spices and flavourings, the sink a melée of potato-skins, tea-leaves and dirty dishes. Two small shoes and stockings on the floor, she bent to pick them up, James entered behind her.

"Did no one take your coat? Where's Barbara?"

"I'm here. She knows well where to leave her coat. Dinner in a few minutes. James why don't you set a fire in the sitting-room."

He changed into slippers and began to pass back and forth with a coalscuttle. Something about the slippers disconcerted Catherine, repulsed her. Barbara gave the impression of being absorbed with the dinner preparations, yet in control.

"Want a drink, Kate? I can't touch it you know, damn, all the sacrifices I make just for kids. I'm sure you were surprised when you heard that I was pregnant again, well, they're nicely spaced anyway. Leave those, sit down, rest yourself. I'm glad you've come, at least a new face, someone to talk to. Nothing strange I suppose? Has Mam been moaning to you too, I nearly ate her on the phone the other night, what the hell is wrong with her, she was never as well off, as if I didn't have enough to worry about, but she wouldn't say she'd come over and stay for a while, give me a break, I get so tired, especially in the afternoon and Niamh is a handful, very difficult child. I'd better run up again, lately she has started to climb out of her cot. . . . Would you? If she makes strange call me, she can be such a little bitch."

Catherine found the room, its dim light, probably afraid of the dark. Niamh is stretched fast asleep, the little fingers wrapped round the rag doll. Catherine is amused, rather flattered, that the doll she made for her should be so particularly accepted. The breathing is somewhat heavy, the mouth partially open. Stray strands of hair glisten on the pillow. She kneels, watching. She ought to steal away, if the child wakens she is bound to be upset. But there is something gripping about the child, lost in her own little dream, overcome by the day's round, the meals, the sounds, the stumbles, the daylit places at once known intimately and terribly unknown. Yet she is Barbara's child, a stranger really, imbibing the tone, having the common characteristics painted within. Dyed in the genes, perhaps. Too easy to be attracted by the sleeping child, the sentimental pose, too easy to forget the reality, the complaining plastic duck, one's own inadvertance. And Catherine drew away from the cot, conquering the wish to touch the delicate skin, the small protruding lips.

"Well, was she alright?"

"Sound asleep."

"That's odd, normally the little devil has to be begged to lie down. Would you call James, he's probably stuck in a book, tell him it's on the table."

Barbara made an effort at acting the gracious hostess, presiding over her dinner-service, silver and cut glass. Wedding presents most likely, brought out on special occasions, perhaps when some of James's colleagues came to dinner, otherwise there can't have been many occasions. But Catherine felt, as with the pretty curtains and labelled jars, a certain playing at *Hausfrau*, grown-up babyhouse, which a normal sane remark might shatter. Like weighing out clay and pretending it was sugar, or mixing mud in a paint-tin and pretending it was sweetcake. If someone, tired of the game or finding themselves outside the circle of make-believe, remarked on the mud, everything would stop suddenly, then pouting, tears, and a smashing of jam-jars on stone.

James almost shattered the effect at times, obviously he needed further practice, but a glance from Barbara saved the moment. Catherine played her part, found pertinent comments, asked about preparations and recipes, admired the design of the cut-glass bowls. It was an attempt at being amiable, at acknowledging the trouble Barbara had so obviously taken. Yet a hug or even a warm handshake would have meant so much, but it would have caused Barbara greater effort.

Conversation fluctuated about the particular, the home, the car, the child existing and the child expected. Catherine helped with the coffee, which was to be served in the sitting-room, washing up was abandoned until the morning. Barbara decided that they did not want to watch the news, James eventually agreed and replenished the fire.

There was some lack of comfort in the room despite the large velvet-covered suite and the wall-length velvet curtains. Television and stereo equipment dominating, a Van Gogh print, an antique writing-desk, a shelf of sitting-room books, children's encyclopedias, the rest loud and mixed, only moved when dusting. Catherine had never experienced the room in such a way before. The encyclopedias especially irritated her, as if they were part of the equipment needed for having children, like prams and soothers, some responsibility had been fulfilled, the intellectual life of the child had not been forgotten. Very likely the house next door repeats the pattern; it is no doubt repeated along the "Drive," a change of colour perhaps, some slight shift of emphasis, a different set of discs or encyclopedias, but the same mental and material specifications.

James, tiring of the domestic preoccupations, brought the conversation round to evolution, some recent reading, Darwin in the Galapagos Islands, long-legged tortoises, iguanas, Barbara cocked an eye and stressed her breathing. Yet he continued. Catherine found the scraps of information mildly interesting but out of context, such an unimaginative attempt at conversation, he must have known he was boring Barbara who reached the limits of her endurance as the flightless cormorants raised their heads.

"James, for Christ's sake give us a break. It's all very interesting I'm sure, but it's not my idea of a relaxed conversation, and I'm sure Catherine is bored stiff; if she's not, well I am. Surely you can keep that kind of stuff for your darling Leaving Certs."

Catherine shifted in her chair. Basically Barbara was correct, but the intolerance of it, the unkindness, while her own topics of conversation were so penetratingly banal. She had grown sharper in tone and feature, even the eyes were too obvious, too protuberant. But James accepted the cut with a feeble effort at humour. Adaptation to environment? Survival of the fittest? Catherine tried to manoeuvre a safe shift, but nothing seemed quite safe in this atmosphere.

"Niamh has got so big since I saw her last."

"I'll soon have opposition. Even as it is . . ."

"And very intelligent, you'd hardly believe it." Of course, Barbara tried to claim responsibility for that.

"Without much hope I should think?" Catherine felt her tone grow bright and artificial, echo of college conversations, pretending an interest.

"Naturally. He is such a clever father. All I seem to have contributed is her cranky moods."

"Her IQ must be way up. You see, Catherine, children have an open pipeline to the seat of creativity, it must be kept open all in the right hemisphere of the brain, you understand functional psychology, very important, and the toys nowadays are so creative, schematised to widen the horizons."

"James is right for once. He brought her this fantastic thing from London—the school trip to Stratford—you should see it, little round things all different colours and sizes, multidimensional, and they all fit into each other in the most striking patterns."

"It even took me a few hours to get the hang of it myself."

"But Kate, I could have strangled her. David and Laura were here too, remember James, she took one look at it, put on a puss and said, 'I don't like it,' and off she went with that bloody awful rag doll."

"But Catherine sent her that doll."

"Oh yes, very nice and all that, but it has got so scruffy."

"Sorry about that . . ." She flushed, sat still, palms pressed to her knees.

"But when I think of what he paid for it, I mean it's intolerable. God, when we were kids . . ."

"Oh it's not the money, Barbara, for goodness sake."

"Your multidimensional fresh from London is meant to find the pipeline to the child's left hemisphere, one supposes. Seat of logic, isn't it?" Her lips were in prim control of the sarcasm, inwardly seething. "But logic, I daresay, is a bad word in the pedagogical junk biz?"

Brother-in-law was not really listening. He missed the shaft maliciously aimed at him.

"Forgive me, ladies, I've got some work to prepare. I know it must sound awfully old-fashioned, but with the lot I have I've got to keep abreast."

"H'm, in order to keep abreast of them I know what I'd do!"

He left. Perhaps he did have some work to do, but she found the emphasized conscientiousness distasteful. The dedicated professional act. Barbara poked the fire, leaned back in her armchair, kicked a stool under her feet. She seemed to expand her stomach, stressing the pregnancy, the acme of the feminine ethos. So aware, the supine position, so much like a pale heroine on a chaise longue, the arm at a pathetic angle and some sal volatile to hand. Something shamelessly typical about the posture, an act that was no act but a choking archetype, now that the male, that necessary irritant, had been driven from the scene.

"Did you hear all that crap about the school, makes me sick. He's more concerned about them than he is about me."

"You're not inclined to over-react are you?"

"So I'm over-reacting am I? Easy for you, you don't know what it's like."

"But surely it can't be that bad, perhaps you're just going through a patch of ill-humour, being pregnant is a strain."

"Oh if you mean that I hadn't wished it."

"Surely some of the methods are dependable?"

"It's not that, Kate, you see I must consider myself lucky to be pregnant at all."

"You can't mean . . ."

"We sleep together, as yet anyway, but I might as well not be there. Oh, I've read the books. . . ."

"Tried the aphrodisiacs I suppose?"

"The lot, from wheatgerm to shock tactics. Then it finally dawned on me. That school, all those girls, even the nuns, it does something to them, I mean it's bound to, siphons off the sexual energy, then he comes home absolutely spent."

"But the job is rather demanding. I imagine that you would feel rather spent yourself."

"I know all that, but this is something extra; now if he were teaching in a boys' school."

"Then you might have other problems."

"No Kate, I'm really convinced, you see during the holidays it's quite different. What man could spent his time among a crowd of girls, mostly nubile, and not be affected, you know what they're like."

"Yes, but you would have expected the opposite effect wouldn't you?"

"All I'm saying is that it's not healthy."

"I suppose Origen would agree with you."

"Please, if that's some authority on educational theory, I don't want to know."

"A very practical man when it came to the instruction of young women. A doctor of the Church. Had himself castrated to avoid temptation. Still, I think that you may be simplifying the situation."

"But I've noticed things, not just once or twice, I still do the washing round here."

"All right, Barbara, let's not be crude. Mind if I go to bed now? I'm mentally drained, must be the journey."

"Sure, why not. I think I might lie on in the morning. Help yourself, Niamh will be running about of course, and James has an early start."

"Goodnight."

"My good nights are over for another few months."

In bed, Catherine tried to relax but jerked awake each time she was on the point of sinking into sleep. Barbara came up, she could hear her mutterings from the master-bedroom as they liked to call it, water, walking, wardrobe doors. Privacy, laths and a skin of plaster. Even from the house next door she heard rumblings, a telephone bell, steps on stairs. Living within earshot of the neighbour. Copulation in one house probably sets up a chain-reaction along the Drive. Barbara's is an end house, she loses half the stimulation. A toilet is flushed next door, a door bangs, silence.

Her book absorbs the restless churning of her mind for two hours or more, still no sleep. She gets up, draws aside the curtain, faces her dim self and a small lit window in the distance. She switches off her lamp and the further houses shape themselves against a diffused light in the sky, a moon somewhere, the gardens form into dark rectangles between cold walls of concrete. The window rattles in a gust of wind, a clothes-line in the next garden bangs off its steel post, metallic sound empty of meaning.

In bed again she relives the thud and rattle of the train. Nerves and wires vibrating. Mechanised universe, mechanised mind. The college course grinding through its gears, the small minds, myriads of them, living blobs of imagination, crushed and ironed out in the mechanism. Not sleep really, but strangled in the recurring nightmare . . .

April, the rustle and scream of birds in morning light. The little face had come close to the edge of her pillow. Doll and hands up tight under the chin, a face oddly shrunk and wizened. Eyes half shut, colourless, lids creased wrinkling the little ancient face from which the eyes squinted at her, in cunning, in curiosity, or in something older than either of them, complicity. Gone silently, she heard the awkward yet determined clop of bare feet down the stairs. Cups and cutlery sounded against each other from the kitchen.

Shepherd's Bush

People looked very weary, May thought, and shabbier than she had remembered Londoners to be. They reminded her a little of those news-reel pictures of crowds during the war or just after it, old raincoats, brave smiles, endless patience. But then this wasn't Regent Street where she had wandered up and down looking at shops on other visits to London, it wasn't the West End with lights all glittering and people getting out of taxis full of excitement and wafts of perfume. This was Shepherd's Bush where people lived. They had probably set out from here early this morning and fought similar crowds on the way to work. The women must have done their shopping in their lunch-hour because most of them were carrying plastic bags of food. It was a London different to the one you see as a tourist.

And she was here for a different reason, although she had once read a cynical article in a magazine which said that girls coming to London for abortions provided a significant part of the city's tourist revenue. It wasn't something you could classify under any terms as a holiday. When she filled in the card at the airport she had written "Business" in the section where it said "Purpose of journey."

The pub where she was to meet Celia was near the tube station. She found it easily and settled herself in. A lot of the accents were Irish, workmen having a pint before they went home to their English wives and their television programmes. Not drunk tonight, it was only Monday, but obviously regulars. Maybe not so welcome as regulars on Friday or Saturday nights, when they would remember they were Irish and sing anti-British songs.

Celia wouldn't agree with her about that. Celia had rose-tinted views about the Irish in London, she thought they were all here from choice, not because there was no work for them at home. She hated stories about the restless Irish, or Irishmen on the lump in the building trade. She said people shouldn't make such a big thing about it all. People who came from much farther away settled in London, it was big enough to absorb everyone. Oh well, she wouldn't bring up the subject, there were enough things to disagree with Celia about . . . without searching for more.

Oh why of all people, of all the bloody people in the world, did she have to come to Celia? Why was there nobody else whom she could ask for advice? Celia would give it, she would give a lecture with every piece of information she imparted. She would deliver a speech with every cup of tea, she would be cool, practical and exactly the right person, if she weren't so much the wrong person. It was handing Celia a whole box of ammunition about Andy. From now on Celia could say that Andy was a rat, and May could no longer say she had no facts to go on.

Celia arrived. She was thinner, and looked a little tired. She smiled. Obviously the lectures weren't going to come in the pub. Celia always knew the right place for things. Pubs were for meaningless chats and bright, non-intense conversation. Home was for lectures.

"You're looking marvellous," Celia said.

It couldn't be true. May looked at her reflection in a glass panel. You couldn't see the dark lines under her eyes there, but you could see the droop of her shoulders, she wasn't a person that could be described as looking marvellous. No, not even in a pub.

"I'm okay," she said. "But you've got very slim, how did you do it?"

"No bread, no cakes, no potatoes, no sweets," said Celia in a business-like way. "It's the old rule but it's the only rule. You deny yourself everything you want and you lose weight."

"I know," said May, absently rubbing her waistline.

"Oh I didn't mean *that*," cried Celia horrified. "I didn't mean that at all."

May felt weary, she hadn't meant that either, she was patting her stomach because she had been putting on weight. The child that she was going to get rid of was still only a speck, it would cause no bulge. She had put on weight because she cooked for Andy three or four times a week in his flat. He was long and lean. He could eat forever and he wouldn't put on weight. He didn't like eating alone so she ate with him. She reassured Celia that there was no offence and when Celia had gone, twittering with rage at herself, to the counter, May wondered whether she had explored every avenue before coming to Celia and Shepherd's Bush for help.

She had. There were no legal abortions in Dublin, and she did not know of anyone who had ever had an illegal one there. England and the ease of the system were less than an hour away by plane. She didn't want to try and get it on the National Health, she had the money, all she wanted was someone who would introduce her to a doctor, so that she could get it all over with quickly. She needed somebody who knew her, somebody who wouldn't abandon her if things went wrong, somebody who would lie for her, because a few lies would have to be told. May didn't have any other friends in London. There was a girl she had once met on a skiing holiday, but you couldn't impose on a holiday friendship in that way. She knew a man, a very nice, kind man who had stayed in the hotel where she worked and had often begged her to come and stay with him and his wife. But she couldn't go to stay with them for the first time in this predicament, it would be ridiculous. It had to be Celia.

It might be easier if Celia had loved somebody so much that every-thing else was unimportant. But stop, that wasn't fair. Celia loved that dreary, boring, selfish Martin. She loved him so much that she believed one day he was going to get things organized and make a home for them. Everyone else knew that Martin was the worst possible bet for any punter, a Mamma's boy, who had everything he wanted now, including a visit every two months from Celia, home from London, smartly-dressed, undemanding, saving away for a day that would never come. So Celia did understand something about the nature of love. She never talked about it. People as brisk as Celia don't talk about things like unbrisk atti-tudes in men, or hurt feelings or broken hearts. Not when it refers to themselves, but they are very good at pointing out the foolish attitudes of others.

Celia was back with the drinks.

"We'll finish them up quickly," she said.

Why could she never, never take her ease over anything? Things always had to be finished up quickly. It was warm and anonymous in the pub. They could go back to Celia's flat, which May felt sure wouldn't have even a comfortable chair in it, and talk in a business-like way about the rights and wrongs of abortion, the procedure, the money, and how it shouldn't be spent on something so hopeless and destructive. And about Andy. Why wouldn't May tell him? He had a right to know. The child was half his, and even if he didn't want it he should pay for the abortion. He had plenty of money, he was a hotel manager. May had hardly any, she was a hotel receptionist. May could see it all coming, she dreaded it. She wanted to stay in this warm place until closing-time, and to fall asleep, and wake up there two days later.

Celia made walking-along-the-road conversation on the way to her flat. This road used to be very quiet and full of retired people, now it was all flats and bed-sitters. That road was nice, but noisy, too much through-traffic. The houses in the road over there were going for thirty-five thousand, which was ridiculous, but then you had to remember it was fairly central and they did have little gardens. Finally they were there. A big Victorian house, a clean, polished hall, and three flights of stairs. The flat was much bigger than May expected, and it had a sort of divan on which she sat down immediately and put up her legs, while Celia fussed about a bit, opening a bottle of wine and putting a dish of four small lamb chops into the oven. May braced herself for the lecture.

It wasn't a lecture, it was an information-sheet. She was so relieved that she could feel herself relaxing, and filled up her wineglass again.

"I've arranged with Doctor Harris that you can call to see him tomorrow morning at 11. I told him no lies, just a little less than the truth. I said you were staying with me. If he thinks that means you are staying permanently, that's his mistake not mine. I mentioned that your problem was . . . what it is. I asked him when he thought it would be . . . em . . . done. He said Wednesday or Thursday, but it would all depend. He didn't seem shocked or anything; it's like tonsillitis to him, I suppose. Anyway he was very calm about it. I think you'll find he's a kind person and it won't be upsetting . . . that part of it."

May was dumbfounded. Where were the accusations, the I-told-you-so sighs, the hope that now, finally, she would finish with Andy? Where was the slight moralistic bit, the heavy wondering whether or not it might be murder? For the first time in the eleven days since she had confirmed she was pregnant, May began to hope that there would be some normality in the world again.

"Will it embarrass you, all this?" she asked. "I mean, do you feel it will change your relationship with him?"

"In London, a doctor isn't an old family friend like at home, May. He's someone you go to, or I've gone to anyway, when I've had to have my ears syringed, needed antibiotics for flu last year, and a medical certificate for the time I sprained my ankle and couldn't go to work. He hardly knows me except as a name on his register. He's nice though, and he doesn't rush you in and out. He's Jewish and small and worried-looking."

Celia moved around the flat, changing into comfortable sitting-about clothes, looking up what was on television, explaining to May that she must sleep in her room and that she, Celia, would use the divan.

No, honestly, it would be easier that way, she wasn't being nice, it would be much easier. A girl friend rang and they arranged to play squash together at the week-end. A wrong number rang; a West Indian from the flat downstairs knocked on the door to say he would be having a party on Saturday night and to apologize in advance for any noise. If they liked to bring a bottle of something, they could call in themselves. Celia served dinner. They looked at television for an hour, then went to bed.

May thought what a strange empty life Celia led here far from home, miles from Martin, no real friends, no life at all. Then she thought that Celia might possibly regard her life too as sad, working in a second-rate hotel for five years, having an affair with its manager for three years. A hopeless affair because the manager's wife and four children were a bigger stumbling-block than Martin's mother could ever be. She felt tired and comfortable, and in Celia's funny, characterless bedroom she drifted off and dreamed that Andy had discovered where she was and what she was about to do, and had flown over during the night to tell her that they would get married next morning, and live in England and forget the hotel, the family and what anyone would say.

Tuesday morning. Celia was gone. Dr Harris's address was neatly written on the pad by the phone with instructions how to get there. Also Celia's phone number at work, and a message that May never believed she would hear from Celia. "Good luck."

He was small, and Jewish, and worried and kind. His examination was painless and unembarrassing. He confirmed what she knew already. He wrote down dates, and asked general questions about her health. May wondered whether he had a family, there were no pictures of wife or children in the surgery. But then there were none in Andy's office, either. Perhaps his wife was called Rebecca and she too worried because her husband worked so hard, they might have two children, a boy who was a gifted musician, and a girl who wanted to get married to a Christian. Maybe they all walked along these leafy roads on Saturdays to synagogue and Rebecca cooked all those things like gefilte fish and bagels.

With a start, May told herself to stop dreaming about him. It was a habit she had got into recently, fancying lives for everyone she met, however briefly. She usually gave them happy lives with a bit of problem-to-be-solved thrown in. She wondered what a psychiatrist would make of that. As she was coming back to real life, Dr Harris was saying that if he was going to refer her for a termination he must know why she could not have the baby. He pointed out that she was healthy, and strong, and young. She should have no difficulty with pregnancy or birth. Were there emotional reasons? Yes, it would kill her parents, she wouldn't be able to look after the baby, she didn't want to look after one on her own either, it wouldn't be fair on her or the baby.

"And the father?" Dr Harris asked.

"Is my boss, is heavily married, already has four babies of his own. It would break up his marriage which he doesn't want to do . . . yet. No, the father wouldn't want me to have it either."

"Has he said that?" asked Dr Harris as if he already knew the answer.

"I haven't told him, I can't tell him, I won't tell him," said May.

Dr Harris sighed. He asked a few more questions; he made a telephone call; he wrote out an address. It was a posh address near Harley Street.

"This is Mr White. A well-known surgeon. These are his consulting-rooms, I have made an appointment for you at 2:30 this afternoon. I understand from your friend Miss . . ." He searched his mind and his desk for Celia's name and then gave up. "I understand anyway that you are not living here, and don't want to try and pretend that you are, so that you want the termination done privately. That's just as well, because it would be difficult to get it done on the National Health. There are many cases that would have to come before you."

"Oh I have the money," said May, patting her handbag. She felt nervous but relieved at the same time. Almost exhilarated. It was working, the whole thing was actually moving. God bless Celia.

"It will be around £180 to £200, and in cash, you know that?"

"Yes, it's all here, but why should a well-known surgeon have to be paid in cash, Dr Harris? You know it makes it look a bit illegal and sort of underhand, doesn't it?"

Dr Harris smiled a tired smile. "You ask me why he has to be paid in cash. Because he says so. Why he says so, I don't know. Maybe it's because some of his clients don't feel too like paying him after the event. It's not like plastic surgery or a broken leg, where they can see the results. In a termination you see no results. Maybe people don't pay so easily then. Maybe also Mr White doesn't have a warm relationship with his Income Tax people. I don't know."

"Do I owe you anything?" May asked, putting on her coat.

"No, my dear, nothing." He smiled and showed her to the door.

"It feels wrong. I'm used to paying a doctor at home or they send bills," she said.

"Send me a picture postcard of your nice country sometime," he said. "When my wife was alive she and I spent several happy holidays there before all this business started." He waved a hand to take in the course of Anglo-Irish politics and difficulties over the last ten years.

May blinked a bit hard and thanked him. She took a taxi which was passing his door and went to Oxford Street. She wanted to see what was in the shops because she was going to pretend that she had spent £200 on clothes and then they had all been lost or stolen. She hadn't yet worked out the details of this deception, which seemed unimportant compared to all the rest that had to be gone through. But she would need to know what was in the shops so that she could say what she was meant to have bought.

Imagining that she had this kind of money to spend, she examined jackets, skirts, sweaters, and the loveliest boots she had ever seen. If only she didn't have to throw this money away, she could have these things. It was her savings over ten months, she put by £30 a month with difficulty. Would Andy have liked her in the boots? She didn't know. He never said much about the way she looked. He saw her mostly in uniform when she could steal time to go to the flat he had for himself in the hotel. On the evenings when he was meant to be working late, and she was in fact cooking for him, she usually wore a dressing-gown, a long velvet one. Perhaps she might have bought a dressing-gown. She examined some, beautiful Indian silks, and a Japanese satin one in pink covered with little black butterflies. Yes, she would tell him she had bought that, he would like the sound of it, and be sorry it had been stolen.

She had a cup of coffee in one of the big shops and watched the other shoppers resting between bouts of buying. She wondered, did any of them look at her, and if so, would they know in a million years that her shopping money would remain in her purse until it was handed over to a Mr White so that he could abort Andy's baby? Why did she use words like that, why did she say things to hurt herself, she must have a very deep-seated sense of guilt. Perhaps, she thought to herself with a bit of humour, she should save another couple of hundred pounds and come over for a few sessions with a Harley Street shrink. That should set her right.

It wasn't a long walk to Mr White's rooms, it wasn't a pleasant welcome. A kind of girl that May had before only seen in the pages of fashion magazines, bored, disdainful, elegant, reluctantly admitted her.

"Oh yes, Dr Harris's patient," she said, as if May should have come in some tradesman's entrance. She felt furious, and inferior, and sat with her hands in small tight balls, and her eyes unseeing in the waiting-room.

Mr White looked like a caricature of a diplomat. He had elegant grey hair, elegant manicured hands. He moved very gracefully, he talked in practised, concerned clichés, he knew how to put people at their ease, and despite herself, and while still disliking him, May felt safe.

Another examination, another confirmation, more checking of dates. Good, good, she had come in plenty of time, sensible girl. No reasons she would like to discuss about whether this was the right course of action? No? Oh well, grown-up lady, must make up her own mind. Absolutely certain then? Fine, fine. A look at a big leather-bound book on his desk, a look at a small notebook. Leather-bound for the tax people, small notebook for himself, thought May viciously. Splendid, splendid. Tomorrow morning then, not a problem in the world, once she was sure, then he knew this was the best, and wisest thing. Very sad the people who dithered.

May could never imagine this man having dithered in his life. She was asked to see Vanessa on the way out. She knew that the girl would be called something like Vanessa.

Vanessa yawned and took £194 from her. She seemed to have difficulty in finding the six pounds in change. May wondered wildly whether this was meant to be a tip. If so, she would wait for a year until Vanessa found the change. With the notes came a discreet printed card advertising a nursing home on the other side of London.

"Before nine, fasting, just the usual overnight things," said Vanessa helpfully.

"Tomorrow morning?" checked May.

"Well yes, naturally. You'll be out at eight the following morning. They'll arrange everything like taxis. They have super food," she added as an afterthought.

"They'd need to have for this money," said May spiritedly.

"You're not just paying for the food," said Vanessa wisely.

It was still raining. She rang Celia from a public phone box. Everything was organized, she told her. Would Celia like to come and have a meal somewhere, and maybe they could go on to a theatre?

Celia was sorry, she had to work late, and she had already bought liver and bacon for supper. Could she meet May at home around nine? There was a great quiz show on telly, it would be a shame to miss it.

May went to a hairdresser and spent four times what she would have spent at home on a hair-do.

She went to a cinema and saw a film which looked as if it was going to be about a lot of sophisticated witty French people on a yacht and turned out to be about a sophisticated witty French girl who fell in love with the deck-hand on the yacht and when she purposely got pregnant, in order that he would marry her, he laughed at her and the witty sophisticated girl threw herself overboard. Great choice that, May said glumly, as she dived into the underground to go back to the smell of liver frying.

Celia asked little about the arrangements for the morning, only practical things like the address so that she could work out how long it would take to get there.

"Would you like me to come and see you?" she asked. "I expect when it's all over, all finished you know, they'd let you have visitors. I could come after work."

She emphasized the word "could" very slightly. May immediately felt mutinous. She would love Celia to come, but not if it was going to be a duty, something she felt she had to do, against her principles, her inclinations.

"No, don't do that," she said in a falsely bright voice. "They have telly in the rooms apparently, and anyway, it's not as if I were going to be there for more than twenty-four hours."

Celia looked relieved. She worked out taxi times and locations and turned on the quiz show.

In the half light May looked at her. She was unbending, Celia was. She would survive everything, even the fact that Martin would never marry her. Christ, the whole thing was a mess. Why did people start life with such hopes, and as early as their mid-twenties become beaten and accepting of things. Was the rest of life going to be like this?

She didn't sleep so well, and it was a relief when Celia shouted that it was seven o'clock.

Wednesday. An ordinary Wednesday for the taxi-driver, who shouted some kind of amiable conversation at her. She missed most of it, because of the noise of the engine, and didn't bother to answer him half the time except with a grunt.

The place had creeper on the walls. It was a big house, with a small garden, and an attractive brass handle on the door. The nurse who opened it was Irish. She checked May's name on a list. Thank God it was O'Connor, there were a million O'Connors. Suppose she had had an unusual name, she'd have been found out immediately.

The bedroom was big and bright. Two beds, flowery covers, nice furniture. A magazine rack, a bookshelf. A television, a bathroom.

The Irish nurse offered her a hanger from the wardrobe for her coat as if this was a pleasant family hotel of great class and comfort. May felt frightened for the first time. She longed to sit down on one of the beds and cry, and for the nurse to put her arm around her and give her a cigarette and say that it would be all right. She hated being so alone.

The nurse was distant.

"The other lady will be in shortly. Her name is Miss Adams. She just went downstairs to say goodbye to her friend. If there's anything you'd like, please ring."

She was gone, and May paced the room like a captured animal. Was she to undress? It was ridiculous to go to bed. You only went to bed in the day-time if you were ill. She was well, perfectly well.

Miss Adams burst in the door. She was a chubby, pretty girl about twenty-three. She was Australian, and her name was Hell, short for Helen.

"Come on, bedtime," she said, and they both put on their night-dresses and got into beds facing each other. May had never felt so silly in her whole life.

"Are you sure we're meant to do this?" she asked.

"Positive," Helen announced. "I was here last year. They'll be in with the screens for modesty, the examination, and the pre-med. They go mad if you're not in bed. Of course that stupid Paddy of a nurse didn't tell you, they expect you to be inspired."

Hell was right. In five minutes, the nurse and Mr White came in. A younger nurse carried a screen. Hell was examined first, then May, for blood pressure and temperature, and that kind of thing. Mr White was charming. He called her Miss O'Connor, as if he had known her all his life.

He patted her shoulder and told her she didn't have anything to worry about. The Irish nurse gave her an unsmiling injection which was going to make her drowsy. It didn't immediately.

Hell was doing her nails.

"You were really here last year?" asked May in disbelief.

"Yeah, there's nothing to it. I'll be back at work tomorrow."

"Why didn't you take the Pill?" May asked.

"Why didn't you?" countered Hell.

"Well, I did for a bit, but I thought it was making me fat, and then anyway, you know, I thought I'd escaped for so long before I started the Pill that it would be all right. I was wrong."

"I know." Hell was sympathetic. "I can't take it. I've got varicose veins already and I don't really understand all those things they give you in the Family Planning clinics, jellies, and rubber things, and dia-phragms. It's worse than working out income tax. Anyway, you never have time to set up a scene like that before going to bed with someone, do you? It's like preparing for a battle."

May laughed.

"It's going to be fine, love," said Hell. "Look, I know, I've been here before. Some of my friends have had it done four or five times. I promise you, it's only the people who don't know who worry. This afternoon you'll wonder what you were thinking about to look so white. Now if it had been terrible, would I be here again?"

"But your varicose veins?" said May, feeling a little sleepy.

"Go to sleep, kid," said Hell. "We'll have a chat when it's all over."

Then she was getting onto a trolley, half-asleep, and going down cor-ridors with lovely prints on the walls to a room with a lot of light, and transferring onto another table. She felt as if she could sleep for ever and she hadn't even had the anaesthetic yet. Mr White stood there in a coat brighter than his name. Someone was dressing him up the way they do in films.

She thought about Andy. "I love you," she said suddenly.

"Of course you do," said Mr White, coming over and patting her kindly without a trace of embarrassment.

Then she was being moved again, she thought they hadn't got her right on the operating table, but it wasn't that, it was back into her own bed and more sleep.

There was a tinkle of china. Hell called over from the window.

"Come on, they've brought us some nice soup. Broth they call it."

May blinked.

"Come on, May. I was done after you and I'm wide awake. Now didn't I tell you there was nothing to it?"

May sat up. No pain, no tearing feeling in her insides. No sickness.

"Are you sure they did me?" she asked.

They both laughed.

They had what the nursing-home called a light lunch. Then they got a menu so that they could choose dinner.

"There are some things that England does really well, and this is one of them," Hell said approvingly, trying to decide between the delights that were offered. "They even give us a small carafe of wine. If you want more you have to pay for it. But they kind of disapprove of us getting pissed."

Hell's friend Charlie was coming in at six when he finished work. Would May be having a friend too, she wondered? No. Celia wouldn't come.

"I don't mean Celia," said Hell. "I mean the bloke."

"He doesn't know, he's in Dublin, and he's married," said May.

"Well, Charlie's married, but he bloody knows, and he'd know if he were on the moon."

"It's different."

"No, it's not different. It's the same for everyone, there are rules, you're a fool to break them. Didn't he pay for it either, this guy?"

"No. I told you he doesn't know."

"Aren't you noble," said Hell scornfully. "Aren't you a real Lady Galahad. Just visiting London for a day or two, darling, just going to see a few friends, see you soon. Love you darling. Is that it?"

"We don't go in for so many darlings as that in Dublin," said May.

"You don't go in for much common sense either. What will you gain, what will he gain, what will anyone gain? You come home penniless, a bit lonely. He doesn't know what the hell you've been doing, he isn't extra-sensitive and loving and grateful because he doesn't have anything to be grateful about as far as he's concerned."

"I couldn't tell him. I couldn't. I couldn't ask him for £200 and say what it was for. That wasn't in the bargain, that was never part of the deal."

May was almost tearful, mainly from jealousy she thought. She couldn't bear Hell's Charlie to come in, while her Andy was going home to his wife because there would be nobody to cook him something exciting and go to bed with him in his little manager's flat.

"When you go back, tell him. That's my advice," said Hell. "Tell him you didn't want to worry him, you did it all on your own because the responsibility was yours since you didn't take the Pill. That's unless you think he'd have wanted it?"

"No, he wouldn't have wanted it."

"Well then, that's what you do. Don't ask him for the money straight out, just let him know you're broke. He'll react some way then. It's silly not to tell them at all. My sister did that with her bloke back in Melbourne. She never told him at all, and she got upset because he didn't know the sacrifice she had made, and every time she bought a drink or paid for a cinema ticket she got resentful of him. All for no reason, because he didn't bloody know.'

"I might," said May, but she knew she wouldn't.

Charlie came in. He was great fun, very fond of Hell, wanting to be sure she was okay, and no problems. He bought a bottle of wine which they shared, and he told them funny stories about what had happened at the office. He was in advertising. He arranged to meet Hell for lunch next day and joked his way out of the room.

"He's a lovely man," said May.

"Old Charlie's smashing," agreed Hell. He had gone back home to entertain his wife and six dinner guests. His wife was a marvellous hostess apparently. They were always having dinner parties.

"Do you think he'll ever leave her?" asked May.

"He'd be out of his brains if he did," said Hell cheerfully.

May was thoughtful. Maybe everyone would be out of their brains if they left good, comfortable, happy home setups for whatever the other woman imagined she could offer. She wished she could be as happy as Hell.

"Tell me about your fellow," Hell said kindly.

May did, the whole long tale. It was great to have somebody to listen, somebody who didn't say she was on a collision course, somebody who didn't purse up lips like Celia, someone who said, "Go on, what did you do then?"

"He sounds like a great guy," said Hell, and May smiled happily.

They exchanged addresses, and Hell promised that if ever she came to Ireland she wouldn't ring up the hotel and say, "Can I talk to May, the girl I had the abortion with last winter?" and they finished Charlie's wine, and went to sleep.

The beds were stripped early next morning when the final examination had been done, and both were pronounced perfect and ready to leave. May wondered fancifully how many strange life stories the room must have seen.

"Do people come here for other reasons apart from . . . er, terminations?" she asked the disapproving Irish nurse.

"Oh certainly they do, you couldn't work here otherwise," said the nurse. "It would be like a death factory, wouldn't it?"

That puts me in my place, thought May, wondering why she hadn't the courage to say that she was only visiting the home, she didn't earn her living from it.

She let herself into Celia's gloomy flat. It had become gloomy again like the way she had imagined it before she saw it. The warmth of her first night there was gone. She looked around and wondered why Celia had no pictures, no books, no souvenirs.

There was a note on the telephone pad.

"I didn't ring or anything, because I forgot to ask if you had given your real name, and I wouldn't know who to ask for. Hope you feel well again. I'll be getting some chicken pieces so we can have supper together around 8. Ring me if you need me. C."

May thought for a bit. She went out and bought Celia a casserole dish, a nice one made of cast-iron. It would be useful for all those little high-protein, low-calorie dinners Celia cooked. She also bought a bunch of flowers, but could find no vase when she came back and had to use a big glass instead. She left a note thanking her for the hospitality, warm enough to sound properly grateful, and a genuinely warm remark about how glad she was that she had been able to do it all through nice Dr Harris. She said nothing about the time in the nursing-home. Celia would prefer not to know. May just said that she was fine, and thought she would go back to Dublin tonight. She rang the airline and booked a plane.

Should she ring Celia and tell her to get only one chicken piece. No, damn Celia, she wasn't going to ring her. She had a fridge, hadn't she?

The plane didn't leave until the early afternoon. For a wild moment she thought of joining Hell and Charlie in the pub where they were meeting, but dismissed the idea. She must now make a list of what clothes she was meant to have bought and work out a story about how they had disappeared. Nothing that would make Andy get in touch with police or airlines to find them for her. It was going to be quite hard, but she'd have to give Andy some explanation of what she'd been doing, wouldn't she? And he would want to know why she had spent all that money. Or would he? Did he even know she had all that money? She couldn't remember telling him. He wasn't very interested in her little savings, they talked more about his investments. And she must remember, that if he was busy or cross tonight or tomorrow she wasn't to take it out on him. Like Hell had said, there wasn't any point in her expecting a bit of cossetting when he didn't even know she needed it.

How sad and lonely it would be to live like Celia, to be so suspicious of men, to think so ill of Andy. Celia always said he was selfish and just took what he could get. That was typical of Celia, she understood nothing. Hell had understood more, in a couple of hours, than Celia had in three years. Hell knew what it was like to love someone.

But May didn't think Hell had got it right about telling Andy all about the abortion. Andy might be against that kind of thing. He was very moral in his own way, was Andy.

Naming the Names

Abyssinia, Alma, Bosnia, Balaclava, Belgrade, Bombay.

It was late summer—August, like the summer of the fire. He hadn't rung for three weeks.

I walked down the Falls towards the reconverted cinema: THE LARGEST SECOND-HAND BOOKSHOP IN THE WORLD, the billboard read. Of course it wasn't. What we did have was a vast collection of historical manuscripts, myths and legends, political pamphlets, and we ran an exchange service for readers of crime, western and paperback romances. By far the most popular section for which Chrissie was responsible, since the local library had been petrol bombed.

It was late when I arrived, the dossers from St. Vincent de Paul hostel had already gone in to check the morning papers. I passed them sitting on the steps every working day: Isabella wore black fishnet tights and a small hat with a half veil, and long black gloves even on the warmest day and eyed me from the feet up; Eileen, who was dumpy and smelt of meths and talcum powder, looked at everyone with the sad eyes of a cow. Tom was the thin wiry one, he would nod, and Harry, who was large and grey like his overcoat, and usually had a stubble, cleared his throat and spat before he spoke. Chrissie once told me when I started working there that both of the men were in love with Isabella and that was why Eileen always looked so sad. And usually too Mrs O'Hare from Spinner Street would still be cleaning the brass handles and finger plates and waiting

like the others for the papers, so that she could read the horoscopes
before they got to the racing pages. On this particular day, however, the
brasses had been cleaned and the steps were empty. I tried to remember
what it had been like as a cinema, but couldn't. I only remember a film
I'd seen there once, in black and white: *A Town like Alice*.

Sharleen McCabe was unpacking the contents of a shopping bag on
to the counter. Chrissie was there with a cigarette in one hand flicking
the ash into the cap of her Yves St Laurent perfume spray and shaking
her head.

She looked up as I passed: "Miss Macken isn't in yet, so if you hurry
you'll be all right."

She was very tanned—because she took her holidays early—and her
pink lipstick matched her dress. Sharleen was gazing at her in admiration.

"Well?"

"I want three murders for my granny."

I left my coat in the office and hurried back to the counter as Miss
Macken arrived. I had carefully avoided looking at the office phone, but
I remember thinking: I wonder if he'll ring today?

Miss Macken swept past: "Good morning, ladies."

"Bang goes my chance of another fag before break," Chrissie said.

"I thought she was seeing a customer this morning."

Sharleen was standing at the desk reading the dust-covers of a pile of
books, and rejecting each in turn:

"There's only one here she hasn't read."

"How do you know?"

"Because her eyes is bad, I read them to her," Sharleen said.

"Well, there's not much point in me looking if you're the only one
who knows what she's read."

"You said children weren't allowed in there!" she said, pointing to the
auditorium.

"I've just given you permission," Chrissie said.

Sharleen started off at a run.

"Popular fiction's on the stage," Chrissie called after her. "Children!
When was that wee girl ever a child!"

"Finnula, the Irish section's like a holocaust! Would you like to do
something about it. And would you please deal with these orders."

"Yes, Miss Macken."

"Christine, someone's just offered us a consignment of Mills and Boon. Would you check with the public library that they haven't been stolen."

"Righto," sighed Chrissie.

It could have been any other day.

Senior: *Orangeism in Britain and Ireland;* Sibbett: *Orangeism in Ireland and Throughout the Empire.* Ironic. That's what he was looking for the first time he came in. It started with an enquiry for two volumes of Sibbett. Being the Irish specialist, I knew every book in the section. I hadn't seen it. I looked at the name and address again to make sure. And then I asked him to call. I said I thought I knew where I could get it and invited him to come and see the rest of our collection. A few days later, a young man, tall, fair, with very fine dark eyes, as if they'd been underlined with a grey pencil, appeared. He wasn't what I expected. He said it was the first time he'd been on the Falls Road. I took him round the section and he bought a great many things from us. He was surprised that such a valuable collection of Irish historical manuscripts was housed in a run-down cinema and he said he was glad he'd called. He told me that he was a historian writing a thesis on Gladstone and the Home Rule Bills, and that he lived in Belfast in the summer but was at Oxford University. He also left with me an extensive booklist and I promised to try to get the other books he wanted. He gave me his phone number, so that I could ring him and tell him when something he was looking for came in. It was Sibbett he was most anxious about. An antiquarian bookseller I knew of sent me the book two weeks later, in July. So I rang him and arranged to meet him with it at a café in town near the City Hall.

He was overjoyed and couldn't thank me enough, he said. And so it started. He told me that his father was a judge and that he lived with another student at Oxford called Susan. I told him that I lived with my grandmother until she died. And I also told him about my boyfriend Jack. So there didn't seem to be any danger.

We met twice a week in the café after that day; he explained something of his thesis to me: that the Protestant opposition to Gladstone and Home Rule was a rational one because Protestant industry at the time—

shipbuilding and linen—was dependent on British markets. He told me
how his grandfather had been an Ulster Volunteer. I told him of my
granny's stories of the Black and Tans, and of how she once met De
Valera on a Dublin train while he was on the run disguised as an old
woman. He laughed and said my grandmother had a great imagination.
He was fascinated that I knew so much history; he said he'd never heard
of Parnell until he went to Oxford. And he pronounced *Parnell* with a
silent *n*, so that it sounded strange.

By the end of the month, the café owner knew us by sight, and the
time came on one particular evening he arrived before me, and was sitting surrounded by books and papers, when the owner remarked, as the
bell inside the door rang:

"Ah. Here's your young lady now."

We blushed alarmingly. But it articulated the possibility I had constantly been pushing to the back of my mind. And I knew I felt a sharp
and secret thrill in that statement.

A few hours later, I stood on tiptoe to kiss him as I left for the bus—
nothing odd about that. I often kissed him on the side of the face as I
left. This time however I deliberately kissed his mouth, and somehow,
the kiss went on and on; he didn't let me go. When I stepped back on my
heels again I was reeling, and he had to catch me with his arm. I stood
there staring at him on the pavement. I stammered "goodbye" and
walked off hurriedly towards the bus stop. He stood on the street looking
after me—and I knew without turning round that he was smiling.

"Sharleen. *Murder in the Cathedral* is not exactly a murder story," Chrissie
was saying wearily.

"Well, why's it called that, then?"

"It's a play about—" Chrissie hesitated—"martyrdom!"

"Oh."

"This is just too, too grisly," Chrissie said, examining the covers. "Do
they always have to be murders? Would you not like a nice love story?"

"She doesn't like love stories," Sharleen said stubbornly. "She only
likes murders."

At that moment Miss Macken reappeared: "You two girls can go for
tea now—what is that smell?"

"I can't smell anything," Chrissie said.

"That's because you're wearing too much scent," Miss Macken said. She was moving perfunctorily to the biography shelving, and it wasn't until I followed her that I became aware of a very strong smell of methylated spirits. Harry was tucked behind a newspaper drinking himself silly. He appeared to be quite alone.

"Outside! Outside immediately!" Miss Macken roared. "Or I shall have you forcibly removed."

He rose up before us like a wounded bear whose sleep we had disturbed, and stood shaking his fist at her, and cursing all of us, Isabella included, he ran out.

"What's wrong with him?"

"Rejection. Isabella ran off with Tom this morning, and didn't tell him where she was going. He's only drowning his sorrows," Chrissie said. "Apparently they had a big win yesterday. Eileen told him they'd run off to get married. But they've only gone to Bangor for the day."

"How do you know this?"

"Eileen told Mrs O'Hare and she told me."

"What kind of supervision is it when you two let that man drink in here with that child wandering around?" Miss Macken said, coming back from seeing Harry off the premises.

We both apologized and went up for tea.

There was little on the Falls Road that Mrs O'Hare didn't know about. As she made her way up and down the road in the mornings on her way to work she would call in and out of the shops, the library, the hospital, until a whole range of people I had never met would enter my life in our tea room by eleven o'clock. I knew that Mr Quincey, a Protestant, from the library, had met his second wife while burying his first at the City Cemetery one Saturday morning. I knew that Mr Downey, the gate-housekeeper at the hospital, had problems with his eldest daughter and didn't like her husband, and I was equally sure that thanks to Mrs O'Hare every detail of Chrissie's emotional entanglements were known by every ambulance driver at the Royal. As a result, I was very careful to say as little as possible in front of her. She didn't actually like me. It was Chrissie she bought buns for at tea time.

"Oh here! You'll never guess what Mrs McGlinchy at the bakery told me—" she was pouring tea into cups, but her eyes were on us. "Wait till you hear—" she looked down in time to see the tea pouring over the sides of the cup. She put the teapot down heavily on the table and continued: "Quincey's being transferred to Ballymacarrett when the library's reopened."

"Och, you don't say?"

"It's the new boss at Central—that Englishwoman. It's after the bomb."

"But sure that was when everybody'd gone home."

"I know but it's security, you know! She doesn't want any more staff crossing the peace line at night. Not after that young—but wait till you hear—he won't go!"

"Good for him."

"He says he's been on the Falls for forty years and if they transfer him now they might as well throw the keys of the library into the Republican Press Centre and the keys of the Royal Victoria Hospital in after them."

"He's quite right. It's ghettoization."

"Yes, but it's inevitable," I said.

"It's not inevitable, it's deliberate," said Chrissie. "It's exactly what the crowd want."

"Who?"

"The Provos. They want a ghetto: the next thing they'll be issuing us with passes to come and go."

"Security works both ways."

"You're telling me."

After that Chrissie left us to go down the yard to renew her suntan. Mrs O'Hare watched her from the window.

"She'd find the sun anywhere, that one." She turned from the window. "Don't take what she says too much to heart. She's Jewish, you know. She doesn't understand."

I was glad when she went. She always felt a bit constrained with me. Because I didn't talk about my love life, as she called it, like Chrissie. But then I couldn't. I never really talked at all, to any of them.

The room overlooked the rooftops and back yards of West Belfast.

Gibson, Granville, Garnet, Grosvenor, Theodore, Cape, Kasmir.

Alone again, I found myself thinking about the last time I had seen Jack. It was a long time ago: he was sitting at the end of the table. When things are not going well my emotions start playing truant. I wasn't surprised when he said:

"I've got an invitation to go to the States for six months."

I was buttering my toast at the time and didn't look up.

"I'm afraid I'm rather ambivalent about this relationship."

I started battering the top of my eggshell with a spoon.

"Finn! Are you listening?"

I nodded and asked: "When do you go?"

"Four weeks from now."

I knew the American trip was coming up.

"Very well. I'll move out until you've gone."

I finished breakfast and we spoke not another word until he dropped me at the steps of the bookshop.

"Finn, for God's sake! Get yourself a flat somewhere out of it! I don't imagine I'll be coming back." He said: "If you need any money, write to me."

I slammed the car door. Jack was always extremely practical: if you killed someone he would inform the police, get you legal aid, make arrangements for moving the body, he'd even clear up the mess if there was any—but he would never, never ask you why you did it. I'd thrown milk all over him once, some of it went on the floors and walls, and then I ran out of the house. When I came back he'd changed his clothes and mopped up the floor. Another time I'd smashed all the dinner dishes against the kitchen wall and locked myself in the bathroom, when I came out he had swept up all the plates and asked me if I wanted a cup of tea. He was a very good journalist, I think, but somehow I never talked to him about anything important.

Because Mrs Cooper from Milan Street had been caught trying to walk out with sixteen stolen romances in a shopping bag and had thrown herself on the floor as if having a heart attack, saying: "Oh holy Jay! Don't call the police. Oh holy Jay, my heart," Chrissie forgot to tell me about the phone call until nearly twelve o'clock.

"Oh, a customer rang, he wanted to talk to you about a book he said he was after. Sibbett. That was it. You were still at tea." She said, "I told him we were open to nine tonight and that you'd be here all day."

For three weeks he hadn't rung. I only had to pick up the phone and ring him as I'd done on other occasions. But this time I hoped he would contact me first.

"Is something wrong?" Chrissie said.

"I have to make a phone call."

After that first kiss on the street, the next time we met I took him to the house, about ten minutes' walk from the park.

"When did you say your granny died?" he asked, looking with surprise around the room.

"Oh, ages ago. I'm not very good at dates."

"Well, you don't appear to have changed much since. It's as if an old lady still lived here."

He found the relics, the Sacred Heart pictures and the water font strange. "You really ought to dust in here occasionally," he said, laughing. "What else do you do apart from work in the bookshop?"

"I read, watch television. Oh, and I see Jack," I said quickly, so as not to alarm him.

"Good Lord. Would you look at that web; it looks like it's been there for donkeys!"

A large web attaching itself in the greater part to the geraniums in the window had spread across a pile of books and ended up clinging heavily to the lace curtains.

"Yes. I like spiders," I said. "My granny used to say that a spider's web was a good omen. It means we're safe from the soldiers!"

"It just means that you never open the curtains!" he said, laughing. Still wandering round the small room he asked: "Who is that lady? Is she your grandmother?"

"No. That's the Countess Markievicz."

"I suppose your granny met her on a train in disguise—as an old man."

"No. But she did visit her in prison."

He shook his head. "The trouble with you—" he began, then suddenly he had a very kind look in his eyes. "You're improbable. No one would ever believe me." He stopped, and began again. "Sometimes I think—" he tapped me on the nose—"you live in a dream, Finn."

And then he kissed me, and held me; he only complained that I was too quiet.

It was nine thirty when I left the building and shut it up for the night: Miss Macken had offered to drop me home as she was leaving, but I said I'd prefer to walk. There were no buses on the road after nine because a few nights before a group of youths had stoned a bus passing Divis flats, and the bus driver was hurt. The whole day was a torment to me after that phone call and I wanted to think and walk.

When I got to the park I was so giddy that I didn't care whether he came or not. My stomach was in a knot—and I realized it was because I hadn't eaten all day. The summer was nearly over—I only knew that soon this too would be over. I had kept my feelings under control so well—I was always very good at that, contained, very contained—so well, that I thought if he even touched me I'd tell him—Oh run! Run for your life from me! At least I didn't tell him that I loved him or anything like that. Was it something to be glad about? And suddenly there were footsteps running behind me. I always listened for footsteps. I'd walked all through those streets at night but I had never been afraid until that moment.

I suddenly started to run when a voice called out:

"Finn! Wait!" It was his voice.

I stopped dead, and turned.

We stood by the grass verge.

"Why didn't you ring me?" I asked, listlessly, my head down in case he saw my eyes.

"Because I didn't think it was fair to you."

"Fair?"

"Because, well—"

"Well?"

"I'm in England and you're here. It's not very satisfactory."

"I see."

"Look, there's something I should tell you. It's—Susan's been staying with us for the past three weeks."

"I see."

I couldn't possibly object since we were both supposed to have other lovers, there was no possibility of either of us complaining.

"But we could go to your place now if you like."

I was weakening. He stooped to kiss me and the whole business began as it had started. He kissed me and I kissed him and it went on and on.

"I was just getting over you," I said, standing up.

"I didn't know there was anything to get over. You're very good at saying nothing."

And before I could stop myself I was saying: "I think I've fallen in love with you."

He dropped his head and hardly dared look at me—he looked so pained—and more than anything I regretted that statement.

"You never told me that before," he said.

"I always felt constrained."

He began very slowly: "Look, there is something I have to say now. I'm getting married at the end of the summer." And more quickly. "But I can't give you up. I want to go on seeing you. Oh don't go! Please listen!"

It was very cold in the park. I had a piercing pain in my ear because of the wind. A tricolour hung at a jaunty angle from the top of the pensioner's bungalow, placed there by some lads. The army would take it down tomorrow in the morning. The swings, the trees and grass banks looked as thoroughly careworn as the surrounding streets.

Lincoln, Leeson, Marchioness and Mary, Slate, Sorella and Ward.

I used to name them in a skipping song.

The park had been my playplace as a child, I used to go there in the mornings and wait for someone to lead me across the road, to the first gate. Sometimes a passer-by would stop and take my hand, but most times the younger brother of the family who owned the bacon shop would cross with me.

"No road sense!" my grandmother used to say. "None at all."

In the afternoon he would come back for me. And I remember—

"Finn, are you listening? You mustn't stop talking to me, we could still be friends. I love being with you—Finn!"

I remember standing in the sawdust-filled shop waiting for him to finish his task—the smooth hiss of the slicing machine and the thin strips of bacon falling on the greaseproof paper.

I began to walk away.

"Finn. I do love you." He said it for the first time.

I pulled up the collar of my coat and walked home without looking back.

It should have ended before I was so overcome with him I wept. And he said: "What's wrong?" and took me and held me again.

It should have ended before he said: "Your soul has just smiled in your eyes at me—I've never seen it there before."

Before, it should have ended before. He was my last link with life and what a way to find him. I closed my eyes and tried to forget, all vision gone, only sound left: the night noises came.

The raucous laughter of late-night walkers; the huddle of tomcats on the backyard wall; someone somewhere is scraping a metal dustbin across a concrete yard; and far off in the distance a car screeches to a halt: a lone dog barks at an unseen presence, the night walkers pause in their walk past—the entry. Whose is the face at the empty window?— the shadows cast on the entry wall—the shape in the darkened door- way—the steps on the broken path—who pulled that curtain open quickly—and let it drop?

I woke with a start and the sound of brakes screeching in my ears—as if the screech had taken on a human voice and called my name in anguish: Finn! But when I listened, there was nothing. Only the sound of the night bells from St. Paul's tolling in the distance.

I stayed awake until daybreak and with the light found some peace from dreams. At eight o'clock I went out. Every day of summer had been going on around me, seen and unseen, I had drifted through those days like one possessed.

Strange how quickly we are reassured by ordinariness: Isabella and Tom, Harry and Eileen, waiting on the steps. And Mrs O'Hare at the counter with her polishing cloth, and Miss Macken discussing her holi- day plans with Chrissie. Externally, at least, it could have been the same as the day before, yesterday—the day before I left him in the park. But I saw it differently. I saw it in a haze, and it didn't seem to have anything to do with me.

"The body was discovered by bin-men early this morning," Miss Macken said. "He was dumped in an entry."

"Oh, Finn, it's awful news," said Chrissie, turning.

"It's the last straw as far as I am concerned," Miss Macken said.

"Mr Downey said it's the one thing that turned him—he'll not be back to the Royal after this."

"We knew him," Chrissie said.

"Who?"

"That young man. The one who looked like a girl."

"The police think he was coming from the Falls Road," Miss Macken said.

"They said it was because he was a judge's son," said Chrissie.

"The theory is," said Miss Macken, "that he was lured there by a woman. I expect they'll be coming to talk to us."

"Aye, they're all over the road this morning," said Mrs O'Hare.

At lunch time they came.

"Miss McQuillen, I wonder?"

A noisy row between Isabella and Eileen distracted me—Eileen was insisting that Isabella owed her five pounds.

"Miss McQuillen, I wonder if you wouldn't mind answering a few questions?"

"How well did you know . . . ?"

"When did you last see him?"

"What time did you leave him?"

"What exactly did he say?"

"Have you any connection with . . . ?"

Osman, Serbia, Sultan, Raglan, Bosnia, Belgrade, Rumania, Sebastopol.

The names roll off my tongue like a litany.

"Has that something to do with Gladstone's foreign policy?" he used to laugh and ask.

"No. Those are the streets of West Belfast."

Alma, Omar, Conway and Dunlewey, Dunville, Lady and McDonnell.

Pray for us. (I used to say, just to please my grandmother.) Now and at the hour.

At three o'clock in the afternoon of the previous day, a man I knew came into the bookshop. I put the book he was selling on the counter in front of me and began to check the pages. It was so still you could hear the pages turn: "I think I can get him to the park," I said.

Eileen had Isabella by the hair and she stopped. The policeman who was writing—stopped.

Miss Macken was at the counter with Chrissie, she was frowning—she looked over at me, and stopped. Chrissie suddenly turned and looked in my direction. No one spoke. We walked through the door on to the street.

Still no one spoke.

Mrs O'Hare was coming along the road from the bread shop, she raised her hand to wave and then stopped.

Harry had just tumbled out of the bookies followed by Tom. They were laughing. And they stopped.

We passed the block where the babyclothes shop had been, and at the other end the undertaker's: everything from birth to death on that road. Once. But gone now—just stumps where the buildings used to be—stumps like tombstones.

"Jesus. That was a thump in the stomach if ever I felt one," one policeman said to the other.

Already they were talking as if I didn't exist.

There were four or five people in the interview room.

A policewoman stood against the wall. The muscles in my face twitched. I put up my hand to stop it.

"Why did you pick him?"

"I didn't pick him. He was chosen. It was his father they were after. He's a judge."

"They?"

"I. I recognized the address when he wrote to me. Then he walked in."

"Who are the others? What are their names?"

"Abyssinia, Alma, Balaclava, Balkan."

"How did you become involved?"

"It goes back a long way."

"Miss McQuillen. You have a captive audience!"

"On the fourteenth of August 1969 I was escorting an English journalist through the Falls: his name was Jack McHenry."

"How did you meet him?"

"I am coming to that. I met him on the previous night, the thirteenth; there was a meeting outside Divis flats to protest about the police in the Bogside. The meeting took a petition to Springfield Road police station. But the police refused to open the door. Part of the crowd broke away and marched back down to Divis to Hastings Street police station and began throwing stones. There was trouble on the road all night because of roaming gangs. They stoned or petrol bombed a car with two fire chiefs in it and burned down a Protestant showroom at the bottom of Conway Street. I actually tried to stop it happening. He was there, at Balaclava Street, when it happened. He stopped me and asked if I'd show him around the Falls. He felt uneasy, being an Englishman, and he didn't know his way around without a map. I said I'd be happy to."

"Were you a member of an illegal organization?"

"What organization? There were half a dozen guns in the Falls in '69 and a lot of old men who couldn't even deliver the *United Irishman* on time. And the women's section had been disbanded during the previous year because there was nothing for them to do but run around after the men and make tea for the Ceilies. He asked me the same question that night, and I told him truthfully that I was not—then.

"On the evening of the fourteenth we walked up the Falls Road, it was early, we had been walking round all day, we were on our way back to his hotel—the Grand Central in Royal Avenue—he wanted to phone his editor and give an early report about events on the road. As we walked up the Falls from Divis towards Leeson Street, we passed a group of children in pyjamas going from Dover Street towards the flats. Further up the road at Conway Street a neighbour of ours was crossing the road to Balaclava Street with his children; he said he was taking them to Sultan Street Hall for the night. Everything seemed quiet. We walked on down Leeson Street and into town through the Grosvenor Road: the town centre was quiet too. He phoned his paper and then took me to dinner to a Chinese restaurant across the road from the hotel. I remember it because there was a false ceiling in the restaurant, like a sky with fake star constellations. We sat in a velvet alcove and there were roses on the table. After dinner we went to his hotel and went to bed. At five o'clock in the morning the phone rang. I thought it was an alarm call he'd placed. He slammed down the phone and jumped up and shouted at me: 'Get up quickly. All hell's broken loose in the Falls!'

"We walked quickly to the bottom of Castle Street and began to walk hurriedly up the road. At Divis Street I noticed that five or six shops around me had been destroyed by fire. At Divis flats a group of men stood, it was light by this time. When they heard that Jack was a journalist they began telling him about the firing. It had been going on all night, they said, and several people were dead, including a child in the flats. They took him to see the bullet holes in the walls. The child was in a cot at the time. And the walls were thin. I left him there at Divis and hurried up the road to Conway Street. There was a large crowd there as well, my own people. I looked up the street to the top. There was another crowd at the junction of Ashmore Street—this crowd was from the Shankill—they were setting fire to a bar at the corner and looting it. Then some of the men began running down the street and breaking windows of the houses in Conway Street. They used brush handles. At the same time as the bar was burning, a number of the houses at the top of the street also caught fire in Conway Street. The crowd were throwing petrol bombs in after they broke the windows. I began to run up towards the fire. Several of the crowd also started running with me.

"Then I noticed for the first time, because my attention had been fixed on the burning houses, that two turreted police vehicles were moving slowly down the street on either side. Somebody shouted: 'The gun turrets are pointed towards us!' And everybody ran back. I didn't. I was left standing in the middle of the street, when a policeman, standing in a doorway, called to me: 'Get back! Get out of here before you get hurt.'

"The vehicles were moving slowly down Conway Street towards the Falls Road with the crowd behind them, burning houses as they went. I ran into the top of Balaclava Street at the bottom of Conway Street where our crowd were. A man started shouting at the top of his voice: 'They're going to fire. They're going to fire on us!'

"And our crowd ran off down the street again.

"A woman called to me from an upstairs window: 'Get out of the mouth of the street.' Something like that.

"I shouted: 'But the people! The people in the houses!'

"A man ran out and dragged me into a doorway. 'They're empty!' he said. 'They got out last night!' Then we both ran down to the bottom of

Balaclava Street and turned the corner into Raglan Street. If he hadn't been holding me by the arm then that was the moment when I would have run back up towards the fires."

"Why did you want to do that? Why did you want to run back into Conway Street?"

"My grandmother lived there—near the top. He took me to Sultan Street refugee centre. 'She's looking for her granny,' he told a girl with a St John Ambulance armband on. She was a form below me at school. My grandmother wasn't there. The girl told me not to worry because everyone had got out of Conway Street. But I didn't believe her. An ambulance from the Royal arrived to take some of the wounded to hospital. She put me in the ambulance as well. It was the only transport on the road other than police vehicles. 'Go to the hospital and ask for her there,' she said.

"It was eight o'clock in the morning when I found her sleeping in a quiet room at the Royal. The nurse said she was tired, suffering from shock and a few cuts from flying glass. I stayed with her most of the day. I don't remember that she spoke to me. And then about six I had a cup of tea and wandered on to the road up towards the park. Jack McHenry was there, writing it all down: 'It's all over,' he said. 'The Army are here.' We both looked down the Falls, there were several mills that I could see burning: the Spinning Mill and the Great Northern, and the British Army were marching in formation down the Falls Road. After that I turned and walked along the Grosvenor Road into town and spent the night with him at his hotel. There was nowhere else for me to go."

I was suddenly very tired; more tired than on the day I sat in her room watching her sleep; more tired than on the day Jack left; infinitely more tired than I'd ever been in my life. I waited for someone else to speak. The room was warm and heavy and full of smoke. They waited. So I went on.

"Up until I met Jack McHenry I'd been screwing around like there was no tomorrow. I only went with him because there was no one else left. He stayed in Belfast because it was news. I never went back to school again. I had six O-levels and nothing else."

"Is that when you got involved?"

"No, not immediately. My first reaction was to get the hell out of it. It wasn't until the summer of '71 that I found myself on the Falls Road again. I got a job in the new second-hand bookshop where I now work. Or did. One day a man came in looking for something: 'Don't I know you?' he said. He had been a neighbour of ours at one time. 'I carried your granny out of Conway Street.' He told me that at about eleven o'clock on the night of August fourteenth, there were two families trapped at the top of Conway Street. One of them, a family of eight, was escorted out of their house by a policeman and this man. Bottles and stones were thrown at them from a crowd at the top of the street. The policeman was cut on the head as he took the children out. The other family, a woman, with her two teenage daughters, refused to leave her house because of her furniture. Eventually they were forced to run down the back entry into David Street to escape. It was she who told him that Mrs McQuillen was still in the house. He went back up the street on his own this time. Because the lights in our house were out he hadn't realized there was anyone there. He got scared at the size of the crowd ahead and was going to run back when he heard her call out: 'Finn! Finn!' He carried her down Conway Street running all the way. He asked me how she was keeping these days. I told him that she had recently died. Her heart gave up. She always had a weak heart.

"A few weeks later Jack took me on holiday to Greece with him. I don't really think he wanted me to go with him, he took me out of guilt. I'd rather forced the situation on him. We were sitting at a harbour café one afternoon, he was very moody and I'd had a tantrum because I found out about his latest girlfriend. I got up and walked away from him along the harbour front. I remember passing a man reading a newspaper at another café table, a few hundred yards along the quay. I saw a headline that made me turn back.

"'The Army have introduced internment in Belfast,' I said.

"We went home a few days later and I walked into a house in Andersonstown of a man I knew: 'Is there anything for me to do?' I said. And that was how I become involved."

"And the man's name?"

"You already know his name. He was arrested by the Army at the beginning of the summer. I was coming up the street by the park at the time, when he jumped out of an Army Saracen and ran towards me. A soldier called out to him to stop, but he ran on. He was shot in the back. He was a well-known member of the Provisional IRA on the run. I was

on my way to see him. His father was the man who carried my grandmother out of Conway Street. He used to own a bacon shop."

"Did Jack McHenry know of your involvement?"

"No. He didn't know what was happening to me. Eventually we
drifted apart. He made me feel that in some way I had disappointed
him."

"What sort of operations were you involved in?"

"My first job was during internment. Someone would come into the
shop, the paymaster, he gave me money to deliver once a week to the
wives of the men interned. The women would then come into the shop
to collect it. It meant that nobody called at their houses, which were
being watched. These were the old Republicans. The real movement
was reforming in Andersonstown."

"And the names? The names of the people involved?"

"There are no names. Only places."

"Perhaps you'll tell us the names later."

When they left me alone in the room I began to remember a dream I'd
had towards the end of the time I was living with Jack. I slept very badly
then, I never knew whether I was asleep or awake. One night it seemed
to me that I was sitting up in bed with him. I was smoking, he was writing something, when an old woman whom I didn't recognize came
towards me with her hands outstretched. I was horrified; I didn't know
where she came from or how she got into our bedroom. I tried to make
Jack see her but he couldn't. She just kept coming towards me. I had my
back against the headboard of the bed and tried to fight her off. She
grasped my hand and kept pulling me from the bed. She had very strong
hands, like a man's, and she pulled and pulled and I struggled to release
my hands. I called out for help of every sort, from God, from Jack. But
she would not let me go and I could not get my hands free. The struggle
between us was so furious that it woke Jack. I realized then that I was
dreaming. He put his hands on me to steady me: "You're having a fit.
You're having a fit!" he kept saying. I still had my eyes closed even
though I knew I was awake. I asked him not to let me see him. Until it
had passed. I began to be terribly afraid, and when I was sure it had
passed, I had to ask him to take me to the toilet. He never asked any
questions but did exactly what I asked. He took me by the hand and led

me to the bathroom, where he waited with me. After that he took me back to bed again. As we passed the mirror on the bedroom door I asked him not to let me see it. The room was full of mirrors, he went round covering them all up. Then he got into bed and took my hand again.

"Now please don't let me go," I said. "Whatever happens don't let go of my hand."

"I promise you. I won't," he said.

But I knew that he was frightened.

I closed my eyes and the old woman came towards me again. It was my grandmother; she was walking. I didn't recognize her the first time because—she had been in a wheelchair all her life.

She reached out and caught my hands again and the struggle between us began: she pulled and I held on. She pulled and I still held on.

"Come back!" Jack said. "Wherever you are, come back!"

She pulled with great force.

"Let go of me!" I cried.

Jack let go of my hand.

The policewoman who had been standing silently against the wall all the time stepped forward quickly. When I woke I was lying on the floor. There were several people in the room, and a doctor.

"Are you sure you're fit to continue?"

"Yes."

"What about the names?"

"My father and grandmother didn't speak for years: because he married my mother. I used to go and visit him. One night, as I was getting ready to go there, I must have been about seven or eight at the time, my grandmother said, 'Get your father something for his birthday for me'—she handed me three shillings—'but you don't have to tell him it's from me. Get him something for his cough.'

"At the end of Norfolk Street was a sweet shop. I bought a tin of barley sugar. The tin was tartan: red and blue and green and black. They wrapped it in a twist of brown paper. I gave it to my mother when I arrived. 'It's for my Daddy for his birthday in the morning.'

"'From whom?'

"'From me.'

"'Can I look?'

"'Yes.'

"She opened the paper: 'Why it's beautiful,' she said. I remember her excitement over it. 'He'll be so pleased.' She seemed very happy. I remember that. Because she was never very happy again. He died of consumption before his next birthday."

"Why did you live with your grandmother?"

"Because our house was too small."

"But the names? The names of the people in your organization?"

"Conway, Cupar, David, Percy, Dover and Divis. Mary, Merrion, Milan, McDonnell, Osman, Raglan, Ross, Rumania, Serbia, Slate, Sorella, Sulktan, Theodore, Varna and Ward Street."

When I finished they had gone out of the room again. Only the policewoman remained. It is not the people but the streets I name.

The door opened again.

"There's someone to see you," they said.

Jack stood before me.

"In God's name, Finn. How and why?"

He wasn't supposed to ask that question. He shook his head and sighed: "I nearly married you."

Let's just say it was historical.

"I ask myself over and over what kind of woman are you, and I have to remind myself that I knew you, or thought I knew you, and that I loved you once."

Once, once upon a time.

"Anything is better than what you did, Finn. Anything! A bomb in a pub I could understand—not forgive, just understand—because of the arbitrariness of it. But—you caused the death of someone you had grown to know!"

I could not save him. I could only give him time.

"You should never have let me go!" I said, for the first time in ten years.

He looked puzzled: "But you weren't happy with me. You didn't seem very happy."

He stood watching for a minute and said: "Where are you, Finn? Where are you?"

The door closed. An endless vista of solitude before me, of sleeping and waking alone in the dark—in the corner a spider was spinning a new web. I watched him move from angle to angle. An endless confinement before me and all too soon a slow gnawing hunger inside for something—I watched him weave the angles of his world in the space of the corner.

Once more they came back for the names, and I began: "Abyssinia, Alma, Balaclava, Balkan, Belgrade, Bosnia," naming the names: empty and broken and beaten places. I know no others.

Gone and going all the time.

Redevelopment. Nothing more dramatic than that; the planners are our bombers now. There is no heart in the Falls these days.

"But the names? The names of the people who murdered him? The others?"

"I know no others."

The gradual and deliberate processes weave their way in the dark corners of all our rooms, and when the finger is pointed, the hand turned, the face at the end of the finger is my face, the hand at the end of the arm that points is my hand, and the only account I can give is this: that if I lived for ever I could not tell: I could only glimpse what fatal visions stir that web's dark pattern, I do not know their names. I only know for certain what my part was, that even on the eve, on such a day, I took him there.

III

Telling

Telling

A very good Irish writer was giving a workshop to a group of possibly fledging writers, all women. He was one of the best, there are twelve bests. "Lucky," M. thought, "four of those twelve are women. Unlucky (because at that time she thought that it was mere luck and not subterfuge which decided these matters), no one else knew that four of the twelve are women." She was glad to be in the same room as this man, not because she thought that she could learn anything from him, and this, not because he had nothing to teach, but because she didn't want to learn what he knew, she was on a slip road from that sort of thing, a hill that would get a better view. Still, she was glad, because his act of speaking to them, even if it was an uncomfortable faraway act, showed a humility that surprised her in one so great.

There were eight others in the room besides M., one who hoped to write a novel, three short story people, already in love with the hurtful intimacy of that form, two possible poets, one poet and one who wished to be a playwright, she hadn't a hope, that is if getting a play performed is an essential part of being a playwright. There may have been others too but M. can't remember them. One of the short story devotees was a lesbian, an honest carefree person, who saw things that the others couldn't hear, and who ran a Women's Disco every Thursday night. The great writer spent a lot of time asking her questions, she answered as if she knew what he was up to. He didn't pass too much remarks on M.

because her desired place of parking made her virtually invisible. The poets had their work cut out for them, even paying attention was hard, and who knew yet if the novelist was prepared to make her task a way of life. After lunch the sun shone, in that contradictory way that it suddenly can in Ireland, and because they were already tired from trying to justify their existences to each other and themselves over lunch, a lethargy descended upon them, an itchiness could be noticed in some legs.

Then the writer told them a story. And told them how to write it. A man and woman in the west of Ireland were married. They had two children. The man was rarely home, because in the summer he spent his time with tourists, showing them this and that, being a great fellow altogether. The tourists thought that he was the salt of the earth and would remember him at odd moments in the middle of England or on an autobahn, for a month or so after their holidays. In the winter he did a little work on his small raggedy farm, but spent most of his time in the pub where things were more jovial than at home. It was dark in the pub, but it was dark everywhere else too. The closing lights and the Guinness made him sullen and certainly going home made him even crosser. What happened behind the door when he closed it after him each night no one knew, because although the roads around were littered with signs proclaiming that this was a Neighbourhood Watch area, this did not mean that people watched their neighbours. If a stranger came and battered a woman that would be serious, but what a local did in his own house was his own business. And something untoward was going on.

The woman got a part-time job in the post office and the contact with every single person lit her up inside, making her remember a little of what used to be her hopes. The post office was the best place, because here she saw the steady saving in small books and how easy it was to hand over a few pounds, how worth it it was to see the numbers climbing up and up. From the very first weeks she put part of her wages into a Savings Account, from the first week was the best way, there would be no great flourish of buying followed by a suspicious drop. She could have been an adviser to bank robbers. As her children grew, fed by the pourings of an invisible, but still active, umbilical cord, so too did her nest egg. Two tourist summers and three unbearable winters later the money was tangible, not much, but it would pay rent for some shabby aching flat that would have three inadequate single beds in it, one for herself and one each for her children when they would visit. Yes visit, because she couldn't afford to take them away. Yet.

When the spring coquetted in she left. Her children too. For the moment. Just until she could afford to move them in with her into a place that would not lose out so badly in comparison to their own bungalow. Her first name was Hope. She left her children too, because what was happening in the hallway of her home with the lights out, was truly untoward, and the light was kept broken in there all the time.

In a matter of months the husband allowed her back into the house in the afternoons. That way she could be there when the children came home from school. And maybe she'd put on a bit of tea while she was there, doing nothing. The joy of seeing them each evening burst out of her spring like lava, making her skin flushed and her hair gleaming. Of course she saw them every morning, she turned up outside the school with extra foosies for their lunch, it was easy, the school only being one mile off the road that led from the flat to the post office. Her savings should have been dwindling fast but somehow she managed to put a finger in the dyke. Yet it would never be enough. And the law was not on her side.

Surprise was the first reaction when a legacy arrived from a cold, tight aunt, followed by the appropriate reaction, an overwhelming, blushing feeling of being a winner, a warmth in the stomach as sure as if coming from an eternal flame. The woman began to lay her plans carefully, secretly, she spoke to her children with a boiling lightness in her voice. Her husband must not know.

But the town was small and word of her luck leaked out. Unknown to her, her husband did find out. It was on a Thursday, this in what was to be her last week, that she was baking bread in the bungalow, her back to the door, answering homework questions on addition, subtraction and wars, when her husband came in. He ordered the children to leave and because the children do not always know how to do the right thing, they did. She was putting raisins in the brown bread, she turned to face him, clenching her hands. "If you go out that door again," he said, "I'll kill you." The woman knew that he meant it. He must not have expected disobedience because as she moved to the door he thought that she was only changing her place in the room. But she bolted out the door, making a run for it like a woman possessed. He got his gun, the one he used when shooting with tourists, took aim and shot her once through the back of the head. When people reached her the wheaten meal and the raisins were still in her hands.

The great writer swallowed. "It's a true story," he said, "and you can use it. I don't want it. Your story is in the wheaten meal and raisins." M. and the rest stared at him, a kind of communal choking smothering their voices. Their rage was too thick to be spread out for examination. "End of session," he said breezily, leaving the room, already oblivious of all those pairs of eyes.

The story of course was not in the raisins, it was in him telling the tale to a room full of women and thinking that it was. Or more than the story, the wonder is that a few of them, the poets perhaps, didn't cry, or that one of them, the novelist maybe, didn't attack him with a brush that the hopeful playwright, being already used to the notion of props, would have just happened to have had handy. But neither is that the story. It is rather what the fledging writers thought of what the great man said. But no, it may not be that either, it may be instead what you think of what they thought of what he thought.

E M M A   D O N O G H U E

Seven Pictures Not Taken

1: Rhubarb

Climbing up the slope behind your house, returning from the river you've been showing me before your fortieth birthday party begins, digging our feet into the unashamed grassy breast of what you call your back yard (though the word yard to me means a hard paved thing), our eyes meet momentarily (by that I mean for a moment, you would mean in a moment's time). Neither of us is English, and our Englishes will always be a word or two apart. Our bodies talk better than our minds, even that first day, when our eyes are spread wide by sunlight.

I like the look of the few downy whiskers on your chin. We are standing beside the hugely overgrown rhubarb bush, some sticks as tall as us, gone black with age, others still new and pink. We both call it a rhubarb bush; good to know we can agree on something.

Though I have only just met you, I want to give you something, to make you remember me. It all begins with vanity, not generosity.

Later you will tell me that you remembered me making rhubarb crumble for your guests. But if you had not met me again, I am sure you would have forgotten my face in a week, my rhubarb crumble in another. It is only in retrospect that strangers seem instantly memorable. I know I would have remembered you, but mostly because my eyes tend to look for pictures to remember. Maybe I invented you, summoned you up as a holiday vision.

All I know is that for a week after your party I had scalding dreams of lying down together on that particular spot, that curve of sundried grass behind your house. The vertical hold becomes a horizontal flow. So by the time you actually laid hands on me, I had drawn out the whole story already.

2: River

This picture is about light on wet skin. I am watching you but the picture is of both of us. Women troop down to the water in the late afternoon; the midges hover, aroused by our heat. I pull black silk up and over my head, step through satin mud and slide in. Under the meniscus I lose my shyness. I watch you as I tread water, kicking off the years. I am a newborn baby in the slip of hills.

How we met was a web of chance rivers, meandering across three continents. If A had not bumped into B in the hottest country she'd ever been in, after (or was it before?) meeting you on the west coast, then driving south with you this summer she would never have introduced you to B's ex-lover C, who happened to bring me (who had made friends with B and C half a world away) to your birthday party. It scares me that if any one of us had stepped out of any one of those streams, I would never have met you, would never even have known there was a you to meet, but I suppose I have to lie back in the current of coincidence, trusting that it has been shaped for us just as the river has been carved through the mountains to reach your house so that I can bathe in it, treading water, looking up at you. Afterwards, as we all dry ourselves on the bank, you tell me that you only own this bit of river to midstream, which must confuse it.

3: Room

The next picture is taken in the dark. No dark is ever entire, of course; there is always enough light to begin to find out shapes. We are practically strangers, at this time of sharing a bed in our mutual friend's mother's house. You could always sleep in the other room, but as I have mentioned to you in passing, the bed there is very hard; we are in agreement that it would not be good for your bad back. This is true but also a barefaced lie. In the dark you ask me if I want to cuddle up, and I do.

In this picture, I am lying awake, marvelling at your strange weight against me, much too aware of you to move. I can't catch a breath; my arm is numb; my arthritic hip is screaming to shift position. I inch it backwards. I do not want to disturb you in case you'll twist away, with the selfishness of the half-awake. I want you to keep resting deeply, coiled around me. I decide to find out how little breath I can manage on, how long my muscles will obey me. I am glad to offer you my discomfort, even if you will never know it.

This room is so dark, fifty miles from a city; no way could a picture of this be taken with an ordinary camera. For all I know this is the only night I will ever spend in your arms.

4: Forest

We are twenty years past wasting time.

The ferns are sharp under the purple cloak I have spread for us, Walter Raleigh style. Their dry fingers idly scratch our hips. Sounds of brass and woodwind leak through the woods from the concert we are missing. Sun slithers through the lattice of maples to lie across your back. My lips, drawn across your shoulder bone, find invisible fur. Desire has twitched and bitten and marked us all day as the brazen mosquitoes do now, here on the forest floor where we are lying.

Seen from high above in the canopy of leaves, we must be pale as mushrooms that have pushed up overnight. Two women, two dark heads, two dark triangles, a maze of limbs arranged by the geometry of pleasure. We press close, my hipbone wedded to your thighs, my breast quilting your ribs, to leave as little body exposed to the insects as we can.

It is hot and uncomfortable and exactly where I want to be. At certain moments what your body is doing to mine wipes away all awareness of the insect bites, the concert, the time, the other women in our pasts and futures, the other days in our lives, all other sights there are to be seen.

5: Body

It is what you call fall, in this picture, and I persist in calling autumn, even though I'm back on your territory again. The patches on your back yard where my ecstatic hands ripped out grass in the summer are covered with leaves now.

We are sitting on your sofa looking through your photo albums in chronological order. You find it hard to believe that I am truly interested enough to turn every page. But I want the whole picture, the full hand of decades. I interrogate you through baby snaps, family crises, teenage hairstyles. I pause on one of you in the first week of your uniform, grinning with an innocent gun; it chills me. You remark that you're glad they kicked you out for being a pervert; you're finally glad. You repeat for me a line from a folk song:

> I will not use my body as a weapon of war
> That's not what any body's for.

I look at the photograph to memorize it. I wonder what this body in the albums, that has come through so many changes in front of my browsing eyes, is for. I'm going too fast. I regret, absurdly, that I was not here to see you grow up. I am having to learn it all in a weekend with the leaves dancing by the window, mocking me with their message of phoenix fire. We have so little time, the most careful picture is a snapshot.

6: Real

The last day of that five-day weekend, I say: I don't want to get in the way of your real life.

Life doesn't get any more real than this, you tell me.

I am momentarily content. But neither of us is sure whether any of this is happening. It seems too good to be actual. Too sure, too easy and unmixed, as bliss goes, to be anything other than some kind of trip.

Down by the river you take out your camera. We sit on rocks and lean over the water, taking turns to pose, laughing at the absurdity of our ambition to capture the moment.

But wouldn't it be worse if photos were better than the real thing? Sometimes I shut a book of fabulous pictures, and my own life seems like a puny little after-image. Better this feeling of overflow. Thank god for times like these when I remember: there is too much life to fit into art.

You take a final photo anyway, with a timer, to prove it happened, that we were in this frame together, that there was no space for light between our faces.

I almost expect the pictures to come out blank. But when you airmail them to me they are full of colour. I look at this middle-aged couple embracing against the sun-polished rocks. Already they are not us. Already they are figures in a collage. Already we are not the same.

7: Frame

In this last of the pictures I never took, it is New Year and I am standing at your window again, looking out at the mountains under their shirt of snow. I make a diamond frame with my hands to shape the picture: dark verticals of trees, angles of snow, some silver birch trees to complicate the contrast. The river is frozen black except for some swirls of white near the bank. It is a beautiful picture, but it is flattening into two dimensions already.

Having flown here for green summer and orange leaves and white snow, and not much wanting to see the mud season, I get the feeling that I am not going to be back. And it turns my stomach to watch myself framing this away, folding it over, when it is still good, before anything has actually happened to put an end to it.

I know I'm speeding, way over the limit, slapping down each image as soon as I catch it, dashing on to the next. Why the hell can't I live in the present, like my friends keep telling me to? They say youth is the hasty time, but I've been in the biggest hurry ever since I entered my forties. I have this craving to see everything I've got left.

The snow fills up the window in this picture, kindly and indifferent.

Maybe this thing needs to be over before I can see it. Maybe in my twisted way I am ending it now so that I can understand and represent it, so the story has an ending to match its beginning. Maybe (what bullshit, what cowardly bullshit), maybe this turning of my back is a version of love.

The Strangest Feeling in

Bernard's Bathroom

Bernard was almost sixty, and still happy. He liked to bring this up in conversation. It was his only vanity.

"I don't expect much," he said. "That way, I'm never disappointed. Other people want the sun, moon and stars. When they don't get them, they become bitter. Honestly, there is so much bitterness in the world. If only people were happy with what they have. That's what I always say."

All his friends in the staff canteen would nod when he said this.

"You're a philosopher, Bernard," they used to say. "You're a wise old bird."

Jack Barrett, his oldest friend, who managed the Curtain Material Section, would chip in here.

"If there's one thing better than an old head on young shoulders, it's a young head on old shoulders," he said, wiping bits of pastry from the corners of his mouth.

And Bernard would come in on that cue.

"The young people want their houses curtained and carpeted before they move in. They want everything at once, just like that. It was different in our day."

"A damn sight different."

Then Carmel Timoney, who worked in the Stationery Department, would bring the whole thing to a close. She would punch out her cigarette at the edge of her saucer, and speak for them all.

"No wonder you look so young, Bernard," she always said. "The right attitude is worth a hundred trips to the doctor."

"Or to the psychiatrist," Bernard would say, but only if the girl from the Information Desk was sitting at another table, because one had to remember, all said and done, that her brother had been in and out of homes ever since the accident on the motor-bike. If she was sitting with them, he would say something else.

"Or to the priest," he would say.

"God forgive you, Bernard Brennan," Carmel would say in mock horror. "Wait until I tell your wife."

That was the pattern of Bernard's life. When you thought about it, there was a lot to be said in its favour. It was all very well to talk about action and adventure, but the truth was you had enough to contend with from day to day. Bernard's life was full of days. It took him all his time just to get through them. Sometimes he thought they would never end. Still, he was good humoured about that too.

"Time probably does fly," he used to say, "but you have to wait a long time to get clearance for take-off."

They loved that.

"You're a laugh a minute," Jack would say to him.

But his wife had heard it too many times.

"Would you ever think of another one?" she said.

So the next time the topic came up for discussion, he changed it slightly.

"Time probably does fly," he said to Janet while she was folding shirts in the kitchen. "But it flies on one engine."

Secretly he preferred it the other way.

Bernard's day began with an erection, and ended with anti-flatulent lozenges. He hated taking them, even the lemon-flavoured ones, because he had to get out of bed to wash his teeth again. If he didn't take them, the inevitable happened. Then Janet would turn over angrily, taking most of the eiderdown with her.

"It's not fair," she would say. "It's just not fair."

His erection she never noticed. Once he had pretended to be asleep, and rolled over to her side. But she never said a word, then or later. Anyhow, that was years ago. There was no point in wondering about it now. Instead, Bernard wondered about other things. Rainbows, for example. They had to do with reflections and the spectrum, but most people never bothered to find out. They just darted home between showers, or gave out about the weather forecast. But they never once stopped to think: how extraordinary rainbows are. In fact, there was no end to what you could wonder about. Teachers nowadays understood that. When he was at school, you never heard about nature trips. And what about the way in which Religion was taught? You didn't just parrot off any old rubbish anymore. You talked about things, you were open to discussion. Of course, certain questions could never be answered. Take a sixty-year-old dead person. Would that person be raised up as a baby, a boy, a man, or an old man? Not even the priests with beards could tell you that. Or take the way people were different. Why was one person a millionaire, and another man with a spastic child? As to sex, you could wonder about that until the cows come home.

Bernard spat out the hydrogen peroxide he had been gargling. Then he rinsed his mouth with warm water.

"You're a great man for questions," he said to his image in the mirror.

A face that was almost sixty, and still happy, looked back at him. Its lips were white with toothpaste.

That was where things stood, the day Bernard walked into the bathroom without realizing Janet was in the bath. He was the kind of man who likes to shave twice a day. Besides, doing it the old-fashioned way with cream and a naked razor gave one a few minutes by oneself after a day spent behind the counter without any real opportunity for privacy. It made you fresh and alert as well. Most of all, it was a good discipline. Bernard had always known when the rot sets into a man: if a chap stopped shaving, he stopped making the effort. He might as well pack it in. His cards were numbered.

It was a good thing Janet had turned on the warm-air heater over the towel rail. Otherwise she might have heard Bernard opening the door. As it happened, she was sitting with her back to him, fiddling with the taps. All her hair was up under the shower cap that had the design of the little Black and White Minstrel men running round musical chords on it. She was bent forward so that her spine stood out. Bernard could see the red mark of her brassiere strap and, just above the water, the thin print that her panty hose had left across the small of her back. It was ten years since he had last seen her like this. Perhaps it was more.

"Janet," he said, and was amazed that he had.

But she never heard him. The taps were going full blast, and the steam was rising in clouds. She started punching the water between her legs, and then whisking it, to make more foam. Bernard could see the slippery corner of her breast, and the white puncture-marks of the vaccination weal on her shoulder. Her body seemed very tired somehow. He felt terribly sorry for it, and for her too. In fact, he had never quite experienced such an odd feeling before; he was at a loss what to call it. He had always been very fond of her, of course, but one assumed that. When they had been married at first, there was the other too as well, for a while at least; and then there was the Christmas feeling, good-will and so forth, from time to time. But that was par for the course. That was run-of-the-mill stuff.

Janet screwed the taps shut with both hands. Now he could hear again the high humming of the warm-air heater, its dry gusts reaching him across the length of the bathroom. He was afraid she might sense him then, or feel a draught, or lose the soap and turn around, groping for it in the bath. She wouldn't understand, she would think he was some kind of Peeping Tom, she would have no idea of the sadness he felt as he saw her sitting there, looking ridiculous and forgotten-about and delicate. He felt if he touched her she would come out in a rash around the mark of his finger. If she fell getting out of the bath, her skin would be bruised. If her ankle knocked against the spigot of the tap, the tissue would blacken. Anything might happen. Without her clothes, she was so terribly naked.

Bernard shut the door quietly behind him, and stood for a while in the passageway. Suddenly everything had gone quiet. He couldn't hear the warm-air heater now. His own body-sounds made the only noises: his heart and stomach juices, his lungs taking in air.

"Janet," he called.

The heater was probably too loud. Or perhaps she had water in her ears. Or maybe she was washing her hair. Would she wash it sitting in the bath or standing beside it, bending over? You could be married twenty-eight years, and not know these things.

"Janet," he shouted.

Finally she heard him.

"I'm in the bath," she called out. "I can't hear you."

Bernard was determined to make more of an effort that evening. It was never too late. If there was one thing people agreed about, it was that. Of course, it would be silly to talk in terms of a resolution. That kind of talk got you nowhere. It would be better to think in terms of giving up cigarettes. When you stopped smoking, you did so quietly. You told no-one. You just hoped for the best. If you made it through Monday, the chances were you would last through Tuesday too. But there was no use worrying, or looking back. The main thing was to stick at it. That would be his approach. Anyway, if he was suddenly to become attentive, she would probably suspect him. It might even alarm her.

After supper, he began to stack the dishes.

"What's got into you?" said Janet.

"I thought you might be tired," he said.

"Thanks very much." But her tone of voice took the good out of it. "I've been tired for twenty-five years. Watch where you let that gravy drip."

Still, she seemed pleased. From the way she swung her sandal by the toe-strap he could tell she was chuffed. That was one thing he knew about her.

"You're in good time for your programme," he said.

"It's on late," said Janet. "That's why I had my bath early. There's some football match on, with a satellite link-up. My programme isn't on until ten."

She cocked her head to one side, and shook it a few times. For a moment, she became strange to him again. He was slopping the dinner plates into the pedal bin, but he stopped to look at her.

"Water," she said, wagging her finger in her ear.

What was the point? After twenty-eight years, you could hardly walk up to your wife, and say to her "I saw you in the bath this evening, and I was shy, but not for the reason you might think. It was because you seemed so small really, so helpless almost. I wanted to put my arm around you, although it was not a sexual feeling. It was more a feeling of sadness."

"You're only making work," she said to him. "You're making a mess."

She was picking peas and a potato-skin off the floor. He let her take the plate from his hand. Then he peeled off the kitchen-gloves. Perhaps it was already too late. Perhaps it would do more harm than good.

Janet examined him closely.

"You're in strange form tonight," she said. "You didn't even shave when you came in."

When she was fast asleep, Bernard put his bedside lamp down on the floor, and turned it on. Then he could look at her without fear of waking her. Something of what he had felt in the bathroom revived in him, but it was not as strong or sudden or strange. In fact, he had to work at it a bit. Face-cream glistened on her cheeks and forehead; her lips were tightly shut. After a while, he experienced a kind of affection, a sort of peace; yet it all seemed willed. What had happened in the bathroom was unselfconscious, and he was wistful about it now. But perhaps it would happen again. Perhaps it would happen more and more often, at the most unlikely times, in the most unexpected places.

Bernard pressed another anti-flatulent out of its foil sheet. He let it dissolve slowly on his tongue. Then he made his way to the bathroom. He could still see the prints of Janet's feet where she had stood under the heater to dry her shoulders and hair, tapping clouds of talcum powder onto her legs to that the white and lemon dust settled around her on the dark carpet. After he had washed his teeth, he sat down on the toilet, and looked at the prints. They were like the marks you see in snow: bird-marks or hoof-marks. There were animals in Asia that had never been seen, Bernard thought. They were known only by the prints of their paws. He had forgotten how small Janet's feet were. They were almost petite. Yet she was not a small woman. She came up to his shoulder.

When Bernard got back into bed, his hands were so cold that he couldn't touch himself with them. He held them away from him until the heat of the bed made them warm again. He knew it would be an hour, perhaps an hour and a half, before he slept. But he was used to that too.

Bernard's third-best suit had a blurred look at the collars and cuffs, and a glazed look at the seat and elbows. In the morning, he put it on, and went to work.

"Have a good day," he said to Janet.

"I don't know how you get away with that suit," Janet said. "Jack Barrett is always dressed like a lord."

He could see that she knew he was behaving differently. It made her uncertain.

"Don't just stand there," Janet said.

He could say it now. He had twenty minutes to spare. Janet was still in her dressing-gown too. It was strange how defenceless people seemed in their night clothes. Their workclothes made them hard again: when they were dressed, they would fight you tooth and nail. But they were clumsy and bashful in their pyjamas, smelling of toast and sleep. He could see why the secret police made dawn-raids. It would be a good thing if the United Nations were to meet in dressing-gowns. Then there would be fewer wars.

"Will you not just stand there?" Janet said. She gathered up the collar of her dressing-gown, and covered her throat with it.

He would say it that evening. Friday night was a good time for speaking out.

"Goodbye so," he said.

A young black in a brightly coloured shirt sat opposite Bernard on the bus. If you look at them, Bernard thought, they imagine you're being critical; if you look away, they suppose you're being contemptuous. He wished he had bought a newspaper on the way to the bus-stop. It might be a time before he could offer his seat to an old lady. The bus was only half-full, and old ladies made a habit of getting up later in the morning. It would be foolish to stand for a young woman. After all, he was almost sixty. Besides, if they wanted to wear trousers, they could go the whole hog, and stand in buses as well.

Bernard stared out the window, lifting his hat from time to time as the bus passed a church. He had never been very consistent in this practice. At times, he liked to raise it at any and every church, whatever the colour of its money; at other times, he would tip it intermittently, once in five perhaps, or once in six. Today, he touched his hat-brim whenever he saw a church; and he was a little surprised, as he had been before, at how many of them there were, on the way into work.

What had happened in the bathroom was not sexual; and if it was, it was also more than that. Seeing a pretty girl sauntering along the street, and wanting, let's call a spade a spade, to reach out and pat her behind, was one thing; but to walk into your own bathroom, to see your wife sitting in the bath, and to feel sad and shy about it, was another. Not that Bernard was a stranger to emotion. He had his feelings, even if he didn't parade them. Only a week before, he had gone out of his way to minimize the fuss when a young woman was caught with a pair of lisle stockings in the Religious Objects Department. Jack Barrett, for all his palaver, would have prosecuted; but Bernard had talked to her nicely, and said it was obviously an oversight, and would she go back to the hosiery section, and pay for the article there. In the end, she made a bee-line for the side-exit.

Bernard looked down at the black hands in the lap opposite him. Why were the hands of black people, and brown people for that matter, so beautiful? Their fingers were long and tapering; they were like pianists' fingers. It was no wonder the blacks had invented jazz. Now if it was Jack Barrett on the bus, he would not have noticed the delicate black hands. He would have saved up some comment about squashed lips and noses. He would not have been open to the beauty that you can see in blacks, if you take the trouble to look. But that was the whole trouble with Jack. He was a very nice oaf, it was true; first and foremost, though, he was an oaf.

Bernard stood up. He had reached his stop.

"I beg your pardon, sir," he said to the black.

The man was confused. His legs were not in the way. Still, he drew them in, and watched the nice old chap with a kind of happy face stepping down off the bus.

When the lunch-hour was almost over, Bernard decided that he would, after all, tell Jack what had happened. Carmel had turned away, and was chatting ten to the dozen to the girl whose brother had had the nervous breakdown.

"I walked into the bathroom last night," he said to Jack, "and I saw Janet just sitting in the bath. I . . ."

"Carmel," Jack called. "Come and hear about Bernard and Janet in the loo."

"Bernard Brennan," said Carmel. "Now at last we know how you manage to stay looking the way you do. I'll have to keep an eye on you, I will."

"But it wasn't that at all," Bernard explained to Jack. "It was the strangest feeling."

"I think I know the feeling," said Jack, winking elaborately at Carmel. "I had a touch of it myself this morning when I went the short way through Trousers, and what did I see?"

"Tell us then," Carmel said.

"A young lady who was nameless and shall remain so, stretched out on the floor of one of the cubicles, with her feet out like so, as if she was having a baby."

Jack pushed back in his chair and swung his legs high. There were whoops of laughter. Bernard gave up, and joined in.

"What was she doing then?" he said.

Jack puffed and panted his answer.

"She was holding her breath, and sucking in her tummy, to get the bloody designer jeans on. But her arse wouldn't go in."

Carmel covered her face, and howled with glee.

"Yes," said Jack in his normal voice, "I know about strange feelings. You're a clever old bird, Bernard. A wise old owl."

Bernard looked at the clock on the canteen wall.

"Time flies," he said.

"Are we ready for take-off?" Jack said, twisting round to squint at the hands.

"No," said Bernard. "We're just coming in to land."

On the way home he had an inspiration.

A priest would listen. In a sense, and without any disrespect intended, that was what they were paid for. It was downright stupid to have even tried talking to someone like Jack Barrett. What could you expect of a man who put brown in his hair, and wore a gold chain around his wrist? Jack had an answer for everything: it was the easy way out. But a priest would understand. At the same time, of course, it would be unreasonable to suppose that a priest would have had any very similar experiences. That was what the whole argument about celibacy was concerned with. On the other hand, they were men who read, and travelled. They knew a lot, and they meant well, even if they did go on a bit about the joy of service, and the joy of faith, and whatever. It was easy known they had never sold a pair of shoes across a counter.

Finally, Bernard got off the bus one stop short. The Church of the Incarnation was only a stone's throw. Anyhow, he would just nip in, and see what happened; if he changed his mind, he could walk home through the park. But he hesitated at the church railing, and was even more unsure in the church porch, where two small boys were playing conkers with a young curate. His fingers stung when he dipped them in the font: holy water had a way of being cold.

Am I behaving oddly? Bernard wondered.

Inside, there was an old woman leafing through a parish newsletter, and a file of six or seven persons waiting for Confession. Bernard sat down at the end of the bench, and shifted farther up it whenever the queue shortened. He used the muscles of his bottom to do this. It was strange how it brought back his childhood, when his legs didn't reach to the kneelers, and he had to shuffle along the seat on his bare thighs, with the waxed wood cold against his skin. That was what Bernard hated most about churches: they always brought you back to your childhood, as if things were not already difficult enough.

And what was he going to say to the priest? That he was a man of feeling? That would be some kind of start, but it might well seem unusual, the more so if the man hearing Confessions was one of the old school, all gate and no garden. In a way, it was odd to be coming to confess at all. It wasn't even a matter of slip-ups or stabs of conscience: it was more the desire to confess the strangest feeling, and one that, in spite of its own bizarreness, Bernard rather hoped to have again, and even again, if that were possible. Because he had no other feeling to measure it against. True, he remembered seeing the blind children coming out of the home the nuns ran, and being emotional about that, especially when they filed across the road at the zebra crossing, each holding onto the one in front, with an albino at the top of the line. Still, he hardly ever thought about that now. Besides, you would want to be a monster not to be upset about blind children. A middle-aged woman sitting in a bath with a shower cap on her head, and no Brigitte Bardot, be it said, was a different thing entirely.

He was almost the first in the queue. This priest was a quick one. Other persons had filled the bench behind Bernard: a policeman in uniform, which was quite extraordinary when you thought about it, a quite young girl with cold sores on her mouth, and a father and son, the son looking rather fed-up, if the truth be told.

Bernard was next. This was ridiculous. He couldn't walk into a Confession box, and rattle off a story about surprising his wife in the bath. The priest would think he was mad. He might even ask the policeman to throw Bernard out. Worse, he might decide to keep Bernard for ages. He might be one of those very young priests who should have been psychiatrists, and would like nothing better than to open the prisons or sell off St Peter's and all its treasures. If he was, and he found out about Bernard not seeing Janet in the buff for however many years, he would probably go on and on, and end up by wanting to see them together. In the meantime, you would have all those people outside, just wondering why on earth this particular confession was taking so long.

The other people in the queue were a bit surprised when the old man who was next, and had a nice, happy kind of face, stood up and walked off. He must have something pretty weighty on his mind; or perhaps he was a crank; or maybe he had left his gloves somewhere, and just remembered where.

Everybody moved down one along the bench.

When Bernard arrived home, and walked upstairs, he found that Janet was in the bath. At least, she was in the bathroom. He listened at the door, but he could hear nothing. The warm-air heater was on.

"Can I come in?" he shouted.

"What?" Her voice was not terribly pleasant. Of course, she hated shouting.

"May I come in?" Bernard said.

"I can't hear you," she cried. She was certainly exasperated.

"Please may I come in?" Bernard shouted for all he was worth.

"I'm in the bath," she screamed.

So he went downstairs again, and hung up his coat, and straightened his tie, and ran a hand through his hair. There were plums in the bowl on the sideboard in the living room, but perhaps they were meant for later. Instead he took a Turkish Delight out of the second layer in the box of chocolates. There were some left in the top layer, mostly nougat, but he didn't care. He would go down to the second, even if she criti-cized him for doing so. After all, who had bought them?

Bernard sat down, and thought about his day. Perhaps it had been impetuous of him to leave the church. Perhaps he would mention the whole thing from start to finish to Carmel Timoney. He had talked to her about other things, personal matters, in the past, and she had always been helpful. When you thought about it, she was a most obliging woman. Why had he not spoken to her instead of to Jack? But perhaps Jack meant well beneath it all. You never could tell.

Bernard went down to the second layer again, and took out a hazel-nut this time. He could hear Janet letting out the bathwater.

Perhaps he had misunderstood himself the night before. Perhaps he had been startled by Janet's plainness and fat. Perhaps he had been a bit appalled that she couldn't make more of herself. No one was asking her to be Greta Garbo, but she might make the effort. Or perhaps he had been tired, or depressed. He had a perfect right to be, sometimes. Maybe it was just as well she hadn't let him into the bathroom with her.

Where was the orange one?

Bernard leaned back, and chewed the chocolate on his good side.

Perhaps it was just as well.

The Story of the German Parachutist
Who Landed Forty-Two Years Late

This is what happened.

The Bowmeester family was sitting down to a late supper. Strictly speaking, this statement is inaccurate: two of the Bowmeesters had, in fact, already sat down; Mr Bowmeester (hereinafter to be called Bowmeester Senior) was folding his Tuesday copy of the *Norwich Chronicle*; and Mrs Bowmeester was having a lot of bad luck with her quick-mix chocolate cake, in the kitchen. But you will have to grant that the inaccuracy is minor; and, insofar as everybody—both Bowmeester parents, the boy Bowmeester, his sister who is called Moninne—is engaged *in the process* of sitting down to supper, the grammatical inclusiveness of the opening sentence may stand.

The main thing is, you get the picture. And you certainly get the name. If you have not got the name by now, you should skip this story, and go on to the one in the library, which is about sudden death, or the one before this, which is about slow death. If you cannot manage Bowmeester, you are not going to be able to cope with Dietrich Fosskinder, who is the person alluded to, periphrastically, in the title of this story.

One last time: a family (of Dutch extraction, but that is not important); supper; a cake that has not worked out; a provincial newspaper. Implications: the family is patriarchal: Mr Bowmeester is reading a paper; it is his wife who has to experience the failed cake-mix. Implication: the kids are hungry. Implication: this is a short story with teeth.

I will have to give you some more details, but only four, since we are already running behind schedule. There is an African beaver coat on the arm-rest of the sofa, which Moninne bought at a swap-shop; it is an all-right coat. There is an oval wedding photograph on the mantelpiece, which is probably the Bowmeester parents' one, or perhaps their parents'. The glass door of the clock on the mantel is a little dirty with flour smudges: whoever has been winding it, has also been working with flour. There is a yellow stain on the edge of the sofa cover nearest the castor: tea or urine. If the first, it can be removed. If the second, it is most likely a dog—a dachshund—but there is no smell of a dog in the place, and, besides, Bowmeester Junior abreacts to dog-hair. Now a human being is hardly likely to have done it. We are dealing, let me tell you, with a very normal family.

"How's the cake coming?"

"The cake's not coming."

"The cake's not coming?"

"The cake's not coming."

"Oh well, if the cake's not coming, the cake's not coming."

Bear with me: I am just trying to establish verisimilitude.

Moninne was still drying her nails. She handled her cutlery with precision. Bowmeester Junior was trying to flick something from his nail onto the carpet, but it kept sticking to his thumb. When he tried to flick it off his thumb, it stuck to his finger. Bowmeester Senior was taking the news about the cake badly.

"Quick mix," he said, rather elaborately.

"Have you ever tried baking?" Moninne demanded.

"Look who's asking," Bowmeester Senior said.

"What's this about?" Bowmeester Junior said. He had finally got the thing off his hand onto the carpet.

"Cakes."

"Is it coming?" Bowmeester Junior said.

That was when they heard the noise. Noise is perhaps too strong a word; sound, on the other hand, is too weak. Everybody heard it. It had come from the apple-trees at the bottom of the garden. The Bowmeester family listened hard. The night had become very quiet. Not a stick cracked underfoot; not a leaf gave up (and why should it? It was, after all, early spring); not a breath of wind disturbed the weather-beaten branches of the Bowmeesters' apple-trees. Things were as still as a mouse.

"Mice are not quiet," Moninne said.

All right. Things were quiet as the grave.

"Who knows if the grave is quiet?" Moninne said.

Point.

"I shall go out to whatever has made the noise," Bowmeester Senior said. He did up the top button of his shirt, and began to knot his tie.

"Don't you set a foot outside this house," Mrs Bowmeester said. "Who knows what it is? What you want to go bringing Things into the house? Dirt on your shoes. Nasty dirt over my carpet."

"Someone might have thrown a bottle over the wall behind the apple-trees," Bowmeester Junior said.

"It might be a meteor, or a bit off a satellite," Moninne said.

"Or an owl doing unforeseen and objectionable things to a rabbit," Bowmeester Senior said.

"It might be someone going to the toilet," Mrs Bowmeester said.

"It will not go away," Moninne said.

"It will go away," Bowmeester Senior said.

"Make it go away," his wife said, running her hand through her hair, and making it all floury.

Mr Bowmeester opened the door. Outside, it was very dark. Strictly speaking, this was not out of the ordinary. After all, it was eight o'clock, and the clocks had not yet gone forward. In two weeks, they would; but not yet.

"It is at times like this," Mr Bowmeester said, "that one realizes the true value of hearth and home. Of domestic plenitude. Of what one has to be thankful for."

They would always remember him like that, the other three decided. Pensive and handsome, standing there, going out to whatever might have made the noise.

"We'll wait for you," they cried, which was, strictly speaking, unnecessary, since the room was not too large.

When he had gone, Mrs Bowmeester looked at the clock.

"It has stopped," she said to her remaining family. "Your father has gone."

Bowmeester Junior examined the hands of the clock.

"It stopped twenty minutes ago," he said. "Just before the story started. It is all jammed up with flour."

Mr Bowmeester walked through the darkness. Here and there, he knocked against roots. Once, his foot walloped off the haft of a rake. In the dark, he could smell apple-blossom and dampness. It had been drizzling. His suede shoes would be ruined. Wasn't there a step there somewhere? He put his foot out cautiously, as if he were testing the water.

High up, a cloud moved over the bit of moon that had been there. Three stars came out. That made twelve. When he was nervous, Mr Bowmeester counted the stars. Where he could, he gave them names. Where he could not, it was another part of the Milky Way. That got over the problem.

Now his heart was beating loudly. Still, the doctor had said that exercise was all right. Sex was equivalent to running five miles, there and back. On the other hand, you could die of shock. He had often heard people saying "He went and died of shock." If it was not true, they would not say it.

"Who are you?" he said to the darkness.

It had nothing to say to him.

"Where are you?" he said to the darkness.

But the darkness was not about to tell him.

Mr Bowmeester decided to go back. He turned slowly. If he went very quietly, nothing would pounce. He could feel the darkness stroking his neck. In front of him, there dangled a pair of boots.

Mr Bowmeester kneeled down. He could hear his heart as if it were coming out of speakers. His head got warm and heavy. The boots went up to legs. The legs joined the rest of a body. There was a face. At least, there was a mask and goggles. Overhead, silk and nylon drapes glistened like polythene among the upper branches of the trees. And above that, all the stars had gone in.

"Are you Jesus?" he said. "Have you come to haunt me?"

"Jesus does not haunt," said the mask. "That is the job of the Holy Spirit."

"Are you the Holy Spirit?" Mr Bowmeester said. It was a fair question.

"I am a German pilot," said the face behind the goggles. "My plane was shot down. I bailed out. Help me to get down from this tree. The wind is piercing. My mind is dismayed by images of conflict. The stars have been put out overhead."

"Are you stuck up there?" Mr Bowmeester said.

"No," said the German pilot. "I landed on open ground, but I had so little to do that I arranged myself up here, the better to appreciate the view of the surrounding countryside under starlight."

"You have not lost your sense of humour," Bowmeester said, "and your command of English is most impressive."

"Where would one be without a sense of humour?" said the German pilot. "One would be totally in the dark. My English is not bad. A trifle bookish, perhaps. But I do not command it. It commands me."

"Where did you learn to speak as you do?"

"Anything can happen in a short story," the pilot said. "My author thought it would be as well if I spoke excellent English. Besides, it was not to be expected that you would be able to converse in fluent German. You can see that he has made allowance for almost every contingency."

"What happens next?"

"For the moment, this moment must suffice. You must stand beside me at the foot of the apple-tree, and meditate the strangeness of this happening. I must remain here, waiting for assistance, my being slumped in obscurity."

Bowmeester had recovered himself. Now he was all efficiency.

"Let me help you," he said. "I can loosen the straps of the parachute. Are you wounded?"

"I am thirsty," said the German pilot.

"Would you like an apple?" Mr Bowmeester said kindly. "It is eighty per cent water."

"That would be nice, but I would much rather an apple-juice."

A suspicion had begun to form in Mr Bowmeester's mind. Then it started to emerge. But this should not surprise you: formation and emergence are the characteristic habits of a suspicion.

"We are not at war," he said. "We are at peace. How can you say your plane was shot down? We were at war with Argentina quite recently, but that is all forgotten. Are you an imposter? Are you a lunatic? Are you a practical joker? Are you a Soviet interloper? Are you something that has welled up out of my imagination? Where are your papers?"

"My name is Dietrich Fosskinder," said the pilot. "I was shot down over Norfolk. I have been falling ever since. Moments ago, I woke up, and I smelled apple-blossom and dampness. Then I heard a noise, the sound of a man stumbling. I thought it might be an animal. I was afraid it would be a Dobermann Pinscher. Then you spoke to me. I knew that my author was not striving for verisimilitude, but I was confident that he would not go so far as to confer human speech-patterns on canines."

"We are in safe hands," Mr Bowmeester said. "We will not be man-handled."

He had unfastened the last of the parachute straps. The German pilot fell the few feet to earth. His ankle twisted fluently beneath him.

"Would I have said 'fluently'?" said Mr Bowmeester. "There is some-body at work here, beside ourselves. I can feel a benevolent presence."

"I can feel pain in my Achilles' heel," said the pilot. "I am bleeding internally."

Mr. Bowmeester put his head under the German pilot's armpit, and hoisted up his trunk. Then he helped him limp among the apple-trees towards the house. It was still there. He had been a little afraid that it might go up in smoke. Stranger things had happened at night. It might just go up in a puff of smoke.

"Not unless the people in the house play with fire," the pilot said.

"I was speaking figuratively," Bowmeester Senior said. "I meant it might be annihilated, dissolved, done away with. I meant it might be pulled up into the sky on wire-strings, like a stage-set."

"We would call that a *Himmelfahrt*."

"I would call it the end," Mr Bowmeester said.

There was great confusion in the house when the pilot was introduced. Mrs Bowmeester wiped her hands on her kitchen-apron, and got off most of the flour. Then she shook hands.

"I have inside staff," she explained to the pilot, who was very dashing. "It's their day off."

Moninne had rushed off next door to smell herself under her arms. She was all right. All she need do was sprinkle a little toilet-water around the collar of her blouse, and behind her ears. She always had her period at the wrong time, she thought. Always. She always felt bottomy at the wrong time.

"How are you?" she said sweetly.

Bowmeester Junior nodded.

"Just drop in?" he said.

First they ate. Then they cleared away. Then they washed. Certain things were not in themselves crucial, but they helped to preserve a sense of the natural order of things. They were more important than ever when you find a German pilot dangling from an apple-tree at the bottom of the garden.

"All I saw was these two feet," said Mr Bowmeester.

He had told the whole story. They were enthralled, even the pilot.

"Did you think I was dead?" he asked.

"Not after I checked your blood pressure," said Mr Bowmeester.

Moninne could not help herself.

"Were you not so afraid?" she said to the pilot.

"I have never been anything else," he said. "One gets used to it."

"When was the worst moment is what Moninne means," said her mother.

"After I baled out. Falling through the darkness. Around me, stars wheeled; the planets spun; my chute flowered above me like a jellyfish. Cold burned my fingers, my eyes stung in the rushing blackness. Hoar hung heavy on my cheekbones. Ice inched upwards on my two greaved calves. Sleep overcame me. Jaded, my jaw dropped on my breastbone. Dozed I did, for all hours. Waking, I wondered. My balls were frozen."

"You poor man," Moninne murmured.

I did not. I said it quite audibly.

All right. All right.

"Why must men suffer so?" she said, and it sounded better coming from her.

"But what were you doing up there?" said Bowmeester Junior.

"I was escorting Heinkels to bomb Norfolk," the pilot said.

"What a mean thing to do," Bowmeester Junior said.

"It *was* somewhat anti-social," Bowmeester Senior said.

"But you were only obeying orders," said Moninne, who had finally opened her third button. It took hours to defreeze a fridge. She knew that, but surely people were different.

"What else are orders for?" said the German pilot.

He was feeling comfortable now, his feed wedged among the fire-irons in the fireplace, and his back leaning against the fattest of the bean-bags. His wine had been sitting at the fire for a half-hour, and it was still ice-cold. Anything can happen in a story; and anything had. Besides, they were nice people, even if slow on the uptake.

But the most important question had not yet been asked.

"Why did it take you forty years to land?" Bowmeester Junior wanted to know.

"Were you that high up when you baled out?" Moninne said.

"It did not seem like forty years," the pilot admitted. "It was more like the wink of an eye. Yet the falling seemed never to end. Far above me, the dead stars glittered. Their light was so tired. They had long since folded up. Their light passed by me. Some of it stuck on my shoulders and sleeves. Some of it spotted my hair."

It was true. It was like paint.

"There are things you cannot ever brush off lightly," the pilot said.

"How will you cope?" Moninne said. "The world is so changed. We have colour photography, sun-lamps, satellites, detergents that kill every germ you can name, Italian and Mexican cuisine, synthetic contraceptives. Most of all, we are at peace. We are not at war."

"This is Problem Number One," Mr Bowmeester said. "You must get used to the thought of peace. You must adapt to the thought of travel. I have been to Germany. I have been to the red-light district in Hamburg, though I did not exactly go in. I have been to Checkpoint Charlie. There is a picture to prove it. I have been to Krefeld, on business."

"Krefeld I know," the parachutist said. "Krefeld is a nice place."

"Krefeld is OK," said Mr Bowmeester. "I am not crazy about it."

"I have travelled too," said Moninne. "To Greece and to Southern Italy. I have never been in Mallorca. I could not even point to it on a map."

She was rather proud of that.

"Problem Number Two is a problem as well," said Mr Bowmeester. "You must see that you do not fit in. You must see that you do not quite belong."

"I will go native," said the German parachutist, looking at Moninne.

"But not completely," she said. "You must always be different. You must always be the man who has fallen for forty years. You must never forget your position. People are forever doing that nowadays. All we are left with is the Royal Family, and even they make speeches."

"Tomorrow morning, I will bury my parachute. Better still, I will burn it." The wine had gone to the pilot's head. How good it was to be warm, to be among people, to smell women, to come into a room and know that there were women in the area. The young one opposite, with the unpronounceable name, had a particularly strong spell.

Smell, you mean.

Smell. She had taken off her boots and placed them beside the poker. She wore tights, with a ladder in the left leg. Left to look at; right to wear. He had been falling for so many years. Now he could begin to climb again. He would like to start by climbing that ladder.

"You mustn't think of burning it," Mr Bowmeester said. "It would be useful for so many projects. I could use it to insulate the rabbit hutches. I could use it to lag the immersion. The Imperial War Museum might want it for their collection. Who knows? Perhaps they have no such thing in their files. Besides, it will bring back memories for Mrs Bow-meester. She used to fold them for the boys."

"Did I?"

"Of course you did. They used you on a poster, you had such a cheer-ful way of going about it. Nothing made you happier than folding para-chutes."

"What did you do, Dad?" Moninne wanted to know.

"Me, I filled sandbags. Thousands of them."

"When I first joined the Luftwaffe," the German pilot said, "it was the proudest day of my life. My father embraced me; my mother put up her face to be kissed. They were not by nature overly demonstrative. You can imagine my embarrassment, my gratification. Then I walked arm-in-arm with my sister around the restaurant area of Dresden. Her behaviour towards me was quite improper; I suspect that she was trying to disguise the fact that we were siblings."

"You must be very striking in your uniform," Moninne breathed. "In my copy of *The Illustrated History of Lingerie* there are photographs of male models in fine Gestapo uniforms, reclining in *dix-huitième* chaiselongues while scantily attired women pull languidly at their boots. One cannot be sure what may or may not occur thereafter. But I doubt that such women would be in a position to go home again."

"Moninne, you are talking very funny," said her mother.

Mr Bowmeester felt that enough was enough.

"Enough is enough," he said. "There'll be time to talk again tomorrow. Our guest, our honoured guest, must be tired."

"I am fresh in fact," said the German pilot. "I have not been getting up to very much for about forty years."

Mr Bowmeester insisted. He felt that this paragraph was running beyond itself. One had to bear in mind the bladder capacity of the average reader.

"There is a time for beginning paragraphs, and there is a time for ending them," Mr Bowmeester said.

They rigged up a camp-bed beside the fire for the German pilot. Moninne brought him a bolster and an eiderdown bedspread; Mrs Bowmeester rummaged about until she found ointment for his chilblains. Bowmeester Junior had walked down the garden to where the slick, translucent folds of the parachute drowsed on the branches of the apple-trees. The moon frosted its tauter parts.

"Until I touch this, I am not going to be deceived," Bowmeester Junior said.

It was not like sail-canvas at all. It was like the feel of women's things as you walked through the undergarment department toward the boys' department. And it was wet.

He ran back toward the house, wiping his fingers madly against his trousers.

Moninne stole in to the pilot round midnight. She took the rubber-band out of her hair, and let it down.

"It suits you down," the pilot said.

"Are you not sleeping?" Moninne said.

"I am asleep," he told her. "I am having a dream. Also, I am being dreamed. In the process, I wake up, and I find a young woman with an unpronounceable name and a strong body-odour kneeling by my camp-bed, letting down her strawberry blonde hair."

"I am going to wash your feet with my hair," Moninne said.

"That would be rash," the German pilot said. "You would go away again with the smell of feet in your hair."

"But perhaps some of the light would rub off on me."

"It has long since dried in," he said apologetically.

"You must make the difference for me anyhow," she said. "I demand that you make the difference in my life."

"I am too afraid," the German pilot said. "I am afraid I will be dreamed in a way I do not want. I am afraid I will be dreamed back on to the apple-tree. I am horribly afraid I may find myself falling again. I want a normal life. I want high-jinks, kids, a choice of vegetable with my dinner, all the Sunday papers."

"How can you do this? Is that what you fell all those years for?"

Her voice was starting to wobble.

"Stop, please," he said. "Tell me what you can smell."

"Nothing," she said.

"Smell harder."

"Myself," she said. "The cake that did not work out. You. The socks drying on the clothes horse beside the fire. Blood in my mouth where I bit my lip to stop crying."

"Up there, there was nothing to smell. For forty years."

He groped for her. But she drew back.

The Bowmeester parents were pillow-talking.

"You see my point," Mrs Bowmeester said. "I don't deny he is very charming. But this is not a novel. In a novel, one has more time. Anything might happen. He might even settle down, and make a match with Moninne. But in a short story, rush is undesirable. I can't simply drop round to this or that person tomorrow morning, and say to them: 'Guess what? We have a house-guest. He dropped in late last night. A fly by night. A ship passing. Come and meet him. He is not going to go away. He is not a tourist. He is a pilot.'"

"I see your point," Mr Bowmeester said.

"Besides, we have been misled by the author. When he said that something would happen, and asked us if he could choose our household as a representative family, we were given to understand that something appropriate would occur. Not that the sky would fall in on us. The surprise I can accept. Surprise keeps you young. It's the *inconvenience* I resent."

"Not to mention the damage to the apple-trees," Mr Bowmeester said.

"Absolutely."

"Why couldn't he have fallen on the road?" said Mr Bowmeester nastily.

"He never thought," she said. "Sheer thoughtlessness."

"Just like a German," Bowmeester Senior said. "Just like Jerry."

"Besides, I never imagined a pilot," said his wife. "I thought a Pools man perhaps; or a solicitor with news of some cousin in New Zealand."

"Solicitors are all the same," Mr Bowmeester said. "Take. Take. Take." He was still thinking about his apple-trees.

"Or a boyfriend for Moninne," said his wife. "I mean a real boyfriend. A nice boy."

"He'll have to go," Mr Bowmeester decided. "There's no place for him here. Did you see the way he just walked in?"

"I knew something bad would happen tonight," his wife said. "My cakes always turn out."

"Typical bloody Hun," said Mr Bowmeester. "Just walked in, out of the blue."

"What this whole episode lacks," Mrs Bowmeester said, "is, to use the most right word that I can think of, a sense of *decorum*."

"You took the word out of my mouth," her husband said.

They told him at breakfast. But they were nice about it, and perhaps a little afraid. Germans were very violent people. So they waited until he had finished his eggs, and was on his second cup of tea. Then they struck.

"This is a bit of a volte-face," he said.

"I never wanted to hear language like that in my house," Mrs Bowmeester shuddered.

The German pilot was distraught.

"I could make myself useful," he said. "I would be an asset."

"You are a liability," Mr Bowmeester said. He was rather pleased that he knew some legal language. "You are a definite liability."

"I can see the way you've been looking at my daughter," Mrs Bowmeester said. "At the part between her throat and her tummy. I've been watching you."

"I was hoping to have relations with her," the pilot explained. "I would find sex with her very fulfilling."

"How dare you talk like that in front of her parents," said both her parents.

"I was expecting the paragraph any page now," the pilot said. "I was going to submit a draft to the author, for consideration."

"What did it say?" Moninne said excitedly.

"'His hands found her, wet and waiting. She thrust against him. "Jesus," she cried. "Jesus."'"

"I would never use the Holy Name in that manner," Moninne demurred.

The last three words are hard to say together.

Rightio.

"I would never say 'Jesus,'" Moninne said. "Who do you think I am?"

"Have a better one?" said the pilot.

"'Again, his hands reached for her. She drew away, frowning. "Not now," she said, "not yet, not here."'"

"Better let the author decide," said the pilot.

This is what I decided.

For a long while, he was content to lick her armpit.

"I love your little tuft," he said.

"You've been there long enough," she said. "Go somewhere else now."

"Enough is enough," Mr Bowmeester said. "This paragraph is going nowhere. The point is, you are not wanted here. Leave us alone. Barge into somebody else's apple-trees. Make a mess of someone else's cake."

"You cannot just throw me out," the pilot said. "Like I was old water, or a broken zip."

"You are a nuisance. You are a domestic incident. You are a shadow thrown over the happiness of our lives together."

"But I cannot leave without my parachute," the pilot said. "I am nothing without it."

"If you do not leave at once," Mr Bowmeester said, "I shall summon the police. I shall call the Rodent Exterminator. I shall call the Drains Inspector. I shall even call a Doctor."

"I'm going," the pilot said. "But you are condemning me to a fate worse than falling. You are condemning me to the existence of a margin. I shall be a crumpled piece of paper: foolscap crushed into a ball for children to kick."

"That," said Mr Bowmeester, "is your look-out."

"But you must see my point of view."

"And what would happen then? Were I to do so, what would be left to me? I would find myself considering the point of view of the veal I consume, of the anthracite I burn, of the apples I gather. Life would become impossible."

"My parachute," the pilot said. "My parachute."

"You must think us simple folk," Mr Bowmeester said. "How can I be sure that you won't drop in on us again? Through the greenhouse panes, or the very roof-tree. What guarantee can you give us? And when did the word of a Kraut mean anything? I have buried your parachute."

"This I cannot believe," said the pilot. Panic was spreading through his syntax.

"I have you foxed," Mr Bowmeester said. "I have you banjaxed. I went out and did it while you were eating your first egg, just before the paragraph started."

"You were too busy looking at bits and pieces of my daughter," Mrs Bowmeester said.

"I appeal to the author," the pilot cried.

Leave me out of it. I am only ghosting this.

"I appeal to the . . ."

Yes?

"I appeal to . . ."

So?

"I appeal . . ."

Get on with it, for Heaven's sake.

"I."

The Bowmeester family was sitting down to a late lunch. Mr Bowmeester was folding his Wednesday copy of the *Norwich Chronicle*. Mrs Bowmeester was having better luck with her sponge gateau. Moninne had stopped bleeding, almost. And Bowmeester Junior had been grinning away.

"Look at this lot," he said.

He opened the holdall, and tipped out the contents. Some of them sparkled and glittered, the way contents should; others did neither.

"German money," Mr Bowmeester said.

"Hitler marks," his son corrected him.

"Are they worth anything?" Moninne said.

"You would have to ask a philatelist," her brother said. "But I should jolly well think they are."

"Bully for you," Mr Bowmeester said. "What else?"

"A comb. A signet ring. A pencil sharpener. Eye-drops. A rubber-band."

"That's mine," Moninne said. "The rotter. He went and stole it."

"When did this happen then?" said Bowmeester Senior.

"Last night," Bowmeester Junior said. "I went through his pockets. I thought he might have had an Iron Cross."

"Him have an Iron Cross?" his father jeered. "They only gave them to men."

Mrs Bowmeester appeared with an immaculate sponge gateau. They all cheered.

"My cakes always turn out," she said.

Mr Bowmeester held up his hand for silence.

"Last night, we heard—or thought we heard—a noise. A sound. A disturbance. Something, we thought—or thought we thought—had happened. Perhaps. It was dark at the time. Sound travels at night."

"I went down the garden," Bowmeester Junior said. "I don't like to say this in front of the women. Somebody had gone to the toilet."

"Big ways or small ways?" said his mother.

"Both."

"Imagine that," said Mrs Bowmeester.

"Did you get rid of it?" Mr Bowmeester said.

"I buried it."

"I went down the garden too," said Moninne. "I found bits of a rab-bit."

"Imagine that," said her mother.

"Did you get rid of it?" Mr Bowmeester said.

"I buried it."

"And I," said Mrs Bowmeester, "I went down the garden too. I found pieces of glass."

"Imagine that," said Moninne.

"I got them up with a rag, and dumped them in the bin," her mother said.

"It is very strange," Mr Bowmeester said. "When I went down the garden . . ."

"Yes?" they all said.

"I noticed nothing out of the ordinary."

Mrs Bowmeester blew dry flour off the hands of the clock. Then she started winding them round anti-clockwise with her finger.

"What time is it?" she said happily.

This was more like it.

ANNE ENRIGHT

What Are Cicadas?

Cold women who drive cars like the clutch was a whisper and the gear stick a game. They roll into petrol stations, dangle their keys out the window and say "Fill her up" to the attendant, who smells of American Dreams. They live in haciendas with the reek of battery chickens out the back, and their husbands are old. They go to Crete on their holidays, get drunk and nosedive into the waiter's white shirt saying "I love you Stavros!" even though his name is Paul. They drive off into a countryside with more hedges than fields and are frightened by the vigour of their dreams.

But let us stay, as the car slides past, with the pump attendant; with the weeping snout of his gun, that drips a silent humiliation on the cement; with the smell of clean sharp skies, of petrol and of dung. The garage behind him is connected in tight, spinning triangles as his eyes check one corner and then the next. There is an old exhaust lying on a shelf in the wall, there is a baseball hat stiff with cobwebs, hanging in the black space over the door. There is a grave dug in the floor, where the boss stands with a storm lamp, picking at the underside of cars. Evenly spaced in the thick, white light that circles from the window are rings set in the stone, to tether cows long dead.

He has a transistor radio. He has a pen from Spain with a Señorita in the casing who slides past a toreador and a bull, until she comes to rest under the click, waiting for his thumb. He has a hat, which he only wears in his room.

He is a sensitive young man.

What are cicadas? Are they the noise that happens in the dark, with a fan turning and murder in the shadows on the wall? Or do they bloom? Do people walk through forests and pledge themselves, while the "cicadas" trumpet their purple and reds all around?

It is a question that he asks his father, whose voice smells of dying, the way that his mother's smells of worry and of bread.

They look up the dictionary. "'Cicatrise,'" says his father, who always answers the wrong question—"'to heal; to mark with scars'—I always thought that there was only one word which encompassed opposites, namely . . . ? To cleave; to cleave apart as with a sword, or to cleave one on to the other, as in a loyal friend. If you were older we might discuss 'cleavage' and whether the glass was half empty or half full. Or maybe we can have our cake and eat it after all."

When he was a child, he asked what a signature tune was. "A signature tune," said his father, "is a young swan-song—just like you. Would you look at him."
     He searched in the mirror for a clue. But his eyes just looked like his own eyes, there was no word for them, like *happy* or *sad*.
     "Why don't cabbages have nerves?"
     "A good question." His father believed in the good question, though the answer was a free-for-all.

If he was asked where his grief began, or what he was grieving for, he would look surprised. Grief was this house, the leaking petrol pump, the way his mother smiled. He moved through grief. It was not his own.

He read poetry in secret and thought his mind was about to break. Sunset fell like a rope to his neck. The Señorita slid at her own pace past the man and the bull and nothing he could do would make her change.

"Come and do the hedges on Wednesday afternoon," said a woman, as he handed her keys back through the window. Then she swept off through the hedges with the exhaust like an insult. The car had been full of expensive smells, plastic and perfume, hairspray, the sun on the dashboard. The lines around her eyes were shiny and soft with cream. Her skin reminded him of the rice-paper around expensive sweets, when you wet it in your mouth.

He rehearsed in his room until he was ready, then came and did the work. He hated her for her laugh at the door. "It's only money," she said, "it won't bite."

In years to come he would claim an ideal childhood, full of fresh air and dignity, the smell of cooking, rosehips and devil's bread in the ditch. On a Saturday night his sisters would fight by the mirror by the door and talk him into a rage, for the fun.

"The place was full of secrets. You wouldn't believe the secrets, the lack of shame that people had. Children that were slow, or uncles that never took their hands out of their trousers, sitting in their own dirt, money under the bed, forgetting how to talk anymore. It wasn't that they didn't care, filth was only filth after all. It was the way they took it as their own. There was no modesty behind a closed door, no difference, no meaning."

To tell the truth, he did not go back for the money, although he knew the difference between a pound note and nothing at all. His pride drove him back, and the words of the man under the hat in his room. "Give her what she wants."

There was a small girl playing football on the grass, just to annoy. They knew each other from school. "Your father is a disgrace," she said in a grown-up voice. "A disgrace, in that old jacket." Then she checked the house for her mother and ran away. The woman sat knitting in the sun and watched him through the afternoon. Her back was straight and hands fast. She kept the window open, as if the smell of chicken slurry was fresh air.

She touched him most by her silence. The kitchen was clean and foreign, the hill behind it waiting to be cleared of thorns and muck. It was the kind of house that was never finished, that the fields did not want. It sat on a concrete ledge, like a Christmas cake floating out to sea.

He liked the precision of things, the logic of their place, the way the cups made an effort as they sat on the shelf. There were some strays, here and there, an Infant of Prague forgotten on the back of the cooker, a deflated football wedged behind the fridge. The cistern from an old toilet was balanced against the back wall, although the bowl was gone.

Waiting for his cup of tea, he forgot what it was he had come for. She was ordinary at the sink, ordinary and sad as she took out the sugar and the milk. When she sat down in her chair at the far side of the room, she was old and looked impatient of the noise his spoon made against the cup.

She asked after his mother, and turned on the radio and said he made a good job of cutting the lawn with the grass still damp. They listened to the tail-end of the news and she took a tin down from the cupboard. "I suppose I can trust you," she said grimly as she opened it up and a swirl of pound notes was seen, like something naked and soft. There was music on the radio.

He fought for the pictures in his room, of a man with a hat, who casually takes her by the wrist and opens out the flat of her palm, as if he understood it. He thought of the taste of rice-paper melting on his tongue, of the things she might wear under her dress. He struggled for the order of things that might happen if he held his breath. She gave him an indifferent smile. He did not understand.

"Women," said his father, "torture us with contradiction, but just because they enjoy it, doesn't mean that it's not true."

There was a soft scratching at the door, and the two of them froze as though caught, with the money trapped in the woman's hand. When it opened he saw an old, fat crone who would not cross the threshold. Her shape was all one, he couldn't tell where one bit ended and the next began. There was a used tissue caught in the palm of her hand. She had a shy face. "Monica, is the creamery cart come?" "Yes," said the woman in a loud voice. "It's a tanker, not a cart." "Oh no," said the old woman, "I'm fine, don't worry about me." She closed the door on herself without turning away.

Her name was Monica. She smiled at him, in complicity and shame. "Deaf as a post," she said, and the room dilated with the possibilities in her voice. She was embarrassed by the money in her hand. She looked at the bob of panic in his throat.

"There was a woman lived up the way from us, the kind that had all the young fellas in a knot. You could tell she wanted something, though probably not from you. She was ambitious, that was the word. It wasn't just sex that gave her that look—like she knew more than you ever could. That she might tell you, if she thought you were up to it. She had an old husband in the house with her, and a mother, senile, deaf, who pottered around and got in the way. And one day the old woman died.

"My father came in from the removal, rubbing his hands. He was a mild kind of man. 'Sic transit,' he said. 'Sic, sic, sic.' He took off the old coat with a kind of ceremony. I remember him taking the rosary beads out of his pocket and putting them beside the liquidiser, which was their place. I remember how ashamed I was of him, the patches on his coat and the beads and the useless Latin. When he sat down he said 'How the mighty,' and I felt like hitting him.

"When someone died, this woman Maureen would wash the body, which was no big deal. She might take any basin they had in the house and a cloth—maybe the one they used for the dishes. I don't know if she got paid, maybe it was just her place.

"'The secrets of the dead,' said Da, 'and the house smelling of fresh paint. Oh but that's not all.' He told me one of those country stories that I never want to hear; stories that take their time, and have a taste to them. Stories that wait for the tea to draw and are held over when he can't find the biscuits. 'Do you know her?' he said, and I said I did. 'A fine woman all the same, with a lovely pair of eyes in her head. As I remember.' He remembered the mother too of course and what kind of eyes she had in her head, as opposed to anywhere else.

"It was the son-in-law broke the news that the old woman had died, and when Maureen came to lay out the corpse, she found the man in the kitchen reading a newspaper and the wife saying nothing, not even crying. She offered her condolences, and got no sign or reply. There was no priest in the house. So Maureen just quietly ducked her head down, filled a basin at the sink, tiptoed her way across the lino with the water threatening to spill. When she got to the door of the old woman's room the wife suddenly lifted her head and said 'You'll have a cup of tea, Maureen, before you start.'

"The corpse was on the bed, newly dead, but rotting all the same. The sheets hadn't been changed for a year so you couldn't tell what colour they should have been. She had . . . lost control of her functions but they just left her to it, so her skin was the same shade as the sheets. Maureen cut layers and layers of skirts and tights and muck off her and when she got to the feet, she nearly cried. Her nails had grown so long without cutting, they had curled in under the soles and left scars.

"'Those Gorman women,' said my father, with relish. 'So which of them came first, the chicken or her egg?' and he laughed at me like a dirty old codger on the side of the road."

After he left the house, the sun was so strong, it seemed to kill all sound. He met her daughter on the road and tackled her for the football, then kicked it slowly into the ditch.

"When I lost my virginity, everything was the same, and everything was changed. I stopped reading poetry, for one thing. It wasn't that it was telling lies—it just seemed to be talking to someone else.

"Now I can't stop screwing around. What can I say? I hate it, but it still doesn't seem to matter. I keep my life in order. My dry-cleaning bill is huge. I have money.

"My father knew one woman all his life. He dressed like a tramp. Seriously. What could he know? He knew about dignity and the weather and words. It was all so easy. I hate him for landing me in it like this—with no proper question and six answers to something else."

ANNE   ENRIGHT

Men and Angels

The watchmaker and his wife live in a small town in Germany and his eyesight is failing.

He is the inventor of the device which is called after him, namely "Huygens' Endless Chain," a system that allows the clock to keep ticking while it is being wound. It is not perfect, it does not work if the clock is striking. Even so Huygens is proud of his invention because in clocks all over Europe there is one small part that bears his name.

Two pulleys are looped by a continuous chain, on which are hung a large and a small weight. The clock is wound by pulling on the small weight, which causes the large weight to rise. Over the hours, the slow pull of its descent makes the clock tick.

The small weight is sometimes replaced by a ring, after the fact that when Huygens was building the original model, his impatience caused him to borrow his wife's wedding ring to hang on the chain. The ring provided a perfect balance, and Huygens left it where it was. He placed the whole mechanism under a glass bell and put it on the mantelpiece, where his wife could see the ring slowly rise with the passing of the hours, and fall again when the clock was wound.

Despite the poetry of the ring's motion, and despite the patent which kept them all in food and clothes, Huygens' wife could not rid herself of the shame she felt for her bare hands. She sent the maid on errands that were more suited to the woman of the house, and became autocratic in the face of the girl's growing pride. Her dress became more sombre and matronly, and she carried a bunch of keys at her belt.

Every night Huygen lifted the glass bell, tugged his wife's ring down as far as it would go, and left the clock ticking over the hearth.

Like Eve, Huygens' wife had been warned. The ring must not be pulled when the clock was striking the hour. At best, this would destroy the clock's chimes, at worst, she would break the endless chain and the weights would fall.

Her mistake came five years on, one night when Huygens was away. At least she said that he was away, even though he was at that moment taking off his boots in the hall. He was welcomed at the door by the clock striking midnight, a sound that always filled him with both love and pride. It struck five times and stopped.

There are many reasons why Huygens' wife pulled the ring at that moment. He put the action down to womanly foolishness. She was pregnant at the time and her mind was not entirely her own. It was because of her state and the tears that she shed that he left the ruined clock as it was and the remaining months of her lying-in were marked by the silence of the hours.

The boy was born and Huygens' wife lay with childbed fever. In her delirium (it was still a time when women became delirious) she said only one thing, over and over again: "I will die. He will die. I will die. He will die. I will die FIRST," like a child picking the petals off a daisy. There were always five petals, and Huygens, whose head was full of tickings, likened her chant to the striking of a clock.

(But before you get carried away, I repeat, there were many reasons why Huygens' wife slipped her finger into the ring and pulled the chain.)

When his first wife died, Sir David Brewster was to be found at the desk in his study, looking out at the snow. In front of him was a piece of paper, very white, which was addressed to her father. On it was written "Her brief life was one of light and grace. She shone a kindly radiance on all those who knew her, or sought her help. Our angel is dead. We are left in darkness once more."

In Sir David's hand was a dull crystal which he held between his eye and the flaring light of the snow. As evening fell, the fire behind him and his own shape were reflected on the window, a fact which Sir David could not see, until he let the lens fall and put his head into his hands.

There was more than glass between the fire, Sir David and the snow outside.

There was a crystalline, easily cleavable and nonlustrous mineral called Iceland spar between the fire, Sir David and the snow, which made light simple. It was Sir David's life work to bend and polarise light and he was very good at it. Hence the lack of reflection in his windows and the flat, non-effulgent white of the ground outside.

Of his wife, we knew very little. She was called MacPherson and was the daughter of a famous (in his day) literary fraud. MacPherson senior was the "translator" of the verse of Ossian, son of Fingal, a third-century Scottish bard—who existed only because the age had found it necessary to invent him. Ossian moped up and down the highlands, kilt ahoy, sporran and dirk swinging poetically, while MacPherson read passages of the Bible to his mother in front of the fire. MacPherson was later to gain a seat in the House of Commons.

All the same, his family must have found sentiment a strain, in the face of the lies he propagated in the world. I have no reason to doubt that his daughters sat at his knee or playfully tweaked his moustaches, read Shakespeare at breakfast with the dirty bits taken out, and did excellent needlepoint, which they sold on the sly. The problem is not MacPherson and his lies, nor Brewster and his optics. The problem is that they touched a life without a name, on the very fringes of human endeavor. The problem is sentimental. Ms MacPherson was married to the man who invented the kaleidoscope.

Kal eid oscope: Something beautiful I see. This is the simplest and the most magical toy; made from a tube and two mirrors, some glass and coloured beads.

The *British Cyclopaedia* describes the invention in 1833. "If any object, however ugly or irregular in itself, be placed (in it) . . . every image of the object will coalesce into a form mathematically symmetrical and highly pleasing to the eye. If the object be put in motion, the combination of images will likewise be put in motion, and new forms, perfectly different, but equally symmetrical, will successively present themselves, sometimes vanishing in the centre, sometimes emerging from it, and sometimes playing around in double and opposite oscillations."

The two mirrors in a kaleidoscope do not reflect each other to infinity. They are set at an angle, so that their reflections open out like a flower, meet at the bottom and overlap.

When she plays with it, her hand does not understand what her eye can see. It can not hold the secret size that the mirrors unfold.

She came down to London for the season and met a young man who told her the secrets of glass. The ballroom was glittering with the light of a chandelier that hung like a bunch of tears, dripping radiance over the dancers. She was, of course, beautiful, in this shattered light and her simple white dress.

He told her that glass was sand, melted in a white hot crucible: white sand, silver sand, pearl ash, powdered quartz. He mentioned glasswort, the plant from which potash is made; the red oxide of lead, the black oxide of manganese. He told her how arsenic is added to plate glass to restore its transparency, how a white poison made it clear.

Scientific conversation was of course fashionable at the time, and boredom polite, but David Brewster caught a spark in the young girl's eye that changed all these dull facts into the red-hot liquid of his heart.

He told her how glass must be cooled or it will explode at the slightest touch.

After their first meeting he sent her in a box set with velvet, Lacrymae Vitreae, or Prince Rupert's Drops: glass tears that have been dripped into water. In his note, he explained that the marvellous quality of these tears is that they withstand all kinds of force applied to the thick end, but burst into the finest dust if a fragment is broken from the thin end. He urged her to keep them safe.

Mr MacPherson's daughter and Dr (soon to be Sir) David Brewster were in love.

There is a difference between reflection and refraction, between bouncing light and bending it, between letting it loose and various, or twisting it and making it simple. As I mentioned before, Sir David's life's work was to make light simple, something he did for the glory of man and

God. Despite the way her eyes sparkled when she smiled, and the molten state of his heart, Sir David's work was strenuous, simple and hard. He spent long hours computing angles, taking the rainbow apart.

Imagine the man of science and his young bride on their wedding night, as she sits in front of the mirror and combs her hair, with the light of candles playing in the shadows of her face. Perhaps there are two mirrors on the dressing table, and she is reflected twice. Perhaps it was not necessary for there to be two, in order for Sir David to sense, in or around that moment, the idea of the kaleidoscope; because in their marriage bed, new forms, perfectly different, but equally symmetrical, successively presented themselves, sometimes vanishing in the centre, sometimes emerging from it, and sometimes playing around in double and opposite oscillations.

(One of the most beautiful things about the kaleidoscope is, of course, that it is bigger on the inside. A simple trick which is done with mirrors.)

Perhaps because of the lives they led, these people had a peculiar fear of being buried alive. This resulted in a fashionable device which was rented out to the bereaved. A glass ball sat on the corpse's chest, and was connected, by a series of counterweights, pulleys and levers, to the air above. If the body started to breathe, the movement would set off the mechanism, and cause a white flag to be raised above the grave. White, being the colour of surrender, made it look as if death had laid siege, and failed.

Death laid early siege to the bed of Sir David Brewster and his wife. She was to die suitably; pale and wasted against the pillows, her translucent hand holding a handkerchief, spotted with blood. It was a time when people took a long time to die, especially the young.

It is difficult to say what broke her, a chance remark about the rainbow perhaps, when they were out for their daily walk, and he explained the importance of the angle of forty-two degrees. Or drinking a cup of warm milk with her father's book on her lap, and finding the skin in her mouth. Or looking in the mirror one day and licking it.

It was while she was dying that Sir David stumbled upon the kaleidoscope. He thought of her in the ballroom, when he first set eyes on her.

He thought of her in front of the mirror. He built her a toy to make her smile in her last days.

When she plays with it, the iris of her eye twists and widens with delight.

Because of her horror of being buried alive, Sir David may have had his wife secretly cremated. From her bone-ash he caused to be blown a glass bowl with an opalescent white skin. In it he put the Lacrymae Vitreae, the glass tears that were his first gift. Because the simple fact was, that Sir David Brewster's wife was not happy. She had no reason to be.

Sir David was sitting in his study, with the fire dying in the grate, his lens of Iceland spar abandoned by his side. He was surprised to find that he had been crying, and he lifted his head slowly from his hands, to wipe away the tears. It was at that moment that he was visited by his wife's ghost, who was also weeping.

She stood between him, the window and the snow outside. She held her hands out to him and the image shifted as she tried to speak. He saw, in his panic, that she could not be seen in the glass, though he saw himself there. Nor was she visible in the mirror, much as the stories told. He noted vague shimmerings of colour at the edge of the shape that were truly "spectral" in their nature, being arranged in bands. He also perceived, after she had gone, a vague smell of ginger in the room.

Sir David took this visitation as a promise and a sign. In the quiet of reflection, he regretted that he had not been able to view this spectral light through his polarising lens. This oversight did not, however, stop him claiming the test, in a paper which he wrote on the subject. Sir David was not a dishonest man, nor was he cold. He considered it one of the most important lies of his life. It was an age full of ghosts as well as science, and the now forgotten paper was eagerly passed from hand to hand.

Ruth's mother was deaf. Her mouth hung slightly ajar. When Ruth was small her mother would press her lips against her cheek and make a small, rude sound. She used all of her body when she spoke and her voice came from the wrong place. She taught Ruth sign language and how to read lips. As a child, Ruth dreamt about sound in shapes.

Sometimes her mother would listen to her through the table, with her face flat against the wood. She bought her a piano and listened to her play it through her hand. She could hear with any part of her body.

Of course she was a wonder child, clever and shy. Her own ears were tested and the doctor said "That child could hear the grass grow Mrs Rooney." Her mother didn't care. For all she knew, the grass was loud as trumpets.

Her mother told Ruth not to worry. She said that in her dreams she could hear everything. But Ruth's own dreams were silent. Perhaps that was the real difference between them.

When Ruth grew up she started to make shapes that were all about sound. She wove the notes of the scale in coloured strings. She turned duration into thickness and tone into shade. She overlapped the violins and the oboe and turned the roll of the drum into a wave.

It seemed to Ruth that the more beautiful a piece of music was, the more beautiful the shape it made. She was a successful sculptor, who brought all of her work home to her mother and said "Dream about this, Ma. Beethoven's Ninth."

Of course it worked both ways. She could work shapes back into the world of sound. She rotated objects on a computer grid and turned them into a score. This is the complicated sound of my mother sitting. This is the sound of her with her arm in the air. It played the Albert Hall. Her mother heard it all through the wood of her chair.

As far as people were concerned, friends and lovers and all the rest, she listened to them speak in different colours. She made them wonder whether their voices and their mouths were saying the same thing as their words, or something else. The whole message was suddenly complicated, involuntary and wise.

On the other hand, men never stayed with her for long. She caused the sound of their bodies to be played over the radio, which was, in its way, flattering. What they could not take was the fact that she never listened to a word they said. Words like: "Did you break the clock?" "Why did you put the mirror in the hot press?" "Where is my shoe?"

"The rest is silence."

When Ruth's mother was dying she said "I will be able to hear in Heaven." Unfortunately, Ruth knew that there was no Heaven. She closed her mother's eyes and her mouth and was overwhelmed by the fear that one day her world would be mute. She was not worried about going deaf. If she were deaf then she would be able to hear in her dreams. She was terrified that her shapes would lose their meaning, her grids their sense, her colours their public noise. When the body beside her was no longer singing she thought, she might as well marry it, or die.

She really was a selfish bastard (as they say of men and angels).

PATRICK McCABE

The Hands of Dingo Deery

 Statement of Det. Insp. Norman Jenkins,
Willesden Police Station.
April 15, '95:9.05 A.M.

To All Staff:
What follows is a truly tragic story. It was found in the pocket of
Mr. Dermot Mooney after he had been remanded in custody following the assault on PC Higgins on the Kilburn High Road last
evening. Initially I had no sympathy for the accused, having witnessed the various bruises on Constable Higgins' face, not to
mention rips both in his tunic and trousers. To be quite frank, I
became exasperated by his insistence that he was a "poet," as he
termed it, and a "cartographer of the heart's secret landscapes." It
was only later, when I secretly observed him alone in his cell, in
the full throes of his oratory, that I began to understand at last
the motivation of a man who goes throwing himself through the
roof of a public building, namely, The Willesden Cinema, not to
mention chuckling and laughing like a man possessed. And, of
course, when challenged, calling an officer of the law "a shite-
hawk from Hades itself!"

It soon became clear to me that this man's journey through
life has indeed been a "Via Dolorosa." It is my considered opin-

ion that we ought to meet his request for an opera cape and two reams of writing paper with magnanimity. Furthermore, although I am not a literary man, I do not believe anyone can read what follows—which is effectively the story of his life— without falling about the place, their eyes welling up with tears. Which is why I bring to you this heart-rending passionate tale of a man's lone struggle with "the capricious vagaries of fate" (Dermot's own words). I defy all staff to read it and then think, "all this man is fit for is punching policemen and drinking cans of McEwan's Export."

Ladies and gentlemen: The Hands of Dingo Deery.

For many years now I have lived alone, within the four grey walls of this narrow room, the tremulous silence intermittently broken as the tube trains cut through the tar-black night with their cargo of ghostly, pallid faces, as if in relentless, heartbroken pursuit of something lost a long time ago, just as the peaceful harmony which once pervaded my entire being has been bitterly wrested from me. How many years now have I paced these accursed floorboards, imploring any deity who cares to listen to return to me the bountiful tranquillity which once was mine and end forever this dread torment which greets me like a rapacious shade each waking day!

And now, as I stand here by the window, watching with leaden, emotion-drained eyes, directly below me in a single line of mocking, waltzing calligraphy, at last they confront me, the wicked, jagged ciphers which, all this time, I have feared would one day rise up from my blackest dreams like wicked flares from the pit of hell: THE SECRETS OF LOUIS LESTRANGE—CAN YOU SURVIVE THE 1,137 WHACKS?

My nightmare began some thirty years ago in a small town in the Irish midlands. I had come to spend the summer with my uncle, who was the headmaster in the local school. He had of late acquired some measure of fame as an ornithologist, and it gave me great pleasure indeed to accompany him on his regular lectures in various halls and venues throughout the county. It is not my intention to imply that my duties were in any way onerous, for in truth, beyond the simple erection of the screen and the operation of the slide projector, there was little for me to do. I carried the briefcase containing my learned relative's notes, it is true, but such was his erudition that he made little use of what he termed "needless paraphernalia," and it was of such insignificant weight that it could have been comfortably borne to The Temperance Hall (in which establishment it was his practice to deliver his orations on the habits of our feathered friends), on the back of the average house fly. What a privilege it was for me to turn the metal disk yet another semicircle as, in *basso profundo*, he would declaim, Slide Please! while his neighbors and friends looked on admiringly.

As I look back on those days now, they always seem to me suffused with the color of burnished copper and within them, time does not appear to move at all.

Afterwards, I would stroll casually through the cooling streets, making the acquaintance of the elderly gentlemen who whiled away their hours on the Summer Seat discussing the imminent ruin of the country and the putative prowess of assorted thoroughbreds in contests that had yet to be.

I would regularly share a lemonade with them, perhaps on occasion pass around a packet of Players. Laughter and an unbending faith in the goodness of our fellow man was a common bond amongst us all.

Little did I know then that already the peace and contentment which only recently had transformed my life would, within only a few short months, have slipped irretrievably from my grasp!

No, at that time, there was little doubt in my mind that where I had the good fortune to find myself was indeed the most idyllic town on earth and had you taken it upon yourself to share your intimations that darker times would soon be discerned on the horizon, I would have extrapolated from your spurious, clandestine philanthropy, nothing more than a bitter, small-minded and wholly despicable envy. I would have scorned mirthfully and packed you off about your business. For, if ever a truth were spoken, it was that evidence of dissension in that sweet little hamlet there was none. Save, perhaps, the awesome figure of a well-known layabout by the name of Dingo Deery, who, at odd intervals, would appear wild-eyed in the doorway of the hall and bellow at the top of his voice, "Shut your mouth, Lestrange! What would you know about it!

You wouldn't know a jackdaw if it walked up to you and pecked your auld whiskey nose off!" Whereupon he would spread his arms and assail the stunned, mute assembly: "You think he knows about birds? He knows nothing! Except how to beat up poor unfortunate scholars for not knowing their algebra! Look at these hands! Look at them, damn youse!"

When he had spoken these words, he would break into a sort of strangled weeping and raise his palms aloft, and indeed there were few present who could deny on first viewing those bruised pieces of flesh that they undoubtedly had seen wear and tear beyond reasonable expectation, even for someone of his social standing. "Cut to ribbons!" he would cry hoarsely. "Cut to ribbons by Lestrange! Him and his sally rods! Oho, yes—you were handy with them all right, Lestrange! But mark my words—you'll pay for what you did to Dingo Deery, I can tell you that!" Then, with a maniacal cackle, his recalcitrant, cumbersome bulk would be forcibly ejected, the distasteful echo of his combative ululations lingering in the air for long afterwards.

But such incidents were indeed rare, and otherwise life proceeded serenely: Yuri Gagarin was in space, Players cost one and six, and John Fitzgerald Kennedy was undoubtedly the possessor of the cleanest teeth in the western hemisphere.

It was to be many years, yet, before the arrival of color television and the first drug addicts.

But how deceptive is reality! For, even as I sat there, my face being gently stroked by the soft and dusty light of the midday sun, drawing deeply, exultantly on the Players, little did I know—indeed, how could I have known—that events were already proceeding apace which would ultimately result in the idyllic calm which I treasured not only being torn apart like a piece of cheap material in some Godforsaken huckster shop, but see to it that I would remain haunted—yes, for there can be no other word for it—for the rest of my mortal days!

The first day I met Mick Macardle, I knew instinctively all was not as it should have been. Deep within me, I heard a timorous voice cry, "Withdraw! Withdraw while you still can!" The languid sunshine, however, and the soothing breeze of the early afternoon conspired in silence to usher away any such uncharitable and unnecessary suspicions.

But now, as I languish here in my one-room prison, forgotten in a city which remembers no names, my heart was crusted over and no such beguiling veils remain to blur my vision, and with staggering clarity I see what ought to have met my eyes in those days of benevolence-blinded myopia, a sight which, had I not been poked in those organs by two large, metaphorical thumbs, should surely have swept through my soul like an arctic wind.

The thin cigar hung insolently out of the side of his mouth. A black raven's wing of Brylcreemed hair fell ominously down over his alabaster forehead. His lips were two ignominious pencil strokes, his mustache not unlike a crooked felt-tipped marker line as might be drawn by a small child. More than anything, however, what ought to have telegraphed to me the imponderable depth of the man's reptilian nature was the slow slither of his arm about my shoulder, the hiss of his silky sibilants as he crooned into my ear, "Don't worry about a thing!" Then, out of nowhere, he would erupt into inexplicable torrents of laughter, the flat of his hand repeatedly falling on the broad of my back as he cried, "You leave it to Mick! I'll take care of it!"

"No prob!" he would cry, sawing the noun in two like some cheapskate magician in a tawdry show.

How I should have loathed the man! But no—my innocence and desire to think the best of all fellows won the day, and even when he passed by my uncle's house in his new Ford Consul, waving through the open window like a visiting dignitary from a Lilliputian puppet state, I chose to ignore the unspoken counsel of my instinct, preferring instead to align myself with the views of those citizens of the town who ranged themselves about him—some, indeed, claiming kinship—as they declared him "One fine butt of a lad!" and insisting furthermore that there was "No better man in this town!"

The abrupt nasal-spurt of his megaphone could be heard far and wide as his glittering consul zig-zagged through the candystriped streets of Summer. "Yes!" it would bark, with metallic brio, "Yes, ladies and gentlemen! Mick Macardle for all your movie requirements! Why not drop along to Mac's Photography Shop and number 9 Main Street? Come along and see what we have to offer! If you want your sprocket spliced, then look no further—Mick's your man! Eight millimeter transfer a specialty! Weddings, christenings, confirmations! Never be negative with Mick Macardle! Mick Macardle's the movie man! No prob! Yes, siree!"

Thus, life proceeded. The church bells would ring out across the morning town, the womenfolk give themselves once more to the fastidious investigation of vegetables and assorted foodstuffs in the grocery halls, brightening each other's lives with picaresque travelogues of failing innards and the more recent natural disasters, delaying perhaps at the corner to engage in lengthy discourse with Father Dominic, their beloved pastor. "That's not a bad day, now," they would observe, the clergyman as a rule finding himself in fulsome agreement. "Indeed and it is not," he would respond enthusiastically, occasionally a dark cloud of uncertainty passing across his fresh, close-shaven features as he added, "Although I think we might get a touch of rain later!"

Observations of similar perspicacity would provide a further ten minutes of eager debate before they would once more proceed on their way, past Grouse Armstrong snuggled up in the library doorway, the single American tourist snapping gypsies in the hotel foyer (*Couldja throw a little more grit on your heads, guys?*) and Sonny Leonard, the local minstrel, rehearsing *I Wonder Who's Kissing Her Now* into the neck of the brown bottle which served as his microphone.

Sadly, even at that transcendent moment, as I gave my heartiest approval to the maestro's impromptu recital with rousing cheers of "Good man, Sonny!" and "More power to your elbow, young Leonard!" disturbing events were already proceeding as the sleek limousine bearing Mick Macardle cruised silently through the streets of Amsterdam, by the side of the ambitious, long-fingered entrepreneur a sinister man of foreign complexion who, within hours, would be outlining his proposition in an outwardly unremarkable lock-up garage, its dimly-lit interior, however, festooned with tattered pictures of young ladies in abbreviated attire. Helpless females of tender years being pursued by villains of the wickedest mien sporting pork pie hats, their misfortunate quarries crying helplessly from the suspended cages in which they would ultimately find themselves. Forced to become slit-skirted temptresses leering through uncoiling cobras of smoke, captured forever in calligraphic captivity as the houndstooth letters whorled all about them in a dizzying, soporific swirl! That same houndstooth lettering that would later choke my soul in bondage like so many miles of barbed wire: EVIL VIRGIN THRILLS! RUN-AWAY GO-GO PSYCHOS! I MARRIED A NAKED MADMAN!

Despicable memories which course through me like a slow-acting poison; the very thought of my Uncle and I adorning that Gallery of the Damned like an eerie step across my grave.

Mick Macardle tapped one eighth of an inch of ash from his thin cigar as The Dutchman ran his tongue along his upper teeth and fanned his fingers on the oil-stained tabletop. "Very well, Mr. Macardle," he began. "That arrangement suits me fine. For each copy you deliver on time, you will receive the sum of five hundred pounds sterling. However, I must emphasize that I can only accept eight-millimeter, as the films are for private distribution. I cannot emphasize how keen my clients are for this type of product, and you may rest assured that demand will constantly outstrip supply. Do you feel you may be able to rise to meet the demands, Mr. Macardle?"

To which the brown-suited businessman responded by paring the nail of his index finger with a marbled pocket knife, flashing his gold tooth, and grinning. "No prob!"

With one wave of his Woolworth's wand began my Golgotha.

To the poor, glorious but innocent souls of the town, he had not been on an evil, self-seeking mission which was soon to shatter forever the harmony that existed amongst us all, but merely, as he cheerfully volunteered, "Visiting the mother in Dundalk! She has a bad dose of the shingles!"

As was their wont in times of difficulty, the commiserations of the local people knew no bounds. Their admiration of such forbearance as he displayed in his time of trial was deep and respectful. "How do you manage to keep going at all?" they inquired of him. "Ah," he would reply, with a modest shake of his head, "I have great faith in St. Anthony!"

Apart from these unsettling events, my life continued as before—setting up the screen, making tea for the various societies who never failed to be impressed by my Uncle's oratory, his statesmanlike imperturbability displaying any hint of fragility only on those occasions when the door would open and a familiar figure appear, crying, "I'll give you Cicinurrius Regius! I'll give you Turquoise-Billed Yellow Jacket! I'll give you Long-Neck Hoppa Tail! Look at these hands, Lestrange! One day you'll pay for what you did to me! Make no mistake, you'll pay all right!"

As the door slammed and the retreating Dingo Deery undulated down the hallway, little did I realize just how prophetic were his words.

It was also my custom in those days to dine occasionally at an establishment known as The Pronto Grill, which was presided over by a gentleman of Italian extraction who busied himself singing selections from the various light operas and furiously polishing drinking glasses. Over a sumptuous repast magnificently prepared by the kitchen staff to whom I had become affectionately known as MORE TAY! because of my predilection for consuming inordinate quantities of the soothing, tan-colored liquid with my meal, I would watch life proceed before me in the warm street outside, at times fearing that such was my ecstatic state that I might collapse in a faint on the formica table before me.

For, in truth, it was not the exquisite quality of the comestibles alone that drew me to my quiet cove adjacent to the steaming chrome of the coffee machine, but the soft voices of the young convent ladies who would converge there in the afternoons, rapt in their sophistry and drawing elongated shapes in the split sugar.

Perhaps I had spent too long in the company of my beloved Uncle—to this day I cannot pronounce upon that with any measure of certainty—but sitting there before me, I knew that beyond all shadow of doubt, I watched them as they became transformed, their splendor now so dazzling and variegated it was as if Gauguin, the master, were himself somehow present, bearing these wonders with him from his Tahitian

Eden. Marvels destined from my eyes alone. And how I gazed upon them, magically lit now by the angled shafts of clear sunlight that crisscrossed the mock terrazzo floor of the restaurant, squatting before me now in their rainbow-hued magnificence, what I can only describe as my Birds of Paradise.

Thenceforward, rarely a day passed but I winged with those exotic creatures across the Elysian Fields of my soul.

Sadly, like The Poet's, and indeed that of the Quattrocentro of the South Seas, my Paradise too was soon to be taken from me.

I was swaying hypnotically in that netherworld of the imagination, partaking of a brimful cup of sugared Brooke Bond when what seemed as nothing so much as the passing of an unseen specter awoke me and I looked up in horror to see Dingo Deery huddled deep in conversation with my pulchritudinous fledglings, their wings folded over as if in protection or a prelude to his spiriting away. How my dream was shattered by the sight of his monochromatic amplitude! Through the crevasse of my fingers, I could see his tiny eyes, phosphorescent with deceit, and in that instant, I watched with a growing sense of unease as he drew the sleeve of the painter's overall across his mouth in a manner that banished the Tahitian genius, perhaps, I considered, never to return.

I fled, despondent, and walked the desolate streets. I felt as if something precious had died on me. I gave myself to Bacchus and that night slept beneath the open skies.

It is hard to say, even to this day, when things began to go wrong between my beloved Uncle and me. Perhaps it was the fact that after my hasty departure from the cafe, he was forced to hire a horse and cart in order to locate me whilst I hopelessly fell from tavern to tavern. His first words to me that fateful night as he came upon me in the open field where I lay beneath the stars were palpably devoid of the affectionate feeling to which I had come to expect in my dealings with him, and we made our journey homeward in silence. There can be no doubt that shortly after this incident, a certain note of sourness became detectable in our relations.

This, however, was just the beginning. Within days, events had taken an even more serious turn. Uncle began to disappear for long periods, without so much as a word of explanation. The only indication that he had returned at all would be the gentle closing of the drawing room door, the soft click to which my ears were to become accustomed as I lay there in the night waiting for the first light of dawn to touch the window. His absences grew increasingly more frequent until, at last, as I stood by my bedroom window watching the silver dawn rise up over the rooftops, I clenched my fist in the pocket of my purple, quilted dressing gown and at last confronted the fact which I could no longer deny: there was nothing for it but to investigate and discover once and for all the mysterious genesis of Uncle Louis's burgeoning eccentricities and the cause of his bewilderingly inexplicable nocturnal peregrinations. There was no longer any doubt in my mind that the animosity toward me was deepening by the day. Night after night I trawled my tormented conscience. Surely a single incident of boorish behavior on my part could not have provoked such a bitter *Volte-face*? Was there something else I had forgotten? Some vile act I had committed unknownst to myself whilst in the grip of the demon grape? A murder, perhaps?

I paled. I wrung my hands in desperation as the greycoated inspector of my mind paced the floor once more, investigating himself with rigorous, indeed fevered, application. But it was all to no avail. The entropy of the vocative served only to confuse me further and the nets of my interrogations were returned nightly, sadly empty once more.

However, as luck would have it, a certain pattern began to emerge. It gradually became clear that my relative's by now seething misanthropy was not directed solely at me. It had begun to extend to almost every citizen in the town.

It was after what I, for the purposes of narrative, shall call "the telephone incident" that I realized that I could no longer indulge in my procrastinations, and that any further dalliance on my part would undoubtedly be construed by future generations as moral cowardice. I had been standing for some time with my ear pressed to the oaken door of the library when, in odd, strangely muted tones, I heard him utter the words, "So, you think I'm at your beck and call, Mrs., do you?" followed by the ringing crash of the bakelite receiver as it was slammed into its cradle and I heard him bellow, "No! I won't be available for ornithology lectures! Tonight or any other fecking night! So put that in your drum and bang it!"

The muffled, indecipherable mutterings which followed seemed to cloak the entire building in a Satanic bleakness.

It was clear that I could delay no longer, and I determined at once to unscramble as best I could this maddening conundrum, this ravelled web of perplexity that enshrouded my dear relative's life. That very night I began my vigil in the doorway of the tobacconist's which was situated directly across the road from the house. For three successive nights I remained at my post, and there were many occasions when I was tempted to swoon into the luxurious, beckoning arms of hopelessness. At last, however, on the fourth night of my vigil, my patience was rewarded and I froze as the massive front door of the house slowly opened and out stepped my uncle into the first, hesitant light of dawn. Hesitantly, he scanned the empty street and then, pulling the collar of his sports coat up around his neck, began to stride briskly into the morning with his binocular case slung over his shoulder.

It was only when he turned left at the old humpbacked bridge that I realized he was making for the woods outside the town.

At once the scales fell from my eyes and I felt myself shrink to no more than five or six inches in height. Silently, I upbraided myself. How could I have been so foolish! To think ill of my dearest Uncle! In those moments, it all became clear to me and I understood perfectly, implicitly, the reasons for his recent erratic behavior. His late night pursuits of his ornithological obsessions had exhausted his body to the point where he had become the victim of an almost Hydesian change in his personality. And, like Hyde of course, he was completely unaware of it. I determined at once to waste no more time. I would explain this to him. I would be brutally frank and honest. Such a decision caused me no concern whatsoever. I knew he would see reason. I knew that within a matter of days he would be back to himself and between us, all would be blissful as before. In that moment of realization, I exulted.

I continued to follow Uncle Louis until he arrived at that clearing in the woods which overlooks the valley, from whence, he had on many occasions reminded me, it was possible at any one time to command a view of over thirty indigenous species of bird.

At first I thought that perhaps my nightly vigils had eroded my resilience to the point where my own mental equilibrium was already affected. Then, through a process of what might be termed cerebral massage, I suc-

ceeded in persuading myself that because of the all-pervasive heat which
we in the town had been experiencing of late, such *hallucinations*—for
what else could one call them—were unavoidable in such weather.

Between my dalliance and my delusions, my fate was sealed.

"Stay right where you are!" a raucous voice snapped. There was no mis-
taking the lumbering rotundity.

The corner of Dingo Deery's mouth curled like a decadent comma of
flesh. I gasped and fell backwards onto a spiky clump of bracken, my
foot, without warning, sinking into the marshmallow softness of a
freshly-manufactured cow pat.

The binoculars fell from my uncle's grasp as a swish of leaves stifled
his cry.

I tried to run, but it was already too late. I found my neck locked in a
vicegrip as a megaphone-wielding Macardle appeared from the undergrowth, flanked by two of his burly henchmen. I watched helplessly as
he stubbed his cigar on a bed of pine needles with the sole of his white
Italian shoe, then slowly approached me, smiling faintly, squeezing the
flesh of my cheek as if inspecting a fattened beast in a squalid market. He
turned from me with disdain.

"Not bad!" he snapped. "He'll do!" before abruptly losing interest in
me and stalking off barking "Action!" into his pathetic trumpet.

I had to avert my gaze, for I could no longer bear to look upon that
gross pantomime of the perverse.

There, before my eyes, were my Birds of Paradise, divested of all but
the most insignificant articles of clothing, howling with glee and rapture
as they cavorted lasciviously on the flattened grass. The bunched, fleshy
fingers of Dingo Deery, like so many pork sausages, caught me just below
the spine as he bellowed, "Go on then—look away, you hypocrite! Pretend you don't see it!" Saliva dripped from his tobacco-stained teeth as
his mocking eyes bit into me. Then he turned to my cowed relative and
snarled, "Louis Lestrange the Peeping Tom! Maybe you could tell us a
little bit about that, Master? How about a lesson on that, eh? Today,
boys, we are doing peeping! Haw haw haw!"

His mirth was unbridled as he continued. "Thought you could get away with it, didn't you? I've been watching you for weeks, spying on us with them binoculars of yours! Oh, yes—I've been watching you, Master Peeping Tom Lestrange, and now, my friend, you are going to pay! You're going to pay for what you did to these—" he paused as the color drained from his face "—these hands." He raised his two hands and displayed for all to see the lesions and contusions which, even after all these years, had not healed, the legacy of so many mathematical and linguistic miscalculations in a chalkdusty schoolroom of the long ago. His head seemed to swell to twice its normal size as all the blood in his body coursed towards it, his two extremities hovering menacingly in front of my uncle's face like two blotched table-tennis bats of flesh.

"I'm sorry," croaked my uncle. "If there's anything I can do to make it up, please tell me!"

But it was too late for any of that. It was clear that no-one could help us now.

We found ourselves bound and gagged and imprisoned in the back of a foul-smelling vehicle which, it instantly became evident to us as we lay there back to back like a nightmarish set of ill-proportioned Siamese twins, had been used in the very recent past for the transportation of poultry.

"Keep them in there until they have manners knocked into them!" I heard Dingo snarl, and the fading jackboot stomp of his Wellington boots was the last sound that came to my ears before I collapsed at last into a dead faint.

As the days passed, our only contact with the outside world was the thin sword of light which shone when the double doors would swing open, a foul-smelling bowl of near-gruel shoved towards us, our only means of sustenance throughout our captivity. How long was it going to go on, that wretched cacophony of sound that assaulted our ear drums daily, like so many aural poison darts, as we sweated in the darkness of our murky dungeon? "Oh my God!" we would hear them shriek in orgiastic delight. "That's great! Keep doing that!" as Macardle's coarse sibilants exhorted those poor, corrupted creatures to indulge themselves to the point of what I knew must be certain destruction. "Come on, girls!" he would cry. "Get stuck in! Put your backs into it!"

In my ears, the sound of bodily fluids intermingling was the roar of some terrible Niagara.

How long we spent in our foul confinement I cannot say. When at last they came to their decision regarding our fate, we were bundled out into the harsh light of day to confront the despicable Macardle, now wearing a white shirt emblazoned with the three lurid rubrics, MAC. A grin flexed itself across his face as he flicked his cigar and stared into my eyes. "Ever done any acting, boy?" he inquired. "No," I croaked, feeling the first faint blush coming to my cheeks, and it was then he raised his hand and slowly opened it to display the photograph of my Uncle Louis, in what has been described as *flagrante delicto*, helpless as he lay in their powdered arms, folded in the delicate wings of my beautiful Birds of Paradise.

"I wonder what the parish priest would make of this?" snickered Macardle, as he secreted the photograph in the inside pocket of his brown leather jacket.

"No, please!" I cried. "Don't send it to the parish priest! Anything but that!"

Macardle coughed and pared the nail of his index finger with his marbled pocket knife.

"And just what's in it for me if I don't?" he quizzed me stonily, his beadlike eyes slowly rising to met mine.

"I'll do anything you say," I said then, resigning myself at last to my fate.

After that, everything is a dream. The nightly agonies of conscience which I suffered, I cannot even begin to chronicle here, for it would be too painful. All I can remember are the sad, hurt eyes of my dear Uncle Louis as the oaken arms of Dingo Deery gripped him once more and hurled him forward with a snort of derision, and the schoolmaster sank once again beneath a flutter of wings and the flying feathers of what once were Gauguin's masterpieces. But etched most of all on my mind is the twisted, salacious expression on the face of Mick Macardle as he distributed a variety of crook-handled canes which he had purchased for a pittance in a London East End market, and with which, through the medium of his barking metal trumpet, he instructed the cast, with unmistakable, lip-trembling glee, to "Bate him harder! Hit him again there, girls! Give him all you've got!"

I hid my eyes as the blows rained down on the reddening flesh of my beloved Uncle, his elderly moons thrust skyward as they continued to yelp excitedly, "This will teach you! You won't be spying on us again in a hurry, you filthy-minded old rascal! Take that!"

The days passed in a black delirium as we were subjected to indignity after indignity; each day another can of eight millimeter film sealed and labeled, just as surely as our fate. Tears come into my eyes as those words return once more, thumbed that day by Deery onto a glinting can: THE SECRETS OF LOUIS LESTRANGE.

I cannot continue. Sometimes I think perhaps it was all a dream, for that was how it appeared when it was all over: the cameras spirited away, the convent reopened, the single tourist gone from the hotel—nothing remaining but the flattened yellow grass and the soft, contented chirp of the chaffinches. I began to think, maybe there had never been a Dingo Deery, a Mick Macardle, a thin mustache?

Would that it were true! I shall never forget the sight of that narrow, mean mouth, the unmistakable smell of cigar smoke that enshrouded me as I felt his hand upon my shoulder: "If you ever breathe a word of this," he hissed into my ear, "the bating Lestrange got will be nothing to what's coming to him!"

I thought of my uncle, his spirit now broken beyond repair, his white-swaddled hands for all the world the blunt stumps of a war veteran as he picked his way sheepishly through the cooling streets.

Oh, yes, Mick Macardle and Dingo Deery existed all right, for in the few days that remained to me in the town, they missed no opportunity to humiliate me, whispering discreetly as they passed close by, "I believe you're a powerful actor, young man!" and "Did you ever try the stage?"

I began to dread these forced intimacies to such a degree that I became a virtual recluse.

The long, hot summer came to an end. Grouse Armstrong met his death in an accident with a Volkswagen Beetle and the only sound to be heard now in The Pronto Grill was that of the proprietor whistling his lonely tune, dreaming of Palermo. Not long after, Mick Macardle opened a supermarket, the very first of its kind in the country, and ever since is to be seen cruising around brashly in his open-topped convertible in streets that are now littered with drug addicts and disco bars. I understand he has entered politics and resides in a magnificent, converted castle on the outskirts of the town, with Dingo Deery resplendent in his blue security uniform by the electronically-surveyed gates, his embroidered extremities now encased in gloves of the softest calf leather.

What bitter injustice there is in this world!

And now in this great city, as beneath my window, the cinema doors open and the hunted, clandestine penumbrae emerge from the subterranean flesh-palace to shuffle homeward like so many tortured specters, I realize at last there is little for me to do now but accept the hand that fate has dealt me. For, having hastily terminated my academic studies and fled the country all those years ago, who am I to complain of a lowly position with Brent County Council? For in truth, they have treated me most fairly, and my supervisor has informed me that the section of Kilburn park for which I am responsible is considered impeccable and utterly leaf-free, and has been singled out for special mention by the visiting inspectors on more than three occasions.

Yes, the old men have long since passed away now, the summer seat taken away and broken up for firewood. To smoke a Players cigarette now is to put oneself in great mortal danger and they say that since Yuri Gagarin returned from space he has become a complete vegetable. But I shall not rest. Deep inside, my quest shall go on, my relentless search for refuge from those terrible memories and the wanton destruction of what was once a beautiful dream.

Which, of course, they shall never know. How would they, those sad, anonymous creatures who shuffle homeward to their waiting, unsuspecting wives, their base desires sated? How are they ever to know that what they have just witnessed on that oblong obscenity they call a screen is the vilest of lies, a distortion, a cruel, ugly trick played by a cheap magician? Would they listen to me if I were to cry out from the very pit of my soul, "THE SECRETS OF LOUIS LESTRANGE! It is lies, my friends! Lies! This is all lies! A pack of despicable, unwarranted lies! Don't believe a word of it!"

No, in my heart I know they would not. So, I have no choice but to go on, with the memory of those days which were once suffused with the color of burnished copper receding within me, nothing more now than a bit player from the last reel of the deserted cinema of life, where a silent, would-be ornithologist, once honored and revered beyond all rustic pedagogues, sits alone in the back row, chuckling to himself without reason as he tries to focus on the past and the way it might have been before a thin mustache, a cruel twist of fate and 1,137 whacks of a crook-handled cane brought an old man and a poor young adolescent boy to within eight lonely millimeters of hell.

R O N A N   S H E E H A N

Telescope

Most nights, after the dining-room was cleared, Patrick took the telescope from the lobby to the roof of the hotel and trained it on the mountain tops, the trees and finally the lake behind the golf course, the pitch-black water. There were canoes there which only guests were supposed to use but since the guests never went to the lake at night the dishwashers and waitresses could relax by paddling about in the dark without much danger of the manager or his wife finding out about it. The forest fringed the northern edge of the lake. Sometimes, at night, bears or foxes could be seen in the undergrowth.

Because he saw so much better this way, he expected to see so much more, so much more than was significant. But he had seen nothing of significance, not yet anyway. Why did he continue with it? he asked himself. Perhaps it was that the glass afforded the illusion of power over the space he surveyed. He could bring things closer to him then make them recede, make them bigger or smaller, as he put the glass to his eye and then put it away again.

Breakfast-time. Mrs Wolfe plodded down the staircase into the lobby and passed the young man at the switchboard whose name she could never remember. There was a long corridor from the lobby to the dining-room and most guests almost ran along it as far as the dining-room door, where they would slow down to make a dignified entrance. Mrs Wolfe knew that her slowness and stiffness were most obvious in the corridor because she, alone of all the guests, could not cover the ground quickly. At least at the point of entrance she did not appear odd or remarkable, because everyone entered slowly. She imagined that sensitive people must consider that it might be better to be even-paced like herself.

Her friend Patrick, the *maître d'hôtel*, was standing as usual at his desk by the door, smiling.

"Good morning, Patrick."

"Good morning, Mrs Wolfe. How do you feel this morning? Did you sleep well?"

"Very well, thank you. I feel fine."

He escorted her to the central aisle among the rows of tables. Mrs Wolfe wished other guests good morning as she passed their tables and they said "good morning" in reply or, when their mouths were full, they raised their cups in salute.

"I think the sun will oblige us today," said Patrick.

"What's that?"

"It's going to be hot today," Patrick pronounced carefully.

"Will it? That's fine!"

"Where would you like to sit this morning?"

"If it's going to be hot I think I would like to sit by the window. May I?"

"Of course! You know I always keep a place for you there."

Mrs Wolfe always sat by the window at the table next to Mr Smith's. She knew that she could have chosen another place if she wished. It was better that she should sit where she did, because she could reach there without walking around another table if she went straight to the centre aisle and turned left. When she walked around other tables she tended to brush against other guests and their children and to lose balance, something which inconvenienced everyone.

Although their conversation followed much the same pattern every breakfast, lunch and dinner, every day, Mrs Wolfe never bored Patrick. Her remarks were spoken with a warmth and sincerity so genuine that he found that his attention was arrested more by her than by any other guest.

At dinner, Mr Smith behaved badly.

"O.K. Patrick, come here. You haven't proved yourself to me yet. Tonight we're going to have a long talk and you're going to try to prove yourself to me. That boy at the desk seems alright. I had a word with him today. But you haven't said anything yet. You're studying philosophy at college, aren't you? Great! We'll philosophize."

He paused for breath. His eyes were glazed, as if he had been drinking too much. At one moment they seemed gay and friendly, the next moment they seemed malicious.

Patrick was uncertain as to how he should respond. His primary concern was to ensure that Mr Smith did not disturb other guests. Perhaps the best way of doing this was to humour him for a while.

"Hello, Mrs Wolfe!' said Mr Smith. "How are you tonight? Getting on alright, eh?"

Mrs Wolfe turned from the window, startled.

"Go on, Patrick. Tell her I was asking for her."

Patrick obeyed. He leaned across Mrs Wolfe's table, putting his mouth close to her ear.

"Excuse me, Mrs Wolfe. Mr Smith says how are you getting on tonight, are you alright?"

"Oh yes," said Mrs Wolfe, her eyes brightening, "I'm fine. I had a lovely day. Thank you so much for enquiring, Mr Smith!"

"Not at all, Mrs Wolfe, not at all. Patrick, you sit down here. What will we have to drink? Where's Jean?"

He snapped his fingers. Patrick winced.

Jean arrived at the table, wine-list under her arm. She looked to Patrick for support. Mr Smith pulled the list from her.

"How are you getting along, Jean?"

Mr Smith inspected the wine-list as he spoke, then stared at her for a reply, cutting across her silent appeal to Patrick.

"I hear you two are hitting it off together all of a sudden, Patrick," said Mr Smith, looking at the wine-list again. "I can see why. She's a real thumper, I'd say. What do you think, Mrs Wolfe?"

Jean stammered something in reply. She knew he was referring to her breasts, which were voluptuous. He made her feel self-conscious about them because he used them against her. Also, she was not "hitting it off" with Patrick—she was going with someone else.

"Are you a real thumper, Jean?" said Mr Smith. "Are you?"

He looked up, leering. He nudged Patrick with his elbow.

"Come on now, Jean. I'm setting a bait for you. Are you going to rise to it? What's the claret like?"

"Very dry."

"Let's have it. You're a vacuum, Jean. Do you know that? I can see why you like her, Patrick. Did you notice that she didn't answer me that time?"

Jean turned and walked away without saying a word. Patrick felt her bewilderment and hurt, her humiliation. These things urged him to answer for her, to avenge her in some way.

"No, she's not a vacuum, you are. Obviously she feels that you're not worth replying to, that's all."

"Patrick, you're a philosopher, right?"

He took a cigarette from his pocket and placed it on the rim of a glass.

"Prove it's a cigarette."

"Why?"

Mr Smith put an arm around Patrick and squeezed him.

"Because you're a philosopher and I want to know the truth."

Patrick knew that the problem was beyond him and that he should change the subject before getting into deeper trouble. But he could not resist the force of Mr Smith's personality.

"Well," Patrick began, "I have an idea in my mind of the genus 'cigarette' to which the particular article here corresponds."

"No! No! What is a cigarette?"

"A cylinder. Say two inches by a half by a third of an inch. It's stuffed with tobacco, wrapped in paper and sometimes has a filter at one end."

"How do you know that's tobacco in there?"

"I know tobacco because I smoke cigarettes."

Mrs Wolfe was smiling. She's lucky, thought Patrick, she can't hear. She can imagine the whole thing as she likes. Jean returned to the table and set the bottle down. Mr Smith ignored her. She left without a word.

"Einstein," said Mr Smith, "would say that you don't know if that's tobacco because you don't know who made the article, you don't know who produced what it contains. In short, you don't know anything about it."

Mr Smith thumped the table triumphantly. Patrick hoped that a submission on his part might achieve some degree of a reconciliation.

"Fair enough," said Patrick. "You've got me there."

"Patrick, you're a fake. You don't know the first thing about logic or argument. You're just ignorant. Now have some more wine."

"And you," said Patrick, "try to shore up your own inadequacies by using the little bit of knowledge and character you do have to insult others."

"You can't hurt me, Patrick, because I've hurt myself so often and so badly that no one can hurt me."

Patrick fell silent. He didn't know what to do.

After dinner he met Jean walking to the lake as the light began to fade. They sat on the sandy patch by the water.

"I know it sounds like a terrible thing to say," said Patrick, "but you'll have to toughen yourself up. It sounds like I'm telling you to become corrupt. But you're good and generous—you trust people. The fact is that when you're like that other people will use you, really hurt you. I hate to say it but it's true. Anyone will tell you the same. Take your face—it's so open!"

"I know. I know. I can't help it."

"Just learn to discriminate. Try to judge which people are for you and which are against you. The ones you can share with and the ones who are on the make. There are people who will take everything from you."

It occurred to Patrick that he might himself be taking something from Jean. He really did want to help her and he felt sure that he was on the right track—but wasn't he effectively trying to persuade her to abandon part of her personality, her gentleness? Yet if he didn't warn her anything could happen to her. . . .

"If you went away more you might learn," Patrick continued, "because you'd meet plenty of tight situations where you'd just have to make up your mind. I think that's the way you could develop."

"I know. Everything is so secure at home, that's why I came here. There's nothing to worry about at home because everyone loves me. Although my mother says I'm a home wolf and an away sheep because sometimes I get really angry. I really do!" Jean's eyes brightened for an instant then, just as quickly, she was crestfallen. "The truth is that I just don't know what to do. I just don't know."

"Look on the bright side," said Patrick. "You still have Michael, don't you? He's a good person and you get on well with him, don't you? I always thought you two looked pretty happy when I saw you together."

"We are. The problem is when I'm on my own. I'm useless when I'm on my own. I have to be with people—sometimes I don't even like who I'm with and I do and say things I don't really want to. I'm just not independent, isn't that what you're saying? I know I'm not."

Darkness fell over the lake, merging shadows, folding up the distinctions between the trees, the shoreline and the water. There in the water, Jean's reflection and his own had disappeared. Their shadows too were gone, part of the general darkness. Patrick lay back and closed his eyes. Satisfaction had eluded him. It was swimming underwater, one of the invisible fish.

He went back to his room and drank himself into a stupor. When he woke he realized that he was going to be late for work, very late. As he rushed through the lobby to the dining-room he heard two guests complaining to the manager. The manager was stalling, refusing to answer their questions directly. His slow, grating drawl followed Patrick along the corridor. In the dining-room the manager's wife was showing guests to their places. Patrick found Mrs Wolfe hovering unattended in the doorway.

"Good morning, Patrick. I was wondering where you were. I'm a little late this morning. Have you kept my place for me?"

"Yes, Mrs Wolfe. I've kept it for you."

He escorted her along the usual route. The manager's wife, her eyes glinting, came half-way across the floor to meet him.

"You're hired to do a job," she hissed. "It starts at seven-thirty, not nine-thirty. Next time you pull something like this on me, you're fired."

Patrick left Mrs Wolfe at her table. He returned to his desk and slumped into the chair. There was a newspaper on his desk. He couldn't read it. It was incomprehensible. In a little while the manager appeared at his side.

"Guests are complaining," the manager said. "The service is bad. I don't think you can do this job. I'm not going to wait much longer for you to get things moving in here."

The manager passed on into the dining-room, greeting guests as he went. Patrick heard him tell Mr Smith a story of Mrs Wolfe's absent-mindedness. They seemed to be deriving some cruel pleasure from considering the old woman's infirmity. It also emerged that they were jealous of Mrs Wolfe's wealth. Her husband was an eminent psychiatrist who abandoned Mrs Wolfe to the hotel for long periods, often failing to make the visits to her which he had promised. Then he would arrive out of the blue, stay a little while and leave at short notice. Since Mrs Wolfe measured time by her husband's movements it was no wonder that her sense of time was askew and that she was absent-minded.

After breakfast Patrick walked in the garden, his hangover swelling in the sunshine. Jean followed him out.

"Something happened," she said. "I don't know whether I should tell you."

"What?"

"It's Mr Smith—he was shouting at me in the corridor last night. He wouldn't let me pass. I only got by when people began to look out of their rooms. I told the manager but he just laughed."

Patrick tried to judge the extent of Jean's upset. He couldn't tell it. She might be terrified or she might be indifferent. He didn't know quite what to say to her.

"I keep remembering what my mother's sister said to me once—'Don't worry, Jean. Take your time. Everything will work out. Don't hurry things.' Do you think she's right?"

It's good advice, Patrick decided. It's calm and sensible and it suits Jean because it presumes a certain benevolence in the outside world. She doesn't have to do anything but hang on. Maybe there is benevolence in the outside world.

"Yes," he said, "I do think she's right."

"I do too in one way, but I'm not sure."

"How do you feel about Smith? Does he worry you? Do you want me to warn him not to go near you again?"

"No. He doesn't really worry me. I think he's just a sick man. I'd say we've seen the worst of him. Anyway you're not going to change him, are you?"

That night Patrick took the telescope to the lake. He couldn't think properly about anything, about Jean or Mrs Wolfe or Mr Smith or the manager and his wife. The sky was bright with stars, the trees cast long shadows over the water. He could hear the grunts of bullfrogs and other mysterious forest sounds which the breeze ushered across the lake. He lay down on his back and trained the glass on the firmament above him.

His mind emptied but his eyes stayed open. Everything that existed was outside—all foreign, all nothing to him. There was no threat from up there, and no promise either. There were shapes and colours, substances. There were no questions to be asked about them. They were there, that was all. He looked up at them through the glass, not knowing when he had started, not knowing when he would stop. They were there, with no beginning and no ending. Shape. Colour. Substance. Space. He felt that he knew these things, certainly. He knew. He felt himself to be superior to them, infinitely stronger than they. Once he felt this he became slowly aware again of his body and the concerns that occupied his mind. When he got up he felt a strange calmness inside himself.

It was almost dawn when he arrived at the shed behind the hotel where the dishwashers lived. They often drank through the night and Patrick knew what their mood would be at this time. He stood in the centre of the floor and took the glass of whisky he was offered.

"It's time to do something," he said. "We're all overworked. They take more guests but no more staff. They won't pay us any more and they haven't even given us the overtime they owe us. It's worse for the girls than it is for you even because they have to take all the complaints from the guests. Anyway, the point is, are we going to put a stop to it or not?"

Everyone joined in the discussion and, although many were very tired if not drunk, the expression they gave to the anger and resentment which they felt was serious. One gave heat to the other until gradually all were engaged. Patrick made certain proposals and left at the height of it, swinging his telescope.

It was breakfast-time when he climbed the stairs to Mr Smith's room. He sensed that he was making an unreal atmosphere, but he didn't care about that. It was his situation—reality was his.

He thumped the door with his fist. He heard Smith mutter as he tumbled out of bed. When the door opened Patrick smashed the telescope across Smith's forehead.

There was confusion in the lobby where the dishwashers thumped the reception desk and shouted at the manager. The manager had lost control. Some guests were demanding refunds and others were clustered together in frightened groups. The girls were relaxing in armchairs. Jean told Patrick that the manager's wife was in the kitchen, washing the dishes herself. Together they tiptoed across the dining-room to glimpse the spectacle through the window in the kitchen door. Patrick couldn't help laughing out loud when he saw her, and Jean did the same.

Mr Smith, head bandaged, suitcase packed, passed Mrs Wolfe in the lobby.

"Are you leaving today?" Mrs Wolfe asked.

"Yes."

"I hope you have a nice time in the future."

"Thank you. Excuse me, but when do you expect your husband?"

Mrs Wolfe did not suspect Mr Smith of cruelty and his dart struck against her innocence as if it were armour, quite harmlessly.

"I do not know," she said. "He comes and goes."

IV

Persona

Persona

A storm was gathering, he could feel it as he drove homeward through the evening city. There was a bitter taste of sulphur in the air, and in the west the sky was blood-stained where the sun had lately fallen. Along the canal the copper beeches stood evil in their vivid stillness, and the water, flowing full and slow, carried on its back a silver metal sheen. At the Four Courts a bent old lady in a black hat stood leaning motionless on her cane and stared intently at the high blind window of a house across the road. Down Winetavern Street a lame dog trotted, sniffing the nervous air, and seven swans were gliding on the river.

The house was silent as he wandered through the empty rooms. Tonight the furniture seemed locked in a new, extraordinary stillness, as though some glimmer of life he had not noticed before had now faded utterly. He sat in the living room and stared at nothing, and into the silence there slipped the sibilant whisper of rain. Light faded from the windows, and the room began to retreat. When the phone rang he started, and gripped the arms of his chair.

A voice came through, scarred and crackling, as though the rain outside were beating and tearing the waves of sound.

—Norman Collins this is God calling you. My child they need you at the theatre. In the pits the lowly populace are muttering darkly and fans are fluttering in the circle. All await your coming. Go forth now my son and fulfil these my wishes.

In spite of himself Norman laughed.

—Mac I can't hear you. Heaven is a long way.

—Can't cod you can I. But listen Norm I'm serious. I mean this is serious. It's late Norman. I've been calling all night and hoping all the time that you were on your way here.

—Mac.

—But you're not on your way are you so what are you doing. As it is we're going to be thirty minutes late. Now I don't like that. The directors like that even less. I mean don't begin to think you're sacred Norman. Bigger men have fallen.

—Mac.

—You can't do this to me Norman. What's the matter with you anyway. I mean you wouldn't want to see me crack now would you. And I don't need to tell you about my nerves.

—Mac.

—Norman please. I'm begging you. Please. Norman. Are you still there Norman. Speak to me.

Norman held the phone loosely at his ear while he gazed down abstractedly into the black pit of the mouthpiece. He said

—It's no use Mac.

—What. Norman. What did you say. Nor—

He placed the receiver gently in its cradle, and heard the voice die. After a moment the little black machine began to howl again. Norman stood up and went away from it.

He let himself out quietly, though there was no one to hear, and on the step he paused to look at the garden. Great glittering arrows were pinning the short grass to the clay, and there was a faint rustling in the lilacs where the rain beat softly on the leaves. Lonely evening weather, stirring the secret pools of memory and sadness. He took the car and drove away from the deserted house.

By the theatre he parked, but did not switch off the ignition. He sat and watched the wipers cut swathes across the windscreen. On the wall beside him the posters gleamed with rain.

Yet another triumph for the brightest talent in Irish theatre. Dazzling. *The Masque of Blackness* marks another giant step in the astronomical career of Mr Norman Collins. Dublin can be grateful for his presence. A colourful, courageous experiment.

His photograph, blown beyond all proportions of life, gazed back at him, a smug light glowing in the smile which somehow he felt had not been there when he sat under the camera. It was not his face, indeed not, but an illustration of what the critics made of him. This year he was fashion, next year perhaps they would ritually slaughter him. Either way it made little difference. If in six months they turned against him then his enemies, and Mac would surely be numbered with them, would have their moment. Never again would they allow him to act in a play under his own direction. He had gone too far too often for them to feel safe with him. No more gambles, no more experiments. Television and radio, and now and then a revue, and there he would wither. Any talent he possessed was immovably based in risk, in gambling against the trends. It was intolerable that he should lose everything now. Intolerable, and yet what he was doing tonight was perhaps the first small step toward destruction. Well, it made little difference. He put the car into gear and drove swiftly away, vaguely conscious of something setting out behind him, a dark implacable pursuer.

While the last light faded, and the rain ceased, he drove out past the limits of the city. The smell of must and decay was replaced as the faint perfume of wet trees and grass sifted into the car.

He stopped at the tall gates and walked up the drive in the darkness. In the ground before him lay pools of water, glittering black, that shivered at his steps. Fire flashed in the far sky. As he neared the house a little breeze came up from the city and sang in the dark trees about him and in the dark grasses. For a moment all the night was singing.

He stood on the black marble of the step and pushed the antique bell, while behind him in the darkness something stirred. Footsteps sounded in the hall, and then light broke out as the door opened.

—Hello Jacob.

—Well by the blessed beard of Jesus but it's Norman. I didn't recognise you. Come in man. Come in. I thought you were a messenger.

He stepped into the bright gold hall hung with mirrors, and Jacob slapped him on the back.

—Well Norman this is grand and unexpected. It must be an awful long time.

—Over a year.

—Christ is it that long. Well well. Look come into the hideout and we'll have a lash of poison.

Norman followed him down the hall past the mirrors with their moving pictures of his striding self. In the kitchen he sat on the table and watched Jacob pour the drinks.

—Now Norman. May the shadow of your prick never grow less. Tell us all the news and leave out nothing salacious.

Norman smiled, and drank, and Jacob grinned at him under his bushy eyebrows. Jacob had not changed, still the vast untidy frame that seemed always on the point of bursting out through the formless clothes. His complexion had progressed a shade nearer to scarlet, but the face was ageless as ever under its unlikely halo of curls. He took a great gulp of whiskey and rubbed his belly, asking

—And how does it feel now to be the child of success.

—You tell me.

—Ah balls. Me—who ever heard of me. Does anybody ever look at them skyscrapers and wonder who put them there. Never. Do I get my name in the papers every second day. Where are all the gorgeous women coming up to me in pubs and making improper suggestions and showing me their little sharp teeth. That's success man. Tell me about it.

Norman said nothing, and Jacob shrugged his shoulders. He finished his drink and poured another, then sat down at the head of the table and lit a cigarette. About them the machines of the kitchen sang an electric song. After a moment Jacob asked

—And how is the family Norman.

—Jo left me. I thought you knew.

Jacob coughed, and took a drink.

—I heard something. What happened.

—I don't know. Everything just fell apart somehow. She didn't like the way I was changing. She started to tell me I was living in a dream world. That I couldn't stop acting even off the stage. But I don't know . . . it seemed to me that I was facing some kind of truth for the first time. Then one night there was a party and I got drunk. I beat the child. I suppose it was the last straw. She left the following day and took the child with her.

—Where is she now.

—In London. With a man I suppose. I hope so. I wouldn't like to think of them alone.

—It's just yourself that's alone eh.

—No. That's why I'm here tonight.

They looked down into their glasses. The form of a smile lay forgotten on Jacob's face. Suddenly he roared

—Ah shit but it's a rotten world. Now is it or is it not.

He looked up, and watching Norman's still face he asked

—What do you feel.

—Nothing. I feel nothing.

—Don't say that Norman.

—It's true.

Jacob went to the cooker. He looked down at the knobs and the little lights, and touched them absently, twisting the glass in his hand. Norman said

—Remember the day I met you Jacob down in Kilrush that day in the pub. The sun on the water and that strange girl singing. You joined her in a chorus and then pinched her bottom and she looked at you so seriously. You talked about America and about despair.

—Did I.

—You laughed so much. I listened to you and I thought this man has something and I covet it. Some secret. You had such force. And in the evening we walked across the fields and you sang a song. Such a strange song. And there was the river and the smell of the sea and a bird flying above us. I could feel you offering that precious thing. Saying have courage.

Jacob had turned away, and was standing now at the sink, looking at the window and the black night pressing against the glass.

—God Norm that was a long time ago. What makes you think of it now.

—Well I needed help then.

—And now.

Norman sighed along the edge of his glass, following the curve with his finger tip.

—Now I seem to have come to the end of something. I seem to have lost the meaning of things. I think that once I was given some fragment or something and out of that I had to construct a—a whole world. But I

must have given up the effort. Does that make any sense. I don't know.
Maybe now I think I'll give up acting.

Jacob laughed.

—Im-possible, he said.

Norman looked across at him. His broad back seemed a wall of
strength that could hold back the darkness at the window, that could
keep at bay the relentless pursuer circling outside.

—Will you tell me something Jacob. A word.

Jacob turned. He put his hand into his pocket and looked at his
drink, considering.

—What do you think of the house, he asked.

—What.

—The house. Since I redesigned it. Jesus did you not notice.

—O the house. Yes. It's very nice.

—I like the stairs. Built it on a ladder motif. Get it.

—Very clever.

—Thanks. Glad you like it. Great man for the enthusiasm.

—I'm sorry Jacob but tonight I can't make conversation.

—Poor Norman is sad and sorry.

—O shit Jacob.

Jacob grinned at him, and he smiled ruefully.

—You know Norman I sometimes think about the old glass boxes I
stick up there and in a way they're like children. Better—they won't
turn around after a few years and kick you in the belly and tell you that
you're nothing but a disgusting old fart. They just stand there and let the
birds of the air shit all over them. But they have their little dignity. Yes.
Old Cohen used to say that all losses are replaced under heaven. I don't
know now but when you get to my age you realize that the world is made
of things.

He lowered his eyes, and smiled, and said again softly

—Things.

Norman rubbed his forehead, and sighed. He asked

—Jacob what are you talking about.

—I'm talking about loss.

—Loss.

—Loss.

—I see. And what kind of loss.

—You can lose things you never had. I'd like to have had a few kids to carry on when I'm gone.

—Jacob I'm still not with you.

—No I suppose not.

Jacob smiling sat again at the head of the table. He pinched his lower lip and nodded slowly, musing over his empty glass. After a moment he murmured

—Loss of the soul.

Norman's legs were swinging over the edge of the table, and when he looked at them they grew still. He laughed nervously, began to say something, stopped and wiped his mouth with the back of his hand. Jacob watched him, and shook his head.

—I'll bet you're sorry you came here tonight, Jacob said lightly.

—I wish you—I wish you Jacob you wouldn't talk like that about soul. The word frightens me.

Jacob crossed the room to put his glass into the sink, but it struck the tap and smashed in his hand with a small sharp ring. He stood quite still and looked at his bleeding fingers, at the glittering shards down in the sink and the worms of whiskey crawling on the enamel. Something happened to his face, and in an instant he was old, tired, and somehow puzzled. He held out his bloodstained hand before him.

—You see it Norman, he asked. The world is made of things. It's all we have. But we cut our fingers and then there's blood.

He turned back to the window, his head bent.

—What is it Jacob.

—When the soul is lost sickness begins. Cohen again.

Norman looked at his hands. They were shaking.

—What kind of sickness.

—O the best there is. The very best.

There were tears on Jacob's face. He came across and laid his hands on Norman's head as though to bless him. He smiled down between his wrists and said

—But I want to die Norman.

—Why.

—I'm tired. You wouldn't understand the—the ease of it.

Norman's voice cracked when he said

—It can't be true Jacob. No I won't believe it.

He stood up from the table, and pushed Jacob's hands away from him. He said

—I'm going now Jacob.

He was at the door when Jacob's voice stopped him.

—I'm sorry Norm old son. I really am. But you know we're all of us on our own in the long run.

Outside the kitchen he stood in the dimness and laid his head against the door. He was trembling. He pushed himself forward and went to the hall. As he was opening the front door he was suddenly conscious of someone watching him. In the partly open door of a room off the hall a small, exquisite child was standing. They were both silent as they looked at each other. Then the child said

—There's something on your hair.

—Is there.

—Yes. It's blood.

—Why do you think it's blood.

The child said nothing more, but stepped back into the room and quietly closed the door, and Norman went out into the night, cold pricking his shoulder blades.

He drove through the night, feeling the darkness press and flow about him on all sides. When he reached his house he swung carelessly into the garage, and in the process tore the flank of the car. He left the engine running and went through the rain to the house. With the door open something came out of the dark hall, a great cold breath of silence from the deserted rooms.

He crossed the garden again, the smell of rain and deathly heat. The storm that had threatened all night was nearer now. At the garage the leaves of lilac brushed against him, and drops of water oiled with sap settled on his hair. He took the car out to the street. Across the road the neon sign of an all-night garage flared once, and died. He drove slowly under the still trees, the silence. Not caring where he went, habit took him toward the river, over the bridge, and he found himself again at the theatre. The last of the patrons were leaving as he went into the foyer. No one looked at him. A few lights still burned inside, and in the corner by the box office a group of stage hands stood in the dimness talking in low voices, hanging on to their cigarettes. He passed them by without a word, and they were silent as he passed. The door of the auditorium opened and McAllister came hurrying out. Norman stopped, and asked

—How did it go Mac.

The producer glanced at him in the shadows and without pausing in his stride he said

—That fucker Collins didn't show. That bastard.

Mac was still talking as he pushed angrily through the doors and disappeared. Norman turned and went into the empty hall. The place was in darkness, but on the stage a dim light burned. He went slowly up the aisle, touching as he went the dusty velvet of the seats.

He stood in the centre of the stage, his hands in his pockets.

—How did it happen Jacob, he murmured. How did it happen. You don't know how much I needed you and you were all I had. You kept me going—did you know that. But you never really knew. Now how can I live.

Echoes came back to him, ghosts sighing from the empty seats.

—Who have I got now Jacob.

Something stirred in the wings, in the darkness. A shadowed figure was there, watching him. He stepped back in terror, and his pursuer stepped back also. He relaxed, and went into the wings, to the great mirror standing there. For a moment he looked at his face dimly reflected, then raised his fist as though to smash the image. But he let fall his hand.

The volume of the rain increased, it pounded on the roof high above him, almost drowning the distant mutter of the thunder.

The Making of a Bureaucrat

I'm going to tell you the story of Frederick. In a way, I know, this is a kind of betrayal, but what do people like Frederick exist for if not to be betrayed by people like me? If it comes to that, I have betrayed him already by everything I am and do.

At least, Frederick, I'm writing this with my left hand. It's late and I'm sitting here in my study, the documents for tomorrow's meetings carefully prepared and annotated. Elsewhere in the apartment, my wife and children are asleep. And I'm sitting here like one of those Chinese bureaucrats a thousand years ago, writing their poems of exile and farewell with their left hands. I know, as you knew, Frederick, that we're living a posthumous existence, the last, miserable, self-deluded days of a civilization that deserves to die but can't. And yet each morning I go to my office and make decisions, evolve policies, as if it were the early days of an Empire, one that will last a year, ten years, a thousand years.

It all came back to me with a rush tonight at the party at the Commission to celebrate Spain's entry into the Community. The place was full of Spaniards rushing around, short, dark-eyed, lit up like children let loose in a playground, full of enthusiasm and energy. Fuelled by lakes of wine, and mussels in a peppery sauce, the noise level rose and once again Spanish filled my mouth and ears. I felt indescribably happy and beamed stupidly on everyone. What was it Charles V said? I speak French to men, Italian to women, German to the horses, and Spanish to God. There is a beautiful Spanish word, *desengano*, that is to say, disillusion, the malaise that afflicted Spain after the fall of its Empire. But *desengano* was the seed of Don Quixote's innocence, and only those who have known *desengano* can embrace illusion as the Spanish do. To have illusions is a blessed state, and it was during my years in Spain that I became illusioned. And of those years, Frederick is the presiding genius.

I will introduce you to Frederick as I first met him. It was one of those nights you get in Barcelona in July, when you can't move without sending rivers of sweat streaming out of your pores. I was tired after an evening's teaching, but I didn't feel like staying in. I showered, put on a dry shirt, picked up an *International Herald Tribune* one of my flatmates had left lying around and went to a bar around the corner from my flat. It was a fairly typical bar for the area I lived in. It only opened at night, serving an exclusively younger clientele, with loud rock music and over-priced beer. I was sitting up at the bar, drinking a bottle of iced San Miguel, reading the *Tribune*, when the paper was rudely wrenched from my hands. I found myself staring into a pair of mad blue eyes six inches away from mine, a face looming huge as in a dream. It occurred to me that the owner of the head must have climbed up on the bar.

"Why are you reading that shit newspaper? You're here with other people. Talk, Englishman, talk!"

The accent was foreign, but not Spanish. I guessed correctly that it was German. I moved my head slightly so that I could see Jordi, the owner of the bar, on his stool at the other end. He nodded at me and smiled-shrugged. Obviously, this maniac was not dangerous. I relaxed.

"What do you want to talk about?" I asked.

"Whuuuh! Whuuuh! These English, they are so cool, UUUH!"

Frederick sprang, bellowing, from the bar and started prancing around, almost banging off the walls. I could see now that he was a big man, tall and squarely-built, dressed completely in black, with black hair and a large, heavy-jawed head. All the bar's patrons treated him with amused familiarity. I knew some of them: Luisa, the fat Argentinean refugee, Merce, the actress who lived down the street, and with whom I had slept once. Around the space invaders machine there was a little group of skinny, long-haired youths, in jeans, sneakers, and coloured cotton shirts. They spent every evening huddled around the machines, or theatrically cradling the telephone, suddenly speeding off on their mopeds to the outer suburbs, on urgent errands.

Frederick bounced back to the stool beside me.

"You! Who are you and what are you doing here?" So I told him, at least to the best of my knowledge. About Frederick and who he was, it would take me a lot longer to figure out. That first evening in Jordi's bar, I learned a few things. He was about forty years old, seemed to have been here a few years. From his English it was possible to deduce a hippy-era past, not to mention the frequent references to events that had taken place in Nepal and Kabul, Marrakesh and San Francisco. He had even spent some time in Galway in the early seventies. But Frederick didn't just talk about his experiences, fascinating as they were. His soundtrack alone would be meaningless: his whole being was a dazzling performance of words, gestures and sheer presence. He dominated every space and every company, even on the street. Part of his technique was the massive attention he focussed on everything and everybody. Once, I was quietly discussing something with him, or at least as quietly as was possible with Frederick, when I made a casual remark about the song playing on the sound system. He jumped up onto the bar with a whoop and pressed an ear against a speaker.

"Listen!" he said, "Listen!" like a poem of Rilke's come alive. And everybody listened, compelled by some tone in his voice, some secret of gesture. I teased him about this air of command, attributing it to his Prussian ancestry. Thus my name for him: Frederick the Great. He was called Andrei. Or rather, as I later found out, this was what he called himself.

I didn't see Frederick all that often. I preferred the demotic bars down near the harbour and only went to Jordi's if I was at a loose end, without the energy or inclination to descend into the cauldron of the city. But every time I met him, we seemed to resume a conversation that had just been broken off. He radiated such sweated intensity that everything else was burnt away like dross, and we could only talk about the big things. As soon as I got used to his hippy dialect, I realised he had read everything, and thought about it.

"Kierkegaard, that Danish shit, man. You know what you do when you read Kierkegaard? You do the same things, but now you're saved! Bullshit! I wipe my ass with it."

Certain words set him off. If someone said the word *politician* he would leap up and grab the word, repeating it slowly, with minute changes of tone accompanied by a pantomime of facial expressions and bodily gestures, suggestive of anal-retentive, wholesome sex, compulsive liar, bumbling stupidity, which had the whole bar in raptures. He could repeat a litany of words like *money, freedom, country, love* and make it seem like the most subtle Czech cabaret. It reminded me of people you can sometimes come across in pubs in Ireland, men who with a little alcohol can make you feel you are in the presence of genius, who can create pieces of performance art which exist only in the sensations of the moment. An art of spontaneity, contemptuous of the bad faith implicit in thinking beyond the moment. In short, Frederick was the first real existentialist hero I had ever met, outside the pages of fiction. He seemed to me a man totally without illusions. Sure, I had had those kinds of conversations with my fellow students years before, but that had been a game, I knew they would end up, despite their professed nihilism, as TV producers and lawyers. With Frederick it was real, and I couldn't but be impressed.

Maybe I was just very impressionable that summer. All that time, in my mind, is tinged with the acrid, sweet taste of hashish or *chocolate*, as the Spanish quaintly called it. Green and resinous, it was brought across the narrow straits from Morocco. I smoked large quantities of it, almost every night. Not for pleasure, because it was not particularly pleasurable, nor oblivion, because it didn't provide it. I like to think now that I was using it medicinally, as cancer patients use it to treat the side effects of radiation treatment. Because that's what I was really doing in Spain: I was exposing myself to another sun, burning away the cancer I was born with, drying out the old damp in my bones. I was using it the way men in the suburbs of my youth used alcohol: as a weapon, as a defense, something to make you pliable so that you wouldn't break. And it helped.

So I usually saw Frederick as we smoked hash in the back of Jordi's bar. Jordi, a plump, affable Catalan, seemed to have adopted Frederick as a brother. Sometimes Frederick would engage in strange, shouted conversations with the youths around the space invaders. Strange because he didn't speak much Spanish, and they, hatched in the dark Francoist womb, didn't speak any English. But they managed to communicate. Frederick would occasionally vanish with them into the night, roaring, his huge frame perched grotesquely on the back of one of the mopeds.

Of course, there was something mysterious about these errands, but I was slow to realise this. One night however, I went into the bar and found no Frederick. I was the only customer. One of the youths arrived on his moped. He came in, nodded to me and started talking to Jordi, who was, as usual, semicomatose on his stool behind the bar. I could barely hear their conversation and wasn't really listening until I heard the word *Aleman*. I paid attention then, but they seemed to be talking about a horse, of all things. After the youth had left, I made some kind of jocular remark about horses to Jordi, as a conversational opener. But he gave me a strange look and didn't say anything. I forgot the incident, until a few days later I was discussing slang with a group of my students. We talked about the slang words for various drugs, and one of them came up with caballo, that is, horse, that is, heroin. I almost laughed at the curious, if typical linguistic jump. But it figured. Of course Frederick was a junkie. But rather than feel sorry for him, I felt vaguely angry, betrayed even.

I consciously avoided the bar for a few weeks after this, but one night I found myself sitting there again. I had just tasted my first San Miguel when Frederick thundered in, a *Blaue Reiter* astride a white horse. As we sat together and talked, the thought uppermost in my mind was that I was sitting beside a man who was slowly killing himself. It was worse than that: he had failed me, had not lived up to the role I had assigned him of the hero without illusions, the man without qualities, unafraid to face the nihilism the rest of us toyed with. He had everything—he was handsome, healthy, intelligent, had an undisclosed and seemingly unlimited source of money, the talent, genius even, to dominate any company he chose—and he chose to sit in a bar in a back street of Barcelona, and die. And absurdly, I found myself trying to talk him out of it. We had a consensus that the workaday world of money, business, politics, success was a crock of shit—but surely there were other things worth living for? What about art? That's how we got around to Joseph Beuys. I admired his work greatly, and Frederick reminded me somehow of him. There was the same kind of energy, the same presence. All he had to do was apply it. But it was hopeless:

"Beuys, sure, it's okay. But in the end it's the same shit. Big professor at the art school, guru of bullshit. Money, money. You know, if he's really so good, why is he so famous?"

I got the point. We had once had a similar conversation about Beckett. But I had sensed a kind of emotional shadow to Frederick's words. Obviously, this had been a temptation along the way. But our conversation was interrupted. Frederick was down on all fours on the floor of the bar, giving a condensed rendition of Beuys's Coyote performance in New York, with Frederick taking the role of the coyote. Ten minutes later, I managed to resume the conversation.

"Why don't you write something?" I asked. Frederick grew almost thoughtful before replying:

"Write, yes . . . you know, if I am going to write something—" and here he sat up ramrod straight on his bar stool—"I do it like this." And he moved his left hand in the gesture of careless writing, casting a hasty, haughty glance at it now and again, as he focussed his attention on his right hand, which was frantically performing a charade of daily life: "Like this, you see? While with the other hand I am eating or fucking or drinking a beer. You see?"

I did see, and I couldn't disagree. I fell silent, as there didn't seem to be much left to say. Frederick's left-handed story was all very well, but what if your right hand was concentrated on sticking a needle into your veins?

Without making any conscious decision, I didn't see Frederick much after this. In fact, I never saw him again. But it was only later that his story, for me, would really begin.

A few months after my last conversation with Frederick, it was Carnival time in Barcelona, as it was all over the Mediterranean. The small streets of the Barrio Gotco were crammed with people dressed in outrageous costumes, and I was no different, my face painted with black and silver greasepaint. In a bar I met a German girl who had a beautiful design of diagonal red stripes painted on her face, arms and breasts. I recognised it from that famous book on body art which spawned a million bad paintings in those years. I told her this and she made a *moue*. She had, of course, copied it from the book. She was an art student, or rather an ex-art student from Dusseldorf. She had left the boring academy to come in search of real life. I had met her type before, the gilded youth of a northern land sojourning in southern squalor. Under the greasepaint, her skin and teeth, her build, told their own story, as much as the semi-derelict studio in the Barrio Chino stuffed with expensive video equipment. The conversation got around to mutual acquaintances. Somehow, I mentioned Frederick, or rather, Andrei. She grimaced:

"Oh you mean . . . Do you not know who he is?"

Frederick, it seems, had gone to school with her brother. A wild man, she had heard much about him. He was the son of a war criminal, a man who had killed enough innocent people to have his name lodged forever in human memory. By this stage, I was so drunk and stoned and caught up in the general frenzy of the night that it hardly registered, it was just one more colourful, grotesque detail of a night in which everything was possible.

It came back to me with a shock as I woke hours later, lying beside her sleeping body. We looked bizarre, our faces still painted in masks, our pale bodies smeared with random streaks of colour, like a map of our love-making. Through the thin walls I heard people coming awake, muttering in the yellow-brown light. So that was Frederick's story. I tried to make sense of it. In our times, the sins of the father are not visited upon the son. And yet, I saw how huge tracts of the world must have been laid waste for him. He could go nowhere without dragging his father with him, do nothing, because to merely exist was in a way to justify his father's cursed existence. The will to self-destruct, to simply not be and in doing so deny not only yourself but the father must have been irresistible to him.

I got up and got dressed, and left as she still slept. I went down the stairs to the street. The debris of the night before was everywhere, beer bottles, coloured papers, the flags suspended between the buildings. A few people were already up and about, scurrying to work. It was starting to rain. In need of some comforting, I went into a place on the Ramblas that opened early, serving fresh *churros* with hot chocolate. As I was eating, a whore came in, a thin, very dark girl with narrow hips.

"The blessing of God on all here!" she sang out as she entered, in her musical Andalusian accent, without a trace of irony.

When I had finished my hot chocolate I walked up the Ramblas and on to the Paseo de Gracia. At the top, there was a huge statue, with its arm raised in a fascist salute, commemorating the victory of the forces of darkness. But now, someone had draped it completely in white cloth, so that it looked like a work by Christo. Its shape under the cloth was benign, the arm could have been raised in benediction.

E A M O N N   S W E E N E Y

Lord McDonald

My name is Michael Coleman and they say I am the finest fiddler that ever lived. They say I put a twist to a tune. I have never been sure of where the twist comes from. I play that way because it is the only way I know. I play because I have to. I do not know where it comes from or what it is going towards.

My home is a small room in the South Bronx. In New York where sometimes it is difficult to see the sky for the skyscrapers. I can't make head nor tail of it. Two of my young nieces landed here last week. They were passing through on their way to look for work. We tried to talk about home but I could not, nor about here either. I took down the fiddle and played a couple of tunes and then there was no gap between me and them or The Bronx or Killavil where I was born and where all the people would fit into one floor of that tenement block across the street. That I have carried around with me all my life.

I could talk to you forever and still say less than the first few bars of "Lord McDonald."

A calm, bright Summer's evening. I got the fiddle out of the pawn once again. Times turned hard years ago. Maybe the boy upstairs is paying us back for the days we were paid a working man's weekly wage for half a morning in the studio. You couldn't have luck.

A cop from some place in the arse-end of Monaghan had hired me to play at his daughter's birthday party. A well-off man who was reputed to be an honest enough one. I spent the week before drinking on the strength of his honesty. A lot of money had been mentioned. It was a short walk in good weather.

The same man had done well for himself. He lived just outside The Bronx in an area where even the sidewalks looked as if someone had got down on their hands and knees and scrubbed them. In a brown stone house with a flight of wide grey steps leading up to it. There was an unsettled feeling in my stomach when I walked up those stone steps, the same anxious feeling I always have before I start to play.

Some nights I sit up and play and then I notice it has got bright in the street outside. Then I find my face is all wet and my jacket is soaked with tears. "Lord McDonald."

I knocked at the door and a beautiful young woman in a blue dress opened it. She looked at me with a face full of puzzlement. There were patches on both elbows of my jacket. There was nothing said for a while.

"I'm Michael Coleman the fiddler, I'm here to play at the birthday party."

The girl still said nothing only looked me up and down for a few more moments. Then she turned on her heel and ran back into the house. It was a quiet house with not a speck of dirt in the hall.

I saw Fritz Kreisler play Carnegie Hall a couple of months back. Wouldn't it be mighty to land back to Gurteen with him? They'd hear some fiddle playing then. And so would he. The like of Fritz have the good life. They didn't sell their music for a couple of dollars back when things were going well. James Gannon, God bless him, knew a lot about music but he never heard of the word *royalties*. He taught me to play "The Boys of the Lough."

I still remember the face of that cop. It was the face of a man who'd take terrible offence if you weren't enjoying yourself enough at his father's wake. A big man, more than six foot tall and still the colour of a man who had spent many a long summer in meitheals. He had the broad hands too with short thick fingers. And a good suit and expensive shoes that squeaked across the lino.

He had more of the American accent than he should have had by rights. I could never manage that trick though I'm not sure as to whether it was much loss.

The cop charged across the lino and tried to catch me by the throat. I sidestepped him and he dropped his hands to his side. The right hand was clenching and unclenching and his left thumb was rubbing against the palm of it. There was no sound in the neat and tidy evening street. He was so angry that his tongue was clashing with his teeth as he spoke.

"Well, Mickeen Coleman, the great fiddler. You have some cheek to show your face here."

I didn't know what was vexing bucky at all.

"My daughter's birthday was this day last week. I had a hundred and fifty people waiting for you. God dammit, where were you?"

It's a whore when you start making those sort of mistakes. It was money I could have done with.

"Well, Coleman, where were you?"

"I made a mistake. I thought it was today I was supposed to be here."

He banged his hand off the jamb of the door. The man was nearly dancing with temper. There were a pair of young women standing in the hall behind him now. They were laughing at his carry-on. It was like prodding an old cross bull with a bit of a short stick.

"I'll tell you why you weren't here, Mickeen, because you were falling drunk around the South Bronx somewhere. I got plenty of warnings about you but I didn't take them, fool that I am. You and your pals are some advertisement for us, drinking and fighting and bringing everyone else's name down in front of the Yanks. Ye think ye're something but ye're nothing."

"I never let on to be an advertisement for anyone only meself."

"With all yer big names, did any of ye ever do enough for a house like this or for a good name, did ye, did ye?"

On about the second "did ye" he struck me into the chest with his right fist and sent me tumbling the wildcat down the steps. I was on my feet before I hit the bottom one. I was always able to land on my feet. When I was a young lad I used to go flying off the ladder in the hayshed and put the heart crossways in them at home. But there was never a loss on me.

I didn't say anything to the cop. I never even saluted him. It was a grand evening. There wasn't enough wind to move grass. I just walked off with the fiddle stuck under my oxter. Safe.

————

It cost people a lot more than their money for the passage when they came over here. The cop wasn't the worst of them. A lot of them wouldn't let you near their house to throw you off the steps. They'd be embarrassed to hear "The Sligo Maid" or "The Kerryman's Daughter." The same people even tried to destroy their accent, whittling bits off it like a man trying to shape a block of wood into something unrecognisable from the original.

There was always a place for us once. At home. A place for those who made others dance. There was food for them and drink for them and company for them. And time for them.

Maybe people don't want to be reminded about what they came from. Because they're scared they haven't moved as far away from it as they think they have.

The fiddle was in pawn again. I was in a saloon. A quiet saloon. Drinking whiskey. I learned to drink at house dances where you'd accidentally break a string if the liquor wasn't landing quick enough. I took my whiskey with laughter and company then. Now I like to drink on my own. In my own company. The drink only makes me feel middlin' these days. Still, middlin' in bad times is good.

The twist. That's what they say I have, what I put into a tune that the others can't. You can't try to put the twist into your playing, it has to be part of it. Some days I think I know what the twist is but I can never catch it because it is caught up in me.

It is what I am. The drinking, the way I could never settle, the blackness I see in front of me some days, the dreams I have in the night. All there on pieces of shellac. Whatever it was that was astray in me leaked out through my fingers and they heard it as the twist.

And sometimes I think I have nothing to do with it at all. When they sold the first 78s I saw men and women dancing and laughing and crying at the same time. At my playing. I am a farmer's son from Killavil. How could it be me that did that? Maybe the fiddle wasn't the instrument at all.

I heard there was men at home who wouldn't eat for a couple of days so they could buy those records. Men who knew me and did that! We had to come to America to record this music from Sligo to be sent back to Sligo for people there to buy even though we'll never see Sligo again. This world isn't half settled, so it's not.

I was never too mad for work. That was well known around the place
at home. All I wanted to do was walk the countryside and play music.
Some men will kill for land, others will die for a woman, I lived for reels
and mazurkas, hornpipes and highlands, polkas and jigs.

Everything else on the face of this earth was forgotten when I picked
up a fiddle. The coldness of the city meant nothing to me when I was
playing well. If I could hear the twist it meant the life I was living was all
right for me.

It's a lonely sway home between pavement and gutter when you run
out of money for drink. This emigration crack is no good for you, so it's
not. You'll always look back at the place you came from and think it was
better. But once you've left your home place at all, then you can never
get rightly back into it.

I was only back in Killavil from London when I came to the States.
Big cars and neon signs, Prohibition and cigars, Vaudeville and dollars.
You couldn't be right in it unless you were born in it. And even then.

We started with an innocent life like we were being broken in gently.
Walking home from dances across dewy fields in Monasteraden, looking
at geese on Lough Gara, playing a tune across the lake in the early morning with no other sound in the clear cold air.

But it was a false life. False because it wasn't right to let people live a
life like that unless they were going to be allowed to stay in it. It wasn't
the right life for people who were already marked to go someplace else. It
didn't do much to leave any of us ready for The Bronx or Camden Town,
South Boston or Moss Side.

There was bitterness and jealousy and poverty at home. And spite.
There's no denying that. But what ever deserved a slow death from a
dripping wound?

Emigration was a big Coney Island carnival too sometimes. But I
looked out at people's faces when they'd hear the names of tunes, "The
Keash Jig," "Famous Ballymote," "The Boys of Ballisodare," "The Plains
of Boyle," and I'd know.

The night the cop threw me down the steps I called to Seamus Anderson's house. Seamus the piper. I was full of whiskey but I knew he had a
fiddle in the house. I wanted to sit up and play music all night. To turn
from "The Longford Collector" into "The Sailor's Bonnet." I needed to

feel that moment in the back of my head I would know I was there. And
then it would disappear before I could catch it and I would have to try
and create it again.

The piper owned a good saloon. Another good house in a good
neighbourhood. I was hitting off garden gates when I hadn't one foot in
the gutter. But I could hear a tune in my head that would cure me if I was
only let play it. I never played a tune badly in my life. The drink would
change around everything in my head but I would still play the same as
ever. The twist would always be there.

I rapped on Seamus Anderson's door. There was light inside but there
was no answer. There were plenty of voices. A light flicked on in the hall
so I tried to concentrate and look sober. Seamus was a religious man
with an awful set on drink though that didn't stop him selling it.

I held my breath and tried to force my eyes to look in the one place at
the one time. All it did was make me dizzy. I fell against the door. A
woman's voice shouting.

"Who's that at this hour of the night?"

"Michael Coleman, tell Seamus Michael Coleman is here to play a
tune, to play 'Lord McDonald,' Michael Coleman is landed, up Sligo!"

"Wait there," she said, and walked away back into the house. I knew
that if I didn't get into the light something woeful was going to happen.
There was a fierce racket inside. It seemed a long while before she came
back.

"Seamus Anderson isn't home tonight, he's out of town."

He had been out of town the last five times I'd landed to the house.
Still, he was a busy man. A businessman. I was still dizzy so I leaned
against the door and hoped that the black ripples in front of my eyes
would disappear. I could hear a man's voice within in the hall.

"Is Coleman gone? That fella is the greatest tyrant when he has
drink."

The voice could have been Seamus Anderson's but I was not certain.
I hammered on the door and shouted for them to let me in. There was
another voice. A harsher, mocking one. Like a circus barker's.

"Get outta here, go on, get outta here, lift them and they'll fall themselves."

In an alley. Me and a rake of bins that were mostly knocked on the ground with their insides spilling round them. And a good few rats. You'll always know rats because they'll sit up and look you straight in the eye to let you know that that's how much heed they have on you. I thought these were real rats, not my rats. "Lord McDonald."

There was a cop walking towards me. I realised my nose had been pumping blood for a while and the front of my jacket was covered in it. The cop was cautiously tapping his night stick against the palm of his left hand, walking towards me in slow, stalking paces. I stepped out from the wall. Into the light.

"Officer, I was only having a rest."

They take drunks down to the station and beat them unconscious. With night sticks. Sometimes they kill them for the crack.

"Jeez, it's Michael Coleman, Michael Coleman, you're the great fiddle player. We've got a whole heap of your 78s at home. What are you doing here?"

"If I knew that, I wouldn't have to drink."

He smiled and steadied me on my feet.

"Good luck, Mr. Coleman. It's good to meet you. You're some bucket of paste when you're poured."

And he walked off. Good Irish. The rats were still there so they were real rats. Not my rats. The night was lovely and warm and there was nothing to be afraid of.

The drink is like music. How can you explain it to someone who has not fallen in love with it? How it floods your head and pushes the blood three times faster through your veins. The blessed moment of the first one the morning after when it starts to clear away the fear and anxiety it put there the night before. Drink makes the world a place of certainty. In every way.

I remember the day I played "Lord McDonald." I sat in a small studio in the South Bronx at noon. Pulled the bow across the strings for a couple of minutes and then it started. I played it through just once and I could feel it pulsing through me. Something. Every second of it was like an hour and the notes were coming from a place so far back in myself I could hardly stand it. I followed the music, chased the music with colours going through my mind and Killavil and my dead brother and the men who taught me to play and the end of all this and the twist in myself and green and brown. It was bringing me somewhere and I finally got there.

I walked away from the microphone when I finished and the two men from the record company walked out into the street after me. One of them pulled a massive roll of dollar bills with a thick brown elastic band around it from the deep pocket of a wide pin-striped trousers.

"A couple of hundred dollars, Michael, for a special performance. No-one ever heard anything like that before. Aw, Jesus."

The sun was shining like it does in New York in the Summer. The rest of the musicians were all sitting in The Tub of Blood, talking about work and spending the money they didn't know they'd never see the likes of again.

I tried to explain what had happened. My hand was shaking and the beer was dribbling into the sawdust on the floor. A ray of sun was piercing through the dark glass of the front window. A blue coloured ray with dust swirling suspended in it. I had got there. I look at my fingers and said that there would be so many more tunes that I would play like this.

But it never came again. Not that way. Just that one day before The Crash for me. "Lord McDonald." My name is Michael Coleman and they say I am the finest fiddler that ever lived.

A Sense of Humour

She sat at the kitchen table and stared out the window to the backyard, where the rain splashed down on the dull metal of the Guinness kegs and spilled into the used beer bottles stacked open mouthed in plastic crates. She was waiting for her father to be finished his breakfast. Without looking up from his newspaper that stood propped against the milk carton, he pushed his cup towards her: "Is there any more in the pot?" he asked, and she filled his cup to the brim, carelessly so that the tea sloshed over into the saucer. It seemed to her that she would always be waiting—waiting for summer or for winter; when the days would be short or fine, waiting for the children to come home from school, waiting for them to grow up, waiting for her parents to grow old; waiting for freedom, for the day when there would be no one left to make her feel guilty.

Her father lifted his tea and she watched him swill the milky liquid round the mug in a slow circular movement, as he always did, before sucking it noisily into his throat. Their neighbor, Maurice Kennedy, was to be buried that morning and he had a few minutes to spare before leaving for the church. Her mother had tried to hurry him over an hour ago coming through the kitchen on her way out, wearing her red woollen coat and the patterned scarf Breda had sent from Medjugorge. "Mind you keep an eye on the clock, John, or you'll be the last in." She paused at the mirror to settle her hair, patting it nervously with a gloved hand, setting loose a waft of scent that drifted back across the room: the *Madame Rochas* that she kept for holidays, weddings and funerals.

"Will you look after things so, Kate?" She glanced quickly about the room, her gaze resting for a moment on the children's toys scattered over the floor: a colouring book, paintbrushes and crayons, a one legged doll sprawled against the table rung. Kate did not turn to answer her mother. She did not want to see the remote, pained expression that came into her face whenever her attention was drawn to the children.

"Robbie Spillane is in the bar this long time," her mother called back as she pulled the door shut behind her.

It was Robbie she had hoped Kate would marry; Jim Spillane's son who farmed a hundred acres or more, Robbie who was single yet, though he could have any girl in the parish for the asking. But Kate had chosen someone else—she had married Liam Lynch who worked in Keynes garage in the town, and so was it anyone's fault but her own that things had worked out as they had?

"Well, I'd best be off if I'm going to get there at all," her father stood up heavily, pushing his chair out from the table, lifting his jacket slowly from the back of it. Would Liam come to this, she wondered, in another twenty years—the pale, bloodshot eyes, the tremor in the speech. Her father did everything cautiously these days; with deliberate effort. Standing by the door in his Sunday suit he looked cramped and foolish; keeping his head lowered, not wanting to be noticed; the raw skin of his wrists, his great hands jutting awkwardly from the smooth serge cuffs.

She began to clear his dishes from the table, carrying them one by one to the sink. She was glad when she heard the latch fall behind him. It was an ease to be alone, out of reach of people's voices, of her mother's gaze. Though she did not know why she should still care what her mother thought or said. She told herself that her mother was an old woman, set in her ways—a woman who had always known hardship and had learned only to bear it without complaint. But from childhood she had been controlled by her mother's face; by her eyes that turned away from you with an expression of injury and surprise that made you feel, whatever it was you had done, it was something else she had wanted. You could not argue with it. To understand you could only watch and listen very closely; listening especially to the things she would not say and to the small unimportant affairs that she made much of. She had never cared for Liam, though she would not say so. And perhaps it was for the reason Kate had gone out with him in the first place, goaded by her look of silent disappointment.

"Mammy, Deirdre has taken my paints."

Her youngest daughter, Maireid, was standing in the doorway, her pale cheeks mottled by tears. She pulled a strand of her corn coloured hair to her wet mouth:

"Robbie told her to give it back to me, but she won't."

Robbie. Kate had forgotten him. He would be inside waiting still. She did not want to see him, not this morning. She had not the energy for making herself pleasant. She had hoped to get the laundry done while her parents were out. That way she would have a little time to her-self in the afternoon. She dried her hands on the back door towel:

"Didn't I tell you not to leave your toys all over the room, Maireid," she said, "you know how it annoys your granny." She walked out of the kitchen and through the small back sitting room that led to the bar. Maireid came skipping along after her, her shoes slipping on the pol-ished linoleum.

The saloon bar was a long narrow room; a concrete extension built onto the main house ten years ago when there was still profit in the bar trade. Her mother had expected great things from it. She had wanted to attract tourists and the young men who had made money from salmon fishing and from work on the building sites in England. But that was in the boom time of the early seventies. Things had changed. It was only the old men who came now—the old and those who had no work. The young had emigrated for good and the visitors, such as they were, pre-ferred the new resort hotel at the strand. But empty or crowded Kate hated the place. She hated the smell that always hung in the air of stale cigarette smoke and the odour from damp clothes. She hated the bare, beige coloured walls and the light that shone from two fluorescent bars on the ceiling. She disliked most all of their customers; the men who came every day whether they had money in their pockets or not. The idle and the shiftless who sat at the Formica covered tables or leaned against the bar drinking until they were stupid with it and could no longer remember why it was they were here and not in their own homes. Customers who knew well that her father had never been heard to refuse anyone a drink. A decent man, as they all said of him.

Robbie sat at the bar drinking a pint of stout. He was a black haired, heavy set man with lazy, good-humoured eyes.

"How are you Kate, you didn't go to the funeral so?"

Kate went behind the counter and lifted down a couple of glasses.

"No," she said, "Maireid is coming down with a dose of flu. I thought it was best to keep her home. And did you hear Deirdre fell off the bike yesterday on her way from school."

Robbie took a mouthful of stout and gave a low snort of laughter that made his shoulders shake:

"Is that so—by God it seems you're lucky to have them in one piece."

He always laughed in this way as though her troubles were a comfort to him, making her feel for a moment that there was not so much wrong with the world. She set another glass under the tap for him. Maybe her mother had been right after all. Maybe she should have married him. A farmer's wife she would have been. She could have kept hens and a few goats. She would have liked that well enough. She could have had a little money of her own. She looked at his mild blue eyes and tried to imagine them distorted by anger. She could not. But then who would believe it of Liam? Even her mother who never approved of him would not accept the picture she painted. Two sides to every story, was all she would say. Kate looked at his big, square hands closed around the belly of his glass. Was there anything you could tell from a face? Who knew what a man was like at his own fireside?

"There's a session at Grogan's tonight Kate, it should be good crack."

She took a box of peanuts from the floor and pulled open the cardboard lid. Let him go to Grogan's she thought. There was nothing stopping him. It had nothing to do with her anyway. She glanced over at the girls who were playing under a blanket beside the Kosangas heater, squirming about under cover, tickling each other's feet, giggling with pleasure. How easy it was for children to make up; they moved from grief to joy as quickly as clouds blown from the sun. No time but the present was real to them. Maireid was four and Deirdre six. It would be another ten years before Kate would be free to do as she pleased. Robbie set a five pound note on the counter:

"Will you have one with me, Kate?"

"No thanks, Robbie, not now."

The peanut packets were attached in rows of four to a sheet of cardboard. She took one from the box and stuck it with a drawing pin to the wall beside the till. What was the point of it, she thought, of his coming here day after day staring at her with his big soft eyes as though there was an understanding between them? What understanding could there be? He might smile as much as he liked—it changed nothing. She was a married woman and would be for the rest of her life if she were never to set eyes on Liam again. She took the note Robbie had given her and putting it into the till slammed the door shut.

"Maireid—Deirdre," she called, "will you go inside and clear up the kitchen before Granny gets home." Seeing their startled faces as they pushed the blankets from their heads, she felt contrite and softened her tone:

"Robbie will you look after yourself," she said, "I'll be inside if you want me."

In the kitchen she began sorting the clothes for the washing machine. She lifted them from the yellow plastic laundry basket and divided them according to fabric and colour, setting them in bundles at her feet. With so many things needing to be done separately it hardly seemed worth using the machine. She carried a pair of blue jeans to the sink and held them under the cold tap to rinse out a blood stain. She watched the foaming soap run red and trickle over her hands into the basin. Fifteen years of this behind her and maybe another fifteen to go. Where did her body find the energy for this ceaseless activity? Month after month purging and renewing itself, cell by cell. And for what? What use had she now for the whole process? It made her irritable to think of it. She piled the clothes roughly into the machine, sheets and towels first. She would have to do two runs at the least. She poured in the detergent and pushed the starter button. Once in action the steady whoosh and whirl of the water spun back and forth soothed her. She sat on a chair and stared vacantly at the white froth bubbling behind the curved glass door.

"It was a great send off, Kate, the whole parish turned out." Her mother had come home ahead of her father. She was standing at the stove drinking a cup of tea, her coat on still and her scarf loose around her collar.

She looked almost like a city woman, Kate thought, done up like that; ten years younger, her cheeks flushed with excitement, little gusts of perfume rising still from her neck and tightly permed hair.

"Even Tim O'Connor—I haven't laid eyes on him for years."

Tim O'Connor was an elderly bachelor who lived alone by Rinnmor. Kate remembered how as children they used to tease him. They would climb the wall into his yard and chase the hens, clapping their hands so that the creatures flew squawking against the wire of the coop. It was not the fowl they were after but himself. It amused them to set up such a din that he would come running from the house, half dressed sometimes, to see what the matter was. When he caught sight of them he would hurry back inside, bolting the door behind him. He had a mortal fear of children, no one knew why. His mother was long since dead and he was one of the many ageing men who lived on remote farms, going without human company for so long that they lost the power of speech altogether or took to wandering the roads talking aloud.

"He looked like a scarecrow with that old black coat on him," her mother laughed, "but sure God help him, there's not a bit of harm in him."

That was what they always said. Even those known to be violent were spoken of in this way, indulgently, as a little simple but meaning no harm. Their existence in the community seemed a reassurance almost; as if their loneliness and dissolution provided a visible proof that God had intended no man to live unmated.

"Was Tim there—that's a wonder alright," Kate said and smiled, making an effort to share her mother's mood. It was rare enough to see her in high spirits. She passed a packet of biscuits across the table to see her and looked at the rough, swollen fingers that reached out to take it. She had once been a tall, goodlooking woman, with dark brown hair falling almost to her waist. Kate could see her still carrying one of the little ones to bed—Breda or Michael—lifting them high in her arms so that their heads brushed the ceiling. "Catch a baby—catch a baby," they would squeal with delight. Now everything about her seemed to have shrunk; her skin, her bones, her hair that was cut short and had grown white, her eyes that had dulled and faded. There was a knowing pride in her smile as she crumbled a biscuit to dip in her tea:

"Did I tell you I had a letter from Breda this morning?"

So it was not only the excitement of the day out that had her in good humour. She had heard from Breda.

"How is she?" Kate asked. Breda, her youngest sister, had done well for herself. She had left home two years ago and worked now as a trained nurse in London renting her own flat in Kentish Town. The good news would mean that she had mentioned again the young doctor she had been seeing. Her mother had gone over for a visit in the summer and since then she had not ceased singing Breda's praises: the stylish life she led, her fashionable clothes and well paid job. To hear her talk you would think it was a credit to herself that Breda had made such a success. Kate listened and marvelled that she could forget so easily.

"I'd say she'll have great news for us shortly," her mother said now, casting a rapid glance about the room as though fearful of being overheard.

Kate stood up and fetched the kettle from the stove. She refilled the pot with boiling water and poured a fresh cup for herself. She remembered all too well what her mother chose to forget. Breda had left home on New Year's Day. She had brought one suitcase and enough money to tide her over for the first week. She had had her hair set the day before and had borrowed the belted grey raincoat that Kate had bought for her honeymoon. They had seen her off at the boat.

"It's only a visit," she had called down from the rail of the deck. "I'll be home in the spring." But they had all known that she would not be. And her mother, Kate thought, suspected more than that; suspected what Breda refused to confide to any of them. She had made no comment. The least said the soonest mended was her policy in all trouble, great or small. What went unspoken, for her, did not exist, and she had not laboured all these years to build about her children a life she thought fitting, to have them rupture it at a stroke. No, Breda must find her own solution, and whatever she chose, it must rouse no trace of scandal. All this was conveyed clearly without a word exchanged.

Kate looked at the rain dribbling down the window. It would continue like this for days now. She would get none of the clothes dry. She remembered that night; Breda's anxious eye and forced smile, waving her white scarf from the deck until long past harbour and she wondered why it was she herself had offered so little in the way of help. She was, after all, the eldest and already a married woman. But she had been cut off from Breda by her own worries, and caught in the net of silence that was cast over all their lives. She looked at her mother who was sitting opposite her now on the far side of the table, her legs crossed, her hands joined in her lap, the line of pink lipstick broadening the line of her clenched lips. Reality, she thought, was made up of the things men did, what could be spoken of in public without lowering the voice. And the rest—all that concerned women only was veiled; a secret, so that even sisters lied to each other.

"Will you let me at the stove for a few minutes, Kate, 'till I put on your father's dinner." Her mother did not stir from her chair but she lifted her eyes to the china clock on the wall above the range. The hands stood at twenty to one. Kate heard the dogs set up a wild bark of greeting and she recognized her father's footsteps in the yard.

"Sit where you are—I'll do it, Mam."

She went to the fridge and took out a packet of frozen chips. She cut open the wrapper and turned the stiff blonde straws of potato onto a dinner plate. Then she lifted the frying pan down from the press. Her father came through the door carrying a newspaper under his arm.

"There was a fierce crowd above in O'Rourkes," he said as though to explain his delay. "John Pat was losing the run of himself altogether." He took off his cap and loosened the buttons of his jacket before sitting down in the armchair that was kept free for him. He turned the pages of his paper, banging them roughly into place with the back of his hand. When he had it folded into a neat square he reached into his pocket for his reading glasses.

"Will you want beans with your chips Mam?"

"Heat them for your father I suppose but don't bother for me. A drop of soup is all I want."

A drop of soup—don't bother for me! If she had not her father to see to, Kate thought, her mother would not bother to cook a meal again. She would live on bread and tea.

"Did you see Breda's letter?" her mother fixed her eyes on the back page of the paper. She spoke lightly; casting the words vaguely into the air but Kate felt the barb in them. If her father's attention was to be caught at all it had to be done before he reached the racing results.

"Give it over to me so," he said, lowering the paper impatiently, "while I have on my glasses."

Her mother took a small blue envelope from her bag and passed it across to him.

"Well?" she asked at last, when he had finished reading and sat holding the letter in his hand.

"Well what?"

"Her news of course, what else?"

"What news?"

"Isn't it plain as day that she intends marrying Martin?"

"Maybe so," he replied, "I saw no mention of engagement plans."

"Maybe so, maybe so—is that all you've to say? You wouldn't notice the sun itself, John Dillon, unless it fell out of the sky and hit you. Give it back to me if that's all you can manage on the subject." She leaned over and snatched the letter from his grasp. He did it intentionally, she knew, to torment her. For years he had gone on in this manner, resisting her in everything. Nothing she did or said could make him show a moment's attention to the affairs of his family. "Your children," he called them. It was his revenge, of course, for coming between him and his pleasures. She had fought him in the past, bitterly; pleaded with him to spend one evening at home at his own fireside. And this was how she was rewarded. He had given up drink and life with it. She was left with the ghost of a man who could do nothing, only read his paper and brood over the hearth.

"Kate," she turned with a look of angry appeal to her daughter. But Kate refused to be drawn in. She set her father's plate on the table, a knife and fork beside it.

"Your soup is in the pot, Mam, it's nearly cooked." She would go upstairs; the beds had still to be made.

As she climbed the back steps she heard the silence settle behind her, heavy and corrosive. Without her as witness there was no point for either of them in continuing.

She opened the door of the bedroom that she shared with Maireid and Deirdre. The light was dim because of the rain, and the small north facing window had misted over. She made up each of the three beds in turn, tucking the covers in tightly. She tidied away the clothes the girls had left strewn about the floor and crawled on her hands and knees under Maireid's bed to retrieve the hot water bottle. When she was finished, she sat down for a moment to catch her breath. Her gaze was drawn to a tangle of blue crayon marks at the bottom of the wall. A wave of depression came over her. Did other people live like this, she wondered, in such disorder and purposelessness? Could a life be made up of no more than this—of making meals and clearing up after them, of washing and ironing, of watching the television, of eating and of going to sleep? Maybe she had her life. Maybe there was only one real event in anyone's, and she had had hers—marriage and the birth of her children. Was that it? She remembered her wedding day—the hope and excitement of that morning eight years ago. Spring; the twenty-fifth of April, a blue sky when she woke, the sun shining, the laughter and fuss of her sisters as they helped her to dress in this room. She remembered the drive to the church, the primroses growing all along the roadside and the lambs in the fields running back from the car. Her mother had said that she was too young but how could anyone, she had thought, be too young for happiness?

She looked at her face in the mirror of the dressing table. Her pale hair fell limply about her shoulders. She looked at the little furrow that had come between her brows and the two deep lines running on either side of her mouth. She used to wonder as a child how it was some women let their face grow hard and bitter. She had thought it would be an easy thing to prevent. She made herself smile, but the line stayed fixed on her forehead. She gathered up her hair and held it in a loose knot behind her neck. She had been goodlooking once. The beauty of the family, they said. She could look alright still if she could have a little happiness, a bit of laughter and fun. Perhaps she should go out with Robbie, it was not as though he was like Liam, anyone could see that. He had a kind face and gentle ways. He would be good to her, spoil her, make her smile again. Why should she care what they said? She had been patient long enough and got no thanks for it. They said she was lucky because she had food on the table and a roof over her head. Because she had children who kept her busy running after them from morning to night, they thought she had no time to be lonely. But the feeling you had for your children only kept alive the appetite for love without satisfying it.

She went to the wardrobe that stood by the window and took from it two woollen jerseys. They were her best—a blue lambswool with a deep vee neck and the other cherry red with small white buttons on the shoulder. Looking in the mirror, she held each to her face in turn, holding the sleeve to her outstretched arm. She liked the red best but maybe it was a bit harsh for her complexion. She swept her hair up again and tried the blue. Yes, it brought out the colour of her eyes—she would wear it and her red skirt with it. She would go to Grogan's with Robbie. And maybe afterwards they could go on to the Strand Hotel. It was lovely there. They had pink shaded lamps on the wall and a candle on every table. There would be music and dancing. It was years since she had danced. She began to do a little step about the room, holding out her arms as if dancing with a partner. She sang—"Some enchanted evening, you may meet a stranger, you may see him smiling across a crowded room," and she laughed aloud. Then she heard the slam of the back door below. It must be nearly two o'clock. She would go down and make something to eat.

The kitchen was empty. Her father had finished his meal and gone out to the fields. The dishes were stacked neatly in the draining tray. Her mother must be inside in the bar. She would have a while to herself. She could listen to the radio in peace. She listened to the programme they had for women at this time most days, if her mother was not in the room, and if the girls were quiet. It made her feel better somehow to hear other women talking about their problems—things she had not had to face herself. Women from all over the country came on to it: ordinary women, housewives and mothers like herself. But it was the girl who introduced it that Kate liked. There was such sympathy and understanding in her voice, it seemed as though she were talking just to Kate. She switched on the transistor radio that stood on the shelf over the sink.

"The great thing, of course, is communication," a woman with a northern accent said, someone Kate had heard before—a social worker or journalist.

"It really is essential to sit down and talk things through."

They always went on like this, people on radio and writing in magazines—about dialogue and the importance of trust. She tried to picture anyone else she knew making time to sit down and discuss their feelings. She could not. The weather and the price of cows, who had died and who had married, that was what you talked about in the country. No one ever mentioned feelings. Maybe it was too dangerous in a place where the same families lived heaped on one another like cattle in a barn, generation after generation. If she had been able to talk to Liam would it have made a difference? Could anyone have found words capable of stemming the tide of bitterness that was in him?

"Kate, have you seen the floorcloth, I want it for a minute?" Kate heard her mother's footsteps coming along the corridor, her slippers making the soft shuffling sound of a spade through wet sand. She did not want her to come in. It would only irritate her to find Kate listening to the programme. She would say nothing, but she would come into the room and potter about making noise while she cleared up; rattling the cutlery in the sink, opening and closing the fridge door. She did not like to hear women discussing their personal lives in public. "Are they never done complaining?" she had asked once when she heard a woman on the television telling about a rape case. There was only one person a woman should turn to in time of trouble and that was the priest. When Kate had come home first her mother had asked her to go and see Father Cusack. "Would you not have a word with him," she had said, "he has experience of these things." You should confide in a priest because he had heard it all before and because he had no one belonging to him to whom he could repeat it.

"I don't know where I left the cloth—I only left it down a minute ago."

Kate tilted back her chair, inclining her head towards the radio so that she could hear it still above her mother's voice.

"It depends on whether the local G.P. is sympathetic or not, unfortunately," the northern woman was saying, "it's very difficult still for rural women and those in small communities." Rural women—they meant people like herself. It was strange to think that she fitted into some accepted category. There were so many different labels these days—city women, suburban women, single women, working women, professional women. It seemed that everyone had a name, could be slotted in under some special heading. Why was it, then, that she felt she belonged nowhere, that she felt completely adrift in the world?

"Kate, did you hear me? I said we needed another case of Coke in from the yard." She made no reply but she got up from her chair. There would be no peace until she turned off the radio. She would go into the bar and listen to it there.

She carried a crate of minerals from the yard through the side door of the bar. Maireid and Deirdre having finished their lunch were sitting by the Kosangas playing with jars of water and some flowers they had brought in from the fields. Robbie was at the corner table with Mossy Sheehan and Tom Walshe dealing cards. They had six pints lined up beside them. They were shouting and laughing, banging the cards down on the rickety three legged table. The smoke from their cigarettes filled the room, hanging in clouds beneath the low ceiling. Kate wiped little streams of beer from the counter with a sponge cloth and dried a few whiskey glasses. Neither the men nor the children noticed her presence. She switched on the radio; an old fashioned one with a netted front they used to call the wireless.

"It's something you can't explain to anyone till it happens to themselves," it was a different woman now, from Dublin she thought, speaking slowly and deliberately, "you live in fear day and night. There's no one you can talk to. The first time it happened was Christmas Eve. The thing I remember was Mary, the youngest, standing at the top of the stairs screaming. He did not even seem to see her. He just went on hitting me across the face with his open hand." Kate set down the glass she was polishing. She was afraid she might break it. Her hands were shaking. The voice came on from the radio, haltingly, as though it were a great effort to get out the words. It was dull and monotone; like a child repeating a lesson, only no child's voice could hold such hopelessness.

"After that, it happened again. Always after the pub. Shouting and yelling, beating me about the head and chest. One time my face was so bruised and swollen I could not leave the house for days. I did not mind for myself. I could have put up with it, it was only when he started on the children I had to do something."

Each word came at Kate with the force of a blow. All her nerves tightened, her senses contracting as she tried not to hear, not to see. And yet she stood fixed, listening as the words came on relentlessly, driving against a barrier in her; the barrier she had erected so as not to feel, not to remember. But she recognized the language as if it had been cut from her own flesh. "Once I tried to escape. He caught me and threw me down the stairs. I had a broken arm that time."

She stood with the dishcloth in her hand, trembling. Ten years confronted her in this stranger's grief. She burned with shame as if it were her own life revealed to the world in these harsh broken phrases. She reached to the shelf and turned the radio off.

"Kate."

Robbie was leaning against the bar staring into her face. She had no idea how long he had been there.

"I'll be with you in a minute—I have to see to the girls," she said, forcing herself to speak calmly and then walked quickly out through the bar door though the children were still playing on the floor. She sat down in the hall on a chair beside the phone. Her breath came in short painful gasps. She bent her head towards her knees and covered her face. She tried not to think—to make her mind a blank. She could not bear to have it all come over her again today. She had been happy. She was to go out tonight. She would wear her new jersey. She would dance. The children were inside playing, she could hear their voices. Her mother was working in the kitchen. She was in her own home now, safe, she told herself. No one could harm her, there would be no shouting, no violence. No one would ever raise a hand to her again. Liam could not come here. It could never be like that again; like the first time. Like the first night he had struck her, so drunk he could hardly walk across the bedroom floor. Struck her with all his force, opening her lip. She had got away from him—locked herself in the bathroom with a chair against the door, sat on the cold tiles until it was morning. It could not be like that again. Like the time she had forgiven him—all those times; made up with him because she could not bear to see only the violence. She had told no one. It was their shame—only theirs. The hurt was buried inside her and only he could comfort it. In the end she did not even try to escape. She knew she deserved it. He would not beat her and abuse her unless she did; unless she was all the things he called her. The pain was final then. She knew that she was stupid, vicious, ugly; everything he named her and when she slept with him again it made her the whore he said she was. But only he could absolve her because only he knew how base she was. That knowledge was what had kept her with him so long.

"Mammy."

Maireid had come and put her arm around her, pushing her head along her cheek. Her hair where it parted in the middle had the sweet sharp smell of apples.

"What's wrong, Mam?"

"Nothing love," she kissed Maireid's hair drying her eyes in it and held her close to her breast. Nothing would ever harm her again, she wanted to promise that. Maireid pulled open her clenched fingers. There was a fifty pence piece inside her palm. She had picked it up from the counter as she had left the bar. The woman had given a number to call—she had heard it just before she switched off the radio. Seven o six something—a Dublin number. She could ask the operator or ring the station. She could call that woman and tell her there was an escape. She could call her just to talk to her. They said that helped.

"Mam, come back in, Robbie wants you."

It was Deirdre standing at the other end of the hall. Kate stood up and, taking Maireid's hand, walked back along the corridor.

Robbie was at the counter still. She smiled at him.

"Kate, fill another for me," he pushed his glass towards her, "and have one yourself."

"Thanks—I'll have a Harp so."

She took two glasses from the shelf and put one under the Guinness tap and one under the Harp. She filled the Guinness first. She watched the brown foaming liquid crawl up the curved side. Robbie was talking still, telling her something that made him laugh. Between each sentence he threw back his head and roared with laughter. The stout was settling in the glass, the froth slipping down again changing to dark black.

"Just imagine it Kate—wouldn't it make you die laughing?"

She looked up at him. His wide fleshy shoulders were shaking, his eyes squeezed tight but although he was laughing they had lost their good humour.

"What's so funny Robbie?" she said making an effort, putting a smile on her lips, wanting to see the joke.

"Amn't I just after telling you girl—where have you been at all? Tom O'Brien, that's what's funny."

"What about him?"

"What I said of course. Look will I go over it again from the start—slowly?"

"Go on."

"Well, I told you about him before. Didn't I tell you about him bringing the gear home from London? The stuff he gets in Soho and places like that—the red light district, you know," he winked at her and took the first swallow of his pint. "Well as I was saying, the last time he decided to bring home a bit extra. He had the videos as usual and a few other gadgets. But this time seemingly he decided to buy a blow-up as well."

"A what?" Kate stared at him.

"A dummy—you know—an inflatable woman; one you blow up, like the boats." He laughed again and wiped the stout from his moustache. "Well, like I told you, he had this great idea for her, for a bit of crack and to make a few bob out of her. He had her down in the cowhouse and he was charging the lads a fiver a go. Jesus Kate, she had tits on her the size of melons, only massive, I'm not joking you. He had the lads lining up. Anyhow there they all were yesterday; Mick Hogan, Peader and Jim Murray down in the shed, having it off—taking turns, you know, when who should come in—who should come in, in the middle of it; not a word of a lie, flinging open the door so that they were nearly knocked from their standing, only the mother. Julia O'Brien herself. Well bejasus Kate, when she saw what they were at she let a shriek out of her like a scalded cat. Poor Mick—I never saw a lad taken so short. He couldn't get the trousers on fast enough. I tell you Kate, he lost almost more than his turn that day." His broad face was contorted, he held his hands across the flesh of his belly as it shook with laughter.

"Did you ever hear such crack—wouldn't you give your right arm to have seen it?"

Kate stared at him; at his quivering body, at the tears running down his cheeks. She saw what he meant now. She saw it all, the whole picture rising clear before her. She saw Mick Hogan, in the old black sweater he never left off, she saw Peader Walsh's thin, lugubrious face, she could see them gathered in the cowhouse at the back of O'Brien's yard, leaning against the wooden stalls, smoking. She saw them laughing, as Robbie was laughing now, their faces red and swollen, as they pushed against the rubber body. She saw their hands grasping at the breasts until the flesh squeaked under them. She saw the blank face of the doll, without eyes or mouth; a thing to be used, to be pushed and mauled, their pleasure beaten from her. A woman's face, dumb and blind as hers had been, a body passive and unresisting as her own.

"Jesus, Kate, you're not laughing, girl—have you no sense of humour at all?"

She did not see her hand lift the pint glass from the counter, she did not feel herself thrust it forward. She did not know what she had done or that she had done anything at all until she saw the yellow foam streaming down Robbie's forehead, the dark stout running into his eyes and down his cheeks that were still spread with laughter.

"Fucking Jeezus," she heard the roar that came out of his wide mouth, but she did not see the men behind him lift their heads from their stupor over the cards and stare at her in bewilderment and horror. She did not see that her daughter came running after her, crying out to her as she herself ran from the bar.

"Kate—what is it? Kate?"

She saw her mother standing by the sink barring her way to the door. She saw the small shrivelled eyes, the look of sorrow and accusation they carried in them always. The look that had grown into her own face, that had tied Kate to her, to her husband, to this kitchen, to the smoke and tumult, the raucous laughter of the bar where they drank before going back to their wives.

"Kate—for the love of God . . ." she said, but Kate pushed past her, her hands grasping the thin bone of her mother's shoulders.

"Let me alone—let me out of here," she said or shouted as she pushed by her and away from the door, the door that opened to the fields. She ran then through the darkness, through the drenched, thick grass, out across the land until she stood alone in the silence of the spread night.

She looked up and saw the sky, with its thousand glittering points of light. She opened her mouth wide and drew down great lungfuls of the sweet, cool air. She breathed it in until the shivering in her body was stilled, until she was calm again. With the corner of her apron she wiped away the spatters of beer that she felt suddenly wet on her face and hands. She looked at the stars. She looked at the distance between them, measuring the time and space that divided them; the space and time their light must traverse to reach her eyes. She felt herself slipping outwards into the lit, clear, sheltering darkness. She closed her eyes, her face uplifted, as though to bathe in it. And the stars stood still, shining though she could not see them, precise and brilliant, each one defying time and space to reach her. A wave of exultation rose in her, a burst of consciousness so swift and sudden that she almost jumped from the ground where she stood and heard herself in the same instant cry aloud for joy. She opened her eyes and gazed about her, marvelling. What a little thing had held her captive—what a small, insignificant, scarcely visible thing had kept her prisoner! She had believed in place. She had believed in circumstance, she had allowed herself to be bound by the trappings of situation: this sky, these patched, stony fields she could hardly now discern, a circle of hills, a house, a voice, a face, a pair of hands. The trivia of place—furniture, that could be found anywhere. She stood still, every nerve in her body attending. She heard the sea roaring at the cliff. The sea that edged each night closer to the land she stood on. The wind ripped at her, froze her cheeks so that she could scarcely part her stiffened lips to smile. For she was smiling; her head thrown back, her eyes wide open. She heard the sound of a car passing below her on the blackened road. A car travelling to Dublin. There were always cars passing on the road, every day, every night, driving away out of this place to another. Going from here to somewhere else.

The Garden of Eden

In the end Eric simply said, "I am going." And Carmelita knew what he meant.

"All right," she replied. She had been waiting for this announcement for twelve years. She had feared it, postponed it, protested against it, and also—at other times of course—wanted it, craved it, paved the way for it. Now—this now, this minute, sitting appropriately, at the kitchen table (*ad mensa* . . . what's the Latin for *at*? she wondered idly), it was nothing but a bald fact, like the sun that shone on the lawn outside, like the marigold in the window box, like the wine glass of water on the blue checked cloth.

Eric stood up, leaving a little food on his plate, and went upstairs. Carmelita sat gazing absently out the window. The laburnum was dropping black pods on the yard. The lobelia had withered. A few montbretia bloomed, with their characteristic brilliance, in the euphemistically named rockery, but mostly the garden was on the wane. Middle August, and hardly a thing left in it. After nine years in the house. And garden. Eric usually did the latter. The split would be mainly *ad hortis*, actually, she thought calmly, pleased to remember this word, if not its cases. He'd never done anything much at the table except eat the food she'd cooked.

She considered the garden next door, as she often did. It was the horticulture *tour de force* of the neighbourhood: tender velvet lawn, bright but not gaudy borders, shrubs in all the right corners, flowering or leafing in a happy sequence of colours, scents and textures. Patio, arbour, roses clambering over trellis, geraniums in great carved terracotta pots. A conservatory. Carmelita envied them, those next door. She coveted that garden. She craved it passionately.

Eric popped his head in and said, "I'm off now. Goodbye!"

His heavy step sounded on the hall floor. The door opened and then shut slowly and sadly, but firmly.

Carmelita stopped thinking about the garden next door. She got up and plugged in the kettle and made a cup of tea. When it was ready she carried it out to the garden, her own garden, and sat down at the table there. A white plastic table with a green sun umbrella and a few odd, mismatched lawn chairs surrounding it. She sat and looked at her shrubs, her flowers, her trees, and the sky. Evening in middle August. The sky, the little bit of western sky she could see, was pale pink. The sun had already disappeared behind the roofs of the houses on the next road.

The summer is over, well and truly over, she thought. A dreadful last-rose-of-summer sentiment of loss and bereavement overwhelmed her for a few minutes. But she did not wallow in it; she waited for it to pass, because she was so accustomed to it. Periodically, every year from about the tenth of August to the beginning of September, she got her last-rose-of-summer depression—she was very sensitive to seasonal cycles, like a lot of women who live in suburbs. The beginning of nice ones, like spring or summer, brought jubilance. The end of nice ones—and there is only one season that really ends—seemed like a great tragedy that experience exaggerated rather than assuaged. And in August it seemed much more over then, much gloomier than in September, which had its own character and self-confidence, which was the beginning of something again, even if it was something not very good. School, frost, long, dark nights.

Carmelita and Eric had been married for twelve years. Oh yes, how time did fly. It seemed that no time at all had passed since their wedding. Since that time of being in love with Eric. There is no time as far as the emotions are concerned, perhaps. On the other hand it was aeons ago; its trappings belonged to history. That ceremony in the registry office in Kildare Street. The drinks afterwards in Buswells, with everyone dressed up somehow. The bridesmaid in white pants and a navy striped T-shirt looked odd, certainly, Carmelita could have killed her, but most of them had made a respectable effort with flowery dresses and hats. Outmoded. Dated. Ancient.

Eric had been as always: smiling broadly, jocular and in full control. He was smart and quick-witted, Eric. She had basked in that, in his protection. He was never at a loss. His decisions were almost invariably the correct ones. And he never regretted them, as a matter of principle.

The decision to get married had not been his, of course, but hers, and her decisions were frequently wrong she had found out as her life progressed. Usually they were irrational whereas Eric's would as a rule be the opposite. It had seemed terribly necessary to marry him at the time twelve years ago, though. She had been pregnant, but that was not why. It had seemed necessary before the pregnancy, which was an effect, not a cause, of the need. Marriage to Eric had seemed to be her only salvation, the only course open to her in life. Life without him, she thought, was unthinkable. She would die without him, she would wither up and cease to exist.

And indeed her expectations had been fulfilled. Marriage had brought happiness and activity. Life had been full as a tick, it ticked all day, all night, there was never a moment's idleness. She had been so busy, so very busy, for several years. So busy that she had not time to consider whether she was happy or not. Now she knew she had been happy during that hectic time. Not having time to think of it, that had been her happiness, it seemed. Not having time to bless herself.

Now she was not busy any more. The garden was empty before her eyes. Friday evening, she had the weekend free, three nights, two whole days, for herself.

She walked over to the fence dividing her garden from the Garden of Eden. She did this every night, because the neighbours were away on their fortnight's holiday in Greece. There was a broken place on the fence—God knows how they had let it remain broken—over which she could peer and get a perfect view.

The first sight of it broke upon her like a peaceful oriental vision. There was a quietness in this garden, partly because it *was* quiet, there was nobody in it, but in greater part born of its perfection. The greenest grass. The fluid forms of the bushes. The pale pinks, yellows, lilacs of the flowers. It was in no way a busy garden, although it required much business to achieve the effect it created. Like a beautiful, rich room upon which endless attention and expense had been lavished, it looked natural and spontaneous.

Eric had driven off in the car. She had heard him starting it, she remembered, just after the door shut. He was possibly far away by now. The thought that there was no longer a car crossed her mind, like a slight shadow, and disappeared. Who needs a car?

She began to climb the fence. It was not easy because it was a thin Swedish fence. But it was not difficult because it had wires attached to it, a bit of broken chicken wire up which she had once tried, futilely, to grow woodbine. She swung herself over the narrow top and jumped onto the pale red paving stones of the patio next door.

At first she stood and looked around at everything she had seen so often from the other side of the fence: the palm and elephant grass just where the patio met the lawn; the green hose lying on the slabs; the pots of deeply pink geraniums all around. She breathed deeply and perfume from mignonette, honeysuckle and escallonia filled her lungs, along with a headier, more intoxicating air: something like incense.

She walked slowly along the lawn. The greenness of it soaked into her skin, she could feel her body absorbing it. It was like swimming softly, breaststroking through a long aquamarine pool. Or through a cloud. Although, naturally, she had never swum in a cloud. She sat on the grass for a minute. It was dampish. She could feel the wet seeping into her skirt. A ladybird came and crawled on her leg. It was a great year for ladybirds. All the gardens were infested with them.

She stayed there for a long time. Then she got up and left, using the same route and technique she'd employed in entry. Before she left she cut three slips from the pink geraniums, which looked like hot, fluttering butterflies resting on a turgid foliage. And when she got to her own side of the fence she potted the slips in terracotta plastic pots, in peat moss, and put them on the windowsill to root. She had heard from a woman she'd once met on a plane to London that stolen slips did best.

She went to bed. The house creaked a lot. Some doors banged because a window was open. She thought about burglars. She believed in burglars, but her image of them, like her childhood images of God and the devil, was vague. They were male, they would break glass, they would burst into her bedroom and . . .

Lulled by such creaks and bangs and ideas, she fell asleep.

The next day would have been long and empty had she not decided in the morning that she really must go shopping. So she took the bus into the city centre and spent the whole day walking around the shops, trying on clothes, examining furniture and rugs. Time passes very quickly in town and she remembered the Saturdays of her youth, her later youth that is, when she had lived with her mother and had had her job, the job she still had. Shop after shop, garment after garment. Bought, worn a few times, discarded.

She bought a white linen suit. And a bag of peaches. And a packet of incense sticks. And several small terracotta pots.

That evening she watched television and cut three slips of escallonia in the garden next door. She burnt the incense, thinking how Eric hated incense or anything that seemed cheap and eastern, like curried eggs and the novels of Hesse and Indian rugs. She drank some red wine but it was sour, as it usually is if you buy a cheap bottle in a supermarket, and she couldn't take more than one glass.

Her thoughts were less of burglars, as she lay in bed, and more of the past. Not the past with Eric, which hardly seemed like past. But of her childhood, of her teenage years which seemed, in retrospect, serene and carefree. She also thought about her slips and planned the future of her garden. Every mickle makes a muckle, she thought, and eventually it will look like theirs next door. Patience is a virtue.

Carmelita was not an especially patient woman and on Sunday she went to a garden centre and bought a palm tree and a blue hydrangea (she'd never fancied the pink) and came home and planted them on the back lawn. And that night—after dark—she stole a large carved terracotta pot from the garden next door. But for the time being she put it in her bedroom where the next-door neighbours were not likely to see it.

That night as she lay in bed she thought of the next-door neighbours. They would not have seen the pot if she'd put it in the hall or the living room, she thought, because they did not visit her house. The reason was that she and Eric had had such fearful rows in the year or two after the accident. Carmelita had been given to screaming loudly in the middle of the night. She used to accuse Eric of all kinds of awful things: not caring about her, letting her waste her life, never doing any housework, not fulfilling her. She had ranted and raved and sometimes Eric had hit her.

Battered. She had been a battered wife, according to a certain point of view. In her own estimation, in retrospect but even at the time, she could justify Eric's hitting her. They always say they've been provoked. But in his case it was, she suspected, true. Anyway, invariably she had hit him back and not infrequently she had hit him first. They had been like two boys scuffling in the school playground.

Except that the sound effects were higher pitched and more alarming. They heard. It was so embarrassing for them and for Carmelita. She hadn't wanted to speak to them. She didn't speak to them, or have cups of tea with them, or invite them in for a drink on Christmas Eve. It had all stopped long ago. There was no noise, no screaming. No fighting at all. But the pattern was set. No neighbourliness. No visits.

Lulled by these thoughts, she fell asleep.

The next morning was Monday and she was supposed to get up and go to work. She worked in a bank. She was a cashier. It was not as boring to her now as it had been when she'd started it; she enjoyed saying hello to the customers, she liked to be nice and friendly and make them feel at ease, which is not how most people feel in a bank. And also she had grown, over the years, fond of her colleagues and of her salary.

But this morning she did not go to work. She got up at the usual time of eight o'clock, went down and had her coffee, but when the time for leaving the house came she did not go. Instead she went into the garden. She examined the slips: none of them had withered so far, which she took to be a good sign. Now she had fuchsia, escallonia and geraniums on the go. She climbed over the fence and looked around. The garden next door looked even more wonderful than usual in the early morning light. The fresh, clean sunshine, the unsullied air of start of day, suited its own spic-and-span, cared-for character. It was in its element.

Carmelita walked all around it, simply admiring. She no longer felt any envy or covetousness, she realised, and supposed it must be because she knew that soon—or at least eventually—she was going to have her own beautiful garden. As beautiful as this. Or more beautiful? No. Just the same.

What would she take? She remembered that they were due home the day after tomorrow so her time in the garden was limited and she would have to choose exactly what she wanted now. She looked at dahlias and lupins and tea roses. Broom and rose of Sharon and a shrub she did not know the name of, that had greenish-reddish leaves and huge fluffy red balls. She looked at elephant grass and marram grass and cordyline.

In the end she cried, "Ah!" Because she saw it. Just exactly what she had wanted all the time. How odd that she had not seen it before, how very odd.

In the corner of the patio, propped up against the wall, a small tricycle belonging to the youngest child next door: there were three children, two girls and a boy. The boy was the youngest. He was four and this was his bicycle. She grabbed it and let it down over the fence as gently as she could. Then she climbed over herself and carried the tricycle up to her bedroom where she put it on the floor just beside the bed.

After the accident all Raymond's things had been given away. Absolutely everything; Eric had thought it was better that way. It was all as bad as it could be, they didn't need reminders, he had said, packing the toys and the clothes and the things, Raymond's things, into boxes for the travellers who called to the door every Saturday, regular as clockwork. There were the photographs, of course, but only in albums. None out on the sideboard, none displayed with the other photographs on the mantelpiece. They had to get over it. They had to forget.

She lay in bed for a while, thinking about her slips and glancing at the bicycle from time to time. Then she searched in the drawers of Eric's desk for the albums. She selected three of the nicest pictures, showing Raymond at one, three, and seven and a half, just after he'd made his First Communion and just before he'd died. She propped them up on her dressing table where she could see them at night before going to sleep and in the morning as soon as she awoke. She'd get some frames for them later. Later today, or maybe tomorrow, or maybe she'd ask Eric to get them.

Because of course he was going to come back. They always come back, Carmelita knew, unless . . .

And Eric came that very night, because he'd rung the office and she hadn't been there and because he couldn't cook and for various other reasons. His decisions were usually rational, Eric's, and usually correct, and he hardly ever regretted them, on principle.

The Long Way Home

Ray Priest came tiptoeing down the stairs at ten to midnight on the thirty-first of March and he walked out the front door to his car. Very gently he turned the key and the engine began to hum. He looked up at the window of the room where he had left his wife sleeping. He hesitated just for a moment, and then he pulled out from the kerb.

Ray Priest didn't know where he was going that night. But he knew he was going somewhere, and he knew he wouldn't be coming back. For weeks now, since their last big fight, he had been moving his clothes and his papers out of the house, a little at a time, stacking them up in cardboard boxes in his brother's garage.

At twelve-fifteen his brother was waiting in the garden, with a flashlight, as they had arranged. He looked cold in his tartan dressing gown. Ray Priest got out of the car. He looked up at the sky and said the forecast was for heavy rain.

"Jesus, I don't know about this, Ray," his brother said, "can't you give it one more go? I don't like to think of you running of in the middle of the night like this."

"Shut up, Frank," said Ray Priest.

"You're forty years old," said his brother, "you're a grown man."

"And you're my brother," said Ray, as though it was an accusation.

"I'm your brother," he said, "but that doesn't mean I have to like it."

"I told you already," said Ray Priest, "everything's over with Maria and me."

"But how do you know, Ray?" said his brother. "Give it one more shot, just for me, please?"

"I'm sorry, Frank," said Ray Priest, "but my shooting days are over with that woman."

They loaded the boxes into the back seat of the car, and then his brother sighed, and they shook hands under the streetlight. Ray Priest heard dogs barking. His brother asked him where he was going, and Ray Priest said he didn't really know yet, but he'd be just fine. He'd be in touch as soon as things settled down a little.

"It's better this way," said Ray, "it'll hurt her less."

"Man, I don't know," said his brother, and he scratched his head. "She'll kill me, Ray, if she ever hears about this."

"She won't hear," said Ray, "if you don't tell Anne."

"Are you kidding?" asked his brother. "I think one broken marriage is enough for this family."

Ray Priest drove until the lights of the city were behind him. He came down onto the dual carriageway at Dolphins Barn and he swung out onto the open road, by the canal. He felt better now. He felt so good that he surprised himself. Speeding through Clondalkin he flicked the radio onto a country music channel. Every song seemed to be about broken promises, so he changed to the World Service. Things were looking bad in Liberia, they said, it might be war any day now. He turned off the radio, rummaged in his glove box for a cassette, and put on Waylon Jennings singing "Blue Suede Shoes."

He sat up straight in his seat, with his hands locked on the wheel. He thought about what would happen next morning when his wife would wake up and find that he was gone. She would be upset, he knew that. But after all this time, and all these arguments, they would be better off. He knew that too. They were destroying each other, not to mention the kids. He couldn't bear their life together any more. And neither could she. Sometimes, he told himself, you have to be cruel to be kind.

The dual carriageway was wide and empty, flanked on both sides by the racing fields and stud farms of the Curragh. A strong wind was blowing up and it made the car shake a little at the high speeds. The night was white and hazy. He would miss her, that was for sure. But something in their lives together had disappeared now, and there was nothing more they could do. They had to face that much. He tried to stay alert by counting the horse boxes, all lined up against the white rails by the road. But after a while, the scenery grew dull, and flat. Ray Priest opened his eyes wide and blew air through his lips.

Passing Rathcoole, he began to feel tired. The road was too straight and the blur of the yellow helium lights all down the way was hurting his eyes. And the road was lonely too, with only the overnight truckers and the tape machine for company. Drizzle speckled his windscreen. He watched a police car come speeding towards him in the opposite lane, heading towards Dublin, with its blue light flashing. Then he pulled off the carriageway and drove up the tiny uphill roads into a little town called Clane. He parked outside the fire station, and he went to get a hamburger and a black coffee in a tiny joint that was still open on the main street.

He sat on the window ledge looking out at the clouds, and trying to make sense of the crumpled map. Behind the counter a young girl with red lipstick was listening to a walkman, bopping her head from side to side in time to the music. A cigarette hung from her lip. Lightning ripped down the sky. Thunder cracked over Clane. Rain came hammering down against the chip shop window. Ray Priest sat looking at the coinbox telephone while he chewed slowly at his hamburger and sipped his bitter coffee.

Rain was falling hard now. Gusts of wind blew litter through the streets. A dustbin overturned with a crashing sound, spilling its contents into the wind. Ray Priest sat in his car for a minute, thinking. He flicked on his wipers, double speed.

"Oh boy, oh boy," crooned the DJ, in a warm and husky voice, "that's going to be a wet one tonight, people. Now that's a night for shutting out the world, and smooching on down with the one you love."

Ray Priest pulled up his collar and lit a cigarette. He started up the engine and pulled away, down through the main street of Clane, taking the side road that went south, and avoided the dual carriageway. A little scenery would do him the world of good, he thought.

Ray Priest drove on, through the towns of Rathangan and Kildare and Monasterevin and Old Lee, and the green dark spaces between them. He sped past abandoned thatched cottages with their walls beaten in, castles brooding in the fields, dancehalls with broken shutters and corrugated roofs. Coming into Portarlington he slowed down to a crawl. He looked at the pink flashing light in the hotel window. WELCOME TO PORTARLINGTON, it said. NO VACANCIES.

This was a town he knew. He remembered the night that he and his wife had stayed in that hotel, after his sister's wedding. He remembered the way his wife had looked at him that evening, the way they had danced together in the red ballroom, and the way the crazy light from the mirrorball had shone in her dark hair.

He stopped outside the hotel and stared up at the windows. He listened to the rumble of thunder, and he wondered what might be going on in that hotel, right now—if only it was made of glass, and he could see right in. Then he moved on again, through the town, past The Dublin Bar and Mick Manley's Pub, slowly over the bridge at the other side. The river was churning now, white with froth underneath the bridge. Ray Priest felt alone.

He wondered where he was going. He stared down at the foaming water, then he eased into first again, and began to drive once more.

Then suddenly, in the still of the road, Ray Priest saw something move. Out of the shadows by the gate of the Protestant church stepped a young man in a leather jacket. Ray Priest swerved. The young man had a rucksack, which he held tight to his body, and long black hair, straggly with rain. He stared at Ray Priest's car, with a hopeful look. He stuck his thumb in the air, and jabbed it up and down.

Ray Priest drove straight past him, feeling a little guilty. But twenty yards later he slowed down, thinking what the hell, maybe it might be nice to have some company on his journey.

Ray Priest stopped and he flashed his emergency lights. In the mirror he watched the man pick up his bags and run towards him. Rain seemed to roar in his ears. He pushed open the passenger door and looked at the young man's shiny pink face. Wind screamed across the bog, rattling the flagpoles in the church grounds.

"Where are you going?" said Ray Priest. Thunder boomed. He had to shout, to be heard above the sound of the storm.

The young man's face was thin, and his skin looked unhealthy. His nose was a little crooked. He had a black scar across his upper lip, and his eyes were bright. Lightning crackled.

"Anywhere," laughed the young man, "you name it."

"I'm thinking of Cork," said Ray Priest, and the young man said Cork would be just fine. He sat into the passenger seat, dripping all over the floor.

"Good Christ," he said, and he sniffed. He wiped his face with the back of his sleeve and he pulled out a pack of cigarettes, looking at Ray Priest with a question in his eyes. Ray Priest could feel the cold from the young man's body. As the car began to move, he noticed a tattoo on his passenger's wrist, shaped like a Spanish dancer.

"Go ahead," said Ray Priest, "the ashtray's in the door."

The match flared. Ray Priest smelled sulphur. The young man's fingers shivered as he lit his cigarette. His nails were dirty.

"Whore of a night," said the young man. He sounded like a local.

Ray Priest said it looked like it would get worse before it would get better. The young man nodded, but he appeared to be far away in his mind and thinking about something. He pulled on his cigarette and did not speak.

"So," said Ray Priest, "what are you running away from?" The young man looked at him.

"Oh, I'm running away from reality," he said, and he laughed.

"Yeah?" said Ray Priest. "I'm just running away from the wife."

"Oh," said the young man, "why are you doing that?"

"That's a long story," said Ray Priest, and he felt himself blush. He glanced at the young man. "I'm just kidding you," he said. "I'm not doing that. Not really."

"No, you're not kidding," said the young man, "what about all that stuff in the back there?" Ray Priest smiled.

"Holiday," he said, "I'm going to see my brother."

"She know you're going?" said the young man.

"Who?" said Ray Priest.

"Mother Teresa," said the young man. "Who did you think? Your wife, of course."

"Oh yeah, oh yeah," said Ray Priest. "Her idea."

"I see," said the young man, "her idea."

"Oh yes," said Ray Priest, "I mean if it was up to me I'd stay at home, but, you know, it isn't. My brother is very sick. He had a heart attack. I don't want to talk about that too much."

The young man said he was sorry to hear it. He began to whistle through a gap in his front teeth, and to drum his fingers on the dashboard.

"Sickness is a terrible thing," he said, and he shook his head from side to side, running his fingers through his long wet hair.

They drove on in silence for some minutes. The towns got smaller and the lights more infrequent, and after a time Ray Priest began to wish that he had not stopped after all. Something about this silent young man gave him a bad feeling.

"Terrible about Liberia," the young man said suddenly, and Ray Priest agreed that things were not looking good. But the young man did not answer him. He just stared straight through the windscreen, nodding, whistling through his teeth, saying nothing at all.

"So what about you?" said Ray, eventually. "What's your story?"

Ray Priest tried to sound interested. It was not that he really wanted to know anything about this young man. It was just that he did not want to sit in silence, feeling edgy, all the way to Cork.

The young man said that he was looking for work. He had just got engaged to a girl from Mullingar. They had been going together for a year, and they planned to get married the following September, live with her father for a while, then get a place of their own. The girl did not get on too well with her father. But they had no money just now. The young man had no work, and his girlfriend had just been made redundant from her job at the factory, and she was having trouble finding something else. So the young man was travelling south, to find some work, and see if his luck would change.

"It's kind of late to start hitching now, isn't it?" said Ray.

The young man had taken a paperclip from his jacket pocket and was twisting it round and round in his fingers.

"Well, I was planning to leave at seven or eight," he smiled, "but I went to see her and say goodbye." He paused. "And you know how it is."

The young man was grinning again. He pursed his lips and nodded.

He pulled a half-bottle of whiskey from his pocket, and began to sip from it.

"Yes," said Ray Priest, "yes, I know how it is."

The young man offered his bottle, but Ray Priest shook his head and said, "No thanks." Sheet lightning lit up the whole sky.

"I thought I might get a waiter's job," said the young man, "there's plenty of those down around Kerry. It's the tourists."

"Yes," said Ray Priest, "that's easy work to find."

"Not for me it isn't," said the young man, quietly.

"Oh yeah," said Ray Priest, "why's that?"

The young man stared out through the windscreen. He wiped away the condensation with the back of his hand.

"I'm not good with work," he said, "this'll be the first real job I ever had."

"Yes," laughed Ray Priest, "I have a son like that. Spent four years in college, now he doesn't seem to know what to do." The young man laughed.

"I wasn't in college," he said, "I was in jail."

Ray Priest swerved around a dark corner.

"Oh yeah," he said, as casually as possible, "what were you in jail for?"

"For killing somebody," the young man said, in a matter-of-fact voice, and he looked at Ray Priest, and he smiled. His teeth were yellow. "For hammering somebody's brains in," he said, "with a spade." He threw back his head and slugged from his bottle of whiskey.

"Jesus," said Ray Priest.

"Yup," said the young man, "I came in one night to find the guy with my girlfriend, so it was wham, bam, thank you mam." He smiled again. "With the spade, I mean," he explained, "not with my girlfriend." Then the young man laughed, in a high-pitched way, like the whinny of a horse.

"Well," said Ray Priest, uncertainly, "how come they let you out?"

"Oh, I escaped," said the young man. "What I did, I dug this tunnel, you see, and I escaped, and went down to South America for a while. Then I came back here, and nobody recognised me."

"Nobody recognised you?" said Ray Priest.

"Yeah," said the young man, "with the face change." The young man began to laugh. He snorted with laughter, then he leaned over and slapped Ray Priest on the thigh. "April Fool, man," he cackled, "it's after midnight, it's April Fool's Day."

Ray Priest glanced at his watch. The young man was right. It was April the first. He sighed with relief.

"Fuck it," laughed Ray Priest, "you had me worried then."

"Heh heh heh," laughed the young man.

"I mean," giggled Ray Priest, "I thought, Christ, here I am stuck in a car with a guy I don't know who's a fucking murderer."

"Heh heh heh," laughed the young man, and he wiped his eyes.

"So you weren't really in jail then?" said Ray Priest. "I mean, you didn't really kill somebody."

"Oh, come on, Ray," smiled the young man, "I mean, what do you think?" The gearbox made a churning sound.

The young man slowly held his hands up in front of his face. He stared at them, as though he had never seen his own hands before. He flexed his fingers, making his hands into fists, then into claws, staring at them all the time.

"Do these look like a killer's hands," he smiled, "to you, I mean?"

"I don't know," stammered Ray, "I wouldn't know about that."

"Take it from me, Ray," the young man grinned, "they don't."

"How do you know my name," said Ray Priest, "just as a matter of interest?"

"Oh, just a guess," the young man said, his face cracking into a grin. He tapped the side of his nose, and winked. Then he laughed out loud, and he said, "No, I'm just kidding you, Ray, I saw it written there, on your suitcase, in the back."

Ray Priest smiled, but he felt a little uneasy. They were moving through dark and tiny roads now, with no light, and high hedges on either side. They drove on through the lashing rain for some time, and the young man kept laughing, "Heh heh heh," and staring at his hands. Ray Priest didn't want to admit it, but he was scared, and he knew that he was lost too. He stopped his car, flicked on the light and began to read the map, glancing from the corner of his eye at the young man.

He was drumming on the dashboard again. He held the whiskey bottle to his lips and blew across the rim. It made a lonely sound.

"Do you fight with your wife, Ray?" he said.

"I'm sorry?" said Ray Priest.

"Your old lady, Ray," he said, "do you fight with her?"

"Sometimes," said Ray Priest, after a moment. "I mean, we're married."

"What do you fight about, Ray? Tell me."

"I told you, we're married, we fight about the usual things."

"That's a terrible thing, Ray," said the young man, and he shook his head ruefully. "A gulf between a man and a woman is a terrible thing." The young man's fingers tapped on the bottle.

"Look, I'm trying to read the map here," said Ray Priest.

A thick mist was coming down now. When the car began to move again, Ray felt the tyres splash through mud, and he heard long branches hammer on the roof. The car turned a corner. And then very suddenly the yellow mist was so thick that Ray could not see the road in front of his eyes. He slowed down quickly into first, and inched carefully along the track.

"We're lost, Ray," said the young man, "we could be anywhere."

"Yes. Maybe we should go back," Ray laughed, "I really don't know about this."

"Don't be afraid, Ray," the young man whispered, and he reached over and touched the back of Ray Priest's hand. "I'm here."

Suddenly there was a loud crash, and a sound of breaking glass. The car shuddered and stopped. Ray Priest heard a low screaming sound, and something heavy falling over out on the road.

"Christ," said Ray Priest.

Ray Priest and the young man sat very still for a moment. When they got out of the car, they were in a tiny bog track, with thick trees and undergrowth on both sides. The young man pulled a torch from his pocket. The rain roared. In a few seconds Ray Priest was soaked to the skin. And the air was thick with fog, so that he could barely even make out the young man's body. The young man faced the road, in front of the car. He stood very still, with his hands on the back of his head. Even with the fog lights on, they could see nothing, except the thick, yellow fog, swirling. The young man did not look afraid.

"Who's there?" shouted the young man. "Who's out there?" But there was no reply.

"We were only doing ten," said Ray Priest, "we couldn't have hurt anyone, could we?"

The young man began to walk away. He walked forward, into the fog. Then he seemed to be gone and Ray Priest was alone. All he could hear was the sound of the rain, pouring into the hedges, hissing all around him.

"Stay with me," he shouted to the young man, but there was no answer. Ray Priest laughed, "I mean, Jesus, don't leave me here."

"I'm here, Ray," came a horrible voice behind him, "you don't get rid of me that easy."

Ray Priest turned around quickly, and the young man was standing behind the car now.

"Quit fooling around," said Ray Priest, "this isn't a game."

"April Fool's Day, Ray," laughed the young man, and he shone his torch up onto his face, and leered. "Heh, heh, heh," he sniggered, "that's poetry, isn't it? April Fool's Day, Ray. I'm a poet and I know it." The young man walked to the front of the car again. He bent down low. He squatted, in the mud, and he held his hands over his eyes. Ray Priest stood beside him. He tried to look straight down the road, but he could see nothing in the mist. "I don't know what we hit, Ray," the young man sighed. "Now, that's very annoying."

Thunder roared. Rain came surging down into the backroad, beating against the leaves, so hard that it made a sound like applause.

Then suddenly the fog was full of strange sounds, the sound of men shouting, and animal noises too, on all sides, wild and hysterical. Ray Priest felt the hair on the back of his neck stand up. He was cold and frightened.

"What's going on?" he laughed.

"Shhh," hissed the young man, suddenly, and he put a finger in front of his mouth, listening. He stared straight at Ray Priest, with wide eyes. And after a moment, he smiled. "Cows, Ray. I know that sound. Must be the lightning. That's the sound of cows, going crazy."

Ray and the young man stood still on the road, trying to gauge from where the sound was coming. In front of the car they could still see nothing. Then, behind them, the wind lifted and the mist began to clear.

They walked back down the road a little, and the rain was falling so hard that they could not hear their footsteps on the road. Rain poured down the back of Ray Priest's shirt. His damp jeans clung to his thighs.

He looked over the hedge at one side of the road, and the young man looked over the other.

"Cows, Ray," shouted the young man. "Come over here. I knew it."

Lightning flashed through the sky, huge forks of lightning.

Black and brown cows were dashing up and down the field, with no direction, crashing into haystacks and trees, stumbling to their knees in the mud. Thin men in black oilskin coats were running through the field too, waving their arms, trying to stop the cows from escaping. The beams of their flashlights moved through the darkness, like the beams of many lighthouses, all gone mad. Rain was lashing down now. The men ran around the field, falling over each other in the dark.

"Look at that, Ray," shouted the young man, and he pointed his shaking hand. Up on the hill behind the field, the little barn was on fire. Great plumes of dark blue smoke rose into the sky. Inside the barn was glowing red and purple. Behind the barn was a house, and all the lights were on in the windows. Everywhere men and women seemed to be running, shouting. A thunderclap boomed across the fields. "Isn't that something?" Wind screamed through the trees. Rushing water gurgled in the ditches.

"Let's get out of here," said Ray Priest, "I don't like this one bit."

The young man and Ray walked back to the front of the car. Now the mist had drifted a little from there too. The road was dark, but in the fog lights, something was moving. Ray Priest and the young man walked forwards.

"Fuck," said the young man.

"Oh my God," said Ray Priest.

A fat white cow was lying on its back in the ditch, wrapped up in barbed wire, with its legs in the air. Its eyes were terrified. It made a whimpering sound, like a baby crying. When it saw Ray and the young man it took a sudden fright, and began to struggle. Barbed wire bit deeper into its flesh, at the udder, and it opened its jaws and howled.

"Oh, Jesus," gasped Ray Priest, "what'll we do?"

The young man seemed not to even notice that Ray Priest was there now. He stared at the cow. He took a step towards it.

"Cool it, lover," he said. He ran his hands over his soaking leather jacket. Then he stretched out his fingers.

And then, with one sudden lunge, the cow flipped itself over onto its belly and clambered out of the ditch, ripping a gash in the side of its leg. It looked terrified. Thick blood stained its white coat. It staggered from side to side on the road, its heels sliding on the wet stones. It charged into the hedge, but could not get through. Its eyes were wild now. It bent its head low and ran at the hedge again. It hit its head on a fence post and staggered backwards, staring at the young man with fury in its eyes.

The young man stepped in front of the cow and he held up his arms.

"Whoo there," he said, "easy now, girl." The cow reared up on its back legs, clawing at the air, like a wild horse. It opened its mouth and bellowed. The young man lunged forward and grabbed its ears. "Whoo now," he said, "you're alright, babe," and he slapped the cow gently on the haunches. The cow screamed again. The young man grabbed the cow's head and swung backwards, putting all of his weight on the cow, so that it could not move.

"Let's just get out of here," stammered Ray Priest.

"We can't do that, Ray," panted the young man, "these cows are somebody's bread and butter."

Ray Priest ran his hands through his soaking hair. He found himself wondering about what his wife was doing right at that moment. Rain spilled down his face. Again the thunder came crashing through the sky. Ray Priest turned and looked straight down the road. What he saw there made him wish that he was anywhere else.

A gang of cows came around the corner at the end of the track, snorting, moving along in a frightened mass, lowing mournfully. They were moving along quickly now, trotting, jostling one another, heads down low, splashing through the mud, and the sound they made was like the sound of some terrible engine. Ray Priest stood very still, listening to the cold and fearful sound. When he looked at the young man, he was staring back at him.

"Fuck," shouted the young man, "do something, Ray, will you?"

Ray Priest didn't even stop to think. He stepped into his car, breathing hard. He turned the key and roared. He jammed it into first, started to three-point-turn it. The front wheel clanged into the ditch, and when Ray Priest tried to move, he heard the wheel whirring round in the mud. He turned and stared over his shoulder. He was panting hard. Although he was cold, sweat pumped through his face. The young man was standing in the middle of the road now, in front of the cows, waving his arms again, jumping up and down. The cows were screaming, charging at him. Steam came streaming from their nostrils. They bellowed and roared. As they got closer, the young man went down on his knees. Ray Priest glanced at his steering wheel. He hit his horn, hard.

The sound of the horn blared through the backroad. The cows stopped, began staring up at the sky, looking confused. One or two kept running. They passed the young man, knocked him over sideways into the ditch and loped along, snorting. But Ray Priest's car was blocking the track now, and there was no escape for them. They stared at Ray Priest, sniffing at his car.

Then men in black seemed to come tumbling over the ditches, forcing their way through the hedges, brandishing flashlights and sticks, their breathless faces and their clothes cut to shreds. They ran up and down, hauling at the cows, tying ropes around their necks, bellowing orders at each other. Ray saw one of them help to drag the young man out of the ditch and lift him to his feet. Cows' faces leered in at him through the window of his car, stupid, curious, blank. Their faces bumped against the windows. Their long pink tongues licked at the glass.

"Fuck off," shouted Ray Priest, "get out of here." He lifted his hands to his wet face and found, to his surprise, that he wanted to cry.

Then, through his fingers, he saw an older man come weaving through the bewildered cows towards his car.

"Who are you?" shouted the dark-faced, unshaven man, shining his flashlight into Ray Priest's eyes. He had a double-barrel shotgun slung over his back, and underneath his oilskin he was wearing pyjamas. When he leaned forward, rain spilled from the brim of his hat. Ray Priest rolled down his window.

"I'm Ray Priest," he stammered, "I'm nobody. What happened here?"

The farmer said that lightning had struck his barn, and the cows had gone wild. He was very grateful indeed to Ray, he said, for acting so quickly, moving his car like that, to block off the road. If they'd made it as far as the dual carriageway, he said, his cows would have just run amok and killed somebody.

Ray Priest sighed. He said that it was the least he could do.

The farmer said the fire was out now. It was just a flash fire, something you saw in the country when the weather was strange as it had been lately. No real harm was done, he said, everything had blown over now.

"And who's that?" the farmer said then, nodding at the young man.

"Oh, that's just a friend of mine," said Ray. The young man came over to the car. His face was grazed, and he was holding his left wrist, but he was still smiling. He nodded at Ray and the farmer, then he put his hand across his forehead and he stared up at the smoking barn, with a weird kind of amazement in his eyes.

The farmer pinched his nose and began to laugh, guiltily.

"You know, when we saw you down here on the road, we thought you might have been those two prisoners," said the farmer, "those two that broke out of Portlaoise tonight. The IRA boy, and the rapist."

The young man turned around very slowly. He stared hard at the farmer. He began to laugh. He threw back his head and laughed hard, "Heh heh heh," and he clapped the farmer on the back.

"Now that's a good one," laughed the young man, "you and me, Ray, desperadoes, isn't that something?" He looked in the window of Ray Priest's car, licking the rain from his lips, and he smiled.

The farmer laughed too, a little nervously. Ray Priest shivered. He felt his heart stop, and then start beating again.

"We don't know anything about prisoners, do we, Ray?" smiled the young man.

"No," said Ray Priest, quietly, and he swallowed hard.

The farmer looked a little embarrassed. His men were pointing at him, from under the trees, and giggling together.

"Well," the farmer muttered, "it's late. I suppose you want to be getting back to Dublin now."

"Yes," said the young man, "us hardened criminals have crimes to do, don't we, Ray?" He punched the farmer playfully on the shoulder, then he grabbed the farmer's hand and shook it hard.

"I thought you were going to Cork," said Ray Priest.

"I never said that, Ray," said the young man, looking surprised, "I said I was going wherever you were going."

"Well, I'm going home," said Ray Priest, "I've changed my mind." The young man shrugged, and he smiled again, and he looked around at the wet fields.

"Well, that's me stuck, isn't it?" he said.

"Maybe we could give you a bed here?" said the farmer, and the young man stared at him, very intensely.

"Well," said the young man, "that would be very kind."

"Sure you won't stay, too?" the farmer said to Ray, putting his hand on the handle of the car door. "You'd be more than welcome."

"No, no," said Ray, "I have to get home."

"Yes," smiled the young man, "Ray has a family, don't you, Ray? We wouldn't want anything to happen to Ray's family, would we, Ray?"

"Where am I?" said Ray Priest. "I'll need some directions."

"Well," said the farmer's son, "you need to go back the way you came, into Abbeyleix, straight through the other side, and you're on the road for Dublin."

"You're going to be taking the long way home," the farmer laughed, "I'll warn you that much. Come on now, do stay with us."

"No, no. That's OK," snapped Ray Priest, "I'm in a rush." The farmer looked sad.

"Oh well," he said, "if you insist."

"He insists, he insists," smiled the young man, "Ray has his responsibilities to think of, don't you, Ray?"

"Yes," said Ray Priest, "yes, I do."

Ray Priest sat in his car for a while, watching the farmer and his helpers and the young man, as they walked up through the fields and back towards the house. The rain had stopped now, and had given way to the lightest of drizzle. But the wind was still whistling hard and cold, down from the mountain and in across the bog.

He drove back slowly into Abbeyleix, then up through Arderin and Mountmellick. He ground his foot into the accelerator and began to drive faster then, small towns flashing past the window of his car, Kilcomer, Rathangan, Naas, until the orange haze of Dublin was within his reach again.

When he walked into the bedroom, his wife sat up suddenly. She leaned on her elbows and gaped at him. Her eyes were wide. She looked a little frightened.

"Ray Priest," she said, "where were you?"

"Don't start now, Maria," he said to his wife, "I'm warning you." His wife looked like she was about to cry. She said nothing. Ray Priest sat on the edge of the bed, with his head in his hands, staring into the mirror. He felt bad for speaking to his wife like that. "I just went for a drive, I needed to think."

"It's five-thirty," she said, "what were you thinking about?"

"I fell asleep," Ray Priest said. "I was sitting up on Killiney Hill, watching the lightning. I was thinking about you and me."

"Your clothes," she said, "you're covered in mud, Ray."

"I fell over," he said, "I tripped outside and I fell." His wife smiled.

"You're such a dreamer, Ray Priest," she laughed, "but I don't suppose I'd want you to change."

His wife lay back in the bed. She watched while Ray Priest opened his shirt, screwed it up and threw it on the chair. She watched while he pulled off his boots, his socks, unzipped his muddy jeans, peeled them over his wet thighs. When he crawled into bed, shivering, she turned away from him, and he lay close to her, with his chest against her back. She flicked out the light. For some minutes, they lay very still, without speaking. Ray Priest felt the warmth of his wife's body spreading through his limbs. His feet smelt bad. His throat felt sore. When in the end he spoke, his voice was hoarse.

"Did you hear the news?" he said.

"Yes," she answered sleepily, "things are bad in Liberia."

"Did you hear anything about the prisoners?" he said. "Escaped prisoners, something like that."

"Mmmm," she said, "they caught them an hour after they got out, in some pub in Portlaoise."

The shadow of the rain on the window danced up and down the bedroom walls.

"You sure?" he said.

"'Course I am," she sighed, "all safely tucked away."

His wife yawned a laugh. "I thought you'd left me, Ray Priest," she said. "I thought you were never coming back."

She moved her feet against his, took his arm, wrapped it around her body, placed his hand on her stomach. Ray Priest's face felt hot.

"You know I'd never do that," he said, softly, "I just got lost for a little while."

"You're a fool," she teased him, "an old April fool," and then sud-denly she was asleep again. The last rolls of thunder rumbled over the faraway mountains.

Ray Priest leaned over his wife's body and he pushed her hair away from her sleeping face. He gazed at her, with love in his heart, and then, very gently, he kissed his wife on the side of her mouth.

"I'll always love you, Maria," he said.

"Mmmm," she sighed, in her sleep.

Ray Priest clung to his wife's body. As he drifted into sleep, he began to see things clearly. He thought about his night, about the loneliness of a man who finds that he has to run from love. And he knew in those moments that love is not always about freedom. He could see it then, with the clarity that only half-sleep brings. He could see that love is often just a homecoming, and little more. And that the journey home of the heart is sometimes the longest of all.

V

The Sloe-Black River

Fishing the Sloe-Black River

The women fished for their sons in the sloe-black river that ran through the small Westmeath town, while the fathers played football, without their sons, in a field half a mile away. Low shouts drifted like lazy swallows over the river, interrupting the silence of the women. They were casting with ferocious hope, twenty-six of them in unison, in a straight line along the muddy side of the low-slung river wall, whipping back the rods over their shoulders. They had pieces of fresh bread mashed onto hooks so that when they cast their lines the bread volleyed out over the river and hung for a moment, making curious contours in the air—cartwheels and tumbles and plunges. The bread landed with a soft splash on the water, and the ripples met each other gently.

The aurora borealis was beginning to finger the sky with light the colour of skin, wine bottles and the amber of the town's football jerseys. Drowsy clouds drifted, catching the colours from the north. A collie dog slept in the doorway of the only pub. The main street tumbled with litter.

The women along the wall stood yards apart, giving each other room so their lines wouldn't tangle. Mrs Conheeny wore a headscarf patterned with corgi dogs, the little animals yelping at the side of her ashy hair. She had tiny dollops of dough still stuck under her fingernails. There were splashes of mud on her wellingtons. She bent her back into the familiar work of reeling in the empty line. Each time she cast she curled her upper lip, scrunching up the crevices around her cheeks. She was wondering how Father Marsh, the old priest for whom she did house-keeping, was doing as goalkeeper. The joke around town was that he was only good for saving souls. As she spun a little line out from the reel she worried that her husband, at right-halfback, might be feeling the ache in his knee from ligaments torn long ago.

Leaning up against the river wall, tall and bosom-burdened, she sighed and whisked her fishing rod through the air.

Beside her Mrs Harrington, the artist's wife, was a salmon leap of energy, thrashing the line back and forth as deftly as a fly fisherwoman, ripping crusts from her own loaves, impaling them on the big grey hook and spinning them out over the water's blackness, frantically tapping her feet up and down on the muddy bank. Mrs Harrington's husband had been shoved in at left full-forward in the hope that he might poke a stray shot away in a goalmouth frenzy. But by all accounts—or so Mr Conheeny said—the watercolour man wasn't worth a barman's fart on the football field. Then again, they all laughed, at least he was a warm body. He could fill a position against the other teams in the county, all of whom still managed to gallop, here and there, with young bones.

Mrs Conheeny scratched at her forehead. Not a bite, not a bit, not a brat around, she thought as she reeled in her line and watched a blue chocolate wrapper get caught in a gust of wind, then float down onto the water.

The collie left the door of the pub, ambling down along the main street, by the row of townhouses, nosing in the litter outside the news-agents. Heavy roars keened through the air as the evening stole shapes. Each time the women heard the whistle blow they raised their heads in the hope that the match was finished so they could unsnap the rods and bend towards home with their picnic baskets.

Mrs Conheeny watched Mrs Hynes across the river, her face plas-tered with make-up, tentatively clawing at a reel. Mrs King was there with her graphite rod. Mrs McDaid had come up with the idea of putting currants in her bread. Mrs O'Shaughnessy was whipping away with a long slender piece of bamboo—did she think she was fishing in the Mis-sissippi? Mrs Bergen, her face scrunched in pain from the arthritis, was hoping her fingers might move a little better, like they used to on the antique accordion. Mrs Kelly was sipping from her little silver flask of the finest Jameson's. Mrs Hogan was casting with firefly-flicks of the wrist. Mrs Docherty was hauling in her line, as if gathering folds in her dress. And Mrs Hennessy was gently peeling the crust from a slice of Brennan's.

Further down along the pebbledashed wall Mrs McCarton was gently humming a bit of a song. "Flow on lovely river flow gently along, by your waters so clear sounds the lark's merry song." Her husband captained the team, a barrel of a man who, when he was young, consistently scored a hat trick. But the team hadn't won a game in two years, ever since the children had begun their drift.

They waited, the women, and they cast, all of them together.

When the long whistle finally cut through the air and the colours took on forms that flung themselves against the northern sky, the women slowly unsnapped their rods and placed the hooks in the lowest eyes. They looked at each other and nodded sadly. Another useless day fishing. Opening picnic baskets and lunch boxes, they put the bread away and waited for the line of Ford Cortinas and Vauxhalls and Opel Kaddets and Mr Hogan's blue tractor to trundle down and pick them up.

Their husbands arrived with their amber jerseys splattered with mud, their faces long with defeat, cursing under taggles of pipes, their old bones creaking at the joints.

Mrs Conheeny readjusted her scarf and watched for her husband's car. She saw him lean over and ritually open the door even before he stopped. She ducked her head to get in, put the rod and basket in the back seat. She waved to the women who were still waiting, then took off her headscarf.

"Any luck, love?" he asked.

She shook her head: "I didn't even get a bite."

She looked out to the sloe-black river as they drove off, then sighed. One day she would tell him how useless it all was, this fishing for sons, when the river looked not a bit like the Thames or the Darling or the Hudson or the Loire or even the Rhine itself, where their own three sons were working in a car factory. He slapped his hands on the steering wheel and said with a sad laugh: "Well fuck it anyway, we really need some new blood in midfield," although she knew that he too would go fishing that night, silently slipping out, down to the river, to cast in vain.

Cathal's Lake

It's a sad Sunday when a man has to find another swan in the soil. The radio crackles and brings Cathal the news of death as he lies in bed and pulls deep on a cigarette, then sighs.

Fourteen years to heaven and the boy probably not even old enough to shave. Maybe a head of hair on him like a wheat field. Or eyes as blue as thrush eggs. Young, awkward and gangly, with perhaps a Liverpool scarf tied around his mouth and his tongue flickering into the wool with a vast obscenity carved from the bottom of his stomach. A bottle of petrol in his hands and a rag from his mother's kitchen lit in the top. His arms in the beginning of a windmill hurl. Then a plastic bullet slamming his chest, all six inches of it hurtling against his lungs at 100 miles per hour. The bottle somersaulting from the boy's fingers. Smashing on the street beneath his back. Thrush eggs broken and rows of wheat going up in flames. The street suddenly quiet and grey as other boys, too late, roll him around in puddles to put out the fire. A bus burning. A pigeon flapping over the rooftops of Derry with a crust of white bread in its mouth. A dirge of smoke breaking into song over the sounds of dustbin lids and keening sirens. And, later, a dozen other bouquets flung relentlessly down the street in memorial milk bottles.

Cathal coughs up a tribute of phlegm to the vision. Ah, but it's a sad Sunday when a man has to go digging again and the lake almost full this year.

He reaches across his bedside table and flips off the radio, lurches out of the bed, a big farmer with a thick chest. The cigarette dangles from his lips. As he walks, naked, towards the window he rubs his balding scalp and imagines the grey street with the rain drifting down on roofs of corrugated iron. A crowd gathering together, faces twitching, angry. The boy still alive in his house of burnt skin. Maybe his lung collapsed and a nurse bent over him. A young mother, her face hysterical with mascara stains, flailing at the air with soapy fists, remembering a page of unfinished homework left on the kitchen table beside a vase of wilting marigolds. Or nasturtiums. Or daisies. Upstairs, in his bedroom a sewing needle with ink in the very tip, where the boy had been tattooing a four-letter word on his knuckles. *Love* or *hate* or *fuck* or *hope*. The sirens ripping along through the rain. The wheels crunching through glass.

Cathal shivers, pulls aside the tattered curtains and watches a drizzle of rain slant lazily through the morning air, onto the lake, where his swans drift. So many of them out there this year that if they lifted their wings in unison they would all collide together in the air, a barrage of white.

From the farmhouse window Cathal can usually see for miles— beyond the ploughed black soil, the jade-green fields, the rivulets of hills, the roll of forest, to the distant dun mountains. Today, because of the rain, he can just about make out the lake, which in itself is a miniature countryside—ringed with chestnut trees and brambles, banked ten feet high on the northern side, with another mound of dirt on the eastern side, where frogsong can often be heard. The lake is deep and clear, despite the seepage of manured water from the fields where his cattle graze. On the surface, the swans, with their heads looped low, negotiate the reeds and the waterlilies. The lake can't be seen from the road, half a mile away, where the traffic occasionally rumbles.

Cathal opens the window, sticks his head out, lets the cigarette drop, and watches it spiral and fizzle in the wet grass. He looks towards the lake once more.

"Good morning," he shouts. "Have ye room for another?"

The swans drift on, like paper, while the shout comes back to him in a distant echo. He coughs again, spits out the window, closes it, walks to his rumpled bed, pulls on his underwear, a white open-necked shirt, a large pair of dirty overalls and some wool socks. He trundles slowly along the landing, down the stairs to make his breakfast. All these young men and women dying, he thinks, as his socks slide on the wooden floor. Well, damn it all anyway.

And maybe the soldier who fired the riot gun was just a boy himself. Cathal's bacon fizzles and pops and the kettle lets out a low whistle. Maybe all he wanted, as he saw the boy come forward with the Liverpool scarf wrapped around his mouth, was to be home. Then, as a firebomb whirled through the air, perhaps all the soldier thought of was a simple pint of Watney's. Or a row of Tyneside tenements with a football to bang against the wall. Or to be fastened together with his girlfriend in some little Newcastle alleyway. Perhaps he was wishing that his hair could touch his shoulders, like it used to do. Or that, with the next month's paycheck, he could buy some Afghan hash and sit in the barracks with his friends, blowing rings of Saturn smoke to the ceiling. Maybe his eyes were as deep and green as bottles in a cellar. Perhaps a Wilfred Owen book was tucked under his pillow to make meaning of the whistles on the barbed wire. But there he was, all quivery and trembling, in London-derry, his shoulder throbbing with the kickback of the gun, looking up to the sky, watching a plume of smoke rise.

Cathal picks the bacon out of the sizzling grease with his fingers and cracks two eggs. He pours himself a cup of tea, coughs and leaves another gob of phlegm in the sink. The weather has been ferocious this Christmas. Winds that sheer through a body, like a scythe through a scarecrow, have left him with a terrible cold. Not even the Bushmills that he drank last night could put a dent in his chest. What a terrible thought that. He rubs his chest. Bushmills and bullets.

Perhaps, he thinks, a picture of the soldier's girlfriend hangs on the wall above the bunk bed in the barracks. Dog-eared and a little yellow. Her hair all teased and a sultry smile on her face. Enough to make the soldier melt at the knees. Him having to call her, heartbroken, saying: "I didn't mean it, luv. We were just trying to scatter the crowd." Or maybe not. Maybe him with a face like a rat, eyes dark as bogholes, sitting in a pub, glorious in his black boots, being slapped and praised, him raising his glass for a toast, to say: "Did ya see that, lads? What a fucking shot, eh? Newcastle United 1, Liverpool 0."

All this miraculous hatred. Christ, a man can't eat his breakfast for filling his belly full of it. Cathal dips a small piece of bread into the runny yolk of an egg and wipes his chin. In the courtyard some chickens quarrel over scraps of feed. A raven lands on a fence post down by the red barn. Beyond that a dozen cows huddle in the corner of a field, under a tree, sheltering from the rain, which is coming down in steady sheets now. Abandoned in the middle of the field is Cathal's tractor. It gave up the ghost yesterday while he was taking a couple of sacks of oats, grass clippings and cracked corn out to the swans.

Shovelling the last of his breakfast into his mouth, Cathal watches the swans glide lazily across the water, close and tight. Sweet Jesus, but there's not a lot of room left out there these days.

He leaves the breakfast dishes in the sink, unlatches the front door, sits on a wooden stool under the porch roof, and pulls on his green wellingtons, wheezing. Occasional drops of rain are blown in under the porch and he tightens the drawstrings on his anorak hood. Wingnut, a three-legged collie who lost her front limb when the tractor ran over it, comes up and nestles her head in the crook of Cathal's knee. From his anorak pocket he pulls out a box of cigarettes, cups his hands, and lights up. Time to give these damn things up, he thinks, as he walks across the courtyard, the cigarette crisping and flaring. Wingnut chases the chickens in circles around some puddles, loping around on her three legs.

"Wingnut!"

The dog tucks her head and follows Cathal down towards the red barn. Hay is piled up high in small bales and bags of feed clutter the shelves. Tractor parts are heaped in the corner. A chaotic mess of tools slouches against the wall. Cathal puts his toe under the handle of a pitchfork and, with a flick of the foot, sends it sailing across the barn. Then he lifts a tamping bar, leans it in the corner, and grabs his favorite blue-handled shovel.

Christ, the things a man could be doing now if he wasn't cursed to dig. Could be fixing the distributor cap on the tractor. Or binding up the northern fence. Putting some paraffin down that foxhole to make sure that little red-tailed bastard doesn't come hunting chickens any more. Or down there in the southernmost field, making sure the cattle have enough cubes to last them through the cold. Or simply just sitting by the fire having a smoke and watching television, like any decent man fifty-six years old would want to do.

All these years of digging. A man could reach his brother in Australia, or his sister in America, or even his parents in heaven or hell if he put all that digging together into one single hole.

"Isn't that right, Wingnut?" Cathal reaches down and takes Wingnut's front leg and walks her out of the barn, laughing as the collie barks, the shovel tucked under his shoulder.

He moves back through the courtyard again, the dog at his heels. As he walks he whisks the blade of the shovel into the puddles and hums a tune. Wonder if they're singing, right now, over the poor boy's body? The burns lighted by cosmetics perhaps, the autumn-coloured hair combed back, the eyelids fixed in a way of peace, the mouth bitter and mysterious, the tattooed hand discreetly covered. A priest bickering because he doesn't want a flag draped on the coffin. A sly undertaker saying that the boy deserves the very best. Silk and golden braids. Teenage friends writing poems for him in symbolic candlelight. The wilting marigolds jettisoned for roses—fabulous roses with perfect petals. Kitchen rags used, this time to wipe whiskey from the counter. Butt ends choking up the ashtray. Milk bottles very popular amongst the ladies for cups of tea.

He reaches the laneway, the wind sending stinging raindrops into the side of his face. Cathal can feel the cold seep into his bones as he negotiates the ruts and potholes, using the shovel as a walking stick. In the distance the swans drift on, oblivious to the weather. The strangest thing about it all is that they never seem to quarrel. Yet, then again, they never sing either. Even when they leave, the whole flock, every New Year's Eve, he never hears that swansong. On a television program one night a scientist said that the swan's song was a mythological invention, maybe it had happened once or twice, when a bird was shot in the air, and the escaping breath from the windpipe sounded to some poor foolish poet like a song. But, if it is true, if there is really such a thing as a swansong, wouldn't it be lovely to hear? Cathal whistles through his teeth, then smiles. That way, at least, there'd be no more damn digging and a man could rest.

He unlatches the gate hinge and sidesteps the ooze of mud behind the cattle guard, and tramps on into the field. Water squelches up around his wellingtons with each step. The birds on the water have not seen him yet. A couple of them follow one another in a line through the water, churning ripples. A large cob, four feet tall, twines his neck with a female, their bills of bright yellow smudged with touches of black. Slowly they reach around and preen each other's feathers. Cathal smiles. There goes Anna Pavlova, his nickname for his favorite swan, a cygnet which—in the early days of the year before the lake became so choc-a-bloc—would dance across the water, sending flumes of spray in the air. Others gather together in the reeds. A group of nine huddle near the bank, their necks stretched out towards the sky.

Bedamned if there's a whole lot of room for another one—especially a boy who's likely to be a bit feisty. Cathal shakes his head and flings the shovel forward to the edge of the lake. It lands blade first and then slides in the mud, almost going into the water. The birds look up and cackle. Some of them start to flap their wings. Wingnut barks.

"Shut up all of ya," he shouts. "Give a man a break. A bit of peace and quiet."

He retrieves the shovel and wipes the blade on the thigh pocket of his overalls, lights another cigarette and holds it between his yellowing teeth. Most of the swans settle down, glancing at him. But the older ones who have been there since January turn away and let themselves drift. Wingnut settles on the ground, her head on her front paw. He drives the shovel down hard into the wet soil at the edge of the lake, hoping that he has struck the right spot.

All of them generally shaped, sized and white-feathered the same. The girl from the blown-up bar looking like a twin of the soldier found slumped in the front seat of a Saracen, a hole in his head the size of a fist, the size of a heart. And him the twin of the boy from Garvagh found drowned in a ditch with an armalite in his fingers and a reed in his teeth. And him the twin of the mother shot accidentally while out walking her baby in a pram. Her the twin of the father found hanging from an oak tree after seeing his daughter in a dress of tar and chicken feathers. Him the twin of the three soldiers and two gunmen who murdered each other last March—Christ, that was some amount of hissing while he dug. And last week, just before Christmas, the old man found on the roadside with his kneecaps missing, beside his blue bicycle, that was a fierce difficult job too.

Now the blade sinks easily. He slams his foot down on the shovel. With a flick of the shoulder and pressure from his feet he lifts the first clod—heavy with water and clumps of grass—flings it to his left, then looks up to the sky, wondering.

Christmas decorations in the barracks perhaps. Tinsel, postcards, bells and many bright colours. Pine needles sprayed so they don't fall. A soldier with no stomach for turkey. A soldier ripping into the pudding. Someone chuckling about the mother of all bottles. A boy on a street corner, seeing a patch of deeper black on the tar macadam, making a New Year's resolution. A teacher going through old essays. A girlfriend on an English promenade, smoking. A great-aunt with huge amounts of leftovers. Paragraphs in the bottom left hand corner of newspapers.

Another clodful and the mound rises higher. The rain blows hard into Cathal's back. Clouds scuttle across the morning sky. Cigarette smoke rushes from his nose and mouth. He begins to sweat under all the heavy clothing. After a few minutes he stubs the butt end into the soil, takes out a red handkerchief and wipes his forehead, then pummels at the ground again. Go carefully now, or you'll cut the poor little bastard's delicate neck.

With the mound piled high and the hole three feet deep, Cathal sees the top of a white feather. A tremble of wet soil. "Easy now," he says. "Easy. Don't be thrashing around down there on me." He digs again, a deep wide arc around the swan, then lays the shovel on the ground and spread-eagles himself at the side of the hole. Across the hole he winks at Wingnut, who has seen this happen enough times that she has learned not to bark. On the lake, behind his back, he can hear some of the swans braying. He reaches down into the hole and begins to scrabble at the soil with his fingernails. Why all this sweating in the rain, in a clean white shirt, when there's a million and one other things to be done? The clay builds up deep in his fingernails. The bird is sideways in the soil.

He reaches down and around the body and loosens the dirt some more, but not enough for the wings to start flapping. One strong blow of those things could break a man's arm. He lays his hands on the stomach and feels the heart flutter. Then he scrabbles some more dirt from around the webbed feet. With great delicacy Cathal makes a tunnel out of which to pull the neck and head. With the soil loose enough he gently eases the long twisted neck out and grabs it with one hand. "Don't be hissing there now." He slips his other hand in around the body. Deftly he lifts the swan out of the soil, folding back one of the feet against the wing, keeping the other wing close to his chest. He lifts the swan into the air, then throws it away from him.

"Go on now, you little upstart."

Cathal sits on the edge of the hole, with his wellington boots dangling down, and watches the wondrous way that the swan bursts over the lake, soil sifting off its wings, curious and lovely, looking for a place to land. He watches as the other swans make room by sliding in, crunching against one another's wings. The newborn settles down on a small patch of water on the eastern side of the lake.

Somewhere in the bowels of a housing complex a mother is packing away clothes in black plastic bags. Her lip quivers. There's new graffiti on the stairwell wall down from her flat. Pictures of footballers are coming down off a bedroom wall. A sewing needle is flung into an empty dustbin where it rattles. Outside, newspaper men use shorthand in little spiral books. Cameras run on battery packs. Someone thinks of putting some sugar in the water so that the flowers will last longer. Another man, in a flat cap, digs. A soldier is dialling his girlfriend. Or carving a notch. Swans don't sing unless they're shot way up high, up there, in the air. Their windpipes whistle. That's a known fact.

Cathal lights his last cigarette and thinks about how, in two days, the whole flock will leave and the digging may well have to begin all over again. Fuck it all anyway. Every man has his own peculiar curse. Cathal motions to his dog, lifts his shovel, then leans home towards the farmhouse in his green wellingtons. As he walks, splatters of mud leap up on the back of his anorak. The smoke blows away in spirals from his mouth. He notices how the fencepost in the far corner of the field is leaning a little drunkenly. That will have to be fixed, he thinks, as the rain spits down in flurries.

VI

The Dream of a Beast

The Dream of a Beast

When I came to notice it, it must have been going on for some time. I remember many things about that realisation. Small hints in the organisation of the earth and air, the city. Everyone was noticing things, remarking on things around them, but for me it was critical. Change and decay seemed to be the condition. It wasn't always like that, people would say while waiting for the white bus or circumventing the mounds of refuse that littered the pavements, but from the tone of their voices it seemed just a topic of conversation; the way once they talked about the weather, now they talked about how "things" got worse. It was during a summer that it all quickened. There was the heat, first, that came in the beginning and then stayed. Then fools who for as long as I had known them had been complaining about wet Junes and Julys began to wonder when it would end. The pavements began to crack in places. Streets I had walked on all my life began to grow strange blooms in the crevices. The stalks would ease their way along the shopfronts and thick, oily, unrecognisable leaves would cover the plate-glass windows. And of course the timber on the railway-lines swelled, causing the metal to buckle so that the trains were later than ever. The uncollected bins festered but after a time grew strange plants too, hiding the refuse in rare, random shrubberies. So they had plenty to complain about, no doubt about that. For my part though, I didn't mind too much. I had always liked the heat. I took to wearing a vest only, under my suit, and walking to work along the buckled tracks. Those trains that did arrive I took advantage of, but for the most part I took advantage of the walk.

But then I've always been a little simpler than those around me. By that I mean that people somehow, even friends of mine—perhaps mostly friends of mine—would find plenty of chances to laugh at me. I had never minded their laughing. I accepted it. Things they seemed to take for granted I found difficult, and vice versa. Tax-forms, for instance, I could never fill out properly, so I would put them off until the writs began to arrive. Neither has gardening ever been my strong point. But give me a set of elevations, give me a thumbnail sketch, give me a hint of a subject even and I can work wonders with it. I often wondered: had my eyes been given a different focus to most others, so that while we looked at the same scene of all we saw quite different things? And of course people laughed, they will laugh, even get indignant, as when the tea you make is weak or you burn the toast only on the one side.

So when other people noticed the heat, what I noticed were the soldiers. I often wondered if they thought they could control the heat by having more of them around. Or were people succumbing to the leaden days in ways that were alarming? They were getting younger too, with that half-shaved look that kids have in their teens. Mostly on their own, never in groups of more than two or three, you'd see them keeping guard by the tiphead shrubberies, or walking the opposite way to everyone walking home from work, as if obeying some other plan. Is there a reason for it all, I wondered, that they don't know but that those who have plotted their movements know? And my memory of the time of my first realisation is connected with one of them.

2   There must have been a white bus that day. I didn't walk along the tracks anyway because I was walking up the roadway from the concrete path by the sea. I was walking up past all the gardens to my left and there was the sound of all the sprinklers hissing when I saw one of them inside the gate. He was as young as the rest, and dark-cheeked, bending over a rose tree. His khaki shirt was damp all over the back and

under the arms. I could see his nostrils almost touching the petals. He is as alert as an animal, I remember thinking, or something inside me thought. There was the smell of just-cut grass. All the gardens stretched away from him, like wrapped boxes waiting to surrender the scents of their rose-trees. Then a door in a house opened and the soldier straightened himself, but not fully, for he slouched out of the garden and down the road. Underneath the rose-tree, I could see now, there was a pile of cut grass and a dog curled in it. I saw his long cheek and his glistening nostrils. They were flaring with the smell. Do they smell more keenly than mine, I wondered? Then suddenly I knew that they didn't. I was riddled with this extraordinary scent, moist and heavy, like a thousand autumns, acres of hay longing to be cut. I stared for a long time before walking to the house.

My garden curved, like a segment of fruit or a half-moon, from the gate to the front door. The house itself was square. It had been built in the days when houses were getting rarer and the ones that were built assumed ever-more-manageable forms. I walked through that curve of garden, past our roses, carrying that strange new sensation. I stopped then, just beyond the roses. I became conscious of a sound. It was a whispering, liquid and lispish, and it grew. I was carrying a briefcase, as I always do. I looked down to my left. All the gardens seemed to sing at once, a symmetrical hum of praise to that afternoon that would have been forgotten by anyone but me, and even by me, had the thing not begun. They curved away out of my vision and I imagined the last garden overhanging the sea, the same dullish hot blue that it had been for months, ivy trailing down a broken brick wall and touching the glimmering water. There must be a reason, I thought, the gardens are opening their pores. Then I walked towards the glass door, realising that the smell was cut grass and the sound was the hissing of sprinklers.

3   Of course I wondered would Marianne's friends be there, talking about the heat, about the weather. I would not have been surprised to see, through the hallway and the open living-room door, the

Ambroses sitting round our glass-topped table drinking weak coffee from our long, thin cups. I would have said something inconsequential I suppose, and retreated to the conservatory to think. There I could look out on the back garden and watch the shadow creep round the sundial, the broad leaves of the knee-high grass glistening in the hot light, the garden which was by now a whispering, torrid tangle of olive-green. I could think there about the changes, without panic or despair.

But there were no Ambroses and Marianne was standing alone in the dark of the hallway. She glanced up when I came in and mouthed my name with that slight diffidence in her voice which was by now familiar to me. There had once been nothing diffident in our love. Her red hair was falling around the nape of her neck, so white that it always reminded me of china. She was turning and turning on her finger her band of gold.

Matilde is sick, she said.

I touched her neck, where the hair curled round it. She withdrew slightly, and shivered.

She's been calling for you.

Marianne walked through to the living-room. I turned upstairs and saw my fleeting shape in the mirror over the first steps. I stopped and walked back down. That shadow had for some reason disturbed me. I saw my shoulder enter the left-hand corner of the mirror and stared. I hardly recognised the stranger who stared back at me. Had I not looked for so long, I wondered. I stared for a long while and concluded that I mustn't have. Certain moods of self-loathing had in the past kept me from mirrors, but never had the gap between what I remembered and what I eventually saw been so large. Marianne moved into the living-room. Matilde called my name. I left my image then, carried on up the stairs and into her room.

Matilde lay curled on the bed, her hair tracing the curve of her child's back. I touched her forehead and felt the heat there. She turned and looked at me, her eyelids seemed heavy with the weight of her long lashes. The almond green of her eyes was flecked with gold. They stared at me, knowing more about myself than I ever could. She lifted her head slightly and her lips brushed the hairs on the back of my fingers.

I was dreaming of you, she murmured.

She seemed not yet out of sleep, or feverish. I could see my reflection in her pupil, ringed and flecked with almond. I was curved there, my cheekbones and forehead were large, the rest of me retreating into the darkness of her gaze.

Read me a story.

The stories she favoured were of unicorns and mythical beasts. She would drink in every detail of those creatures, the bulging arch of their brow, the skull the skin of which is so thick it could have been scaled, the luxuriant hair along each arm and palm of hand. So I read once more of the merchant with the three daughters, the sunken ship, the sea journey to the garden and the waiting beast.

After a while her eyes closed and her breathing became a long slow murmur and the blush on her forehead faded a little. I looked out through her window and saw the sun had vanished from the fronds of grass. I made my way out there and listened to the hissing of sprinklers from neighbouring lawns. I could see the mauve haze descend on the town, somewhere beyond my garden. There was the hum of night machines beginning, taking over from the last roars of day. I touched my finger off the sundial, so hot with the day's sun that it burnt the skin. I rubbed the burnt spot, noticing how hard it was. I rubbed finger after finger then and found each of them hard. Again I wondered how long since I had done this, or had this leathern hardness suddenly appeared? I looked around for no reason other than impulse and saw Marianne in the kitchen window, staring at me. I saw what she saw then, which was me, hunched and predatory, bending over a sundial to stare back at her. Her red hair glistened and her eyes shone. I shambled towards her through olive-green growth. There was the smell of burnt meat.

The radio was crackling when I went in. Let me help you, I said to her. I took the hot plates from the oven. Again my flesh stuck to the surface, but I felt even less than before. The meat was smoking gently and the smell of flesh drifted round the room. Sit down, I said to her. The word love, which I wanted to utter, froze on my lips. When I touched her neck, just where the red hair met the white, she pulled back sharply from my hand.

We ate the vegetables first and then the meat. The voice on the radio crackled on, bringing as it always did the slight panic of the outside world. Turn it off, I asked Marianne, but she didn't want to and so it drifted on like a voice between us, making our conversation for us. What is happening, I asked her after a while. I don't know, she answered.

While I washed the things, I heard her inside, tinkering on the bass notes of the piano. It was quite late by then, since we always ate late. I walked from the kitchen into the living-room. Can I play with you, I asked her.

She made room for me around the higher notes. We played the Chaconne in D minor, in a duet form we had worked out in the first months of our love. She played the bass as smoothly as ever, almost without a thought. My fingers found it hard to stretch, though, and an awkward rhythm crept into the tune. She was annoyed, understandably. She stood up swiftly after the end of the tune and lit a cigarette. I stared at my fingers, which were still holding the white keys. I heard the note hang in the air long after it should have died. Will you come to bed, Marianne asked me.

We made love of course. I watched her undress and thought of all the words to do with this activity. My mind soon exhausted itself. I took her white throwaway pants in my fingers. She was lying under the feather-down sheet waiting for me. She turned off the light. I buried my face in her paper pants, then took off my own clothes.

There is a halo round you, she said. I looked down at myself. There was light coming through the window. Each hair on my body seemed isolated by that light like a bluish gossamer, a wrapping. It is a trick of the light, I thought. I made my way to the bed and felt her hand reaching out for mine. It rested on my arms.

Her fingers were long and bony, but soft, with the softness of her white neck. I had known them in so many ways, clutching the pillow, rubbing my cheek, scouring my back, that the fact that they felt different now didn't seem remarkable. Something was happening, I knew, with us as well as with the rest of it. She ran them down my arms and all the small hairs there sprang to attention. I touched her eyes with my fingers, which miraculously seemed to have lost all their hardness, they were like pads, responsive to her every pore. Her eyelids fluttered beneath them and so I drew my fingers down her cheeks to the bone of her jaw and down to that white neck. I learned my face forwards and kissed her lips. My mouth seemed larger than human, able to protect hers in its clasp. I felt her tongue beating against my lips and opened them and soon I felt her saliva in mine. My mouth crawled down her body and she opened her vagina for me. Her murmurs seemed to fill the air. Her knees were bent around the small curve at the back of my head, pressing it downwards. We seemed to twine round each other as if our limbs had lost their usual shape. We made the beast with two backs then and somewhere in between our cries another cry was heard, a little more urgent. Matilde was standing in the doorway, still in her dream.

You go to her, Marianne said, turning over. I rose from the bed and took her in my arms, which seemed no longer pliant, but heavy and cumbersome in every movement. Matilde whispered parts of her dream to me as I carried her to bed.

Marianne was asleep when I got back. I looked at my body in the dark and saw all the tiny hairs glistening in the moonlight. I began to dream, standing there. There was a skylight and the moon in my bedroom shifted above me, for I was a child, with face pressed to the skylight, staring down below. There were women, crossing and recrossing a parquet floor. Each woman carried a cup. The cups glistened with liquid. They entered a tiny arch and came out again with each cup empty. I inched my way down the glass to see better and for the first time noticed my shadow below, marked-out by the moon, much larger than I was. They noticed it too, for they all pressed into a circle and stared at me together, their raised faces like a large ageing daisy. The glass below me melted slowly and they each held a cup up to catch the drops. I melted in turn and an arm gathered me in a raised cup and a woman's face with two soft, feathered lips bent towards me to drink.

I awoke and the moon was outside the gauze curtain once more and Marianne was beside me, a swathe of crumpled blanket between us. Her slightly tilted nose and her upper lip jutting out from her lower looked strange, strange because once so familiar. How I would dream when we first met of that full petulant rose of her upper lip, the dreaming wistfulness it gave to her face. I would try to describe it in words, as if talking to a stranger. But no stranger could have understood.

I touched her long athlete's back and she shivered in her sleep, drew the sheets around her. She pulled away as if from a stranger. I looked at my hand on the white sheet that covered her white skin. It was much darker than it should have been. The skin was wrinkled and glistening, like the soft pad that is underneath a dog's paw. The nails were hard, thicker than they had been in the afternoon, the points curling round the tips of the fingers. There were five blisters there, from the burning of the sundial and the hot plates. I covered my hand with what was left of my end of the sheet and lay with my mouth close as it could be to her hair without waking her, my breath shifting the strands at ever longer intervals as sleep overtook me.

4   When I awoke the sun was coming through the gauze curtains, cutting the air in two with a beam that hit the edges of the sheet wrapped round my legs. The dust wheeled in the beam towards the green carpeted floor. I heard the sound of the front door closing and of Matilde making her way towards school. There was the sound of clattering dishes and of the lawn sprinklers starting on their circular motion. Marianne came down the corridor and as she neared the room I wrapped myself in the sheet as a cover. I saw her in the mirror when she entered and she must have caught my glance for she turned and told me in that soft brusque voice that it was late. When she left the room again I rose. I kept my eyes from my body since sunlight is so much more revealing than nightlight. Both hands fitted through my shirtsleeves only with extreme difficulty. I dressed fully and slowly and made my way to the kitchen.

The moods that were between us were almost richer than speech. I sat watching her eat, eating only occasionally myself. However much I loved to watch her, I knew there was nothing I could do to dispel this silence. It had its roots in things done and said and it was like ivy now, twining round me. I spoke a few words, but my voice sounded harsh and unnatural. I then rose to leave and tucked my hands round my leather case, walking backwards towards the door. She told me that the Ambroses would be dinner-guests tonight. I will come home early, I said, and talk to you. There's something I must say. Do, she answered.

But what had it been that I had intended to say, I wondered, when I passed through the gate and began the walk down the long sequence of lawns. The heat had brought a mist from over the waters, it clung to the edges of the lawns and the grass borders of the pavement. There was a steady movement of people from the lawns, down the pavement, towards the city.

The sea glistened from beneath the mists and I left the crowds waiting for the trains which I knew might never appear and walked along the tracks. Wisps of haze clung to the sleepers. I walked calmly, but inside me was building an unreasonable joy. This joy was nameless, seemed to come from nowhere, but I found if I gave my thoughts to it it answered back, asking nothing of me. It frothed inside me. The leather of my briefcase seemed moulded to my palm. I brushed back my hair. My tough nails scraped off my forehead and my hair leapt apart at the bidding of my fingers. The joy abated then and became still water. I knew I must keep it as much a secret as my monstrous hands. I heard a sound behind me and leapt back as a train thundered past.

I walked through the smoking piles on the outskirts of the city till the tracks tunnelled beneath the ground. I let the sleepers guide me through the void. I emerged in a long corridor of glass with listless crowds below, waiting for trains. I made my way to the silver escalator, which had been still for some years now.

In Nassau Street the tendrils of plants swung over the railings and brushed off the crumbling brickwork. The gaps between buildings gave a view of clear blue sky. The haze was dispersing now. I knew Morgan would be sitting in the office we shared, with his green eyeshade jutting from his forehead, his sharp observant eyes fixed on the drawing-board. I feared what those eyes would notice and so stopped off at a tailor's shop. I bought a pair of gloves there, several sizes too big for what I once had been. I fitted them on behind a tailor's dummy while the assistant busied himself with labels. They made two large white, knotted lumps of my hands, more noticeable to me, I hoped, than to anyone else.

I reached our office in Crow Street. There was a games parlour downstairs that opened out onto the street. I saw the screens glowing dimly inside, lit every now and then with flashes of white, the shadows of youths bent over them. I made my way upstairs to where Morgan sat, his eyeshade cutting his face with a half-moon of green.

Having been partners for years, we talked very little. Whether we didn't need to or didn't want to had become unimportant, since it was comforting just to know each other's movements, to be allowed room in another's presence, to work in alternative rooms and make coffee on alternate days. We liked each other, and I rarely heard Morgan complain about the heat. From his window he could see the wide street spill over to the giant building opposite where the paper-sellers would crowd with each new edition calling the days' news. He would talk about the quality of coffee I made, about the crossword puzzles and the state of trains, but he would never question, senses of panic and unease were unknown to him. He did the elevations, the line-drawings, the fine-pencilled work. I would do the colours, the storyboards, the broad sketches.

He told me a woman had called, and would call again later. I walked past him and picked up, besides the acrid smell of his sharpened pencils, the smell of something quite different. As I entered my room it seemed to follow me, or I followed it. I knew that smell, though I hadn't met it before.

I had been given details over the phone. She represented a perfume firm who wanted to advertise a thing called musk. She had described the associations she wanted the odour to carry in the minds of the public. It was to be feminine, seductive, yet to carry a hint of threat, like an aroused woman surrounded by a threat she cannot touch, feel or even see. So I had sketched a long rectangular drawing, almost Cinemascope in shape. On the left-hand side was a white, porcelain bath. There were ornate brass taps, a female leg crooked between them, dangling over the floor, the rest of the body beyond the picture's confines. A fine-boned hand was soaping the leg. Water trickled over the arch of the foot and gathered in drops at the perfect heel. The floor was patterned in black and white tiles, of which I'd forced the perspective a little, so the lines seemed to run like a web to the farthest wall. The dripping water from heel to floor then carried your eye over the chequerboard tiles to an open door and a corridor outside. On the open door was a gilt mirror. Full-length, turned in such a way that the bather couldn't see it, it reflected the corridor outside. And there I had sketched in a marble table, a telephone, a discarded bathrobe just thrown on the carpeted floor. There was an empty space, in the vague outline of a figure. That was to be the threat, awaiting definition.

It was odd to see my work on the boards, a product of yesterday's thoughts. I was different now, and found myself looking at it with a certain nostalgia. That threat, which seemed to be one thing yesterday, would be quite another today. I took my pen in my swollen hands and began to draw. Soon the pain of bending my massive fingers eased and the lines came. The lines of that fallen bathrobe seemed to clash with anything vertical and so I knew he would be prone, whatever else he was. I lined in a sinuous passive object almost touching the robe. The shape became bunched like a fist and the nails sunk into the carpet went deep, like claws. Hardly human, the curves of that bunched fist went backwards, always close to the floor, more a stretching leg than an arm. It began to rise then, with all the majesty and sureness of a sphinx. There was a torso there, waiting to emerge. I sat there, feeling it grow. It was all sensation, no line could have drawn its image. My back rippled and arched, there was a scent everywhere. There was the sound of a door opening.

She was wearing a hat, with a black fringe of lace round it. There was a small smile on her lips which showed that one upper tooth was cracked and angled inwards slightly. She walked slowly through the room, leaving that scent in the air behind her. I stayed at my board with my pen in my hands and my hands between my knees. I glanced at her every now and then. She had mumbled a word or two of greeting, hardly listening for an answer. She traced an arc round my things, picking up a sketch here and there and an odd finished drawing, the way professionals do, tilting her head as if to assess it, but already I knew her interest was more than professional. I find it difficult to explain how I knew this; my hands began to feel damp, as if they were sweating copiously under the bandages. Most of all it was the scent, which seemed to hang in the air like figures of eight. I felt that creature in my drawing in the empty shape in the corridor begin to grow, like a growing-pain. I could not yet see the form it would take, but I knew now that I would recognise it when it came, as I recognised that scent, which carried the name musk.

She pulled over the swivel chair and sat down beside me.

This is it, then, she said, looking at my drawing.

I said it was as yet only an idea. My voice sounded strange to me. Not so much hoarse as furred. I told myself I should not be embarrassed. But that scent, when she was close, was overpowering.

We need something extraordinary, she whispered. Things are so bad, firms are on the line. They want me to bring them a miracle.

I said nothing. I was a professional after all, not a miracle-worker. But I felt the pressure of something extraordinary, too extraordinary to be talked of. I felt a throbbing, like a pain, in my back, beginning in my left shoulder-blade, then creeping its way round my ribs. There was a knot of fur in my throat.

She changed from talk of the picture to talk of herself. I listened while she told her story. She came from the country intending to be a nurse but found all the hospitals overstaffed. I could see what a wonderful nurse she would have made. She had beautifully long bones in her arms and hands that folded with this restfulness. Her hair was auburn under the black lace and would have swung around her face as she bent over each bed and, together with those hands, would have given the bandaged heads a sense of heavenly reassurance. She told me how she wandered from job to job, mostly on the fringes of artistic worlds. Her tall figure and her auburn hair were considered a suitable adjunct to galleries and theatre foyers. She felt outside the events that went on there and yet people seemed to think, she told me, that she embodied their essence. Her present job had been foisted upon her out of the same misapprehension.

She had finished her story. Her odalisque eyes were wide open on mine all the time she spoke. They were by no means beautiful, but they gripped me. I fell into the dream again, with the daylight all around me, I saw a long, golden stretch of desert. Nothing moved except occasional flurries of sand which rose in tiny whorls, as if filling vacuums in the air. The sand was sculpted in hillocks, which could have been the length of miles or the length of a fingernail. My eyes sped over these stretches, the outlines hardly varying till the expanse was broken by a jagged rectangular shape, pure black, sinking at an angle into the sand. It was marble, porphyry, or some alloy of glass. Inside I could glimpse a face, barely visible in that blackness of ice, hair frozen in statuesque, perpetual disarray. I had never seen the face before. One of the teeth was cracked.

She saw the half-drawn shape by the bathrobe as some kind of beast. I told her that was the obvious form for such a threat to take, but what kind of beast? She mused about it for a while, and began to enumerate species. I stopped her, telling her it was unwise to presume, one must let it assume a form of its own, one that we could never anticipate. She suggested a visit to the zoo tomorrow, to muse further. I agreed. She left then, tipping my arm ever so slightly, as if to impart some hidden message, or to imply some secret we shared.

I drew a few more lines. Soon my arms became extraordinarily heavy. My head was swimming with images. I let the pencil fall, let my arms hang by my sides and breathed deeply. Slowly and inexorably, the rush of joy built up. It was like a gathering wind. I sat there with my back slightly bent, my hands dangling and swinging gently as if to the sound of late afternoon traffic outside, the smell of musk in the air. The windows were rattling with the wind and beneath all sounds I could hear the deepest one, the one that was at the base of all sounds. I had never heard it before, but recognised it instantly. It came from below the building, from the earth itself. As if the roots of being stretched down, so deep down like a tuning-fork and sang with an eternal hum.

Morgan must have come in then, for my interest was diverted and the joy slowly subsided. He had taken off his eyeshade, the first of the signals of his imminent return home. I rose from my chair. My arms felt light once more. Outside, night was coming down on the full street.

5   Night had begun to fall with a disturbing swiftness. Without any of the change from summer to autumn, around 1800 the sky would begin its wheel from cobalt to blue, and down in the streets faces, buildings and vegetable growths would be lit with a strange, lurid glare. It was the glare of changing, of heightened shadows, it threw darkened shadows under the eyes of passers-by. There was this yellow, febrile glow until the night lights took over.

The hot air seemed to enclose the crowds in a continuous bubble of movement. They arched their bodies, embraced, queued, made talk and love against the peeling brick. They seemed to glory, for a few brief moments, in the heat, in the sense of lost time and future. Their brightly coloured shirts and skirts moved towards me, the women indistinguishable from the men.

Morgan turned left at the river. I could see the bands of youths gathered outside the game halls. I could hear the buzzing of innumerable machines. I crossed the bridge. The crowds always seemed about to engulf me but clove apart as I approached. I suddenly felt older than any of them, older than anyone I could possibly have met. My steps became halting, my neck scraped off the collar of my suit with the roughness of what felt again like the pad beneath a dog's paw.

I found myself outside the station. The artificial palm fronds which passed me on the escalator seemed limp with the day's heat. Inside on the platform the crowds were there again, waiting for the train's arrival. The eaves on the corridor of glass above each held a drop of moisture which grew to fullness only to fall and be imperceptibly replaced by another. It seemed so much like rain, but I knew that to be an impossibility. And sure enough I saw a man in a blue uniform standing between the tracks holding the nozzle of a hose and sending a high arc of spray over the glass skylight and the artificial fronds alike. Walking on sleepers when the light is gone is foolhardy, I knew, so I stood in the shadows waiting for the train. The spray cleared the grime from the glass above and made the light and shade harsher. The man walked past me with his arc of water, dragging the pipe behind him in an arc of black.

The hall filled up with steam then and glass was obscured by billows of smoke behind which liquid flashes still managed to glint. In the shadows of the palm frond I rubbed my cheek with my left hand. I saw a series of tiny flakes twirl towards the ground, displaying a rainbow of colours in the half-light. I saw the crowds press from the platform into bunches round each door. I moved out from the shadows and pressed my way amongst them. I held my face down. I was disturbed at the thought of what it might reveal to them. Knowing how each one of us assumes that what is seen of him by others is not what he knows to be the truth but a mask, I felt a sudden terror that the whole of me was about to be laid bare. Whatever adjunct of our persons it is that maintains this demeanour, it was slowly leaving me, I realised that now. The skin of my person was being shed to usher in a new season, a new age. It would peel off me slowly and inexorably as if pulled by a giant hand.

My main concern, though, was that others should not see what I knew now to be the case. I pressed myself behind the last backs at the door nearest to me. I have always been considerate of others. My urge to spare their feelings will drive me to outlandish lengths. So I took my place some distance from the doorway, my face to the wall. When the train lurched forwards, our bodies swung to one side, then the other. The last of the evening light bled in both windows.

The movement slowly lulled us all. I felt the cramped space between windows easing a little. I let my eyes take in the shapes around me. Bowed shoulders and heads led in waves to the window opposite. The angular city drifted by the glass, then gave way to the tips and heads of the outskirts and behind them a steady thread of blue sea. This blue slowly came to fill the window and to outline, and darken by contrast, the face that was nearest it. It belonged to an ageing lady. She had cascades of lines round her eyes and a fullness round the cheekbones that softened these with warmth. As the blue sea faded from the window a white, rich light slowly filled her face. She was remembering, I sensed. Her eyes were creased with those tiny wrinkles and had the wistfulness of everything that is best in humans. I knew I would either meet her again, or had seen her before. Then slowly recognition dawned. She was my mother.

6   I twisted my body so I faced the opposite window. I heard a loud rending sound and several heads turned. I kept my face down, but from the corner of my eye could see that she had noticed nothing, she was in a world of remembrance all of her own. I remembered the poplar trees at the end of our garden and the plaid rug she spread beneath me. I looked down at my right arm and then my left. My sleeve had split below the elbow and the bandage was now in shreds. The change had spread to my wrist and then must have raced in a sudden surge towards the knot of muscle in my forearm. She would roll up the sleeves of her dress to let me count the freckles on her skin. I knew she lived upon the route but had never seen her take the train before. I would count the freckles till my eyes swam. My weekly visits had become an embarrassment of late with the gloom that swept over me in waves. I thought of how she must have missed me. In one full moment I felt how much I had missed her. My longing to touch her seemed to fill

the carriage like a soaking cloud, like steam. A strange warmth rose from the whole of my body. I felt a dry rustle on my forearms and heard a soft fall on the floor, as if innumerable flakes were drifting downwards. I imagined them on the metal, in an untidy pile. They would be swept away on the return journey, perhaps by that porter with the water-spray. He would drown these shards of me without a thought.

I saw my mother's expression changing. From her window she could obviously see the platform approaching. The train halted and she left, with several others. There was more room, but I stayed pressed in the shadows. I imagined her walking down the blue-lit street towards the house I grew up in. I wondered would the time ever be right to call. I suspected it might not be.

My platform crept through that window, the train halted, I walked up the concrete steps. The liquid blue lay like a shroud over the tracks, the undergrowth beyond them and the rows of houses above. I walked, trailing my torn sleeve and bandage behind me.

The sprinklers were uttering their last whispers. Small piles of grass lay gathered beneath each rosebush. A dog barked from the third garden. A door opened and then closed again. I saw a car outside our house, with sounds coming from it. They were bright, chattering voices, so brisk and hopeful that for a moment I imagined they belonged to the Ambroses themselves. But as I drew nearer I heard the metallic crackles of the airwaves and saw the red light of the radio flashing on the dashboard.

7   The front door was open. I heard voices coming from the kitchen. I walked quietly past, up the stairs and into the bathroom. My cheeks had begun to discolour in blotches, the skin ridged and bumped along them, puckered with holes. I put plasters over each one and I wrapped a long white bandage over my forearm, which was by now unrecognisable. Everything had changed or would change, I knew, and this knowledge made my efforts to hide it even more pathetic, and yet I pressed on with them. Such is the persistence of the human, I thought, and made my way downstairs again.

The voices seemed involved, like those on the car radio, in some common human drama. James's was the loudest and yet I could not distinguish the words. I heard a sound that was like an insect's hum for his, with an odd, irregular climax. I heard a more plaintive note for Marianne. Mary's sound I could not hear at all. I saw all three of them turning towards me when I entered. James rose and the hum became more and more irregular as if the insect was beating its wings fiercely, to escape. I avoided shaking his hand. I noticed for the first time how awkward his bones were, how he was all bumps and angles under his sleek black suit. His temple lobes were too long and his nose too sharp. Mary turned and smiled but her eyes were wide open in a stare that seemed as if it would never lose its amazement. Her pupils throbbed with the beating of her heart. Marianne looked up momentarily and smiled. Then the fringe of her hair covered her face as she held out a plate to me.

I heard all three sounds start at once, in conversation. There was tongue on the plate before me. I ate slowly, something of the flavour of the creature disagreed with me. James's hum throbbed on, swinging round towards me now and then like a pendulum. I heard the sound of Marianne's voice answering for me. It was soft, conchlike, falling like a wave, as if to protect me. I continued to eat. The soft threads of tongue on my own tongue made me feel as if somehow what I ate was myself. I looked up and saw Mary's eyes fall.

James hummed and rose an interval or two, then soared up an octave. Was it because I could not distinguish the words that I felt the need to talk? Or did his tone enrage me to the point of utterance? I knew I had embarrassed them, I knew it was all wrong, but I felt the need to tell them about the joy. You could not believe the joy of what has happened, I said to them, though everything may point to its opposite. Let me describe to you that unreasonable beauty that fills up my soul, unreasonable only because so unexpected. . . .

I stopped when I saw my words were not helping any. There was absolute silence for a moment, then the sound of the tongue on James's plate being rent and lifted to his mouth. Then the sounds of conversation began again. They were coloured this time with a deep blush, as if with shame for something that had happened.

I rose with difficulty and excused myself. I crossed the long distance to the living-room door. The silence kept on. I closed the door behind me then and made my way across the hallway. I could hear the sounds raising themselves again. I went into the music-room. I looked at my bandages, which were now stained in places with a dull, rust-coloured liquid. I suspected I was sweating. I sat down at the piano and began to play. Though my fingers were cramped by the swathes I did get through, slowly and haltingly, the first part of the Chaconne. The long, full bass notes seemed to throb through the piano's frame, to mine, to the floor itself. I thought of the question, as I played, of why music soothes the restless soul.

I heard the sound of voices at the doorway, then Marianne's footsteps back along the hall and the sound of a dinner evening ending. I stopped. I had lost the urge to play. I saw the liquid had seeped from my fingers on to the keys, staining the white ones with irregular threads. It made highlights on the black ones too. It looked like weakened syrup, but I suspected it might taste of salt. It was not at all unpleasant. I heard Marianne's footsteps up the stairway and the sound then of large, heavy rustling from upstairs. I followed, soon after.

The weight of my form must have shifted towards my head and torso, for walking up the stairs I had to grab the rails every now and then to stop myself falling backwards. The house was silent now but for a rustling of bedclothes somewhere and the tiny hum of Matilde's breath. I stood on the landing, listening to the new quality of this silence. Slowly it came to me that silence was not what for years I had supposed it to be, the absence of sound. It was the absence, I knew now, of the foreground sounds so the background sounds could be heard. These sounds were like breath—like the breath of this house, of the movement of the air inside it, of the creatures who lived in it. They seemed to wheel around me till I heard a piece of furniture being pulled somewhere, too much in the foreground, and the spell was dispersed.

I knew I must wash myself before the next move. Now was not the time to approach Marianne, and when that time came cleanliness would be essential. The bathroom, like that of most of our neighbours, was our pride and joy. The taps were gleaming silver, with handles and spigots elaborately wrought, with an elegant adjustable arm fixed to one side, holding a shower nozzle. The spray that came from this was fine and hard, with a lever at its base which changed the water gradually from cold to the sharpest heat. I thought of the countless times I had stood beneath it, in a different season, and the water had stroked me with its heat, washed away all the grass cuttings till Marianne sometimes joined me, her hair bundled beneath a cellophane cap, closing her eyes with pleasure and pain at the heat and her mouth puckering as she did so, waiting to be kissed. I would kiss her and let the water palm us both and her eyes would open as much as they could under the streams, her spare lashes looking like drowned kittens, her fingers, each one, edged into the ribs of my sides. The kiss would last until the hot water ran out and it would be a test of each other's endurance to wait through the cold till it came back, for the heat came in cycles.

So I remembered as I undid my hands how it was she who taught me to be excessively clean and how there are some lessons one should never unlearn. Now my hand was not my own, I saw the ridges and tufts of flesh come clear of the bandages, the hair matted with liquid and the muscles like scallops leading up to the forearm. I peeled off the other hand and the rest of my sodden clothes and ran the bath as I did so. The shower water would be riddled with memories; I thought I was wise to bathe in preference but discovered my mistake when the enamel filled enough to still the liquid and my reflection became clear. I had come to accept that I was not myself but had no conception of the enormity of the disparity between me and the being who confronted me. He was arresting, without a doubt, his forehead was tall, his nose broad and somewhat pushed in as if some afternoon, years ago, it had been broken in a fall. His hair was luxuriant and thick and swept back in clumps from his crown. His eyes were almond-shaped, fronted by even bushes of hair, white round the edges of the almond, streaked a little with red, then amber, gathering into black. Beneath his neck, which was ridged with two angular tendons, was a sharp V, then a scalloped expanse which swept in sharply then to his stomach which in turn swept in towards a tiny whorl. Beyond his stomach my vision was blocked by the edge of the bath but that was enough to see what a piece of work I had become. I stepped into the steaming water and dispelled my image with ripples. I found my changeable limbs floated with a strange bouyancy and took no stock at all of the heat. It filled them with ease, dispersed all thoughts of strangeness from me, everything found its place. How natural it seemed to loll in that water, to turn and face the air again and turn again. The steam rose in the darkness like versions of myself and the lapping water seemed to echo round the lawns. I held it in my monstrous hands and let it drip down to the whorl on my stomach, where it gathered till it spilled over my flat sides. I couldn't have noticed the door opening, for I saw a shape in the corner of my vision then, a white shape, and it seemed to have been there some time. It was Matilde, in her nightgown. By her wide-open eyes, I knew she was still in her dream. Her dreams of beasts were never nightmares, for her stare had all the fascination of a child for an object of wonder. Her eyes travelled down the length of this body that jutted in and out of water, that filled her dream, that perhaps even was her dream. A knotted hand clutched the edge of the bath and she blew soft air out of her lips to ruffle it. I raised both hands and turned her then in the direction of the door. She walked out that way as silently as she had come.

I heard the rustle of her bedclothes and her turning over to sleep. I raised myself from the water and hammered the bath with the droplets that fell from me. I searched for a towel in the dark, but could not find one. I walked outside into the hallway and lay down in the thick carpet, letting it absorb the moisture. I turned on my back, then on my front, stared back towards the bathroom door. It was open. The gilt mirror fixed to the doorway held the reflection of the bath, but none of myself.

Within minutes I was dry. I rose and walked down towards the bedroom. The corridor seemed shrunk, as if the angles had become forced in upon each other. Through the bedroom door I could see the moon behind the gauze curtains. Marianne was asleep on the bed, the blankets rolled tightly about her. She had thrown two blankets on to the floor at her feet. I reached out my hand to touch her shoulder, but saw its texture against her white skin and withdrew it again. I rolled myself in the blankets at her feet.

8   When I awoke Marianne was above me. She had thrown more blankets down, whether because of the excessive heat, or from the impulse to cover my shape, I tried not to think. I had all the appearance of sleep and so didn't move when she threw one leg over my shoul-

der to stretch for her stockings. I watched her cover herself with pants and then sheath each leg with nylon and saw her breasts vanish under a brassiere. She raised both hands in the air and drew on a flower-patterned blouse. She slipped her feet into two white high-heeled shoes, then drew her heels back sharply, grazing my cheek with a metal tip. She wrapped a kilt around her and walked from the room.

I lay on. I had awoken, but my dream was still with me. The moon shone through opulent French windows on to a parquet floor. The resinous gleam from the floor was similar to that over which the women had traced their circles. I was suspended from above, swinging inches above that gleam. The hairs of my cheeks brushed off the varnish. My eyes followed the rope which bound me, a vertical climb up to a creaking pulley, then a long sagging angle away. My eyes followed the rope down that angle to the floor, where it was knotted round the heel of a high-heeled shoe. There was a leg in the shoe which gave it weight and substance, immensity even, and yet strangely fine proportions with its line of ankle moving smoothly to the swell of calf. I swung my body on the rope. I rocked myself in ever-widening arcs towards that heel. I held out my arms to grip at the ankle but could never quite reach. Then the foot walked off abruptly, as if its owner was tired of waiting. I was swept quickly to the ceiling. I shattered the skylight through to the moon.

Marianne came in again. She unwrapped the tartan kilt from around herself and pulled on a skirt instead. When she had gone, I pulled the blankets down. My body responded only slowly to my efforts to move. My veins seemed sluggish and all my muscles seemed grossly over-stretched. I made it over to the wardrobe and sought out my largest suit. This was a dress-suit, with adjustable buttons for waistcoat, jacket and trousers. I found a white starched shirt-front which I tied around my neck, since none of my shirts, I knew, would cover me. The problem of shoes I solved by slitting the sides so wide that my feet could splay through the opening. I then tore one shirt into strips for use as bandages, since my stock had quite run out. I waited then till I heard Matilde leave for school, then made my way downstairs.

Marianne was sitting with her face to the window. There was coffee across the table from her, with a bowl for me. I sat and ate as quietly as possible. She didn't turn or speak. Her red hair fell away in strands from her cheekbones. Her mouth expressed both hurt and horror, but most of all a kind of outrage. When I had finished the bowl I got up to leave. She turned her face towards me as I was at the door. There were tears rolling down each cheek.

She asked me how I could do this to her. I replied that it was not me that was doing it. Again the sound of my voice made me not want to say anything further. She said she would like to kiss me, but could not bring herself to. Will I kiss you then, I asked. When she nodded, I walked towards her. My shadow reached her first. I bent down and brought my lips to her cheek. Her tears moistened my lips and brought them some relief. I stood up then and thanked her, and made my way to the door. I didn't look back.

Such is the complexity of the human, I thought, as I made my way to the station. My appearance attracted attention, but I kept my eyes rigidly ahead. Anger, pity, love, hate, the names we give to our emotions signify a separateness, a purity that is rarely in fact the case. She had stared with anger, pity, love and hate. I walked, again, along the buckling tracks. The sea was leaden today, like a pit of salt, with only a little mist. The fronds of the artificial palms, when I came to them, were still fresh and erect after their night watering. Morgan's eyeshades touched the drawing-board in greeting when I entered.

I sat down to work. I began with tiny details, put the major questions quite out of my mind, and as often happens when that is the case, the details themselves began to answer the questions. I filled in the highlights and shadows of the enamel bath. This led me to her leg, which I lit with an almost porcelain finish. The shadow fell from an unseen lightsource, cutting an angle between the side of the bath and the carpeted floor. I followed the tuft of carpet the way one does a wheat field, with a series of vertical strokes nearest the eye, followed by a ruffled expanse. The sun was falling on the left-hand side of my face. I rubbed my cheek occasionally, because of the itching of the heat, causing a shower of flakes to litter the page, which I each time duly blew away. And in this way I was led to the figure. He extended himself from the tufts of carpet, with a shape that was indeed sphinxlike, two noble paws pressed deep into the pile. Sphinx though seemed too common a name for the creature he was becoming. I teased my mind as I drew with names for him, but any others that occurred seemed equally inadequate.

I had him half-sketched when I suddenly broke off. I found myself exhausted without knowing how or why. The sun had nearly crossed my drawing board which was, I surmised, more than two hours' journey. I remembered my appointment. I rubbed my face and snowed the drawing once more. I went to Morgan's room, but he was out. His room was eerily silent, as if he had never been there. I decided to walk.

I wrapped my bandages round my hands, arranged my shirt-front so it covered the widest possible area and ruffled any further flakes from my hair and face. I then borrowed Morgan's eyeshade, the shadow of which I hoped would be more than enough to cover my visage. Then I ventured out.

9   How long was it since I had walked between morning and night? The city seemed to curl under the sun like a scalded leech. The shadows were tall and black, the pavements white and empty. I crossed Westmoreland Street alone, the only movement the rustling in the patches under the walls. Is the world to be left to me, I wondered, and such as me? A statue of hot bronze pointed nowhere, his finger warped by the years of sunshine. I walked through the sleeping city, blinded by the glare, meeting no one. I came to the river, which had narrowed to a trickle in its caked bed. I walked beside it up by Parkgate Street. The Wellington Monument jabbed towards the white haze, I passed through the parched Hollow towards that long avenue, whose perspectives seemed to beckon towards splendours unseen. I saw then, after some time, a shape approaching out of the melting tarmac. I heard the clip-clop of hooves and readied myself to spring into the bushes, in case I met horse and rider. But no, it was a deer which walked down towards me and stopped some feet away, as I did, to stare. I noted the grace of his rectangular jaw, the dapples that led from it to his sprouting horns. Do you see things differently from me, I felt like asking, are your perspectives wider than mine, have you two planes of vision to carry everywhere you go? Whether I thought this or phrased it, he seemed to hear, for his

lower jaw moved at odds with his upper and he bounded past me, in two neat, langorous leaps, as if inviting me to imitate him. I merely watched him, though, disappear into the city haze.

As I walked on, the shape in front of me defined itself. I could see a glittering white façade with two proud pillars and the whorling fingers of a wrought-iron gate between. Walking further, more pillars defined themselves, white ones, stretching in pleasing harmonies from the façade of the house. It slowly dawned on me that it was the presidential palace. Then the memories came. They flooded in on me, like the dreams, the avenue was full of them. I leaned against a slim tall tree, with no foliage at all except for an umbrella at the top. I saw my mother, walking towards it. She was wearing a narrow pleated jacket, with a flowered skirt. She was walking down the avenue, holding my hand. I was pulling her towards the hedge beyond. She wished to view the palace from behind the gates, but I wanted to see—what was it I wanted to see? The zoo, I realised. And I stepped out from under my tree-trunk, remembering. Enclosed by those hedges, I remembered, the animals would leap at that tall barbed wire, lining the path to the presidential palace.

I crossed the avenue and walked along the hedge. I heard a few mournful snarls, as if of creatures woken for the first time in years. I came to a turnstile and walked through. The Swiss-style cottage was still there, but now it gave out no afternoon teas. The wires were everywhere covered in ivy, the bars were twined in eglantine, honeysuckle and in thick trembling vines that lined the roofs of the cages. I walked through the empty zoo and heard a few parakeets squawk, I saw the flash of a pink flamingo rising from a pool, I saw a treetop swarming with small green monkeys, but all the great animals seemed vanished. I felt a sudden wash of disappointment and realised then that I had come here to find my beast's prototype. He was no cousin of those chattering monkeys or those squawking birds. I came to a pool then and saw a ripple break the covering of thick green slime. A seal's shape curled out of it, its back speckled, even coated in this weight of green. His glistening, troubled eyes made me feel more akin to him. Then he dived and left the surface unbroken once more.

I was walking through a tunnel of vines when I heard footsteps. I bent beneath the hanging branches, as fearful as before. The gardens were free now, to animals as to humans, and yet my fear kept me cowed.

There was the dusty odour of evergreen leaves. Then another scent crept through it, the scent of quite a different place. I ventured out to those approaching footsteps and recognised her walk.

She was carrying a black handbag, swinging on the crook of her arm. She did not seem to be aware of it. She was wearing a fawn hat which made a circle of shadow round her face. I swear I could smell the perfume from where I was. Her high heels clacked and clacked as she walked nearer, her eyes searched around constantly. She was on time, I gathered, as I must have been. When I stepped out in front of her path, she didn't show fear or surprise, only a familiar gladness.

I took her arm without any hesitation. We walked through the vines and out the other side, where once there was a reptiliary. The shed skins of its old inhabitants lay scattered about, colourless and wafer-thin. Her heels clattered off the tiled floor. She told me more about her life, but asked no questions at all about mine. Why I found this so comforting, I wasn't sure, but walking round the glass cases, my arm fell about her waist and hers around mine. We came to the exit sign and walked through, finding ourselves on a long green lawn. Even under the rolls of bandage and under her cotton dress, I could feel the bones of her hips and the movement of her skin above them. We sat down on the lawn.

Take it off, she said, pulling off my eyeshade.

Don't you mind, I asked, feeling drops of sweat fall down my outlandish forehead. She had a matter-of-fact air, however, that made such questions seem redundant.

You look tired, she said.

I was tired. She took my head between her hands and laid it on her lap. She stroked my forehead and my matted hair then, while talking in a deep, hypnotic voice about the project and herself. While she talked, although my back was to her, I could see the limpid shapes of her eyes before me. She talked of the complaints of everybody around her, of the hundreds of minor dissatisfactions they gave voice to daily. She herself, she told me, felt a dissatisfaction that was deep, but that she knew would never end, so what was the point in voicing it? She told me how heat appealed to her, she could wear light cotton dresses and always kept a colourful supply of wide-brimmed hats for going out in the sun. She told me how her life to others seemed to follow no shape, since she never worried or guarded against the diminishing future. But she said that the fact was that while she did accept most of what happened to her, she would have a premonition of important events some time before they occurred, as if to prepare her for them, so she could take advantage of them. She had felt that when she first heard the name *musk*.

I turned my head and looked up into her face. I put my hand on her knee as I did so. Take it off, she said, and began to unroll my bandages. I protested, but she whispered, in this persistent voice, that it could do no harm. She unwound it and unwound it till the first hairs began to appear between the white, and then the huge fist was exposed. She put my hand on her knee then and wrapped my elongated fingers round it. I felt her whole knee in the cup of my hand.

She told me more about herself. I could see long machines cutting corn in swathes as she talked. She talked of herself as if she were describing an acquaintance she had known for years, but never well enough. There was a girl, I gathered, before the woman. The thought that we all had some past was becoming difficult for me. But looking at her I could see her face diminish into the other she must have been. She stretched out her leg so that her knee straightened under my fist. Some bright green-coloured birds flew out of the cedars. I felt her knee change shape once more as she bent her long leg at an angle under my chin and began to talk about the beauty. My voice sounded deeper than ever and so I turned my head to see if it had alarmed her. What I found was her eyes staring wide at me in a way that left no doubt that each was understood. I told her about the sounds I had discovered beneath the surface of things, the hum from the girders, the mauve twilight. As the surface of everything becomes more loathsome, I said, thinking of the thing I was, the beauty seems to come from nowhere, a thing in itself.

She leaned towards me and again I knew I had been understood. But the pleasure of that thought brought an anxiety with it, as to whether she had been. She took my face in her hands, she was smiling. How long was it, I wondered, since I had felt uncalloused skin against my own? The beauty came in a rush. *Joy* was the word I thought of, *joy* I knew then was that word for when beauty was not only seen or heard, but felt from inside. The sound of it was all around me. Her eyes were the brown of burnt heather, with tiny flecks of gold in the dark. They glowed as she bent her head down towards me and rested her lips on mine.

The green birds must have flapped closer, because I heard their cries, one after the other so that they became a throaty purr. How I admired her boldness, in meeting my lips which must have changed beyond recognition. The rest of me must have learnt a new suppleness, however, for while still lying on her lap I managed to turn and raise her above me in the same embrace. Can I describe the garment that wrapped round the top of her legs? She murmured again and smiled, and again I thought of her descriptions of herself as not herself. She gave a small cry as of a bird released and all the green parrots flew into the air at once. Her limbs wrapped round me, each one seemed interchangeable, always with the same texture, and I knew then that I had a soul for she met it, embraced it and breathed on it with her own. We lay there, brute and beauty, a small curtain of pollen seeming to fall on us as if cast off from the blue skein above. There was a dry flowered smell.

It was some time before we rose. My soul had twisted itself into a knot that it would keep, for ever, I thought. We walked back through the arboured tunnel. Her heels clicked once more against the path. She told me that the insides of her legs were wet. She rested her hand on the crook of my arm. Behind us tiny animals followed, unseen, only present by the noises they made, small whisperings and rustlings as if to celebrate the hour that had passed. We agreed to revisit the reptile parlour, then to go for the time being on our separate ways.

Even as we walked through the shattered awning, I was made aware of further changes, by the minute. The skins of dead reptiles hung off the vines and as we walked beneath we set them swinging, collapsing the remaining panes into shivers of crystal. How wise of that genus, I remarked to her, to cast off a surface with each new season. She rubbed her nail up and down my forearm and told me more about her childhood.

I listened as she talked about books, how an unlettered farm girl would remove them from a large tea chest beneath her father's workbench and phrase to herself the long words, few of which she understood. They seemed a secret knowledge to her, and when she came to work in galleries, her surprise at the fact that others shared it was only matched by their surprise at the freshness her childhood knowledge had retained. Several times I tried to answer but found my voice retreating once more to the deep cavern of my throat. As the words went, then panic came that the essence of that hour we had spent was vanishing, shedding itself in turn. She turned to me suddenly, as if noticing this, on instinct. It is time to go, she said.

Before leaving she wrapped me carefully once more. We left by different entrances. I walked back down the long avenue and knew that each change that happened was reflected in that bowl-like essence that lay somewhere beneath the skin. The avenue was empty of people, the shadows slept at the feet of the trees, long and somehow full of ease. My feet moved over the grass, faster and then faster, I felt abandoned beneath those trees and dared to move out into the open fields. I saw a mark on my wrist and made out a number, in stately blue ink, barely smudged. She had written it there. Everything would be for the best I felt, having no knowledge of what awaited me.

10 Travelling in the mauve light at the irregular time that I did, the train was quite empty. The city barely rippled in that light, the soldiers had left it, the water lay still to my right like a sheet of well-tempered glass. My vision was obscured with a fringe of hairs to the left and right of the oval it had become. I sensed this was caused by the growth round my temples. But it lent a charm to that seascape, fringed by rainbows that threw into relief that gunmetal blue. Then all the light bled from the carriage, my shadow came to match the tint of the metal floor. I felt suddenly darker. The train lurched on its sweep forwards, as if dragging me towards some armageddon.

And small gusts of spray blew over me when I came to the gardens. There was wind at last. I thought of the conversations that wind would make around evening tables. There was a slow dull pain in the palm of my hand. I looked down and saw that my fingers were curled like clams. I had mislaid my briefcase.

The front door was ajar. I made my way through the house. I could hear Matilde or Marianne or both moving round upstairs but I didn't call. I felt they had heard me. Something moved me through the house and out of the French windows on to the lawn. I stood by the sundial amid the mounds of cut grass. I felt Marianne's eyes approach the window upstairs but didn't turn or look. I tried to imagine what she must see below her, but no effort on my part could make that leap. Sure of what I felt like, all images of what I looked like were beyond me. Was I rotund, I wondered, did these luxuriant clumps of hair spill out from the crevices of what served as my garments, intimating the chaos inside? Or was the hair in fact quite sparse, did the flakes that I left behind me like gossamer cover my cheeks, my fingers, every centimetre of available flesh that wasn't hidden by cloth? I remembered that my skin at times had made her uncomfortable. Did she remember that now, I wondered, and then realised how futile it was. All I could gauge was that whatever creature was filling her gaze had his left hand placed upon the disc of the sundial, the two largest fingers supporting the weight of his leaning body. I didn't dare return it. All I could bear was to call her name, my eyes fixed on the digits of the sundial, and wait for a reply.

I must have waited a long time for her voice, because when I became aware of my surroundings once more I was encircled by a halo of tiny insects. They hovered over the dial's copper surface, then up along my forearm, into a lulling, shifting crown around my head. The light that came through their penumbra was green, that strange pea-green aura I remembered from the first days of spring. Their combined hum was like the murmuring of angels. Their eyes were bright and green, and to my huge blue the magnificent swathes of their wings reduced to just that transparent glimmer. I remembered a glen, and her red hair surrounded by them, her long fingers flicking them from her face. I took my fingers from the sundial and began to walk back towards the house. They followed me, like a retinue all of my own, but then they thinned as they approached the French windows, as if their proper home was outside. I entered the house with some sense of loss.

There was no meal in the kitchen. Once more I waited. I stood by the range feeling that to impose myself any further might be a mistake. I sensed a presence and heard a footfall behind the door, but could only see the door's gentle swing and the ghost of a shadow on the floor.

Have I become repugnant to you, I wanted to ask, as gently as the tilt of that door. But I feared the sound of my voice. So I waited to see would she enter, of her own accord.

The shadow departed and the footsteps retreated up the stairs. I kept my silence for a moment, and then thought of Matilde. The longing to say goodnight made me move once more. I crossed tile after tile of the kitchen floor. The scalloped shape of the soles of my shoes no longer suited my posture. I would have thrown them off and walked barefoot, but felt that would have worsened things. I pushed open the kitchen door and felt the resistance of tiles change to the softness of carpet. As I reached the bannisters there was a rustling above. I heard her voice.

Don't come up, she pleaded, Matilde's not asleep.

Please, my darling, I said, but the words sounded like heavy drops of oil, don't be afraid. I want to kiss her goodnight. I would have said more but I could feel her fear rush down the stairs towards me like a wall of water. I could by no means blame her, but that fear served to goad me even more.

Matilde, I called, hoping I could pronounce at least that. Marianne's sob answered me from above.

Come up then.

The top of the stairs was bathed in light. Marianne was there, a spiked baking tin in her fist.

Say goodnight from the doorway, she said.

Your voice, I tried to say, sounds as foreign as mine must be. Again the words curled beyond speech. I walked up slowly. She kept her metallic shield thrust towards me. I placed my palm against the spikes. The landing seemed unnaturally narrow. I followed her covered hand to a door.

Goodnight Matilde. I attempted the syllables slowly. The broad *a* reminded me of a field of grass and the *ilde* made me think of a thin bird flying directly upwards. I tried to picture both of these as I phrased her name, the thin bird flying directly upwards out of the sea of grass. To raise the timbre of my voice I contracted all of my throat muscles.

I heard no reply. I drew as quiet and deep a breath as I could and began again. Before I reached the first consonant, however, I felt a blow from behind. The metallic spikes scraped me like a claw, I fell headlong, I heard a door slam and a key turn in a lock with a short reverberant click.

11 The house fell into its evening mood, that mood of which one might remark how quiet it is. On the contrary, it was a harvest of sounds. I lay with my cheek on the carpet and listened. I knew now that I was not in Matilde's bedroom but in my own, or, to use the terminology of the past, our own. My fingers touched off a gossamer substance which seemed for a moment or so to be castaways of mine but which I discovered, as I pulled it towards my lips, to be a long silk stocking. I drew it through my lips and the smell of her skin came to me with a strength that it never had had before. I recognised the odour of the drops she added to her bath. Woman and the world that word implied seemed as strange a bestiary to me as the world I had become. I listened to the sounds and tasted the memories that smell brought to me. The moon was swelling into the rectangle of the window. I was in a bar with oak and gold-coloured fittings, waiting for her entrance. There was a door adjoining which led to a dancehall, and dancers surrounded me, some awaiting their partners, others already joined. I stood a little on my own, as if to express the pride I felt, knowing that when I held her in my arms I would want no other. I glimpsed myself in the bar-room mirror, quiet, saturnine, but above all, proud. They surrounded me in couples but none would be as beautiful as she. Then she came in, wearing what she called her disgraceful dress. It was white, glittering with spangles, slashed all over with half-moons that showed her flesh. The dark silk of this stocking glowed beneath it, flashed black as she moved towards me and one leg parted her dress's sheath. We kissed at the bar, before the mirror, and moved towards the dancehall; even before we had approached it our movements blended into dance. We wove through those thousand couples and that perfume was our own.

The memory of that perfume was easier than her name. One by one the lawn sprinklers stopped their hissing. The insects that had thrived on the long heat beat against the window-pane, lit by the globule of blue light that the moon had become. The perfume waned and ebbed in my senses through the chorus that I once thought of as silence. My arms were tough as beetle-hide beneath me on the carpet. My lids were heavy but took a long time to close. Slowly, though, that chorus changed from bluish to black and I fell asleep.

12

There were curtains of dark like curtains of silk, the blackest furthest away. There was one lone hair on an expanse of tan, which swathed off from me like a desert. At its base the earth swelled a little like a pore, then sucked inwards. And as I stood there it grew. Grew so much that it bent away near its tip, under pressure from its own weight. A tiny drop formed there, fell away and splashed at my feet. I began to walk over that undulating surface, through the curtains of dark. What had seemed darkest from some way off melted, as I approached, into the hue of what I had left behind. There were no humans in this landscape, though all about me was the aura of humanity. The darkness dispersed as I walked towards it, then formed again in the middle distance. I felt I would meet a woman here. Another smooth basilisk grew some way off, soaring from its pore beyond my field of vision. Around it grew neighbours, too smooth to be a forest, too separate to be a field. A drop splashed beside me, so large that it wet my ankles. Then another fell and another, so much so that the water rose to my waist, surged in a current and drew me away. Its colour I would have registered as blue, had the light been clear enough. I hardly swam, I was borne with it over that landscape that sank under its even progression. There were threads of hair beneath me, stroking my body like moss or water weed would, but of a more silken texture, long, flowing with the water, as if each strand was endless. I dared to put my feet down and felt the fleshly surface. I walked to a bank and raised myself up. The water ran below me now, the hair wafted with the flow. There was a woman some yards beyond me, on the bank. Two great webbed feet caressed the woman, her hair made fury with the water. All above me was the beating of wings. A white neck curled from the sky as if on a sudden impulse, its predatory beak turned this way and that. Was it the sight of me, I wondered, that made the sound of wings more furious, that caused those feet to rise, that white neck to coil about that woman, bearing her upwards? Her hair dragged itself from the yards of water and soared, whipping my face with droplets before it was gone. The bank from which she'd risen flooded with water, forming a pool. I made my way to it and bent. I saw my monstrous head reflected there, ringed by a circle of eggs. Were they the swan's, or the woman's, I wondered and lifted one of them out. The heat of my unruly paw was anathema to it, for the droplets of water began to sizzle and steam and a crack sped across the white surface. The sheaves of egg fell away and a cherub stood there, creaking its downy wings. One by one the other eggs split and the cherubs beat their way to the ceiling. They settled into niches in the plasterwork. There was the sound of falling water.

13 When light finally spread over the contours around me and the clusters of colour gathered at each eyelid I found I was on the floor no longer. The bed was beneath me and the sheet was crammed into a ball, shredded in parts where my fingers had clutched it too ardently. There was a sound in the air which I could not immediately divine. I got to my feet and it was all around me, a steady thudding like the feet of many children. I went to the window where the light was. My eyes were unsteady as yet but when I pulled back the gauze curtain and gazed out on the unfamiliar, I saw it all. It was raining.

The water came in straight threads, the darkest ones furthest from my gaze. Had I dreamed that liquid, I wondered, from the constant sky. But I saw that in the gardens all about me the sprinklers had stopped and gathered that others must hear it too. There was moisture in the air, the scent of dryness had vanished. My bandages clung like a mask.

There was the sound of a table being laid downstairs. I was not at all hungry. I squatted, held my knees close to my chin and listened to the downpour. Each echo that came from downstairs was different now, muffled by the falling water. Towards evening I heard music and the sounds of guests. I rocked backwards and forwards by the window. There was a rhythm to the falling water to which I responded. A kind of sleep came.

I dreamt I was in the room downstairs. A metronome ticked from the piano, with the sound of dripping water. I played, keeping my fingers on the black notes. Marianne stood above me. Matilde danced, in her confirmation dress, the white frills spreading as she turned. The liquid beat spilled over the piano though and soon my hands began to sweat. My bound fingers stretched for the notes, so that Bach was slowed to their shape. I knew it was going badly. Can we not try it again, I asked Marianne, but the russet stain was creeping from the black notes to the white, making them indistinguishable. The liquid thud from the mahogany frame began to wilt then, to melt into a gurgle. Matilde turned bravely but the wafer-like stiffness of her confirmation dress became sodden in turn. It hampered her movements, it clung round her knees like whipped cream. She twirled and twirled, but could not defeat it. Her tears made matters worse and soon her Crimplene elegance was plain grey, clinging to her sides. The greyness oozed from the keys, the same as the colour that bound me, and soon music, room and all of us were buried in its path. I saw their hair, twined just above that matter, in the shape of a fleur de lys. It bound and unbound itself as if in final parting, then too went under.

14 The rains merged day into night and night into day again. The dull throbbing and the whispering of rivulets outside and the distant cascades of trains enveloped me. A light fungus grew on the walls, a furred coating of gossamer. I would loll against this vegetable surface, my breath wreathing the room in billows of steam which dripped in tears from the ceiling. So my room wept at intervals and the carpet vanished beneath a film of grey. My lungs, like sodden sponges, inhaled their own moisture. At intervals a plate was pushed through the door. I ate, but hardly noticed the textures. Each dish grew a web of its own. I slept and woke and slept again, lulled by those watering noises. My limbs ceased to concern me. There was a kind of peace in this moisturous world and I wondered once how it was regarded by the world outside. Morgan's eyeshade would be dispensable, I gathered, since the hard sunlight was no more. The streets would have changed from a dusty tan to a shimmering grey. I dreamed that perhaps my condition might have lessened. Then the rains stopped and I knew that I could dream no more.

15 There was a calm, willow-green evening light. All the drops had finished but their liquid echo lasted for some time. Old sounds gained precedence, old but fresh because so long unheard. There was the crackle of burning fat from below. A plate clattered. Then came the hissing of sprinklers, like barely-discernible strings.

I rose, very slowly. My limbs stretched at their coverings, having grown in the interval. I knew there would be no reversal. Certain tendons felt like wads of bunched steel. I walked to the doorway. It was locked as before but I gouged round the keyhole with my nail. The wood splintered easily, the door swung open. Now that crackle of fat sounded louder and the pall of singed flesh slowly filled the room. But stronger than that was the pall of memory. I heard the front door open, the sound of voices, of entering guests. The door closed again and the voices fell to a murmur, broken by the occasional soft ringing of glass. I stepped on to the carpet. I thought of my appearance, but looked in no mirror, as mindful of my own terror as I was of theirs. The landing, which had once been planes and angles, throbbed as I walked through it, the ceiling seemed to congeal beyond me into a closed mouth and yet raised itself as I came forwards, as if parting its lips to let me through. The stairs whorled below me in turn. I followed the glimmer at the end of them, through which the sounds seemed to emanate. My fingers gripped the rail and my new hands left palm marks on the cedar wood. There was the door then, tall, soft-cornered and ringed with light. I stopped, listening to the voices. I meant to enter, but knelt first on the carpet and put my eye to the keyhole of light. I saw the dim shapes of figures round a table. Then the handle turned, the door fell from me and I collapsed inside.

There were kitchen tiles by my cheek once more. I saw the foot of Marianne, the long black heel rising to her ankle, and her hand, clutching the doorknob and her face, far above me. Her voice was raised, but the words I could not distinguish. I understand your anger, I said, I have become an embarrassment to you, I can see that clearly. But from my prone position on the tiles those words didn't sound like words. My darling, I tried again, perhaps it's better that I leave. Through the curve of her shoe's instep I could see the table, the dinner-lamp hanging low and the Ambrose couple, male and female, staring towards me with curved, craned heads. Marianne's foot rose and fell again, nearer now to my eyes. I inched backwards away from it as I felt I should. It rose again and the heel sang off the tiles. I gathered myself on to all fours. Do you remember that evening we danced, I began, but that heel numbed me into silence. I craned my head round and stared up at her face, which seemed larger than a full evening moon after wet weather. Should I go, I mouthed and the eyes, though they didn't seem to hear me, seemed pregnant with the word Yes. I backed away and sidled round the doorway, still longing for a contradiction. But the heel clacked off the doorway and the doorway clacked shut. I heard the rustle, the regretful whisper of the key turning. I raised my weighty palm to that door and gouged some words on the cedar. Goodbye.

16 The dark had brushed all the gardens outside. Each lawn swam with what the rain had left and the cuttings of grass lay like moss upon the surface. I walked. I was watched only by the moon, which shone silver above me, swollen, as though it could contain any number of dreams. When I reached the tracks a few restful stars had joined it. The sleepers had swollen into giant sponges and between the lines of track, glowing dully with the rust it had gathered, a steady stream of water ran. I found night so much more comforting than day, each shape seemed like a disguise, each shadow a mask. A reptile slid down towards me through the waters, passing under my legs to the sleepers behind me. The city, when I reached it, gleamed with the metal of new rain. I walked along the river, glistening at last, laced with ropes of fungus and the pads of lilies. The bridge barely curved above its growth. It seemed now hardly necessary, the river at points spawned a bridge of its own, vegetable and massy, beneath which it remembered its liquid state. There was the steady moan of travelling water and a film of moisture followed its curve to the bay, and beyond to dimness. My feet padded over the metal bridge and their muffled echo seemed to come from beyond. A fish leapt clear of the lilies, gripped a moth in its jaws

and plunged downwards once more. I walked, with no knowledge of where I was heading. Somewhere, I felt there was a place for me. And the bridge led me, as it only could, to the empty street alongside. There was a cobblestone archway ahead. A tangle of foliage hung from above. Through the olive-green leaves I saw an edifice glowing. I brushed the leaves apart with my arms and walked on towards it.

17 As with creatures whose bone structures enclose their flesh, ants, crabs and armadillos, lending support from without rather than within, so the girders of this structure bound the planes of concrete and glass. It was square-shaped, beetling over the tiny streets around. It threw more a mood than a shadow on its environs. Not a soul walked on the pavements around it and the mists, which were now dispersing elsewhere, seemed to cling to the brickwork for comfort. How had I not noticed it, I wondered, in what I was at last beginning to think of as my former life. I had the dim memory of waiting under that Dutch-style façade beyond for a cream-coloured bus. How long must that have been, I wondered, and how long did this immensity take to build and under what conditions of secrecy? It was a seat of some power, I sensed. The surface of the brick was smooth, even metallic, and it tingled gently under the pads of my fingers as if to give just a waist, close to the wall. I walked along it, feeling that tremulous whisper. I reached a corner. It was sharp, seemed dropped like a plumb-line from the stars. I could then see large steps and a concrete patio leading to the miniature street. The dimensions of that street, once so snug and human, now seemed absurd. This giant that scraped the stars had winnowed any purpose it might have once had. There were vast globes on the patio that lit it from the front. The building rose beyond their beam though, and vanished into gloom. The steps rose to plate-glass doors, higher than any human frame. They would have sufficed even for me.

I walked back beyond the corner to the girder-point. I removed the bandages from my palms and I began to climb.

Soon the mist was below me, and the patio, and the street. My cloths unwrapped as I rose. They made white flags in the breeze beneath me. Then even the clouds dispersed and the moon rolled yellow next to the clean line of brick. My shadow came with it, darkening the streets. The stars pricked the sky all over, the moon ladled over them and the wind whipped round my loosened limbs. It tore at my bandages, set them free then in one long roll from my waist. I had come to the end of the girder. There was a parapet above me. I paused, clinging with both hands to an overhang.

The last piece of white unravelled from my calf. I let loose one hand and grabbed the cloth with it, swinging freely. I was naked, I realised, but observed by nothing but the moon and stars; for one moment my body sang. I hung on, and each tendon felt at home. I looked up at the moon and whispered a sigh of thanks. The stars glowed brighter for a moment. I heard the wind and the furling of cloth. I let my eyes follow the bandage, which billowed in a long white arc, drawn into a curve by the high wind and tracing figures to the ground below me.

It was no longer empty. A small boy stood there. His hand was stretched in the air for the white end. It hung above him, moving back and forth. I considered what he would have seen and felt proud of myself, his eyes watching. He had the calm concentration of all children. I let the bandage go, as a message or gift, and swung myself in one movement over the parapet.

I thought of wheat fields at night, their yellow tips gleaming as the full sweep of the night sky came into my vision. All the stars had cleared themselves of mist for me, like hard bright cornheads waiting to be gathered. I balanced on that parapet without much difficulty. My toes gripped the edge while my heels still hung over the void. There was humming in the air. It had two pitches, bassy below and thin and wavering above. Did it come from those stars on this building, I wondered. I let my eyes fall with it from the wheat fields to what lay at my feet.

The roof was of plain cement with a spiral staircase jutting out into the skyline. Many yards away, near the opposite parapet, was a rain trough. I stepped down on to the roof and felt the cement beneath my feet.

The staircase was made of thin steel which sang when I plucked it. It made a dark half-segment through the roof. I climbed down, into the building below.

I found a long, low-roofed storeroom. There was a rolled carpet against the wall. Through the slim rectangular windows the wheaten stars could be seen. I crawled inside the cylinder of carpet and was soon asleep.

18 My dreams were of humans. I was smooth once more, my hair was cut close to my temples, I was wearing a suit I had never seen, it is tighter in fashion than in my day I remember saying. Absolutely unfamiliar with myself, like one who has drifted off and been suddenly woken in mid-afternoon, I knew obscurely that what I carried under my elbow, pressed to my side, was a brief of some kind. I walked down a long corridor with flowers on the floor, there were sweeps of light coming through successive windows. When I came to the fourth door I knew that this was where my assignation was, though there was no indication that doors down the long corridor beyond were any different. I knocked, heard no answer but entered anyway.

She was standing by the window with some beads on the high-frocked dress which gave her figure the repose it had always promised. She was twisting the beads in her fingers. She did not look up when I entered, allowing me to see to the full what a woman she had become. The creature I had left, so small, so unformed, with those long ribbons of years ahead of her, had emerged, both bound and unwrapped by them, the child I barely knew so changed as to be almost hidden and quite another creature revealed.

Matilde.

She turned when I called her name. Like those exotic birds in whom, by reason of acquaintance with their more prosaic cousins, we recognise some characteristics, I could see in that long neck; in that tiny ruffle which seemed to spread from it to the crown of her short cropped hair, some ghost of her childhood movements.

She came towards me and kissed me. The kiss was a brief one, but in the quick withdrawal of her face from mine I sensed a torrent of emotion. I looked into her eyes and saw them at once angry and pleading for kindness. I knew then she was in love, she had been in love and felt mishandled. I felt pity, but even more, a sense of great misplacement that her body had touched another's, her soul had met another's. She called me by a name then, not my own, and it dawned on me that she was in love with me.

She asked me to reconsider my feelings. She told me no one but me could fill her life, now or for a long time to come; perhaps for ever. My coldness she could not understand, but she could live with it if I were to give even a hint of my former affection. Nobody could have been like me, she whispered, during those moments.

I wondered what I had done, how I had met her, how I had kept my identity secret. But the light that came through the great plate-glass window from what seemed to be a workaday, silver-lined city outside imposed its own order on my words, my movements. I felt the great age-ful wash of guilt, I must have known, obscurely, in the pit of the consciousness with which I performed whatever acts I had performed, who and what I was. It inhibited my words even more. She was bathed in that light, so proud and vulnerable, shifting backwards and forwards, her tall comely shape like a product of it, so statuesque and proud, waiting for words I could never utter now I knew who I once was, what I later was, to her. At last she took my silence with finality. She became as shapely, as functional as that light.

The light surrounding her was oblong and tall, suiting her proportions. Then the light changed and all the angles softened and I was staring now at a circular orb as rich as morning. There were rainbows in front of my eyes and the multitudinous curve of those hairs once more. Like sedge-grasses or rushes sweeping down a dune, they glistened with pinpoints of moisture as if Morning herself had bestowed them upon her, sucked through that invisible line between light and dark. I knew then it was my arm, on which my large head was resting. The long funnel of carpet was up there, a mouth of light. The morning sun filled it almost totally, distorted only by the grime on the plate-glass window. I stared at this sun for a long time. It was golden as ever, but no longer an orb. It was blessedly elliptical, as if the lenses of my new eyes had given it depth. Then the sun was eclipsed by a shape that entered its curve abruptly and hung there, wavering slightly, its edges blurred. Was it cherub or flying creature, I wondered, hovering just beyond the edges of that plate-glass; until it spoke then, and in a boy's voice.

I brought you your things, sir.

The voice was high-pitched and eager, with a slight hint of the Americas. I wondered what being would call such as me sir. I dragged myself towards the light. His face withdrew somewhat, then approached again. A hand stretched.

I kept these for you. The way you climbed that building was really something.

His hand was firm and surprisingly strong. It grasped mine until I clambered out. I rose to my full height and stretched myself. I could feel his eyes on me constantly, admiring and awestruck. I almost shared his wonder at my movements. The air was cut in half with the light which slanted in one rigid plane, darkened my upper half and lightened my lower. There was a plain white marble block by the window. I sat on it, my knees became half-orbs of grey. The marble was cool, chalk-smelling. I placed my chin in the palm of my hand and looked up from the repose of myself to his face.

I kept them for you, he repeated. They're as good as new.

He held the bandages in his tiny hands. The first stirrings of haze began in the city behind him. The bandages were amber-coloured; last night's rain had sullied all the white. He held them out as if presenting a gift. And when I took them from him I felt the mood of my last self rise like steam off them, they carried an odour like the juices of a thousand memories, if memories could have been crushed like grapes or rose petals. I let them drop to the floor and a cloud of dust rose from them, as if they were unwilling to say goodbye.

Is there anything you'd like? he asked.

I had been reluctant to speak, remembering the loathing that my voice once produced. But I trusted in his trust of me. I told him slowly and carefully that yes, I did feel hungry.

What do you eat?

And I realised for the first time that I was not sure. I had the memory of what had once been a tongue shredded on a plate, and of murmuring voices. Had I not eaten since then? I told the boy I was not sure. He described, his eyes wide open and eager, the various kinds of foods that he could get me. His father grew sweetcorn in the basement, where the heat from the immense boiler that he stoked let them grow to "that size"—and he stretched out his arms. There were leftovers from the office canteen. He could even get me whole dinners, at a pinch.

I imagined the broad green leaves of the sweetcorn and so asked him for that. He ran to the door then, but stopped there and turned. He stared at me. His brown eyes seemed almost embarrassed.

Is there something wrong? The timbre of my voice was by now like whole forests. His eyes flashed towards me and away.

I want to see you walk.

So I rose from the marble block and took his hand in mine and walked to the plate-glass window. Every tendon seemed to stretch like never before. The light filled me when I reached it. I let go of his hand and pressed both arms against the glass. The glass, which transmitted such heat, was itself like ice. My forearms blazed with colour. I turned to see was he happy, but he was gone.

I felt the light come through me. I walked up to the spiral staircase and climbed outside.

19 The city had grown its coating of haze, so thick that the skyline imitated a horizon, an even murky blue, but for the largest buildings which soared above it. Periodic gusts of hot winds spread across it, dragging me now in one direction, now in the other. I was drawn towards the cement pool and there saw myself again, with wonder now and a touch of delight. The water was miraculously still, maybe four feet deep. I was fawn in colour, strange elegant angles like curlicues whorled where my elbows were. Underneath the tawny sheen my limbs seemed translucent, changed into some strange alloy, gelatin perhaps, opaque where the bones might have been. I could have stretched for an age. I slid into the water then and assumed its element. Threads of gold flowed out from me, shifting with the ripples. I rolled my head under and around and came to the surface again, dreaming of that hair again that flowed towards a bank. Two great webbed feet were splayed above it. There was the sound of flapping wings, the sky was muddied by white and the feet slowly rose, underneath the bales of beating feathers. A large egg rocked there, backwards and forwards. A line streaked across its surface, then a regular crack which grew, emitted

small bursts of chalk dust. The sides of egg split, two wings struggled to light and a Phoenix head above them, a jabbing, mareotic beak turned this way and that. I grew to fullness then flew, again flapping bales of feather drew the webbed feet upwards. The fragments of shell tumbled into the water and hissed there, bubbling gently. Something green floated among them. I gripped it between two fingers. It was a head of corn.

The boy stood by the pool's edge, his thin arms folded round a host of green corn-tips. He smiled and I saw for the first time a gap between his teeth. I slid from the water to the pool's edge. I ate the corn slowly and he ate one too, as if to share the moment with me. I peeled the broad green leaves which the wind whipped away over the parapet into the haze beyond. He told me how the corn struggles through its envelope of green and only throws it off when it attains perfect ripeness. Has that happened to you, he asked. I answered that I could not be sure.

He told me then how his brown complexion came from stoking the enormous stoves which powered the building which his father, the boiler-man, kept under his charge. He had stoked them for six years, and was now aged twelve. He asked me my story and I told him of the changes, the bandaged dinner-parties and the escape into the night. He nodded, and seemed to understand. I remembered Marianne and Matilde, and standing by the sundial underneath the fencing, and my cheeks moistened with tears. I felt a pain where my heart should have been and my shoulders began to heave with uncontrollable sobs. He put his hands on my temples and laid my head on his minute shoulder. He told me of dreams he had of changes, that his father was in fact a king who lorded over quite a different building in a large suite, serviced by a glittering lift.

Will nothing bring you back? he asked.

I told him I was not sure. He spoke to me then of wizards, of magic potions and maiden kisses. He kissed me on the fingers, as if to see could that effect a cure, and his eyes took some time to change from hope to disappointment. Then he confided in me that his disappointment would perhaps have been greater if I had changed back since nothing could be as splendid as what I was now.

There was a rumble in the building then and the liquid in the pool broke into ripples. That sound started up, both high and low at the same time. They were the boilers, he told me, starting up for the day. He would be needed to run errands and stoke them. Was there anything else I needed?

And I remembered her then. Like a clear liquid that one drinks with very special meals, the taste brought back that perfume, that dark hat moving among the drawing boards, those long knees in the reptile house. We had both shared the changes. My longing to see her was as sharp for a moment, as brutal, as all that had happened. I held my pliant wrist, remembering the bandage she had written on. I told him there was a number, written on the bandages down by the carpet-roll, could he ring it and tell her I was here.

I saw him run across the large empty slabs below, the white bandage streaming after him. He stopped at the edge of the street to roll it in a ball, but it unwound when he ran on again, trailing through the morning crowds. I sat on the parapet, feeling somewhere that I should think of things, but my thoughts resisted any shape. Each minute brought a mood of its own to which I succumbed.

So morning passed in a series of changes. Every moment presented a different vista. The winds blew in one and died down in the next. The sun kept its heat but moved perceptibly, bringing all its shadows with it. All the creatures of the air seemed to cling to the shadows and move with them too. Towards noon they settled as if the heat had lulled them at last and they knew that the shadows, decreasing since daybreak, could only grow. The pool steamed gently. I began to walk. I paced around my rectangular home and the creatures rose in flurries with each step. They seemed to anticipate each of my movements and cleared the warm concrete under my feet before each of my footfalls. I paced the concrete for what seemed an age. Each brick was infested with life. More creatures whispered from the crevices in the parapet. I stared over the edge at that great sweep of concrete and glass, and that whisper became a roar.

There was the sound of footsteps and I turned as she emerged from the spiral staircase. The wind came from below now and tugged at her dress and the straw basket she was carrying. The boy came out behind her. He stood watching as she walked towards me past the pool. I stood with my back to the parapet. She had a flowered dress. A stick of bread jutted from the basket. I went to move but none of my muscles would answer. The wind lifted her dress in gusts like the bowl of a hyacinth over the stems of black stocking which covered her knees. I felt strangely transparent under her gaze, as if she could see as she approached every cranny of me, down to that strange heart of mine still woven into a bowl from that afternoon of animals.

My darling—

She held out her hand and touched mine. Slowly the whole of me rose to attention. The boy stared from behind her. Her only expression was a smile.

You are different again.

She drew me down beside her to tell me about the world. The company Musk had gone bankrupt, the product vanished without trace. And Morgan? I asked. She had called three days in succession, she told me, found the office closed and then transformed into a manicure salon. Do things change so fast out there? I asked. Everything, she answered.

I thought of Morgan and how our years together would vanish without trace. The wind lifted her hair and transformed it utterly.

Can I embrace you? I asked her.

When she smiled in reply I put my arms around her, felt how they stretched with ease down below her spine to the tops of her thighs. She stroked my back, which seemed to mould itself into her hand's movement. I could picture the shape it assumed, a scallop, ridged to its base by her five long fingers. She drew one finger from the hollow of my temple down the long plane of my cheek and buried it in the golden strands of my torso. I lifted her in both hands, one beneath the small of her back and the other behind her knees, and walked with her to the parapet. She laid her cheek on the concrete and her eyes followed each one of my movements. Behind the flame of her hair the city steamed in its haze. My largeness was apt at last, my three fingers stretched the fabric of her dress, they exuded a warmth that filled her eyes, I was nothing that I had ever known or imagined. I carried her to the pool and dipped her slowly just beneath its surface. The green corn leaves floated everywhere, clinging to her body as I lay with one arm stretched on the bank, the other rippling the water. She made a crown of thick dark olive with the leaves. And as she played with me I changed, the hair of my forearm became sleek and shining, my fingers bunched like the feet of cattle. She nudged against my ear and drew one arm around me, wrapping the long strands of my tail about her neck. The boy made a wide fan of the corn-leaves

and beat the air repeatedly to cool her. We played all afternoon under
the boy's slow, quiet eyes. They filled with our delight and delighted us
in turn. I saw a band of gold glistening in the water. I brought it to the
surface and saw it was a wedding-ring. Long, slow tears coursed down my
face then. She brushed them clear with her hands, but they kept on
coming. And as if they understood my need, they held me while I wept,
filling the pool to its brim, tears spilling over the sides. By evening, the
whole parapet was wet.

She left with the last of the light. It held on barely, very barely, while
she travelled down the core of the building. I saw her make that short,
hesitant run across the piazza below and on to the empty street. The
darkness slowly filled the air behind her, as if only my gaze had been willing it back. The way the inky blue of Matilde's palette gradually merged
with and swamped the pink, that way the night invaded each yard of
street as she passed over it.

20

The moon then came up and spread its own brand of light,
and its image in the water was rippled by the wind. I was content to lie and measure its ascent and observe the gradual appearance of
the stars. The spiral staircase became etched with silver. In my naivety,
my joy, I had neglected to ask either of them about what lay below. That
anonymous hum which even now persisted seemed to imply any number
of worlds. I made my way to the staircase, swung myself on to the whorl
of metal and crept downwards. I saw the concrete room and remembered
my bedding in that roll of carpet. Below that again I found a hall of
wires. They spread in all directions, all shapes and colours, from the tini-
est to cables the circumference of my torso. The humming, so anonymous above, had grown a certain depth down here, as if each wire
carried its own note, from the thinnest soprano to the basso-profundo of
the thick-set cables. I thought of the music of insects, so ravishingly
conveyed to me that garden afternoon. Each sound then had seemed
bred of chance; no graph, no logical architecture, could have determined the glorious chaos of that chorus. But here, purpose seemed to

reign. The wires sang in unison, with a constancy that had an end in view, an end I could only guess at.

The end must have been in that building, or perhaps the building itself was an end. With this in mind I made my way across the hall of wires to what had the appearance of a lift-shaft. The array of white buttons was discoloured with age. Too small for the pads of my fingers; I had to press them at random several all at once. I saw hawsers glisten through the metal grid, I heard the clicking of grease and the whir of a motor. And then the trellised box of the lift rose towards me.

We sank downwards through the building, the lift and I. Those dim halls rose to my vision and away again, each much like the one before. The buttons I had pressed must have determined our passage, because we stopped, unaccountably, in a felt-lined corridor without much distinction. I stepped through the trellised doors. I was half-mindful of going forward, half-mindful of going back again, when the doors slid closed. The lift whined and the light on the panel sank downwards.

I walked forwards. There were doors off this corridor, with rooms leading to more doors. What I had assumed to be devoid of life I soon found to be a bestiary. A deep-piled room seethed with mice. A moth watched me from a filing-cabinet. His eyes, full of the wisdom of ages and the fierceness of his few hours here, seemed to require my attention. My ears swelled with a sensation I could hardly feel as sound, let alone speech, and yet I felt from his quivering wings the urge to converse. I brushed him on to my palm. His glance seemed to harden—with disdain, it seemed—and his wings beat their way skewwise towards the doorway.

I followed. His uneven flight, irritating but somehow alluring, drew me down stairways, passages, lit only by the fierceness of his glare. We were now in low-roofed concrete tunnels, similar in texture to the ones I had left, far above. He blundered into walls and cables, but somehow always kept ahead of me. Then that jagged flutter changed to a spiral of panic. I heard an unearthly trill, like the vibration of a toughened tongue in a mouth of bright leather. I turned and saw the scythe-like wings of a bat swoop by me, then change its flight into those jagged arpeggios the moth was now weaving. They traced each other in counterpoint for a moment and it seemed a second cry rang out with the bat's, a cry that was soft, like the sound pollen would make brushing off a wing, but yet a cry with more pain in it than any I had heard. Their paths merged into one then, the bat's mouth opened, then closed, and the bat flew on alone.

The corridor seemed like a tomb to me afterwards. That ashy cry seemed to echo down it, bringing tears to my eyes which made the walls glow. I made my way to the corridor's end, hoping for a lift or concrete stairs. The tunnelled walls curved and were lit by a glow that seemed brighter than the rainbows of my tears. It was yellowish, it flickered, there was a rhythmic, scraping sound. I heard voices then, one old and masterful, the other young. I came to the corner and saw the boy in the distance shovelling coal into a furnace. The heap he shovelled from was replenished from a source unseen. His shovelling was too tender to keep his heap down to size; it kept growing until it almost engulfed him. He was goaded on by shouts, coarse and violent. Then a dark-skinned figure in dungarees appeared, shovelled furiously with him for a moment, sent him spinning towards the furnace with a blow and left again, admonishing him to work faster.

21 When the boy appeared the next morning with his arms full of cornheads and that glad expression on his face, I didn't mention what I had seen. I breakfasted on the corn and watched the leaves whirl over the city on the early-morning wind. Even that wind seemed to partake of the savagery of last night's events. The mists slowly disappeared, revealing the tiny beads of the morning crowds. I bathed in the pool and as he washed each sinew, I noticed weals on his body where before I had been aware only of that dusky tan. I questioned him on the rules of the building, though. He told me that he worked by night, and by day the building fed upon the heat he had generated. The corridors were peopled by secretarial ranks and the whirr of office machines took over from the more ancient machines of the night. I asked him was he tired by day and he told me that he was, but the pleasure of my presence kept him awake. I told him that once my presence brought very little pleasure, to man or to beast, and he answered that he could not imagine

how this could have been so. After a time he slept in my waterlogged arms. I wrapped myself round him, to accommodate his dreams.

I awoke to find her standing above me. It must have been early afternoon. I whispered at her to be silent and placed him beneath the shade of the parapet. We became lovers once more, then many many times. The concrete bubbled with our perspirations and we took to the pool for refreshment. She floated there, staring into the sky as I told her of the bat and the helpless moth. She told me that life had its own laws, different for each species. Does one law not rule us all? I asked her. How can it, she answered, or else we would have seen it. I asked her was there a law for me, as distinct as those for the bat and the moth. If there were, she asked me, would you obey it?

I had ceased to think of thoughts as thoughts, for the effort to separate them from the clouds of sensation that germinated them was mostly beyond me. Now, however, I pulled at this thought, I needed it clear, abstract and separate so as to find an answer. Her head played around my armpit then gradually fell asleep. I remembered dimly a tale of a beast who cried to the world to reveal him his destiny, to send him a mate. If there was a law for the bat, for the moth, for the woman, there must be a law for me, a law as succinct and precise as those laws I obeyed when walking past the whispering gardens each day to work. But how to find out this law, and the destiny it implied? But then, it occurred to me, walking by those gardens, along the torrid tracks, I had been no more aware of what law I obeyed than I was now, obeying no law at all. If asked then, was there a pattern, a plan, I would have said no, categorically no. So law, if law there was, revealed itself in retrospect, like a sad bride coming to her wedding too late to partake in it.

My efforts at thought exhausted me and these fancies gradually sank into that well of sensation from which they had emerged. The darkness seeped around me, like a torpor brought on by my mood. It was indeed night. She still slept in the niche of my arm. I lifted her head and placed it at my navel, and curled around each of her limbs to make her sleeping easier. The wind ruffled her tangled clothing and set the down along her cheekbones alight. I thought about what laws bound us and she opened her eyes then, as if in answer to that thought. Her lids parted slowly to reveal my curved reflection in her pupils. I stared at myself for a time, for perhaps too long a time, seeing me, seeing her, seeing me in her. Only when her eyes were fully open did I become aware of her expression. She took a sharp intake of breath. The horror filled her limpid eyes as the night had filled mine. She drew backwards. I raised my hands to clutch her, too roughly. Please, I whispered. It's the night, she said, you're different. No, I cried. She was standing now, walking backwards towards the staircase. You should never have let me sleep, she whispered. The dark moulded her like a curtain, her hair glowed like sullen rust. I can't help my fear, she whispered, you should never have let me sleep. Her hand searched for the metal staircase. No, I whispered again, but my whisper gathered like a roar. She ran from that wall of sound. Somewhere above me, stars began to fall.

22   I lay for a long time. The darkness weighed on me. Who would remember the extraordinary length of her legs, I wondered, who would delight in that softness of skin at the joint of her knee, if not me? The changes came with such rapidity. Was the air never to be still, I wondered, from one moment to the next? To whom could she tell those stories, of the large tractors swathing through the meadows, of the young girl walking through the dew-soaked stubble? And even now the pace of my grief was such that I could feel it entwining me in a skin of its own. She had seen something, I remembered, something that caused the fear, and I rose slowly to my feet and staggered to the water. All I saw there was a shadow, like some more essential shade of dark than that which surrounded me. And I managed the thought that even what she had seen was now part of the past. Yet the desire to see what she had seen persisted. I made for the building below, searching out a mirror.

The lift was made of trellised bars of metal. None of its surfaces conveyed the ghost of a reflection. I pressed the buttons for some level below. I heard the whine of the motor, and with it a sound that was not a sound, that was above sound, that was a sensation, around my skull, my cheekbones, like the needle-points of a sandstorm. I raised my hands to my cheeks to locate it. Then this sound took shape, flowed into vowels and syllables, into sentences. It spoke.

You operate this lift, it said, like someone remembering what it was to travel in it. And yet you look like—

What do I look like? I asked. I closed my eyes. The voice began again.

You take your texture from whatever surface you inhabit. In this lift you belong to that odour of grease, hawsers and trellised metal. Outside it, I would have no idea.

I opened my eyes. I saw opposite me, clinging to the bars, a bat. His eyes were bright with reason. I remembered the arpeggios of fear and the death of the moth. That leatherish mouth didn't move, and yet his voice sang all around me.

Can you fly? he asked.

I shook my head.

Each animal function, he told me, has its sister emotion. Loathing, he said, has been your companion for some time.

He moved his head and seemed to smile. Do you wish to fly?

I nodded.

Take us up, then.

I pressed the buttons. He stared as we swayed upwards once more, a stare full of brightness, whimsy, intelligence.

23   He clung to the matted hair on my arm as I walked from the staircase. I placed him on the parapet. His sightless eyes turned in their sockets. I could feel his voice again, prodding me like gorse. Forget wings, he told me. Watch!

He moved both arms as if stroking the air, stepped off the parapet and plummeted like a dead weight. I cried out in alarm, but saw his fall, of a sudden, transform into a grace curve. It became a figure of eight and slowly drew him upwards once more. He hovered above me for a moment, full of cries.

Wings are quite useless, he said, mere symbols of our activity. Birds, being vainer than my species, love to proclaim their importance, cover themselves in feathers and tails they can fan. But all one needs to fly with is desire.

And I thought of how swallows always reveal themselves in spring like small threads of longing and as the heat grows they become rushes of memory, filling the air with their curlicues, never touching ground, symbols indeed of desire.

Do you desire? he asked me.

I had hardly thought before I flew. The parapet swung above me and piazza grew larger, swum before my eyes till I left it behind and moved in a long curve down Dame Street, barely at the level of the second windows, piercing the rim of that layer of heat that the night hadn't yet dispersed. I took the breeze on my left side at Nassau Street and swept down that channel of air. Some instinct drew me towards the river. I felt his voice all around me again and glared up to see him at my shoulder, his wings dipping easily and gracefully with my infant movements.

Lead the way, he whispered, so I swung him down the steaming river and then left, face above the railway tracks, under the long glass awning, through those arcs of spray that splashed on the night trains. We kept close to the rails as sleeper after sleeper sped below us, each like a resinous wall. I smelt the odour of cut grass then and rose and skimmed above garden after garden till at length I came to one where the blades had not been cut and recognised it as mine. I headed over the tips of the nodding grasses, barely able to see through the pollen. There was an immense triangle jutting from a metal plinth. I hovered over the heiroglyphs on the disc below and saw how the moon's cast upon time was at variance with the sun's. I saw a large ball of light somewhere up ahead. I left the sundial and made my way through the grasses once more. The ball of light beckoned through the clouds of pollen and then the air suddenly froze. I beat myself against it, but to no avail, the light was there, but sealed behind it, impenetrable. I had almost exhausted myself when I recognised the frozen air to be glass, the ball of light a flickering bulb. I slid downwards. A large jewelled palm wiped moisture off the pane. Through the swathe that was cut in it I could see a glass, half-filled with liquid and the same hand lifting it to the crescent space between lips. I was indeed home. I watched Marianne for what seemed an age, from below. In my absence her lips had changed from deep cherry to rust, her hair had been shorn tight, the corners of her eyes had grown two black triangles. Two fingers indented themselves on her cheek and the dome of another's head descended for another's lips to meet hers. I recognised James.

There was a letting-go and a sensation of ice sliding past my cheek. I fell down among the grasses below. Her lips, though larger to me than ever, were still those lips I remembered. Down among those roots of green I could still picture the kiss, too long, far too long for the desire that had carried me here. I tried to beat myself upwards but not a whisper of movement ensued.

I felt the air stroking my face then in soft hushes, and his voice sang round me once more.

You know now why bats are what they are, poised between strutting and flight. To fly cleanly you must learn pure desire, a desire that has no object. Any attachment to things of the world leaves you earthbound once more.

I held a pure blade of grass between my palms and imagined pure desire. I could picture nothing, and soon nothing was all I pictured. Slowly, very slowly, the memories left me. The house, the hissing sprinklers, the sundial. That window was the last memory to go, and the kiss drifted away like a whorling water, and I rose, to hover inches over the lawn. He chirped with a pleasure that made me soar. Soon the house became a tiny dot in the palette of the blue earth below us.

24 The city sank, like a glass bead into a muddied pool. The air was pure above it, with the ethereal blue of a wedding-gown. He seemed not to move, but yet was all movement, rising above me. Desire, he said, when purified; becomes desire no longer. I felt his voice and soared with the certainty. Loathing, when purified, becomes loathing no longer. I felt all affirmation and drifted towards him, his eyes glowing sightless in the gloom. Through blindness, his voice sang out, we cultivate the vision, through sensation we reach it and yet what we reach we still cannot see. He drifted around me like a thread of silk. Yet the feeling, he whispered, is our only road there, so can we doubt that the feeling is all?

He drew his limbs about him and let himself fall. I fell to his pace, just above him. The air thickened and the streets billowed out below. There is a city, he whispered, to whose shape all cities aspire. And when the sheaves of our city fall away, we shall reach it. When will that be? I asked him. Tomorrow, he sang. He curled his furred body and sped downwards.

25 I stood alone on the parapet under the moon. Alarth—for that was his name—had vanished into the depths of the lift-shaft. The streets were empty and silver, like a dream that was now dreaming itself. I slid down from the parapet and walked towards the trough. I saw my face there, as limpid and clear as the moon beside it. Each breath I took was like a sliver of lost time. I inhaled and seemed to drink in hours. To each beginning there was an end, I knew, and each change hurried it nearer. I walked down the staircase to the comfort of the lift. I pressed the buttons and felt the gradual slide downwards. The cables of the lift swung, shifting their curves as they did so. I thought of the gardens, through the long heat and the rain, of Marianne's face with its triangles of black. That change, so miniature, had brought an ache to me as large as that the chaos of myself had brought to her. There was a law, I now knew, and its resolution would come to be. I pressed the buttons with the stumps of my arms. The door slid back and a corridor faced me, like all the others. There was no moonlight here to illuminate my way, but the discs of my eyes soon accepted the black and the dark became light of its own. A swarm of midges hovered round a door. I entered, and saw a room in the chaos that work had left behind. There were paper cups, the rinds of cheeses and a bottle of mineral water. There were drawing-boards ranged against the walls and across the slope of one of them a figure lay sleeping. I recognised the crescent of the green eyeshade and moved myself closer. Beneath the dull green shadow I saw Morgan's face, his lips immobile, a day or two's growth on his chin. He had vanished when she called, she had told me, and must have found different employment. I saw drawings crumpled beneath his head, those buildings of concrete and glass that had come to litter the city, half-finished. Conceived by nobody, it was generally imagined, and built in the owlish hours. Yet their source was here, in these immeasurable

rooms. Spanning the wall behind was a miniature of the city as it once had been. I looked at those squares in their measured movement towards the river, their proportions so human, yet so perfect to the eye. I saw the park, etched out in strokes of green, the zoological gardens at its centre. I remembered the textures of pavements under my feet, of grass round my ankles, the doorways that once stared at my child's eyes, the balanced stone of their arches and the fanlights of glass. I saw drops splashing on Morgan's clenched hand and drew my lips down to taste the salt of my tears. The hand shifted then, the fingers stretched and touched my movable skin.

It is you, he said, after a moment's pause.

I nodded. His reddened eyes flashed under their arc of green.

What is it like, he asked, to be away from it all?

I shook my head. If I could have spoken I would have asked him not to talk, reminded him of our days without words in adjacent rooms. He rubbed his eyes and gestured round the room.

Each afternoon, he said, I draw the city for them. And each morning my instructions change.

Who are they, I would have asked.

I work for them now, he added. He gripped a paper cup and began rubbing it to shreds.

Do you remember the time, he asked, when we used to work until five and walk down the river to our separate trains?

Yes, I said. The word came out round and true.

I sleep here now, he told me. I wake and I work and I sleep again. I keep the shutters down so that the light is the same.

I asked him would he mind if I pulled them back. He shook his head slowly and watched me as I did so.

A horse walked down the street below, moved sideways to avoid a bollard. A large poppy filled the window of a haberdashery.

I stretched out one arm and touched his green eyeshade. My palm, like a mucous membrane, let his face glow through it.

Is it fair, he asked me, to have given us the memory of what was and the desire of what could be when we must suffer what is?

I heard the gravel of dust in his voice, I saw smudges of graphite on his fingers. I phrased his name slowly. Morgan.

He looked up. I felt the wind of his despair. I rose slowly till my thighs

were level with his face. Goodbye now, he whispered. He stepped forwards with me and opened the window. I heard it close behind me as I
sank through the gloom outside.

The horse was walking slowly, his dark grace etched against the
sweep of College Green. I felt tired, I had lost even the memory of
desire. I sank into the poppy in the haberdasher's window. I clung to the
pistil and the petals billowed round me, settling gradually into a pillow
of red.

26   I awoke to the sounds of people. My arms were curled round
      that thrust of pistil with the dewdrop at the tip. The morning
sun had stiffened the petals, the red pollen covered me as if their lips had
bunched into a kiss. The early crowds passed by, but as I stretched my
limbs groups of them gathered to stare. I drew myself upwards, bending
the pistil towards me. The dewdrop fell on my face. They murmured as
they watched, about portents and signs. Two soldiers pushed to the
front. The pistil slipped from my hands then, I rolled down the petal and
came to rest at their feet.

A man in the livery of a hotel commissionaire called on me to stand.
One khaki leg prodded me, gently, but not without authority. Whom do
you belong to, a voice above me asked.

I saw a small face thrusting through the thighs about me, a pair of
arms full of cornheads. I gestured, but was unwilling to speak. Is he
yours, the same voice asked, when he made it to my side. The boy nodded, with childlike pride and vigour. He pressed a cornhead into my
hands.

I ate, and listened. You must keep him inside, one of the soldiers said,
phrasing the words carefully, as one does with a child. The boy nodded,
took my hand and led me forwards.

The crowd parted in front of us, but followed from behind. The commissionaire protested from amongst them. The solider reached forward
and the boy began to run. I ran too, over the grass above the paving-

stones, and as the crowd followed faster, I gathered him in my arms and lost them.

We wove our way through the desultory streets. We came to a hotel with a park beside it. There was a waterless fountain there. We climbed into its stone flower and feasted on the cornheads. Soon the petals were littered with green.

27 He told me he had searched for me through the depths of the building. He had waited for her, but she had never arrived. I told him I had flown, guided by a feeling that was nothing but itself. I had seen the city become a dot on the landscape and a blade of grass become a tower of green.

He told me then of Jack, who had planted a stalk that made a ladder to the skies, of how the story never told him what Jack found there. I would dearly love to fly, he said, turning his face to me. We will wait till evening, I told him, till the magic hour when our desires can picture the image that retreats from us. Will you fly to her? he asked, but I didn't reply.

All day we waited, while the sun moved the shadows through the empty grass. Some shadows walked and stopped by the fountain, gazing at us before walking on once more. He told me how the shadows thrown by the fires he stoked reminded him of the lives other boys must lead, lives he would never know anything about. Sleeping, never far from his father's calloused hands, he had longed for a friend, but could never picture what that friend might be like. A siren wailed in the distance and the city's hum rose like a final breath. What is happening? he asked, and curled his fingers round me. Nothing, I answered. Be calm.

Towards afternoon I must have slept. I imagined a moth fluttering towards the sun, the dust on its wings crackling with the heat, the flame spurring him on to his own extinction. When I awoke the mauve light had softened the shadows and given each colour a life of its own. It was evening.

The boy stood on the stone petal staring at the sky. I swung my way towards him, wrapped one arm around his torso and flew. I held his face close to mine to see the passing wonders echoed in his eyes. I bore him round at random and my desire became delight. The rush of wind drew my hair around him in a silken cloak. We flew together, out by the southern suburbs. We went far up into those realms of pure air where the rose-coloured clouds hung over the city I had loved like a brooding mushroom. The winds were fresh and keen up there. The air was aquamarine. I could see the lines of the bay very dimly, and another line too, between the metal green I knew to be the sea and the brownish mass that was the city. I sped down towards it and found not one line but two, both of which crossed at intervals, in slender figures of eight. It was the railway-track, which traced the curve of the bay. I had heard tell of these tracks, but had never yet seen them. His eyes were alert to every passing shape, as if the shadows his flaming coals threw had taken on true life. This side of the city was foreign to me, with its multitude of cramped, cracked villas tumbling towards the sea. I bore us closer to the land and found the houses gave way to a slope of trees. Though there was foliage at the tops, the trunks were quite bare and so I whipped between them, grazing the peeling bark like a swallow. The dance of those trees I apprehended without thought as I threaded my way through them and crept upwards again. We burst through the foliage and the odour there— thicker than steel wool, richer than pollen—brought to mind the one I had last held this close. I thought of musk once more. The mountainside sang of it and told me my desire had an object. The slope became a cliff, wreathed in fog. The fog bled downwards and I followed to the sea where our reflections rippled with our movement. Then there was fog no more and tracks beneath us. We passed scattered villas, imitiative of a style I could not now remember. They led to a bridge, and a station beyond.

I felt the panic of a desire that had led me truly. I traced a large arc over the eaves of the station. There was a line of pleasure-parlours by a crumbling promenade. In one of them a yellow light glimmered.

28 She was standing by the dodgems in a blue smock. There were blotches on her face and runnels of hair along her arms. The changes, she told me, were so rapid that each day was a source of sometimes wonder, sometimes terror, sometimes both. She had longed to see me, but had been unwilling to approach, since she felt the need of a partner to delight in them. Could you now? she asked, and came towards me, the pits and shallows of her face raised in expectation. Yes, I said, but the word that emerged did not seem affirmative. So, she said, I must find another. She brushed my translucent face with her bunched fingers. Business was even worse, she told me, in the realms of entertainment than in the realm of perfume. Her friends had shunned her, she told me, seeing her as a sign, of a happening they would never allude to or define. And yet I am glad, she said. Tell me why I am glad. The fact, I told her, is a relief from its anticipation. And the feeling is all. She drew her swollen lips into a smile. Once more, she understood. A soldier entered then, his head bent low, his hands thrust deep into his khakis. You must leave now, she whispered. She drew her smock around her face and walked towards him.

We slipped through the shadows, the boy and I. I drew him over the awning in one sad curve. The soldier parted her tresses below us. She sighed with anticipated pleasure. We hovered above them, like uninvited guests, until I drew him towards the sea once more.

29 The waters were calm, a long shallow pit of salt. All hint of reflection had now vanished. They were graced by a thin pall of mist.

You cannot blame her, the boy said. His voice bounced over the waters.

No, I replied. I sank with him to just above the mist.

She loved you, he said. But only for a time.

His wisdom was comforting. I fell with him into the sea and held him there, buoyed by an excess of salt.

He remarked on how it tasted like tears. I agreed with him. We let the sea carry us, and the night.

30 When day came up, we saw that the city with its crumbling cubes was far behind us. The waters steamed gently. The liquid rose in a diaphanous haze and left behind pure crystals of salt. They stayed poised beneath the surface like a thousand eyes. I twined myself into a vessel beneath him and moved us forwards with my broad fingers. He told me of the mermaid who had ventured on land and to whom each footstep was like the thrust of a blade. Soon my arms became covered in a crystal sheen.

The sun moved slowly on the waters. At its pinnacle the haze was such that it multiplied itself. I swam on. The boy wondered whether the sun moved backwards out here. But no, it was merely the illusion of haze.

I felt little need to speak. The sound of the water, oddly reverberant in the ever-present vapour, made speech enough. The boy talked as the spirit moved him. He had strands of my hair wrapped around his fists, in excitement or anticipation. Then night came down and the light gave way quite unobtrusively.

31 We must have slept, for I awoke to moonlight and a sense of turbulence. The sea all about us was calm, however, and the moon was brilliant in the absence of haze. The boy still slept. I heard a prodding all around me which merged into a voice. I saw Alarth winging towards me across the waters. Come, come, he whispered. A winged fish broke the surface, twisted silver under the moonlight and enveloped him

in its maw. Then a white flash filled the air from the city we had left. It was paler than any white that had been and was followed by others, each paler again till the white seemed permanent. Then the sounds came, all the sounds at once, from the deepest to the thinnest in a circular boom, they sang towards us in waves, and hard on their heels the waters followed. I covered the boy and was dragged by the mountain of water.

32 What came was not quite daylight and not quite night. The waters were calm and strewn with debris and cut grass. I had twined myself into a pouch round the boy. Far behind us that cloud, shaped like a phoenix, glowed with that terrible mauve. I stroked my fingers and moved us towards a promontory beyond.

A marble arm lay on the whitened sand. The boy was sick, I knew. His translucent lips tried to speak, but couldn't. I rose with him from the waters and made my way across that sand. There were the marks of feet. A fish twined its way round a clump of seagrass, its gills moving easily. I followed the webbed footprints.

When the time came that I knew the boy was dying, I wrapped myself fully round him, assumed him into myself. We both walked onwards, though my steps were weary with the knowledge that I would never see his face again. I remembered the cornheads, but felt no need for food. After a time those footprints were joined by others.

Each knew where to go, with no need of direction. With the mareotic sea far behind me, I took their advice. Many, many footprints later I came to a pool. The boy in me drew me to its surface. I put my lips to it and drank and felt his satisfaction. When the rippling caused by my lips had settled, I saw a reflection there, no less terrible than mine. A hand rubbed white sand away from a mouth. It was like mine in its shape and texture. Her hair, unmistakably female, was a whey-coloured fan in the constant wind. I raised my head and the boy inside me leapt. Her lips moved slowly and creased themselves upwards. My lips moved too. I recognized Marianne.

33 We spoke for a while, by the pool. Once accustomed to each other's voices, we both walked together, following the footprints before us. We had similar memories of the maretoic lake. She told me of a fish that walked and of a tree that shed its covering of scales. Matilde, she told me, was inside her now. I put my arms down to her waist and felt her. The boy kicked with pleasure at the touch.

Once a large beast flew above us and her hand gripped mine. We followed the footprints, but met no others. Soon the sands gave way to a vista of grass. The labour of our feet was lessened then, that soft cushion drew us onwards. The footprints had ceased, but we followed our own path. We crossed a hill and found a landscape of tall poplars. Planted years ago, it seemed to speak of quieter times. If things lead us to anything, she said to me, they surely lead us to realisation. Each happening bears a message, as surely as those poplars speak of whoever planted them. She curled her fingers round my hand once more and I saw the translucence was slowly fading, being replaced by something like a tan. The line of poplars led us to a signpost reading: HOPE ETERNAL. The arrow had wound itself into a circle, though, the point of which pressed into its rear. There was a garden up ahead. The gates were unattended and the grasses wild. The sundial seemed bleached by an eternity of light and the sprinklers moved so slowly that they whispered. Can I kiss you, she asked and I answered yes, in a voice that had become like hers. She had to tilt her head to reach my lips which I found were once more soft. The kiss was long, long enough for the sun to cross the dial, for the moon to traverse it and for the sun to rise once more. I saw the globes of her eyes and in my visage reflected there saw something as human as surprise.

In the Tradition of the Irish Short Story

Barr, Fiona. *The Wall-Reader*.
Beckett, Mary. *A Belfast Woman*.
Beckett, Samuel. *More Pricks Than Kicks*.
Berkeley, Sara. *The Swimmer in the Deep Blue Dream*.
Bowen, Elizabeth. *Look at All Those Roses*.
Boyle, Patrick. *A View from Calvary*.
Cooke, Emma. *Female Forms*.
Corkery, Daniel. *The Hounds of Banda*.
Daly, Ita. *The Lady with the Red Shoes*.
Higgins, Aidan. *Felo de Se*.
Joyce, James. *Dubliners*.
Kelly, Maeve. *A Life of Her Own*.
Kiely, Benedict. *A Letter to Peachtree*.
Lavin, Mary. *A Memory*.
MacMahon, Bryan. *The Red Petticoat*.
McCabe, Eugene. *Heritage*.
McGahern, John. *The Collected Stories*.
McLaverty, Michael. *Collected Stories*.
Moore, George. *The Untilled Field*.
Mulkerns, Val. *Antiquities*.
O'Brien, Edna. *A Scandalous Woman*.
O'Brien, Kate Cruise. *A Gift House and Other Stories*.
O'Connor, Frank. *Collected Stories*.
O'Faolain, Julia. *Melancholy Baby and Other Stories*.
O'Faolain, Sean. *The Collected Stories*.
O'Flaherty, Liam. *The Mountain Tavern and Other Stories*.
O'Kelly, Seamus. *The Golden Barque and The Weaver's Grave*.

Park, David. *Oranges from Spain*.

Plunkett, James. *The Trusting and the Maimed*.

Somerville, E. OE. and Martin Ross. *Some Experiences of an Irish R. M.*

Stephens, James. *Etched in Moonlight*.

Strong, Eithne. *The Collected Stories*.

Treacy, Maura. *A Sixpence in Her Shoe and Other Stories*.

Trevor, William. *The Collected Stories*.

Of the Contemporary Writers Collected Here

Banville, John. *Long Lankin*.

Binchy, Maeve. *London Transports*.

Boylan, Clare. *Concerning Virgins: A Collection of Short Stories*.

Conlon, Evelyn. *My Head Is Opening*.

Devlin, Anne. *The Way-Paver*.

Dorcey, Mary. *A Noise from the Woodshed: Short Stories*.

Enright, Anne. *The Portable Virgin*.

Hogan, Desmond. *The Diamonds at the Bottom of the Sea and Other Stories*.

Jordan, Neil. *A Neil Jordan Reader*.

Kelly, Rita. *The Whispering Arch and Other Stories*.

MacLaverty, Bernard. *Secrets and Other Stories*.

Mathews, Aidan. *Adventures in a Bathyscope*.

McCann, Colum. *Fishing the Sloe-Black River*.

Ní Dhuibhne, Éilís. *The Second Blackstaff Book of Short Stories*.

O'Connor, Joseph. *True Believers*.

O'Loughlin, Michael. *The Inside Story*.

Sheehan, Ronan. *Boy with an Injured Eye*.

JOHN BANVILLE, fiction writer, critic, and dramatist, was born in Wexford in 1945. He lives in Dublin with his wife and two sons. He has received the Guinness Peat Aviation Literary Award and has been nominated for the Booker Prize. He is currently Literary Editor of *The Irish Times*. A critical introduction to his work was written by Rudiger Imhof in 1989. "Nightwind" and "Persona" first appeared in *Long Lankin*, a collection of short stories published in 1970. His other fictional works include *Nightspawn* (1971); *Birchwood* (1973); *Doctor Copernicus* (1976), which won the James Tait Black Memorial Prize; *Kepler* (1980); *The Newton Letter* (1982); *Mefisto* (1986); *The Book of Evidence* (1989); *Ghosts* (1993); *Athena* (1995); and *The Untouchable* (1997). *The Ark*, a children's book (illustrated by Conor Fallon), was published in 1996.

MAEVE BINCHY, novelist and short story writer, was born in Dublin in 1940 and gave up her original career as a teacher to take up a position (which she still holds) with *The Irish Times*. She now lives in London. Her first attempts at fiction were short story collections based on her observations of the people around her: *Central Line* (1978), *Victoria Line* (1980), and *Dublin 4* (1982). "Shepherd's Bush" first appeared in *London Transports*, a collection published in 1983. Her novels, which have been translated into many languages and are published worldwide, include *Light a Penny Candle*, *Silver Wedding*, *Echoes* (1985), *Circle of Friends* (1990), *The Copper Beach* (1992), *The Glass Lake*, *Cross Lines* (1996), *Evening Classes* (1997), and, most recently, *Tara Road* (1999). *Echoes* and *Circle of Friends* have been adapted for cinema. Her television play *Deeply Regretted By* won two Jacob Awards and Best Script Award at the Prague Film Festival.

ELIZABETH BOWEN (1899–1973) was born in Dublin and spent much of her childhood at the family home in County Cork. In 1923 she published her first collection of short stories, *Encounters*. Many other collections followed, including *Look at All Those Roses* (1941), which includes "Summer Night"; and *The Demon Lover* in 1945. She wrote the following novels: *The Hotel* (1927), *The Last September* (1929), *Friends and Relations* (1931), *To the North* (1932), *The House in Paris* (1935), *The Death of the Heart* (1938), *The Heat of the Day* (1949), *A World of Love* (1955), and *Eva Trout* (1969).

CLARE BOYLAN, journalist, short story writer, and novelist, was born in Dublin in 1948. She received the Benson & Hedges Award for outstanding journalism in 1974 and has served as a judge on several literary award committees, including that for the Booker Prize. She has published a number of short story collections: *A Nail on the Head* (1983); *Black Baby* (1988); *Concerning Virgins* (1989), which includes "The Little Madonna"; and *That Bad Woman* (1995). She has written the novels *Holy Pictures* (1983), *Last Resorts* (1984), *Home Rule* (1992), and *Room for a Single Lady* (1997). Her work has also been broadcast on BBC Radio and RTE (Radio Telefis Eireann, the Irish national radio and television network).

EVELYN CONLON was born in 1952 in County Monaghan and was educated at St. Patrick's College, Maynooth, in County Kildare. She spent many years traveling the world, living for a time in Australia and Asia. Conlon is coeditor of *Graph* literary magazine and now lives in Dublin where she works as a writer, reviewer, and occasional broadcaster. Her book *Where Did I Come From?*, a sex education book for children, was published in 1983. She has also written novels, including *Stars in the Daytime* (1989), *Up in the Air*, and *A Glassful of Letters* (1998). Her first collection of short stories, *My Head Is Opening*, was published in 1987 and was followed in 1993 by *Taking Scarlet as a Real Colour*. "Telling" first appeared in the *Cimarron Review* in 1996.

ANNE DEVLIN was born in Belfast in 1951. She won the Hennessy Literary Award in 1982 for her short story "Passages," which was adapted for television as *A Woman Calling*. Her first collection of plays, *Ourselves*

Alone, was published in 1986, and *After Easter* in 1994. "Naming the Names" first appeared in *The Way-Paver*, a collection of short stories published in 1986. The recipient of many awards, she received the Samuel Beckett Award in 1984 and the Susan Smith Blackburn Prize in 1986.

EMMA DONOGHUE was born in Dublin in 1969, where she lived until moving to Cambridge University to study for a Ph.D. on eighteenth-century literary friendships. She is currently based in Canada. Her play, *I Know My Own Heart*, based on Anne Lister's regency diaries, has been produced in Cambridge, England, and Dublin. A nonfiction work, *Passions Between Women: British Lesbian Culture, 1668–1801* was published in 1993. Her novels *Stir Fry* (1994) and *Hood* (1995) received much critical acclaim, and her collection of short stories, *Kissing the Witch*, was published in 1997. *What Sappho Would Have Said*, an anthology of poems of romantic friendship, love, and desire written by women for women over four centuries, edited by Donoghue, was also published in 1997. *We Are Michael Field*, a literary history, was published in 1998. "Seven Pictures Not Taken" first appeared in the *Cimarron Review* (1996).

MARY DORCEY was born in Dublin in 1950 and has lived in England, the United States, France, and Japan. She now divides her time between Dublin and the west of Ireland. An active feminist, she was a founding member of Women for Radical Change, Irish Women United, and the Irish Gay Rights movement. She has published the following poetry collections: *Kindling* (1982), *Moving into the Space Cleared by Our Mothers* (1991), and *The River that Carries Me* (1995). Her first collection of short stories, *A Noise from the Woodshed* (1989)—which includes "A Sense of Humour"—was awarded the Rooney Prize for Irish Literature. Her first novel, *Biography of Desire*, was published in 1997.

ANNE ENRIGHT was born in Dublin in 1962, where she still lives and works as a producer at RTE television. Her novel, *The Wig My Father Wore* (1995), received much critical acclaim on publication, and her collection of short stories, *The Portable Virgin*, was awarded the Rooney Prize for Irish Literature in 1991. Her stories reprinted here were taken from *The Portable Virgin*.

DESMOND HOGAN was born in Ballinasloe in County Galway in 1950 and was educated at University College, Dublin. He has worked as an actor and as a teacher but now writes full-time. His plays include *A Short Walk to the Sea, Sanctified Distances,* and a radio play, *Jimmy,* which was produced by the BBC in 1977. He has published many novels including *The Ikon Maker* (1976), *The Leaves on Grey* (1980), and *A Curious Street* (1982). Among Hogan's other publications are the short story collections *The Diamonds at the Bottom of the Sea* (1979)—from which "The Bombs" is taken—*Lebanon Lodge,* and *Children of Lir,* as well as his autobiography, *A Farewell to Prague.*

NEIL JORDAN, writer and filmmaker, was born in Sligo, in the west of Ireland, in 1950. He now divides his time between Ireland and America. In 1974 he was a cofounder of the Irish Writers' Co-operative, which published the work of young writers. *Night in Tunisia,* a collection of short stories, appeared in 1976 and was awarded the *Guardian* Fiction Prize in 1979. Since the publication of his first novel, *The Past,* in 1980, those that have followed, including *The Dream of a Beast* (1983) and *Sunrise with Sea Monster* (1994), have met with widespread acclaim. Jordan has directed many successful films, including *Angel, The Company of Wolves, Mona Lisa, High Spirits, The Crying Game,* and, most recently, *Michael Collins.*

RITA KELLY was born in Galway in the west of Ireland in 1953. She has been writing in both Irish and English for many years, and her writings have been published in numerous collections. *The Whispering Arch and Other Stories,* which includes "En Famille," was published in 1986, and her works of poetry include *Dialann sa Diseart* (1981), *An Bealach Éadóigh* (1984), and *Fare Well / Beir Beannacht* (1990).

PATRICK MCCABE was born in Clones, County Monaghan, Ireland, in 1955 and later he spent some time in London teaching. He is married with two daughters and lives in Dublin. *The Adventures of Shay Mouse,* a children's story, was published in 1985. His first novel, *Music on Clinton Street,* was published in 1986, followed by *Carn* in 1989 and *The Butcher Boy* in 1992. In the same year, *The Butcher Boy* was adapted for stage (as *Frank Pig Says Hello*) and produced by the Co-Motion Theatre Company at the Dublin Theatre Festival; it also won *The Irish Times*/Aer Lingus Literature Prize and was shortlisted for the 1992 Booker Prize. *A Mother's Love Is a Blessing*, a television drama, was screened by RTE (the Irish national network) in 1994. In 1996 *The Dead School* was published to great critical acclaim, and *The Butcher Boy* was made into a film directed by Neil Jordan (author of the novella at the end of this collection). "The Hands of Dingo Deery" first appeared in the magazine *Here's Me Bus!* (1995). The novel *Breakfast on Pluto* was published in 1998, and his most recent collection of stories is *Mondo Desperado* (1999).

COLUM MCCANN was born in Dublin in 1965 and has lived in America, Japan, and Ireland. He currently teaches English in New York City. Honored with two Hennessy Awards (Best Newcomer and Best Overall) in 1990, he also won the Rooney Prize for Irish Literature in 1994 for his short story collection *Fishing the Sloe-Black River* (which includes the stories that appear in this collection). In addition to his novels, *Songdogs* (1995) and *This Side of Brightness* (1998), he has published stories in many periodicals and anthologies including *The Picador Book of Contemporary Irish Fiction* and *Ireland in Exile*.

BERNARD MACLAVERTY was born in Belfast, Northern Ireland, in 1942 and educated locally. He is currently working as a teacher in Scotland. He has published the following short story collections: *Secrets and Other Stories* (1977), from which "Between Two Shores" comes; *A Time to Dance* (1982); *The Great Profundo* (1987); *The Best of Bernard MacLaverty* (1990); and *Walking the Dog and Other Stories* (1994). His book for children, *A Man in Search of a Pet*, was published in 1978. The novels *Lamb* (1980) and *Cal* (1983) were both adapted for cinema. His novel *Face Notes* (1997) was shortlisted for the Booker Prize.

AIDAN MATHEWS was born in 1956 and educated at University College, Dublin, and Trinity College, Dublin. The recipient of the Patrick Kavanagh Award of 1977, he held a writing fellowship at Stanford University between 1980 and 1982. He is presently a radio drama producer at Ireland's national radio and television network, RTE. He has published collections of poetry: *Windfalls* (1977) and *Minding Ruth* (1983); plays: *The Diamond Body, The Antigone, Immediate Man*, and *Exit / Entrance*; a novel: *Muesli at Midnight* (1990); and two collections of short stories: *Adventures in a Bathyscope* (1938) (from which the two stories reprinted here were taken), and *Lipstick on the Host* (1994) (which won Italy's Cavour Prize for best foreign fiction).

Éilís Ní Dhuibhne was born in Dublin in 1954. She has completed a Ph.D. thesis on folktales, and she has worked as a civil servant, librarian, archivist, and lecturer. She is married with two children and is Assistant Keeper at the National Library in Dublin. *Blood and Water,* her first collection of short stories, was published in 1988; and a second collection, *Eating Women Is Not Recommended,* appeared in 1991. Her novel, *The Bray House,* and a book for children, *The Uncommon Cormorant,* were both published in 1990. *Voices on the Wind: Women Poets of the Celtic Twilight* was published in 1995. *The Inland Ice and Other Stories* was published in 1997. "The Garden of Eden" first appeared in *The Second Blackstaff Book of Short Stories* (1991).

Joseph O'Connor was born in Dublin in 1963 and was educated at University College, Dublin, and Oxford University. He became a full-time writer in 1988. His first novel, *Cowboys and Indians* (1991), was shortlisted for the Whitbread Prize. His other writings include the novels *Desperadoes* (1994) and *The Salesman* (1997); *True Believers* (1991), a collection of short stories that includes "The Long Way Home"; a play, *Red Roses and Petrol* (1995); and his nonfiction works, *Even the Olives Are Bleeding* (1992) (a biography of the Irish poet Charles Donnelly), *The Secret World of the Irish Male* (1994), *The Irish Male at Home and Abroad* (1996), and *Sweet Liberty: Travels in Irish America* (1996).

Michael O'Loughlin was born in Dublin in 1958. His poetry has been published in the following collections: *Stalingrad: The Street Dictionary* (1980), *Atlantic Blues* (1982), *The Diary of a Silence* (1985), and *Another Nation: New and Selected Poems* (1995). He published a critical essay, *After Kavanagh: Patrick Kavanagh and the Discourse of Modern Irish Poetry,* in 1982, and a short work on Frank Ryan (a major figure in the Republican movement in the Spanish Civil War), *Frank Ryan: Journey to the Centre,* in 1987. He has also translated works by the Dutch poet

Gerrit Achterberg, including *Hidden Weddings: Selected Poems* (1987). "The Making of a Bureaucrat" first appeared in the short story collection *The Inside Story* (1989). *The Jewish Bride*, a novel, was published in 1999.

RONAN SHEEHAN, solicitor and writer, was born in Dublin in 1953. He has won the Hennessy Literary Award for his short stories. He lives in Dublin, and he worked for many years on *The Crane Bag*, which was one of Ireland's leading cultural and political journals. His novel, *Tennis Players*, was published in 1977. "Telescope" is included in *Boy with an Injured Eye*, a collection of short stories published in 1983. *The Heart of the City*, a celebratory study of Dublin, was published in 1998.

CHERRY SMYTH was born in Port Stewart, Northern Ireland, in 1960 and is presently living in London, England. She is the author of *Queer Notions* (1992), a book charting the rise of urban gay culture; and *Damn Fine Art: New Lesbian Artists* (1996). She performs regularly on the English poetry circuit and in 1993 won second prize in the London Writers' Competition. She has published poetry and short fiction in several anthologies and is currently working on her first novel. "Near the Bone" first appeared in *quare fellas: new Irish gay writing* in 1994.

EAMONN SWEENEY was born in Sligo in the west of Ireland in 1968. He lived for a number of years in London, England, but is now based in Dublin. His short stories have appeared in many publications and anthologies, and in 1995 he won the European/Raconteur Short Story Award. "Lord McDonald" first appeared in *Force 10: An Irish Journal* in 1989. Sweeney's first novel, *Waiting for the Healer*, was published in 1997.

PERMISSIONS ACKNOWLEDGMENTS

Grateful acknowledgment is made to the following for permission to reprint previously published stories:

John Banville: "Nightwind" and "Persona" by John Banville. Reprinted by permission of the author.

Sara Berkeley: "Emily Dickinson" from *Home Movie Nights* by Sara Berkeley. Reprinted by permission of the author.

Maeve Binchy: "Shepherd's Bush" by Maeve Binchy, copyright © 1983 by Maeve Binchy. Reprinted by permission.

Elizabeth Bowen: "Summer Night" from *Collected Stories* by Elizabeth Bowen, copyright © 1981 by Curtis Brown Ltd., Literary Executors of the Estate of Elizabeth Bowen. Reprinted by permission of Alfred A. Knopf, a division of Random House, Inc.

Clare Boylan: "The Little Madonna" from *Concerning Virgins* by Clare Boylan (London: Hamish Hamilton Ltd.), copyright © 1989 by Clare Boylan. Reprinted by permission of the author care of Rogers, Coleridge & White Ltd., 20 Powis Mews, London W11 1JN.

Evelyn Conlon: "Telling" by Evelyn Conlon. Reprinted by permission of Blackstaff Press, Belfast, Northern Ireland.

Anne Devlin: "Naming the Names" from *The Way-Paver* by Anne Devlin. Reprinted by permission of Faber and Faber Limited, London.

Emma Donoghue: "Seven Pictures Not Taken" by Emma Donoghue, copyright © 1996 by Emma Donoghue. Reprinted by permission of the author.

Mary Dorcey: "A Sense of Humour" by Mary Dorcey. Reprinted by permission of the author.

Anne Enright: "What Are Cicadas?" and "Men and Angels" from *The Portable Virgin* by Anne Enright (London: Secker & Warburg), copyright © 1991 by Anne Enright. Reprinted by permission of the author care of Rogers, Coleridge & White Ltd., 20 Powis Mews, London W11 1JN.

Desmond Hogan: "The Bombs" from *The Diamonds at the Bottom of the Sea and Other Stories* by Desmond Hogan (London: Hamish Hamilton Ltd.), copyright © 1979 by Desmond

Hogan. Reprinted by permission of Rogers, Coleridge & White Ltd., 20 Powis Mews, London W11 1JN.

Neil Jordan: "The Dream of a Beast" from *The Dream of a Beast* by Neil Jordan (London: Chatto & Windus), copyright © 1983 by Neil Jordan. Reprinted by permission of Casarotto Ramsay and Associates in association with Lutyens & Rubinstein Literary Agency.

Rita Kelly: "En Famille" by Rita Kelly. Reprinted by permission of the author.

Bernard MacLaverty: "Between Two Shores" by Bernard MacLaverty. Reprinted by permission of Blackstaff Press, Belfast, Northern Ireland.

Patrick McCabe: "The Hands of Dingo Deery" from *Mondo Desperado* by Patrick McCabe, copyright © 1999 by Patrick McCabe. Reprinted by permission of HarperCollins Publishers.

Colum McCann: "Cathal's Lake" and "Fishing the Sloe-Black River" from *Fishing the Sloe-Black River* by Colum McCann, copyright © 1993 by Colum McCann. Reprinted by permission of The Wylie Agency, Inc.

Aidan Mathews: "The Strangest Feeling in Bernard's Bathroom" and "The Story of the German Parachutist Who Landed Forty-Two Years Late" by Aidan Mathews. Reprinted by permission of A. P. Watt Ltd., London, on behalf of Aidan Mathews.

Éilís Ní Dhuibhne: "The Garden of Eden" from *Eating Women Is Not Recommended* by Éilís Ní Dhuibhne (Dublin, Ireland: Attic Press, c/o Cork University Press, 1991). Reprinted by permission of the author.

Joseph O'Connor: "The Long Way Home" from *True Believers* by Joseph O'Connor (London: Flamingo), copyright © 1991 by Joseph O'Connor. Reprinted by permission of Blake Friedmann on behalf of the author.

Michael O'Loughlin: "The Making of a Bureaucrat" by Michael O'Loughlin, copyright © 1989 by Michael O'Loughlin. Reprinted by permission.

Ronan Sheehan: "Telescope" from *Boy with an Injured Eye* by Roman Sheehan. Reprinted by permission of the author.

Cherry Smyth: "Near the Bone" by Cherry Smyth. Reprinted by permission of the author.

Eamonn Sweeney: "Lord McDonald" by Eamonn Sweeney (Force 10 Publishers). Reprinted by permission of the Peters Fraser & Dunlop Group Ltd.